The Winter Queen

Books by Jane Stevenson

SEVERAL DECEPTIONS

LONDON BRIDGES

THE WINTER QUEEN

The Winter Queen

Jane Stevenson

HOUGHTON MIFFLIN COMPANY
BOSTON • NEW YORK
2002

First published as *Astraea* in Great Britain in 2001 by
Jonathan Cape, Random House.

For information about permission to reproduce selections from this book, write to Permissions, Houghton Mifflin Company, 215 Park Avenue South, New York, New York 10003.

Visit our Web site: www.houghtonmifflinbooks.com.

Library of Congress Cataloging-in-Publication Data

Stevenson, Jane, date.
[Astraea]
The winter queen / Jane Stevenson.
p. cm.
Originally published: Astraea. London : Jonathan Cape, 2001.
ISBN 0-618-14912-0
1. Elizabeth, Queen, consort of Frederick I, King of Bohemia, 1596–1662—Fiction. 2. Netherlands—History—Wars of Independence, 1556–1648—Fiction. 3. Marriages of royalty and nobility—Fiction. 4. Africans—Netherlands—Fiction. 5. Yoruba (African people)—Fiction. 6. Interracial marriage—Fiction. 7. Freedmen—Fiction. 8. Queens—Fiction. I. Title.

PR6069.T4535 A94 2002
823'.914—dc21 2002032803

Printed in the United States of America

QUM 10 9 8 7 6 5 4 3 2 1

This book is dedicated to

Hutchinson
Bradshaw
Ireton
Smith
and
The Good Old Cause

Acknowledgements

As usual, friends have come to my assistance in all kinds of ways. Penny Bayer, Andrew Biswell, Peter Blegvad, David Dabydeen, Peter Davidson, Dan Franklin, Maureen Freely, John Gilmore, Arnold Hunt, Pat Kavanagh, Jamie Reid Baxter, Alison Shell, Nigel Smith, Winifred Stevenson and Adriaan van der Weel have all helped matters along with facts, insights, theology and creative criticism of all kinds. I would particularly like to thank Adriaan for a beautiful translation, which, in the end, never quite found its place.

I would also like to acknowledge the help and advice I have received from the staff of Kew Gardens, the Radcliffe Science Library, the Bodleian and the British Library, the Koninklijke Bibliotheek and the Haags Historische Museum in Den Haag, and the Zeeuwse Archief, the Zeeuwse Bibliotheek and the Koninglijke Genootschap der Geschiedenis in Middelburg. For my understanding of the Yoruba in the sixteenth century, I am particularly indebted to the writings of S.O. Biobaku, Robin Law and G.J. Afolabi Ojo; and for what I know of the Ifá Oracle, to the writings of Afolabi A. Epega, Philip John Neimark, Judith Gleason and E. Bolaji Idowu. Ifá is a living tradition, which I have made use of for my own fictional purposes, but I have tried to respect its integrity and dignity: I apologize to anyone who feels that I have not succeeded.

Jane Stevenson
Aberdeen, 2000

Now when the world with sinne gan to abound
Astraea loathing lenger here to space
Mongst wicked men, in whom no truth she found,
Return'd to heaven, whence she deriv'd her race;
Where she hath now an everlasting place.

Edmund Spenser, *Faerie Queene*, V, 1, xi

Ultima Cumaei venit iam carminis aetas;
magnus ab integro saeclorum nascitur ordo.
iam redit et virgo, redeunt Saturnia regna,
iam nova progenies caelo demittitur alto.

Now comes the last age of the Sibyl's song;
The great line of the centuries renews.
The Virgin comes, the Golden Age returns,
At last, a new child, sent down from high heaven.

Virgil, *Eclogue* IV

Nigredo

I

10 February 1639

A woman is sitting in a great chair under a cloth of estate, in a room hung with black velvet. She is dumpy, deep-bosomed and straight-backed as a trooper. Her cheeks are doughy with adversity and time, but her hazel eyes are clear. Dusk is falling outside in the Voorhout, and in the dim, candle-lit velvet cavern of the presence chamber her face, breast and hands shine dimly pale against the black behind her and the black of her dress. Of the tall man standing before her, clad in scholar's black broadcloth, nothing can be seen but the chaste, starched-linen gleam of his collar and cuffs. The hand which holds his black beaver hat is invisible: as she peers into the gloom, she can barely discern his face, let alone his expression. Only a sudden liquid shifting in the gloom makes her realize, with a sudden qualm, that she has been staring straight into his eyes. She turns her head away, settling the black silk scarf around her shoulders against the creeping chill of the Dutch winter, adjusting her rings.

'Tell me a story,' she says, her eyes downcast. Her voice is a strangely youthful one to come from so still and matronly a figure.

'What story do you wish, your majesty?' he responds. His voice is deep and resonant, but husky, like the sound of a bell made of wood.

Still she does not look at him, and when she speaks her tone is wistful. 'Are there truly men in Africa whose heads do grow beneath their shoulders?'

'I have not seen one,' he says gravely.

'Oh, I hoped it might be true. There is a phrase, is there not – "ex Africa semper aliquid novi"?'

'It was Pliny, I believe, who said that. And perhaps it is true. There are many things I saw in Africa which would seem strange here and, doubtless, many strange things there which I have not seen at all. I have seen Oyo Ile, where I was born, Igboho, Ifá, the city of the oracles, and El Mina, the great fortress of the Portugals. I have seen Bornu and Gao of the Songhai Mussulmans, where I went to buy Barbary horses for my father the king. I have seen the jungle and the desert, the plains, and the sea, and animals of many kinds. But all the men I saw in Africa were shaped like men anywhere else.'

'What is the strangest thing which you have seen, Dr Pelagius?'

'If anyone had told me, when I was in my father's house, that he had seen water solid like crystal, burning to the touch, with men walking upon it, I would have called him a liar. That is the strangest thing.'

27 June 1634. A great day for Amsterdam, daughter of the sea. For it was on that day that the spring sailing from the East Indies finally arrived in Holland. The gulls were screaming cheerfully overhead and light dazzled on the waters of the harbour, broken into a million sparkling diamonds. The herring fishermen had spotted the tall ships soon after they entered the Narrow Seas and alerted the port authorities, so an expectant city was standing on the quays to greet them. They came into the great harbour at Amsterdam one after another, great ocean-going vessels, three-masters fitted to fly before the endless winds that girdle the earth in the Roaring Forties, manoeuvring in that narrow space with all the grace of an albatross in a duckpond, clawing their way to haven amid a throng of small boats come out to escort them. As the anchors finally rattled down, a cheer went up from the thronged docksides and a salute was fired from the Admiralty Depot. The wealth of the Indies was coming to the city: the journalists from the courants were there, jostling shoulder to shoulder with wharfingers, investors waiting impatiently to speak with the captains, and pickpockets, merchants, wives, whores and simple bystanders.

In the next few days, as the courants triumphantly reported, 326,733 Amsterdam pounds of Malacca pepper, 297,466 pounds of cloves, 292,623 pounds of saltpetre, 141,278 pounds of indigo, 483,082 pounds of sappan wood; 219,027 pieces of blue Ming ware from China; 52 further chests of Korean and Japanese porcelain; 75 large vases and pots containing preserved confections; 600 pounds of Japanese copper; 241 pieces of fine Japanese lacquer work; 3,989 rough diamonds of large carat; 93 boxes of pearls and rubies (of miscellaneous weight and water); 603 bales of dressed Persian silks and grosgrains; 1,155 pounds of raw Chinese silk; 199,800 pounds of unrefined sugar from Kandy; an elephant and a tiger were all disgorged into the long, waterfront warehouses of the East India Company. This fabulous hoard, as the papers reported, was put on display; and the fashionable, the merely wealthy and the dealers descended like vultures. This is a matter of public record: clearly established, abundantly corroborated fact – recorded, for example, in the Amsterdam *Courante uyt Italien en Duytschland* for 27–8 June 1634, which, since it spoke only to the readers of its day, can have had no interest in deceiving us.

The activities of Pelagius van Overmeer at this time, on the other hand, are attested only by a personal chronicle which he wrote almost thirty years later. His primary concern in this document is to explore the providence of God as it was manifested in his own life. He records no dates and material facts are referred to only indirectly, insofar as they illustrate the subtle directions of God in his affairs. But as far as it can be reconstructed, this is what must have happened. The precise date can be established by juxtaposing two facts: that there was only one sailing from Batavia which could have brought him and that he refers to the curious coincidence that he arrived in Holland in the year of the Elector Palatine's death, which would take place on the morning of 19 November 1634, five months in the future.

Therefore, along with the fabled luxuries of the mysterious East, an unregarded piece of supercargo must have made his own way, not without difficulty, down the great wall of a ship's side on a dangling rope ladder and into a rowing boat. If he had looked up from the uncertain little skiff, deadly dangerous in its near invisibility among those mighty ships, he would have seen the quay walls ringed with broad, fair Dutch faces, avid with an interest which in no way included him. But perhaps his strongest emotion was relief. For the first time in his life, he will have travelled in the relative comfort enjoyed by a passenger rather than chained in the reeking hell of a slave deck, but all the same, after months at sea, he will have been glad to have land under his feet. Once on the dockside, he will have attracted little attention. A tall, soberly dressed, middle-aged black man was no unusual sight in Amsterdam, where the rich had already begun to regard black servants as fashionable accessories: there were too many for one to be interesting and not enough to provoke hostility.

It is even possible, though unlikely, that Elizabeth was on the dockside. The arrival of the fleet was an event, and she was as interested in orient pearls and silks as any other lady of rank: the news would have reached her palace in The Hague long before the fleet actually landed. By June the Elector Frederick had already been away on campaign in Germany for six long months: she may have welcomed an opportunity for a little excursion to break the gentle monotony of her days.

Pelagius, then, landed in Europe without attracting public attention of any kind. He had a little gold in an inner pocket and, sewn into his belt, a few precious stones, pearls and sapphires; the two sailors he had paid to act as his porters were carrying his books and his few clothes. He had a letter of introduction, nearly as precious as the sapphires, and no idea where he was going.

His narrative is a blank about these first days, though Holland must have seemed very strange to him after twenty or more years in the East Indies. It was early summer, so he would not yet have been shivering, and the style of architecture, the tall, flat-fronted houses with their big windows and crowstep gables, would have been broadly familiar to him, since the principal houses of Batavia, the East India Company's headquarters in Indonesia, were built in the Dutch style. The town had even acquired a canal system in 1621, which brought the waters of the Ciliwang through the city in true Dutch fashion, so this would also have been a familiar element in the townscape before him. Amsterdam's Prinsengracht was bigger than the Tijgersgracht, of course, the houses which lined it grander than those of colonial Batavia, but they were essentially similar.

All the same, apart from these meagre points of congruence, the differences must have been inescapable, crowding relentlessly upon him: the relative dryness of the air, the tang of tar, coal smoke, drains, horses, and alien sweat which it carried; the refusal of even the most obviously menial to carry burdens on their heads; the white faces everywhere. The background noises: harsh mewing of gulls, the liquid whistle of starlings, the complacent roo-coo-coo of pigeons, sounds which for some time he did not even associate with birds, and everywhere harsh Dutch voices, unmixed with Chinese, Javanese or Malayan.

So: somehow, Pelagius, Mynheer van Overmeer as he was known, the Man from Over the Sea, got himself a place on a coach bound for Leiden. It is probable that he was cheated outrageously and that the colour of his skin drew impertinent comment, but he does not choose to mention it. For as the slow, unsprung, smelly vehicle rumbled towards Leiden, that dull, provincial little manufacturing town just inland from The Hague, he was taking the final steps towards his heart's desire. He was no longer young and he had been a slave for a long time, too long to be still dreaming of a life which involved him in great events. The prospect before him was in itself a hope bigger than he had had since he was taken from Africa. Having presented his letter to the Rector of the University, a large and genial man who vaguely recalled Pelagius's patron from his own student days, he was successfully matriculated as a student in the Faculty of Theology, the first step to becoming a Protestant minister. He joined the household of Johannes Sambucus, Professor of Theology and author of *De Tertio et Quarto Regno in Prophetia Danielis*, a lengthy and learned commentary on the Book of Daniel, and began his studies.

His intention was that, having completed a degree in theology and added Greek and Hebrew to the languages he already commanded (Yoruba, Dutch and Latin, with a few words each of Arabic, Bantamese, Portuguese and Scots), he would return to Batavia as a fully fledged Calvinist predikant. He had been converted soon after his arrival in the Dutch colony and his faith was the most precious thing he possessed. But it had become obvious to him that the cause of true religion in the colony was under threat because of the shortage of educated clergy prepared to serve in a tropical climate: to him, therefore, and also to his patron Robert Comrij, ordination seemed a path marked out for him by the finger of God. It also promised him a future, dignity, independence. No small thing for a man who had been a slave for more than twenty years.

He was a good enough student to cause no comment whatsoever. For nearly three years, he appears blamelessly in the laconic notes kept by the University authorities, but in the third year he disappears. For this, and how he felt about it, it is necessary to turn to his own account. 'In tertio anno meae novitiatis, Dominus me probat, et temptavit oboedientiam meam. Haud voluntate mea, Lugduni exii. Nam patronus meus, subito revertens in Europam, me vocavit ad Hagiam ut eum adjutaverim . . .' He does not tell us how he felt about this, but it is easy to imagine from the word 'haud': scarcely, hardly. It is the sort of word used by a man committed to understatement, or to classical forms of emphasis by understatement. 'Not exactly at my own desire, I left Leiden.

For my patron, suddenly returning to Europe, summoned me to The Hague in order to assist him.'

Pelagius, in his neat, bare student's room in Sambucus's house on Leiden's Herengracht, turned the letter over and over in his hands. It spelt the death of all that he had hoped to be and to achieve in this second half of his life. But Comrij had taken Pelagius up from the living death of slavery, baptized him and brought him to God, made of him something almost like a son, and, as far as the law went, freed him. But the legal aspect was secondary: regardless of his legal status, both the Yoruba morals which had formed him and the European sense of rights and obligation which he had learned in Batavia told him that Comrij's will could not be gainsaid. But. But, Pelagius thought painfully, his mind moving stiffly in unfamiliar channels as the familiar despair of slavery enfolded him once more, what of the will of God? I hoped, I intended, to return to Batavia to do God's work. Do I have a clear call to disobedience? He laid the letter aside and knelt by his bed, letting his forehead rest on his clasped hands. 'If any man come to me, and hate not his father, and mother, and wife and children, and brethren, and sisters, yea, and his own life also, he cannot be my disciple.' He knelt for a long time, in silent agony. Were these words of the Lord the words which should guide him? Jesus's warning tormented him: was it his will speaking or his duty? Finally his path seemed clear: if God's will was that he should return to Batavia, then this would, in the end, be compatible with answering Comrij's call. If not, perhaps some yet inscrutable purpose was laid up in the bosom of time. As soon as this thought entered his mind, he knew he was lost.

It took a week to disengage himself from Leiden. He explained the situation to Professor Sambucus, who expressed decent regret and good wishes for his future, paid his bills, packed, hired a horse and went to The Hague. On the level of pure sensation, it was pleasant to be riding again, to be out in the fresh air, but this was in itself depressing to him: getting what he could from casual and fleeting pleasures was a habit of mind he had had in slavery, when there was nothing else to keep him from despair. As a free man, a man with hope, he had not needed such moments. As he approached The Hague slowly from the north on a tired old livery hack, the road was straight and unmistakable in front of him, embanked up from the flat lands to either side, under a huge, open sky. But at its vanishing point it seemed to disappear into a wood. Gradually he began to discern church towers rising among the trees, a windmill, and later, the irregular outline of great houses and the gleam of water. The impression of wildness was a false one: the trees turned out to be in regular lines, guarding gardens, market gardens, the banks of the canals. Once in the town – and it was not even that, he knew, but officially speaking the biggest village in Europe, without the civic status the Dutch held dear – he left the horse at the agreed inn, with some relief that he had parted from the poor old beast before it dropped dead, and asked directions.

They were not hard to follow. Like many houses in Holland, the place where his patron lodged was distinguished by a sign. He was looking for 't Groote Vis, near the Groote Kerk, and within less than half an hour he found himself outside a strange door in The Hague, with a battered copper whale swinging on a bracket above it.

The door was opened by a skinny Dutchwoman clutching a broom, her careworn face prematurely aged by anxiety. She curtseyed, goggling at him with a stupefied awe which seemed to derive in equal measure from his preacher's blacks and his black skin. When she had recovered herself and he had enquired after Comrij, she pointed him speechlessly towards the stairs, steep as a ship's companionway, and departed in a waft of soap, lye and honest, housewifely sweat with a breathless ''Dag, mynheer!' He climbed three flights to an attic tenement and knocked again.

A familiar voice snapped, 'Come in, come in.' At the sound, he felt the web of old associations close round him like a net. Comrij was working, as he had always preferred to do, standing, at a tall lectern set in front of the window to catch the light, which turned his flossy, neglected white hair into a thistledown halo. More than a head shorter than Pelagius, he keeked up at him through thick, tangled white brows. 'Aye, so you're here then. They've not been starving you, I see.'

Pelagius looked around him for somewhere to put his heavy satchel, but every surface in the room was already occupied: he set it down beside the door. The rest of his luggage would arrive by carrier in due course. Clearly, not a word of thanks or welcome was to be expected. Such things had never been in Comrij's way, but after more than three years of separation the absence of a greeting struck coldly to his heart. Another thought struck him suddenly. 'Is Mistress Anna with you, Master Comrij?'

'Dead, poor lass. Dead of a fever. That father of hers was after me for her poor body for his heathenish ceremonies – it was Soo-Ming this and Soo-Ming that till I lost my temper. I told him straight, Pelagius, lad. Your daughter was baptized with the name of Anna, she lived with me as a Christian wife and died with Jesus on her lips. Devil take me if I'd let her from my care once she was dead. She's in the Protestant cemetery, with a decent stone over her.'

'I am sorry, master.'

Comrij, as was his way, rejected sympathy. 'It's all one, lad. Providence had it that we should have no child to live after us, so there was nothing to keep me in the East. It seemed to me then that I was called to return and bring my work before the public.'

Pelagius suppressed a sigh. The great *Theatrum Florae Indicae, aut Panarion contra omnes noxias Asiaticas – Theatre of the Plants of the Indies, or, Medicine-Chest Against all Asiatic Ills* – had been in progress for, at a conservative estimate, three decades. It had also occupied more than twenty years of his own life, in which time it had become steadily more complicated without yielding to any systematic principles, not even those of Paracelsus, the acknowledged inspiration of his master's life work. The shabby room, as he looked around it, bore bleak testimony to Comrij's industry: untidy heaps of paper and herbaria – still more untidy albums of dried plants – were heaped everywhere. For all his learning and enthusiasm, which bordered on monomania, the older man was incapable of any kind of organization. It was only too clear, he reflected as he looked around him, what his place in the enterprise must be. Jacob came into his mind; Jacob, who served seven years for Rachel, and, having been tricked by his father-in-law into taking her sister Leah, was forced to serve yet another seven. In his middle years God's purpose was fulfilled in him, but how bitter, Pelagius wondered suddenly, were the feelings of Jacob, as he entered on the second set of seven years? How did he feel, embarking on renewed servitude, in that time when he had confidently expected freedom with his beloved? As the Book tells the story, there was no word from God to comfort him. Hope, Pelagius told himself. Patience. Trust in the purposes of God. 'Master Comrij,' he asked, 'where am I to sleep?'

'I was forgetting. Come with me. There is a closet for you.'

In the weeks that followed Pelagius's worst fears were justified. He had a clear, orderly mind, and after two years of Greek and theology his capacity for organizing and categorizing information was still further developed by experience and training. But the scale of the mess which he faced was enough to daunt the most resolute.

Somewhere, under the mass of details, was, and had long been, a thesis. Comrij was a follower of the philosophical chymist Theophrastus Bombastus, called Paracelsus. His hope and intention was to apply the Paracelsan doctrine of signatures to the alien flora of the East. The wildly proliferating and mysterious plant life of the Indonesian jungle was to yield to a European sense of logic. The withered leaves, shadows of their former selves, which Pelagius turned over in their albums, were preserved as reminders of their shape and characteristics, for according to the Paracelsan doctrine of signatures, each plant should bear in its outward signification its inward virtue, its application to human need. Comrij was seeking to create a whole pharmacopoeia for the East, based on the principles he had learned in his own youth in the medical faculties of Leiden and Leipzig. Mango, with its heart-shaped, reddish fruit, must benefit the heart, that at least seemed obvious. But the nutmeg, enclosed in its red net of mace, was – what? In one place Comrij associated it with the kidney in its protecting cocoon of fat, in another with the testicles held safely in the scrotum. Which was right? Pelagius, who had so often been sent in search of rare plants in the jungle where the tigers coughed and sang in the dawn – the jungle which came up to the very walls of Batavia, as if the Dutch and their programme of orderly colonization did not even exist – found, creeping over him, a chilling failure to believe in the intellectual basis of the project which was eating his life.

Searching for plants for Comrij, he had spoken with Bantamese, slight, shy, fierce people who came up to his chin, explaining in his few words of their language matched with their few words of Dutch, what he was looking for, and as far as possible, why. It was evident to him that they had their own clear sense of what plants were, and were not, good for. In Africa he had been taught to respect hunters' wisdom about plants and animals, and he was inclined to feel that the knowledge of the Bantamese was something to recognize. Comrij's sense of the sufficiency of European theory outside Europe was a position which, he gradually perceived, was tenable because he never went beyond the walls of Batavia. Pelagius remembered all too clearly a conversation, a good ten years earlier, in which he had ventured to express an edited version of this idea to Comrij. The older man had been scornful.

'It's a simple matter of logic. Truth is either true, or it is not. God must set, in each part of the world, the simples appropriate to it: His benign and fatherly care extends over the whole of His creation, of that we may be sure. It is certain that our European herbs are not so efficacious here, where the very water is different and the air brings different influences with every breath. But there must be equivalents to be found, appropriate to the airs, waters, places, times and seasons of the East. These poor silly Bantamese do not know God, so why should they understand His creation? I grant you they may be right from time to time, but they are right without science. What had you in mind, boy?'

'Ginger, for instance, master. The men of Bantam set great store by it. It is heating, they say, and protects the heart against cold and damp. I believe this to be the case, on empiric grounds.'

'Do they so? Well, well, they may be right. Remember the words of our master Paracelsus.' The argument was taking place in Comrij's specimen room on the first floor of his house on the Tijgersgracht in Batavia, a spacious apartment with an airy balcony, lined with tables of bamboo and rattan, where plants dried out in presses or jars of fine silver sand, or stood planted up in temporary pots, waiting to be drawn. Comrij unlocked the red lacquer cupboard where he kept his treasures, produced a fat, vellum-clad folio, and leafed through it, setting it on the tall lectern by the open balcony. 'Consider this passage, from his *Liber de imaginibus*: "behold the Satyrion root, is it not formed like the male privy parts? No one can deny this. Accordingly magic discovered and revealed that it can restore a man's virility and passion. And now we have the thistle, do not its leaves prickle like needles? Thanks to this sign, the art of magic discovered that there is no better herb against internal prickling." If animals can snuff out the herbs which will heal their ailments, why should not the poor Bantamese know what is good for them? But for *chemiatri*, such as we are, it is necessary to consider the powers and virtues of the ginger plant. We cannot be guided by their knowledge, which embodies neither science nor divine guidance. Paracelsus directs us to consider colour as a clue to the nature of plants. What are the colours of the ginger plant?'

Pelagius considered the question thoughtfully. 'The root is pale, straw-yellow inside. When it is very fresh, the tips are pink. The flower is of a pale purple.'

'What are the virtues of yellow and purple?'

'Yellow is the colour of the sun, gold. Purple is the colour of kings.'

'So we have a plant of royal influence. Like the sun, it warms and nourishes; it is sovereign for the king of the body, which is the heart. The Bantamese are well guided, but now we understand.'

Pelagius sighed, tucking his hands into his armpits to warm them as he contemplated the mess of paper before him. When he permitted the thought to cross his mind, he hated the thick, clumsy bundles of fabric in which his body was encased. The moist heat of Batavia was a memory too distant to evoke, but in recalling the conversation, he found himself assailed by a nostalgic recollection of the clean and comfortable loose white robe and drawers which he had worn at that time. With an effort, he returned his thoughts to the present. 'Master Comrij, do you still favour organizing the *Theatrum* plant by plant?'

'That is convenient, certainly, but is it logical?' said Comrij dubiously. 'Man is the measure of all things: perhaps it will be better to follow the antique pattern of *homo microcosmus* and associate my material with the human body and its ills, from head to foot.'

Pelagius swallowed another sigh. 'There is the problem of the engravings, Master Comrij. The engraver must surely make each plate showing all the parts of a plant together. That is very well when a plant has a single use, but when it has many where is the plate to go?'

'True, true. Yet it is a basic principle – since there is no member or part in man that does not answer to some element, some planet, some intelligence, and to some measure and number in the Archetype or first pattern, we would be illustrating the correspondences of the greater with the lesser world. And if I arrange the *Theatrum* plant by plant, how is order to be imposed . . . let me see. Perhaps I should arrange them following the hierarchies of nature. Trees first, then shrubs. Climbing plants, which are courtiers to the great trees, and parasites of the smaller. Small plants . . . or wait a while. Perhaps they should be arranged by influence. Plants governed by the sun, then plants of the moon, and the other planetary spheres in sequence.'

'Master Comrij,' said Pelagius firmly, 'you have tried all these arrangements at least once in the pages before me. All of them have value, but with respect, master, we have come to the time when you must choose one and set your matter in its final pattern. It must be your choice.' He looked at Comrij as he spoke with deep misgiving. His master had aged considerably in a short time: the death of silent, bustling Anna had diminished him. He had been a spry little cockerel of a man more than twenty years before, when they first looked into one another's' faces in the slave market of Batavia. Now, with the thickening of his body and the thinning of his legs, he had lost the jaunty strut of his younger days and called to mind stiffer, slower creatures like the chameleon and the toad. The outward deterioration mirrored an inward reality: the process of decision had become almost impossible for him.

'Perhaps we could send a few sheets to the engraver. The ones that are most certain . . . ?' His voice trailed off.

'Master, with respect, that will not do,' said Pelagius firmly. 'We must have a clear plan of action from the beginning. The plates must be organized according to a definite principle, or no one will be able to use the book.'

'I am tired, lad. Let us speak of this tomorrow. Meanwhile, perhaps, we should work on the general essay. Where had we got to?'

'The notes on the uses of distilled spirits are all but complete. We were to consider tobacco.'

'Tobacco is death to phlegmatic temperaments. In the hot, moist air of Batavia, it is mere poison,' said Comrij immediately, the beginning of a diatribe which Pelagius had heard countless times over the years.

'So you have always said, master,' he said patiently, before the older man got properly under way, 'but how are you to convince the Dutchmen, who are never without their pipes?'

'Let them keep their pipes,' snapped Comrij. 'When they are in the East, I would have them smoke bhang, which is cordial and under the dominion of the sun, and the more sanguine of temperament can smoke opium.'

Pelagius, sorting out the many notes on the evils of tobacco, shot him a very dubious look. If there was one aspect of the indigenous temperament of which he was convinced beyond any doubt, it was that no Dutchman was able to contemplate a life which was not viewed through a drifting veil of tobacco smoke. Rather than accept such a notion, they would seek to dismiss the book as nonsense. It was hard to watch Comrij wilfully crippling his creation before it was even born. His master had been brought up, as far as he knew, entirely in Holland: but his father, in turn, had been a Scot who had exiled himself from his native land in the days of Queen Mary, for the sake of religion. Although Comrij was in no sense Scottish, apart from occasional lapses into that tongue, his background as the child of a resident alien had left him with a sense of apartness from the Dutch which sometimes, as it seemed to Pelagius, left him extraordinarily obtuse about the culture he inhabited.

Pelagius bit back comment, as he had so often bitten it back. In the days of his slavehood, Comrij had been remarkably considerate as the relationship of master and slave went, but he was under no illusion that he had ever been invited to express his opinion as if he were an equal. Now he was a free man, with Comrij as his patron, but the situation was completely unchanged. Comrij's dependence on him was expressed in every moment of their intercourse, but he was sublimely unaware of it, as he had been unaware of his dependence on his wife.

As the weeks went by, some decisions were eventually made. Comrij was gradually talked into organizing the plants by class. He found and hired an engraver; the focus of a whole further round of argument and hesitation before settling on Meester Gerrit in the Turfmarkt. Gerrit's bill for all the plates would amount to as much as would keep the pair of them for six years; a sum which brought Pelagius out in a cold sweat. The risk inherent in the whole venture cost him many hours of sleep. Exhaustive enquiry had established that no publisher was prepared to take on such a project unless the illustrations already existed: thus almost the entire preliminary expense of the project was borne by the author. Pelagius did not know what Comrij's resources were, though he was able to make a shrewd guess: the fifty, full-page plates of the *Theatrum*, especially if a number of fine, hand-coloured copies were made as Comrij clearly envisaged that there should be, were going to make a formidable hole in them. Printing the plates for five hundred copies would be another sixty-five guilders, with more than forty for the paper. More than two thousand guilders in all: he doubted that Comrij owned much more. Even given the limited medical resources of Batavia, the fees gained by so eccentric, opinionated and quarrelsome a man had not been excessive. It did not seem likely that he had saved much. Pelagius had returned to Comrij the remains of the money he had had from him to support his studies, so his own future, his chance of getting back to Leiden to resume his work, and then of returning to Batavia as a free man and a preacher of the word of God, was therefore entirely dependent on the success of Comrij's book, which he was almost powerless to influence beyond imposing what order he could as far as he was permitted to do so.

Comrij, meanwhile, was supremely unconscious of any of this. If he was anxious about his book, he did not show it directly: his nervousness expressed itself through irascibility, and exasperating changes of mind. Pelagius attempted grimly to concentrate on the task most immediately to hand, since he feared that any attempt to take a broader view would immediately result in losing his temper. They lived as cheaply as possible: for a consideration in the rent they had dispensed with the services of Mevrouw Mariken, their landlady. Before beginning his work on the *Theatrum* each day, he took out the slops, fetched clean water, swept the plank floors of the tenement and cooked their simple meals: oatmeal porridge, bread soup, frugal stews of stockfish, kale and onions. Once a week he washed their linen. Comrij clearly grudged the time he spent on this laborious task, but Mevrouw Mariken had been so anxious about the cleanliness of her house that Pelagius dared not let standards slide lest she ask them to find other lodgings. He was obsessed by the need to economize, as if, by saving a few stuivers here and there in the week, he could somehow hope to offset the hundreds of guilders which were seeping from Comrij's purse. For the rest of the day, once the most necessary chores were out of the way, he prepared pages for illustration, pasting up his own and Comrij's meticulous drawings of the various parts of each plant into a single, carefully laid-out page meticulously annotated, for which purpose, he had had to learn to write in reverse, so that all the engraver had to do was copy for the script to come out correctly on the printed page.

One by one, the pages were completed and taken to Meester Gerrit. He charged forty guilders a plate (including, as he was quick to point out, the cost of the copper), a sum which caused Comrij to rave helplessly about thieves and extortionists, though it was clear that the thing could not be done cheaper. It was Pelagius's business to take him the finished drawings, and twenty guilders with each one: the balance was to be paid on completion of the whole.

For his own part, he quite welcomed his visits to the engraver: they broke the monotony of tedious days spent in silence with his own thoughts, a silence broken chiefly by the irritating sound of Comrij's painful, phlegmy cough, which had settled on his chest shortly after his arrival in Europe and never quite left him, and the hard claws of the pigeons rattling on the slates above their heads.

On one such occasion, early in the spring, he looked at his folio page, wrote a final word with care, and laid down his pen. 'Master, this page is ready for Meester Gerrit.'

'Aye, is it so? Let me see.' Comrij came across from his lectern, and looked at the prepared page. 'Flower . . . leaf . . . ripe seed pod . . . root. Preparation of the ground root . . . Aye, not so bad. You have looked at your notes with a mirror?'

'Of course, master.'

'You may as well take it, then. And that bloodsucking bastard will want his money.' Comrij disappeared into his room and Pelagius heard the scrape of his iron-bound chest as he pulled it from under his bed. Meanwhile, he rolled the completed drawing carefully, inserted it into a cylindrical leather carrying case and capped it. He took his cloak and hat from the peg beside the door, and when Comrij came back with twenty guilders in his hand he was ready to go.

Their lodgings were near the middle of town, in a street of old houses near the Groote Kerk which had gone catastrophically down in the world since the building of a new, fashionable quartier around the Vijver and the Voorhout. Meester Gerrit lived on the edge of The Hague, in an area dominated by small workshops and independent craftsmen of one kind or another, many of whose activities were either smelly or noisy. Engraving was neither, of course; but it was convenient on both sides for engravers such as Gerrit to work in close proximity to printers, who were both. It was a pleasant enough walk, even on a sharp morning in early spring with impertinent children cat-calling and yelling 'Swarte Piet!' as he passed by, round the court precincts of the Binnenhof, and down the long canal called the Spuy to the Turfmarkt. Meester Gerrit, like themselves, had a top-floor workroom, in order to catch the maximum amount of light, over a printer's shop on the ground floor. When he knocked on the side door, an answering shout told him to come up, so he went up the vertiginous flight of stairs and emerged in Gerrit's attic.

Gerrit was sitting at his table, with the light falling on the sheet of copper in front of him, burin in hand, his working drawing pinned on an easel to one side. He was a big man, fat rather than formidable, with pale eyes in a pale face and straight, lank, dirty-white hair, abrupt and charmless in his manner, but a very considerable craftsman.

'Hey, it's the black. Brought me another, have you?'

Pelagius bowed without speaking and handed over the case with the drawing. Gerrit wiped his hands down the sides of his breeches, took out the drawing, unrolled it on a spare corner of his worktable and studied it carefully. Finally, he nodded.

'It'll do. No. There's just one thing. Look here. Where the pod's split. Are these meant to be separate seeds, or what's-its, you know, like a raspberry or a blackberry? Or something in between, like you have in a pomegranate.'

'They are separate seeds, not drupes, Meester Gerrit. Brown, with a hard coat.'

'All right. I'll remember that. Let's see the money.'

Pelagius handed over the twenty guilders silently. Gerrit not only counted them, but rang each one on the table and examined it before slipping it into his pocket. Only when he was satisfied with the weight and purity of all twenty coins did he scribble a receipt on a grubby scrap of cheese paper and give it to Pelagius.

'The last one you brought me's done. What was it? – galingale, I think. I've pulled a proof page for the doctor.' As he spoke, he crossed the room and rummaged in a folder, then put an engraved folio into Pelagius's hands.

'Thank you. This is excellent.' It was, indeed, excellent. The galingale and its parts stood on the page crisply, clearly and accurately. At a swift glance, the Latin text appeared to be flawless and probably was. Gerrit was expensive because he was renowned for seldom making mistakes. Pelagius disliked the man for his rudeness and his heavy, sour smell, but appreciated his worth. The engraver had already returned to his work, without even waiting to see if he had any corrections to make, assuming with characteristic arrogance that there would be none. Silently, Pelagius read carefully through the text, put the proof page into his carrying case and bowed formally to Gerrit, who, head bent over his work, his hand moving with crisp, mechanical precision throwing up bright, hairlike curls of copper from the tip of his burin as he sent it ploughing through the metal, neither saw him, nor responded. Pelagius turned away and let himself out.

The banging from the printer's caught his attention and he looked in at the window for a moment to see what was going on. Printing, he knew, would be another major expense: he was interested to know if there was any way of saving money on the job. Three men were at work, one working thick black ink evenly across the surface of a copper plate, while a second was taking ink equally carefully off another until it looked clean again, a procedure which puzzled him, and looked suspiciously like make-work. The sharp, metallic smell of the oily ink, which was keeping warm in a pot over a tiny brazier, exhaled from the window. A third, older man, Claes the master printer, whom he had met once before, was expertly bedding a plate on the press. He looked up, perceiving the occlusion of the light as Pelagius paused before the window.

'It's Dr Comrij's black, isn't it? Want to see what we're doing?' Pelagius opened the door and went in. 'We've got a run of Meester

Gerrit's stuff printing. This is what will happen to your master's plates, if we're all spared.'

'It doesn't look like a press,' said Pelagius, considering the great wooden structure in the middle of the floor.

'Ah. You'll have seen a printer for letterpress. This is a press for copper plates. Look. The plate goes here. The paper goes on top and then these blankets, to even the pressure. Then it goes through the rollers.' The rollers were turned by a wheel with four great spokes, like a St Andrew's cross. Setting his foot on one and hauling the next with both hands, Claes set the machine into motion, putting his whole not inconsiderable weight into the swing. Reluctantly, the bed passed forward between the rollers as the spokes went round. When the plate had fully emerged on the other side he let go of the spoke which he was holding, laid back the blankets and peeled the paper free of the plate, holding it delicately by the top corners. 'There you are. A perfect print, or it will be when it's dry. And it takes all this for every single one. You can tell your master that's where the money goes.'

'How long to print each page?' asked Pelagius.

'Oh, three – four minutes. And that's with three of us on the job. That's why we charge a guilder a hundred. Come on, lad. Get your coat off and send a couple through yourself. Give me a minute to catch my breath.'

Pelagius, nothing loath, took off hat, cloak and coat, and stood expectantly by the wheel of the great press. The two journeymen glanced at him slyly, then looked at each other.

''E should be doing the inking, by rights,' said one under his breath. ''E's black enough already.'

'Hold your tongue, Janneken,' commanded Claes, without animosity. 'That's a good shirt 'e's wearing. And when I want your opinion I'll ask for it.' He set up another page for printing and Pelagius hauled willingly at the spokes of the wheel. It was astonishingly hard work; the muscles of his back strained with the effort and it was only when he shoved down viciously with one foot as well as using his hands that he was able to persuade it into motion. The three printers were cackling at his efforts, with the traditional sadism of workmen watching a gentleman attempting a task at which they are expert. 'Not bad. Keep it going through even,' said Claes sharply. 'Nice smooth pace. There it goes. See? Nothing to it, really.'

Pelagius breathed hard, unbuttoning his waistcoat as Claes rescued the print and hung it up. 'Do you do this all day?'

'All day, son, when there's a rush on. We've a publisher desperate for these plates. Copper engravings are all the rage these days, the public reckons woodblocks're common. Printers mostly contract the work out, like your Mynheer van der Aa. Anyway, with this one, there's twelve engravings in each book and they're printing a thousand copies. There was some kind of mix-up, and Meester Gerrit had to re-cut three plates. It cost someone a pretty penny, I'm sure, and now they're in a hurry. Are you ready for another?'

'Yes.' He took a deep breath and sent the wheel round.

He did an hour's work at the printer's and walked home feeling the better for it. He had learned a great deal about the printing process, which, while not reassuring, at least gave him a clearer sense of what was entailed before Comrij's book came out. The hard exercise of turning the press, though he knew he would suffer the next morning, had done him good. He spent too much of each day immobile on a hard wooden stool working on the *Theatrum*; it made for nightmares, and unrefreshing sleep in which he was haunted by visions which, he feared, might be true sendings. It had not occurred to him before that the printing process was also going to be so expensive; but he could see the work that had to be done, feel it, in his own muscles. Whatever Comrij might think, there could not be a cheap way of doing it.

II

> How can a man who has reached the lowest point in the circle of fortune say: 'Misfortune has cast me down?' Since he himself is responsible? . . . In the end, man himself bears responsibility and guilt for his fate whether it has brought him fortune or misfortune. A man who goes about his task in the proper way, who has intrinsic worth, who is capable and knows what he is doing and displays diligence and care in performing his work, moves ahead. But a man who does not move ahead has no right to complain! For he is worth less than the other, and for this he can blame only himself and no one else.
>
> Paracelsus, *Liber de Mala et Bona Fortuna*

So it went on for the rest of the year. Comrij's cough got worse and seemed, some nights, as if it might shake him to pieces. He wrote and rewrote his text, coughing and hawking sputum which was often bloodstained into an increasingly disgusting handkerchief, and dosing himself with opium. As Meester Gerrit worked his way through plate after plate, the unmentionable necessity of getting the text to a state where it could be described as finished loomed between them, cutting off all other conversation beyond the most basic. Comrij's opium consumption was also causing Pelagius considerable concern. Taken in wine, it certainly helped the cough, but at considerable cost. Comrij, who had always shovelled down his food with the indifference of a man stoking a boiler, clearly now found it difficult to make himself eat at all: he lost weight and spent long hours in a sort of heavy, feverish state between sleeping and waking, in which he could do nothing whatsoever.

Once the last of the plates had gone to Meester Gerrit and summer had given way to the wind and rain of autumn, Pelagius finally ventured a comment, on a morning when Comrij seemed brighter than usual. He had rehearsed the moment so often in his head that he sounded strained and artificial to himself.

'Master, we must speak to a printer soon. Meester Gerrit will be finished in a week or so.'

'Damn it, boy,' snapped Comrij. 'Who are you to dictate to me?'

'I dictate nothing, master, but I am called to speak. My life is worth little, I know, but such as it is, it is bound up in this work. Have I not earned the right to a word, with twenty years of service?'

Comrij looked at him sharply and the anger seemed to dry in his mouth. His shoulders sagged defeatedly. 'Aye, lad. It's no more than the truth. When I gave you your freedom, I gave you the right to a tongue in your head.' He sat down heavily at their battered table and drew a piece of scrap paper over to him. 'What do we owe that bastard Gerrit?'

'A thousand guilders, master.'

Comrij opened his mouth, as if to protest, then shut it again defeatedly. 'It's tight. It's getting very tight, lad. It's enough to break a man's heart. The Dutch are mad for flowers and we're sitting here with the key to the East. Yet we're as poor as rats in a country where a man can make his fortune with one tulip.'

'But master,' protested Pelagius, 'we have nothing to please the florists. It is not just its beauty which makes the tulip so beloved by the *liefhebbers*. It is a plant of the Levant, so it will grow out of doors here in Holland, and God has given it the power to show itself in many forms and shapes, and to break into stripes, flames and borders. So the florists delight in making new varieties and the merchants profit richly. We cannot offer them a plaything of the same kind. Orchids are too tender to stand the Dutch winter and there is nothing else with the gift of mutability.'

'True enough. But it is a bitter jest to chew on, Pelagius. If God had seen fit to give such a gift to the crinum, we'd be living like princes in the Voorhout, not starving in a damned attic.' He roused himself with a visible effort. 'Come on, then. We need to go and talk to that man van der Aa.'

Pelagius bowed, and went to get Comrij's cloak and brush it. Their clothes were appallingly shabby, he thought, looking at it dubiously, but he hoped that if they at least looked clean they would also look self-respecting enough to be taken seriously. Comrij's appearance did not inspire confidence. The wine and opium he consumed had given his skin a sodden, toadlike quality, which the bitter winds of the previous winter had overlaid with red, broken veins. His hair was unkempt and his chin sported a bristly, greyish-white stubble. His whole posture and appearance suggested a man who was already defeated; and Pelagius, who was by now familiar with the ruthlessness of Dutch merchants – honest, as far as their bond went, but not merciful – feared for him.

After a series of negotiations with Sebastian van der Aa, their publisher, it was agreed that the heavy copper plates should be hauled downstairs to Meester Claes and a contract drawn up that he should print five hundred copies, to be delivered to van der Aa's offices and bound in with Comrij's text when that was printed.

Pelagius, who of course played no part in these negotiations, watched in agony as Comrij was driven from point to point by van der Aa. If the final text of his work was not with the publisher by 1 March, the contract was void. And, most crucially, Comrij was forced to undertake either to find a patron or himself to pay the costs of Meester Claes as well as those of Meester Gerrit.

'Master,' he said tentatively, as they walked home in grim silence, a meagre, spiteful rain misting the air and insinuating itself through their clothes, 'how are we to find the money?'

Comrij turned to him, his face rancid with the bitterness of a lifetime's disappointments, an old dog brought to bay, showing long yellow teeth. 'God alone knows,' he snarled. 'If I hadn't been fool enough to give you your freedom, I'd sell you.'

Pelagius's fists clenched involuntarily. He was so angry, he could hear the thin, high sound of his blood singing in his ears. He wanted to strike the man who had so unselfconsciously, unthinkingly, taken twenty years of his life and seemed unaware even that the book which he could not finish was only half his own work. He whirled on his heel and stalked off down a side street with long, angry strides, to keep himself from answering one unforgivable word with another. Pitching oblivious down the street, he gave no thought to where he was going, and was surprised to emerge on the Voorhout.

A moment later, he was almost knocked down: he had erupted from his side street almost under the hooves of a splendid chestnut horse: it reared and curvetted, but the rider controlled the beast well enough, and it resumed its place in line with no more than an ill-tempered jerk of its head, fighting the bit. Its master did not even trouble to shout at him. Stopping to stare, Pelagius saw before him a cheerful procession of nobles, men and a few women, well dressed on handsome beasts, cheeks glowing with exercise and the rain; ostrich plumes nodding bedraggled from fine beaver hats. The court, perhaps returning from the hunt. As they trotted by in chattering groups, glowing with well-being, his guess was confirmed; they were followed by a more sober group of servants, with a milling pack of tired dogs and, bringing up the rear, the corpses of deer slung stiffly over the backs of steady horses. They seemed to him infinitely strange and remote from the sordid details of his life with Comrij: their wealth visible in their shining faces, the lace at their wrists, the well-fed, well-groomed animals.

The whole answer to their problem lay before him. If a noble could be persuaded to act as patron, the book was safe, Comrij's future secured, himself – if he dared hope so far – back at Leiden. But Comrij had quarrelled with everyone who held any kind of position of power or influence. The court, so near physically that some Count had very nearly knocked him down, was as remote in terms of access as the mountains of the moon.

The situation was one which touched his sense of the ironic; since he understood the man on the chestnut horse very well. In his life as a prince, before slavery and Batavia, he had so often ridden out from his father's *afin* to find human flotsam before the gates; the deformed or abnormal who had a claim on the royal mercy, criminals hoping for life, even the existence of a palace eunuch, rather than death. Lives important to the men who lived them, of little significance to anyone else, nothing to the King's eldest son. He knew too well how foolish, how weak, they looked to a man on a horse. One long-forgotten face returned suddenly to his mind's eye, an albino, his skin excoriated by the merciless sun of Africa till it looked like old red leather, who had stood by a pillar of the *afin*, motionless among the clamour, his devastated eyes blank of hope or expectation. Seeing himself through the eyes of this Dutch Count, he knew himself to be a black man clad in shabby black, a nobody, standing neglected and absurd by the corner of a house. He could not begin to imagine how he could interest a horseman, happy and weary from the hunt, who was thinking only of hot water and fresh linen. Defeated, he turned away. He would go back to 't Groote Vis. Comrij would not apologize. Life would continue spinning down the thin cusp of the almost intolerable. And despair is a sin.

He walked for the rest of the day. The chill of the rain gradually cooled his temper, reminded him of his duty, not merely to Comrij but to God and himself. After his encounter with the court, he had kept down the Lange Voorhout, and ended up walking out along the Nachtegaalspad out from the east end of the town, under the strange, club-headed shapes of the pollarded trees which marched like soldiers down either side of the path, a popular walk, though on so nasty a day, no nightingales sang there, and he had it to himself. He was wrestling with his conscience, trying to sift in his mind where the Divine Will might lie. He knew very well what he must do: 'the rule by which a Christian must try himself, is the Word of God. We must judge of our spiritual condition by the Canon of Scripture.' And what did the Word of God say to help him? The psalms are lamps to light the Christian's path: he thought, therefore, of the psalms. Words came dropping through his mind. 'He that chastiseth the heathen, shall he not correct? He that teacheth man knowledge, shall he not know?' He was inclined to take it as a true sending. King David had written this psalm in despair and anguish of mind, but as its conclusion made clear he trusted, nevertheless, in God as his final refuge and was not forsaken. Was this the way he was guided? Another thought. In the pride of his young manhood, his princedom, he had been a heathen. Now, in his bitter anger and humiliation, he was taught, he was corrected, he was chastened by God – and 'he that spareth the rod, hateth his son'. As the dusk began to come down, and he turned his steps towards the westering sun, he thought, finally, of psalm 130, balm for his wounded spirit. 'Out of the depths have I cried to thee, O Lord . . . I wait for the Lord, my soul doth wait, and in his word do I hope.' Comrij in his stupid arrogance, his crass unawareness of his servant's manhood, might yet be a subtle instrument of God's correction and proving of his elect – a way of thinking which at least, made it easier to imagine how he might get through these endless days.

He returned to the attic as the town clock was striking seven, cold, wet and hungry, with muddy feet, but calmer in his mind. Comrij was working at his writing desk as he entered, and paid him no heed as he hung up his damp cloak and took off his dirty shoes.

'Ten copies of this, boy,' he said presently, as if nothing had happened. 'The Stadhouder, the President of the East India Company,

Count Marnix van sint Aldegonde. Secretary Huygens, Cornelis de Witt, the Grand Admiral, the President of the States-General, Dr Jan Dousa of Noortwijk, the Rector Magnificus of the University of Leiden, the President of the Amsterdam Chamber of Commerce. Somewhere in this infernal country there must be a man of vision.'

Pelagius took the rough copy from his master, and sat down on his stool at their rickety deal table, reflecting grimly that, thanks to his burst of temper, he had lost the opportunity to write the thing himself. Thus does God correct the stiff-necked. Glancing through it, his heart sank. The courtesies at the start of each letter were his business: those at least he could improve, but the content was a different matter. Once the preliminaries were out of the way, Comrij had failed to resist the temptation to lecture. 'The physician is only the servant of nature, not her master,' he declared. 'Therefore it behoves medicine to follow the will of nature. It is obvious even to those of mean intelligence that the airs and waters of Batavia are as different as the place, and rife with ills unknown here in Holland: yaws, elephantiasis, ulcers of all kinds bred by the moistness of the air, worms which grow beneath the skin and in the body. Nature has provided here in Europe herbs to cure all the ills which we Europeans suffer, and as He is a tender father to His children, we may be sure that in Asia there are herbs to cure the diseases that lurk there. I, Robert Comrij, licentiate of the University of Leiden, have given my life to the study of the plants that grow in the territories of the East India Company, their nature, qualities and medical uses. The wisdom of the ancients is useless with respect to the diseases of Batavia and the knowledge of the moderns little better. The doctors who have sought to treat the imposthumes of the East with Western simples are little better than murderers: their ignorance is a toll on the Company's servants, and that portion of its wealth which is in slaves. I ask, Sir, for your countenance for my *Theatrum Florae Indicae, aut Panarion contra omnes noxias Asiaticas.* I will put in the hands of every shipmaster and doctor of our great Eastern possessions the means of life and health, to the great profit of the East India Company, and the nation. The sum needed to bring my book to light is trifling and the reward will be great, in this world and the next.'

Pelagius, copying in his best italic, edited circumspectly, reducing the incidence of 'I', adding 'with respect', 'I humbly suggest', where he could, knowing in his heart that only a miracle would get this document past the private secretaries of the various addressees. He was only too well aware that the merchant princes of Holland were not accustomed to being addressed in such a style. And there was no recommendation! The great expected to be approached via some satellite or another: the letter out of the blue disqualified itself on sight.

'Master,' he said tentatively, 'should we not make gifts? We have some plants still living. I know Count Marnix van sint Aldegonde is a lover of tulips. We have a good crinum, one which is not so good, and there are the three cannas. Perhaps if we gave him one of these plants, he might look kindly on your request.'

'We are enjoined to believe, Pelagius,' said Comrij, his voice dripping with sarcasm, 'that this country is not run by idiots or children who can be distracted by a flower. I agree that the evidence for this is not manifest, but damn it, boy. I'm offering this ungrateful nation the means to hold the East. Should I fool about with pot plants?'

'Master, a letter needs a recommendation,' Pelagius insisted. 'If we do not have one, then it must carry its own. The plants are all we have.'

Comrij opened his mouth to argue, but as he drew breath he was overtaken by one of his terrible phlegmy coughs; a cough which convulsed him from head to foot and threatened to fetch the lungs out of his body. The sputum he hawked into his handkerchief was greenish, streaked with blood, nauseating to see. Purple in the face, unable to speak, his eyes starting from his head, he gestured urgently at Pelagius, who had risen and stood irresolutely watching him. Swiftly Pelagius went to the cupboard, got a glass and the flask of wine, and poured, then carefully dosed it with tincture of opium. He knelt by his master and put the glass carefully into his hand. He had to help Comrij get it to his mouth at first, but after a few sips the cough began to subside. When his breathing had finally returned to normal, he sagged exhausted in his chair.

'Do as you will about the damned bulbs,' he said sulkily, draining the glass. 'What do I care? One more drop of blood these leeches must take from me. It will not be missed, among all the rest.' Pelagius could hear from the thickening of his voice that the opium was beginning to take effect. Comrij staggered to his feet and mixed himself another glass: an indication that Pelagius was, in effect, on his own with the problem.

Pelagius, thus abandoned, gave his mind to the question of which of the notables Comrij had chosen to address were most likely to be impressed by the gift of their few flowering plants. It was probably a pointless gesture, but it was the best he could do.

Over the next couple of days, the letters were written, delivered, or entrusted to the posts for Amsterdam and Leiden. Comrij, meanwhile, worked on his *Introductio*, the sum of all that he wanted, or needed, to say.

'Listen to this,' he said with satisfaction, late one afternoon, laying down his pen. '"Habes hic, amice Lector, planissimam descriptionem Plantarum quas haec terra Oriens-India profert, quae ferme omnes suas vires medicas ostentant. Operis sique est laus, eam non sine jure meretur Magister Robertus Comrij, medicus Universitatis Leidensis, inventor ac descriptor huius plantarum secundum methodum principis iatrophilosophorum, Magistri Paracelsi. Nam id omne quod in ea magis concernebat vires plantarum medicas, forma autem earum ejusque partium leviter ac superficiariè exposita ipsae quoquae figurae minus erant perfectae, quam ut formam omnem partium, praecipue Florum, Fructuum, et Seminum exactè exprimerent." This will keep my name in the memory of man for many a year.'

Pelagius looked at him. As so often, the waves of pity and raw fury which rose in him in response to his master ran across each other so that their energy cancelled each other out, leaving him with nothing but silence. The naïve self-importance of this unprotected man was so clearly the medium for his complete destruction that, for a moment, he wished with profoundest seriousness that Comrij had been, however briefly, a slave. Poverty, mockery and disappointment appeared to have taught him nothing; did it take the full horror of descent into the valley of the shadow of death to give a man a sense of reality?

It suddenly struck him that this was not a random thought, but that a serious idea was involved. The principles of alchemy were part of the Paracelsan theory of matter and he had become familiar with the concept of *nigredo*, the death from which comes a more perfect life. He had come to trust it as a postulate, since it had obvious parallels in the natural world: it was a matter of observation that caterpillars begin as lowly creatures, degenerate into a foul, formless soup and are gloriously renewed. The idea also had a clear parallel in the life of the soul, since for most, and perhaps all, the road to true conversion led through a period of spiritual anguish. From which, he thought, it was fair to conclude that God, in permitting him to suffer the horror and grief which had marked so much of his life, had poured upon him the most singular mercies, which He had withheld from Comrij: an idea easier to perceive logically than emotionally.

As usual, Comrij had not stayed for an answer, but had turned away and was tidying up his desk, making an oddly innocent purr of satisfaction through his teeth as he sorted out his papers. The fair copy was put proudly to the side of his work table, while all the other papers which had cluttered its surface for weeks were sorted, docketed and put away.

'You can take the whole lot to Meester Gerrit for setting tomorrow,' he said.

'This is the very end?'

'Aye, lad. The end of an old song.' Comrij got up heavily, went over to his cupboard and rootled around on the bottom shelf. 'Ah . . .' He straightened up with difficulty, holding up a dusty flask sealed round the mouth with wax. 'The last of my old Burgundy, saved for this moment. Two glasses, Pelagius, lad. Drink with me, to the *Theatrum Florae.*'

Pelagius slipped from his stool, found their two real glass glasses (they also owned a number of pottery beakers, but he felt they were unsuitable to the dignity of the occasion) and rinsed them in the drinking-water bucket, regretting the absence of a clean cloth to polish them with. Comrij, hacking inexpertly at the black wax seal with his pocket knife, was evidently unconcerned by such details. Once the flask was open, he poured the wine without ceremony.

'To the *Theatrum.*'

Pelagius stood, holding his glass as custom prescribed by its foot, and solemnly took a long swallow. 'To the *Theatrum.*' It is not wrong to wish luck to an enterprise. Perhaps, he reflected sadly, God, who sees the movements of the heart, will look kindly on His servant Comrij and prompt some lord of this rich land to support this work.

He sat down again, setting his own wine to one side, and refilled Comrij's glass, which was already empty. His master lifted it without acknowledgment and drank deeply. Sprawled in his chair as if he had been dropped there, his face nonetheless looked oddly youthful; the habitual lines of anger and anxiety which marked it temporarily smoothed by the triumph of bringing his work to an end.

His thoughts must have in some way been running parallel to Pelagius's own, for he suddenly said, 'It's been a long time, boy. I mind you in the slave market, what is it? – twenty years ago. No, maybe more. I was looking for a likely lad, a boy with something between his ears, and there you were. Tall as any man there, and strong, but it was your face which drew me. There was a pride about you. The slave master told me then you'd been a prince in your own land, but I could see it in you, without his talk.' Pelagius silently refilled Comrij's glass, which was empty again. There was a boastfulness in his master's words which grated on him. Comrij began to speak again, into the silence which he took for granted. 'Now I think of it, it's twenty-four years since I took you from the market. You cost me a pretty penny. And here you are, with grey in your hair. Not the life you expected, I've no doubt. But it hasn't been all bad, has it, son?'

'You have been good to me, master,' said Pelagius as neutrally as possible, pouring more wine. Comrij expected no less and perhaps he would be satisfied with that. This search for reassurance was a new development since Mistress Anna's death and intensely irritating; he did his best to choke it off whenever it occurred. Bitter words rose to his tongue. Life? he wanted to say. My life ended when I left Oyo. Since then I have been a walking machine, waiting for my heart to wear out. But as always, he set his teeth, forcing the words back into the depths of his mind. Meanwhile Comrij, flushed and a little drunk, was pursuing an erratic tack of his own.

'What was it, now, that you were called then?'

'I beg your pardon?' said Pelagius, surprised out of his deliberate gravity.

'Your heathen name, Pelagius. The slaver told me and I have forgotten. But he had a name for you. Something, from somewhere.'

Pelagius looked at his master with distaste. They lived together in the little attic in a forced intimacy almost like that of husband and wife, they shared their work and their food, they endured one another's odours, but Comrij's absorption in his task had at least allowed him the privacy of his own head. This clumsy probing was like tearing the dressing from an open wound. 'Omoloju,' he said reluctantly, the word falling strangely from a tongue long accustomed to Dutch. 'My name was Omoloju. My father was called Onfinran, and he was the *alafin* of Oyo.'

'And what is that, boy?' Comrij was curious, but barely interested.

'He was a king.' Pelagius spoke more firmly than he had intended and Comrij raised a protesting hand.

'Na, na. No need to snap at me. I was only asking. Well, whatever he was, he's long dead, no doubt.' Pelagius compressed his lips. The last week of what had been his life raced across his mind: he had been at Jebba trading for war horses with the Nupe when one of the royal messengers, a man he had always trusted, had stumbled into camp on a foundering horse to warn him that his father had been forced into suicide by the King's council, who intended to crown his cousin. He had had to desert the caravan and take the best of the men and horses on a desperate race to the *afin* at Igboho, hoping to reach it before Egonoju could be crowned. Only twenty leagues from the capital his force had been brought down; two days later he was sold to the King of the Nupe, who took no small delight in seeing him humbled, and the day after that he was stumbling in a coffle on his way to the Portuguese stronghold on the coast, defeated, gone, forgotten, dead. Comrij knew nothing of any of this, nor would he ever. Can a man tell such things to another man who has opened his mouth and looked at his teeth as if he were a horse? Pride is a sin; he would humble himself in captivity, as Moses and Joseph had done before him. But no further.

The light had faded from their high window. He got up, hoping that the movement would deflect Comrij's train of thought, and lit a couple of the cheap tallow dips they used in the evenings. 'More wine, master?' The flask was light in his hand, there was not much left.

'I may as well,' said Comrij indifferently. The cheerfulness of the earlier part of the day had gone off, leaving gloom in its place.

Pelagius poured the last of the wine into his glass. 'Will you have a little supper, master? There is still some bread, and some of the *stamppot* I made yesterday. I could heat it on the fire.'

'No. Eat, if you like, but I want nothing.' Pelagius went to the cupboard, and found the end of a loaf and a hunk of cheese. The *stamppot* would keep another day. He was not hungry; Comrij's clumsy questioning had stirred up a bitterness in his belly which made food difficult to swallow, but it was, to him, part of the discipline of life that one should eat, soberly and with gratitude. He retired modestly to the other side of the room, with his supper on a wooden trencher on his knees, and chewed solidly through the stale bread and hardened cheese, helping them down with a beaker of water.

Comrij, meanwhile, as he observed from the corner of his eye, was questing in the cupboard. He seemed impervious to the effect of what he had drunk already; though it was considerably more than he usually took. He straightened up again, holding a bottle of genever, and poured himself a glass. The urge to talk seemed to have left him, for which Pelagius was grateful. He sat on, staring blankly into the meagre turf fire they allowed themselves against the autumnal chill, as the last of the day faded from the sky. When Pelagius smothered the fire and went to bed, he was still there, unmoving in their only chair with his glass on the table beside him, the flickering light of the tallow dips fitfully catching the tangled white eyebrows and the curves, folds and hollows of his bristly cheek.

Pelagius rose, as always, at first light. It was frosty in the early mornings this late in the year, and in the tiny cubby hole under the eaves where he slept he felt it as if he were sleeping outside. He went to bed in his shirt, which retained the heat of his body, but when he shook out his carefully folded breeches and put them on, the coarse fabric was so cold as it dragged over the shrinking, goose-pimpled flesh of his legs that it felt actually damp. A moment of private misery every morning. He fastened the belt, nonetheless, and shrugged into his waistcoat, the heavy Dutch clothes settling round him like the chill garments of the grave. As he well knew, his own living warmth would dispel the cold fairly soon, but in those first moments of the day it took the full force of his will to get him moving about like a man and not a sick monkey.

When he went through to the main room, he was not surprised to see Comrij still slumped in his chair, breathing stertorously. His head was at an awkward angle against the chair back, his mouth open with a childish, bee's wing trail of dried saliva depending from one corner, glimmering among the coarse, grey-white bristles. He had left his glass half full when he dropped off to sleep and the room reeked of genever. As quietly as possible, Pelagius coaxed the fire back to life, and put water on to heat. He got a jar of dried willow bark out of the cupboard, shredded some with his pocket knife and put it in the pot on the fire with dried betony, water and a little honey. A bitter brew it would be, but restorative. When it was ready, he shook his master's shoulder gently.

'Master Comrij. It is morning.'

'Eh?'

'Morning.'

'Oh, God give me strength.' Comrij moaned, stumbling to his feet and wavering into his bedroom, holding on to bits of furniture. Some moments later Pelagius heard a heavy splashing as the old man urinated copiously into his chamber pot. After he had relieved himself and drunk Pelagius's willow tea, he began to look less grey. Pelagius, meanwhile, put more water on to boil, and shaved first his master, then himself. He put the last of the warm water in a pannikin and they both washed their faces and hands. Pelagius rubbed his head and armpits with a rough, dampened towel, an exercise which Comrij refused for fear of catching the cold. It was the best they could do. An all-over wash was a major enterprise, when every bucket of water had to come up three flights of stairs, and even Pelagius seldom attempted it. Comrij consented, however, to comb out his wild hair with an orris-scented comb, while Pelagius did his best with their clothes.

Moving more freely as the room warmed and his headache abated, Comrij went to his room and dragged the chest from under his bed. Contrary to his usual custom, he came back in, holding the heavy little chest in both hands, and put it on the table. The key was on a string round his neck; he took it off and opened the chest. Pelagius sat down on a stool to watch. The first thing to come out was Comrij's fat little leather-bound account book, then a number of small wash-leather bags and rolls and some pieces of coarse cloth, evidently intended to keep the contents from rattling.

'This is it, lad,' Comrij observed, untying the strings of a bag with care. 'After this, it's the streets for us. You may as well know the worst.' He tilted the bag, releasing coins gently on to the table, and began to count. 'Sixty-seven guilders left, now that bastard Gerrit's had the last of his money,' he said after a while. 'Four English crowns, eleven doubloons. Now for the silver.' The silver was more miscellaneous, stuivers, thalers, deniers, shillings, pieces of eight. Another two hundred and seventy coins, in all. It looked like a fortune, in terms of what it cost them to live from day to day. It was not enough and he knew that Comrij knew it. Yet his master seemed to have emerged from the other side of despair into a kind of blank cheerfulness, fragile as a bubble.

Comrij pushed the coins to one side and unrolled a little bundle, touching the contents with clumsy care. A pair of jade eardrops, true dark green and lustrous. They seemed to bring dead Anna into the room with them, in her Sunday finery; tiny, slim and upright as a weasel, dressed in black silk, her chignon of raven hair glossy with coconut oil, the jade drops glowing on either side of her brown, flat-nosed face. And she had also worn jade bracelets . . .

'I sold the bracelets to pay my passage,' said Comrij, cutting into his thoughts. 'Got a good price for them. The heart wasn't in me to part with her ear-bobs, she loved them so. I should have sold them in the East, where they understand jade. God knows what they're worth here.' As he spoke, for all the roughness of his voice, he was folding the wash-leather back round the jade drops as tenderly as if they were alive and sleeping. There was another pair of earrings, Indian-made tassels of pearl and coarsely cut rubies, which Anna had sometimes worn, and a packet of loose pearls, poorly matched. The gold hoops she had worn for everyday, a few scraps of silver filigree, mostly damaged, a badly flawed loose emerald in a screw of paper. That was all.

'Meester Claes needs a hundred and ten. We must sell all the jewellery.'

'But, master, what shall we live on after that?' said Pelagius helplessly.

'We will wait and pray that I get an answer to my letters, boy. But it does not matter. Once I have the book in my hands, once the Governor General has actually seen it, I will be vindicated. For myself, I care nothing. I will say with Simeon, "O Lord, thou lettest now thy servant depart in peace, according to thy word." But if it does not produce a pension, perhaps a position as medical adviser to Jan Pieterszoon, well . . .' As he spoke, he began rolling up the jewels, tucking the precious little packet into an inner pocket. 'Your adopted countrymen are no fools, lad, though they are not men of vision. All will be well. Hey-ho, time we were going.'

With Pelagius one step behind, carrying the manuscript in a satchel, they went to a pawnbroker, who gave them a reasonable price for the jewels including the scrap, and on to Meester Claes.

'Glad to see it,' said the printer, after preliminary civilities had been observed. 'I've two shelves full of your plates and I need the space.'

'When will you start to print my illustrations, Meester Claes?' asked Comrij.

'Well, Dr Comrij, I've ordered your fine French paper, it's in the warehouse whenever we want it. We can start whenever you like.'

'When will my book be ready, then?'

'Doctor', said Meester Claes dryly, 'That's for you and Mynheer van der Aa. My work'll take about a month. He could do the letter press printing in a fortnight if he saw fit. Go and have a word with him.'

That was the end of the conversation. Claes was more than happy to be civil, but Comrij refused his offers of genever and tobacco. Shifting in his chair, he seemed so anxious to be gone that he was barely able to answer yes or no. As soon as it was decently possible, he bade an abrupt farewell to the printer, and walked with Pelagius to van der Aa's. His shop and works, with his living quarters above, were in a small but solidly built new house on the Prinsengracht, part of an enclave of recent building redolent of solidly middle-class comfort and security. It formed a painful contrast to the ramshackle medieval building which Mevrouw Mariken tried to keep decent.

'It's plain enough to see that it's publishing the money's in, not the writing,' said Comrij bitterly, as they shivered on the step in a light, spitting rain, looking up at the sparkling windows and newly painted white shutters, trim against the rosy brick of the walls. A spruce manservant came and opened the door to them, making them, despite his professional lack of expression, aware of their shabbiness and eccentricity. Comrij sent in his name with some hauteur, and he showed them past the shop and the print works, and up to van der Aa's business room. After a wait of some minutes, van der Aa himself appeared, fat, pink and clean like an overgrown baby, wheezing a little with the effort of the stairs, blandly smiling.

'Ah, the learned doctor. What can I do for you, mynheer?'

'My book, sir,' said Comrij baldly. 'Here is the manuscript. The plates are with Meester Claes. It awaits only your word.'

'Genever? No? Some for your man?' Pelagius shook his head. 'Perhaps I will, though. Just a little.' He got up, and opened a triangular cupboard in the corner behind his chair, revealing a black flask of genever and a number of glasses. He poured himself a drink, holding the glass judiciously up to the light of the window as he did so, and sat down with it, smiling fatly. 'Well, Doctor. The situation is a little more complex than it appears to you, alas. I fully understand your anxiety, indeed, I share it, but you must realize, my dear sir, that I have a number of books in hand at this time. The Homer and Virgil of our nation, Mynheer Jacob Cats, has honoured my presses with his latest masterpiece. Mynheer Cats, as I am sure you are aware, is a most prominent citizen poet and his work is eagerly awaited. With respect, Doctor, a work which has been twenty years in the making – all the better for it, of course, I am sure! – can wait another little while. For the moment, all my effort must be expended on Mynheer Cats. I will go in person to the Turfmarkt, as soon as I have a moment, and discuss the situation with Meester Claes.'

'But –!' Comrij half-rose in his seat, incoherent with distress.

'Ah, you scholars!' said van der Aa smoothly, with a hint of indulgence. 'You are a fiery breed, Doctor. The life of the mind. Poor drudging men of business like myself must take matters more calmly. Have no fear. Once the plates are printed we will have the letterpress set up as soon as may be.' Van der Aa finished his drink, and stood up. A flabbergasted Comrij, by a gentle, but quite inexorable pressure, was shepherded out of the room, then out of the house, still opening and shutting his mouth, unable to muster the words which he needed. The door closed behind them, quietly but firmly.

It had settled down to rain in good earnest. Comrij led off home, far faster than he usually walked, his mouth set in a grim line. His colour mounted and after a while he began to breathe hard, but he did not slow down. Stopping only to buy more genever, he went straight back to 't Groote Vis, trailed by Pelagius. As they went through the hall, Mevrouw Mariken came out to intercept them, but he brushed straight past her as if she was not there.

'Mynheer Comrij! Mynheer!'

Pelagius turned, and put out a hand apologetically. 'I am sorry, mevrouw. This is not a good moment to speak. I must go to my master.'

'Please, mynheer.' She put a timid hand on his sleeve; when he looked down at it, she let him go.

'Later.'

The incident with Mevrouw Mariken had been a matter of moments, but by the time Pelagius got up the stairs Comrij was already sitting with a glass in front of him.

'I am trapped,' he said, without preamble. 'Consider this. All that we have is invested with Meester Claes. I cannot go elsewhere. I must wait on the pleasure of this smiling Judas, this Pilate, this Herod . . .' Words failed him. He began to cough and drank deeply, his eyes bright with tears perhaps induced by the cough, or the raw spirit, or some other cause. Pelagius contemplated him without sympathy as he took his cloak off and hung it behind the door. Now you know, he thought. I have lived in the hell you have tumbled into ever since you returned to Holland. It was not a generous thought; he chided himself for letting it dwell in his mind.

'Soon, master,' he said patiently. 'Printing a book is no small task. Mynheer van der Aa must print each book as it comes in, surely? And Mynheer Cats is ahead of us.'

'And how long can we afford to wait, boy?' snapped Comrij. 'Can you see yourself as a shore porter, or a rag man? It may come to that.'

'But Mynheer van der Aa does not know this,' pointed out

Pelagius, trying to keep the irritation from his voice. 'We cannot assume that he is of wicked mind. And I do not think we can ask his charity.'

'Charity! Pah.' Comrij drank deeply and coughed again. He looked very small and crumpled, as if the day's disappointments had physically diminished him, still huddled in his damp cloak, which gave off a penetrating odour of wet wool. 'Light the fire, lad. I'm chilled to the bone.' It was cold enough in the attic: the fire had gone out since the morning and they had been so intent on the business in hand that they had not stopped to eat. But though his own fingers were cold-clumsy as he struggled with flint and tinder, he felt a spark of alarm. His master complained lavishly enough about the things he considered important, but he bore physical discomfort with indifferent fortitude. It was a horrible afternoon and what light there was was leaden, but he thought he could see an unhealthy flush on Comrij's cheek.

'Will you eat a little, master?'

'Na, na.' Comrij roused himself and attempted to smile. 'Have something yourself, if you care to.'

'But you did not eat last night, or this morning.'

Comrij sighed and coughed again. 'It does not matter. Heat some water, lad, and make me a toddy with genever.'

'We have no lemon, master, but there is honey still,' said Pelagius apologetically. Comrij paid him no mind. He lapsed into silence, sipping slowly at his hot drink, swallowing awkwardly at intervals as if his throat had become painful. When the last of the light went and Pelagius finally lit a tallow dip, he saw that the old man's face was wet with tears which he seemed hardly to know he was shedding.

By their bedtime it was obvious that Comrij was ill. He had consumed a prodigious amount of hot gin and water, to no apparent effect, but the hands which held his beaker were shaking with the regular tremors of fever and the breath rasped in his throat. At intervals he coughed, his whole body convulsed with the effort he was expending.

'Master, I think you should go to bed.'

Comrij attempted to answer him, but was unable to speak for coughing. When he had fought it down, he whispered hoarsely, 'Opium.'

'Willow tea?' offered Pelagius, without hope.

Comrij's fist clenched: unwilling to trust his voice again, he shook his head. Greatly against his better judgment, Pelagius brought the phial of tincture and poured a measure into Comrij's gin. When he attempted to take the phial away, Comrij reached for it and closed his dry, burning hand round it in silent denial. Without further words, he drank the noxious draught down and allowed Pelagius to help him to bed fully dressed, and to roll such spare clothes as they possessed into improvised pillows so that he could rest without lying flat.

'Can I bring you anything else, master?' Comrij shook his head again, so Pelagius, after checking that the chamber pot was conveniently to hand, wished him good night, and took away the candle.

III

> The sons of Hermes who have commenced in the Highschool of true Magic and Theosophy, have always spake their hidden Wisdome in a Mystery, and have to couch it under shadows and Figures, Parables and Similies, that none can understand their obscurely-clear writings, but those that have had admittance into the same School and have tasted of the Feast of Pentecost . . . a parabolical or Magical Phrase, or Dialect, is the best, and plainest habit and dress that Mysteries can have to travell up and down the wicked world.
>
> Jacob Böhme, *Signatura Rerum*, translator's preface by John Elliston

Pelagius woke early the next morning, wondering if Comrij might need him. There was no sound from his master's quarters, so he left the old man to sleep off his fever. Once he was dressed and shaved, he began on the household chores. Though it would make another trudge up and down the stairs for him later in the day, he left his master's chamber pot undisturbed, for fear of waking him. Taking his own pot and the bucket for clean water, he descended the stairs to the pump in the yard, the only meeting point between himself and the household below, which he had gradually come to comprehend. Mevrouw Mariken kept a stall in the market: a variety of women, daughters, perhaps, or relatives, lived with her, spinning, sewing, making goods of various kinds, and took turns to sit in the market with what they had made. Apart from himself and Comrij, the house was an entirely feminine one, a congeries of drab, clean, desolatingly poor women, supporting one another by their mutual efforts in a way that reminded him of Oyo. Just so, among his own people, widows and wives beyond the age of childbearing banded together to work and sell their wares.

He was standing in the bitter, early-morning cold, pumping the water which they would need for washing and cooking through the rest of the day, when Mevrouw Mariken herself came out to the yard. Wrapped in an old brown shawl, her thin, quill-like nose reddened by cold, she was a bedraggled and pathetic figure.

'Goede morgen, mevrouw,' offered Pelagius, with automatic courtesy.

'Oh, mynheer!' She seemed unaccountably nervous, clutching the shawl round her with both bony hands, her eyes watery and pleading.

'Can I help, mevrouw? You look a little anxious.' Her anxiety, he reflected uncomfortably, was probably about her rent, which had not been paid for some weeks, but one loses nothing by courtesy.

'Mynheer, you are book-learned men, aren't you? You and the doctor?'

'Yes, that is so,' Pelagius confirmed in some surprise.

'It's my daughter,' she confided. 'Not the one you know, the widow; the one who's married. I'm at my wit's end.' Tears began to well in her pink, bald-rimmed eyes and run down her withered cheeks.

'What is the trouble with your daughter?' he asked, at a loss.

'Well, mynheer, she's expecting again. The fifth time and she's not a single one to show for it. She's lost them all – you know what I mean – before they're due. It's hard on her, mynheer. She's got a good man, but he wanted a family, and he's a master mariner, and she's afraid he'll just find someone else in one of the ports and never come home. She came to me yesterday.'

Pelagius considered this story gravely, still leaning on the pump handle. 'I am sorry for your trouble, mevrouw, but how do you think we can help?'

She looked up at him; her eyes full of inchoate hope. 'You're cunning men, Doctor. I've seen all them plants you've got up there. Perhaps you know of something, something to keep little Hans-in-the-cellar where he belongs, till he's ready to come out?'

Pelagius sighed. He had read a little about women's medicine, but there was nothing he knew of in the presses upstairs which would be of the slightest use. There were several plants he knew of which would bring on a woman's courses, but none which had the opposite effect. On the other hand, Mevrouw Mariken touched him. They desperately needed her good will, which was a consideration, but her concern was a proper and decent one, and she had his sympathy: as he stood there, bare headed in the cold, he was racking his brains for a way to help her. A memory of his early life broke suddenly through the flotsam of botany and scientific medicine which he had learned from Comrij. Science had failed him, but human kindness suggested that it was better to try something else than to offer her nothing at all.

'May we go inside, mevrouw?' She led the way to her own quarters and he followed, tucking his frozen hands under his armpits as they went. She took him to the kitchen, an old-fashioned cavern of a room with a huge fireplace hung with mysterious trivets and metal implements. A meagre but cheerful fire burned in the hearth, with a kettle waiting beside it, though no one else was about as yet. She sat him down in a rush-seated chair and looked at him expectantly.

Entirely unsure if he was doing the right thing, he began to speak. 'I am a man of Africa, mevrouw. My people know of a being called Órunmila, who speaks the will of God. I am a Christian man and not a witch, but I think Órunmila is perhaps like a prophet or a messenger of God. There is an oracle called Ifá, of the words of Órunmila, which many have trusted. I learned Ifá, when I was a young man in my own country. Shall I try it for you?' His lack of confidence was not apparent in his voice, which was deep and calm.

'You're sure it isn't magic?' she asked nervously.

'Not in the least. It is not an act of worship, but a way of questioning the divine intention. And it has often worked for my people. It may work here.'

'What do you do, then?' she asked, a faint hopefulness dawning in her voice.

'Can you find me sixteen nuts? Not very large ones.'

Mariken rose and rummaged in a chest, coming out eventually with a bag of hazelnuts. 'Are these all right?'

'They will do very well.' Pelagius spoke more confidently than he felt. The nuts should be palm nuts and he was far from certain he could remember all the *odù*, which he had not thought about for many years. But, he felt, if he performed the ceremony in a sincere spirit and God was pleased to aid him, then all would be well; if God did not wish this to happen then it would not. He took the nuts loosely in one hand and banged the other hand against it. Three nuts dropped out. He noted the number, picked up the nuts again and repeated the performance. Mariken was watching with breathless interest. Once he had eight numbers, he performed the well-remembered calculation which would give him the number of the *odù* which represented, in some way, a solution. Ninety-one. *Odù Ìwòrì'túrúpòn.* How extraordinary. His heart gave a cold little leap: it must be a true sending, as if God had been guiding his hand.

'This is the oracle, mevrouw. There was a man called Ìwòrì, and he was the husband of Òtúrúpòn. She had a baby who died, so she is like your daughter. Ifá says: Òtúrúpòn will bring forth another child who will live, but Ìwòrì must make sacrifice, a hen, a goat, a fish, and eighteen thousand cowries. Òtúrúpòn must drink a soup with the fish, and *èla* leaves, early in the morning.'

'But we can't do any such thing!' wailed Mariken.

'No, indeed', said Pelagius firmly. 'Christians do not make sacrifice. The form of the oracle is proper to its time and place, so we must interpret, as we do with the Book of Leviticus. Your daughter's husband must put some money to charitable uses, with the thought in his mind that he is fulfilling the oracle. What they can afford. And he should send a hen and a lamb to some place for the destitute, perhaps the hospital. The *èla* is a tree of my country, which does not shed its leaves when others do. So let your daughter make a broth of herring each evening, and steep juniper in it, since juniper does not shed its leaves, and let her drink it when she wakes. Has she reached the fifth month?'

'Yes, mynheer,' whispered Mariken, awed.

'Then let her do this each night for the next six weeks and commend herself to God. We are in His hands.'

'Thank you, mynheer.' He rose and bowed to her, and trudged upstairs with his pail, wondering at himself. But when God had given him the words, words unthought-of for nearly twenty-five years, could He be opposed? Works of charity were not significant to salvation, but nonetheless he could not imagine that they could do harm in a situation such as this. And why had God put the oracle into his mind, if he were not to use it . . . ? He plodded on up, deep in thought.

The morning was wearing on. Purposely, he made a certain amount of noise as he swept and tidied, but there was no sound from Comrij. He made some more of the willow tisane, and after a little hesitation, knocked on his master's door and went in.

The old man was resting half-upright on his pyramid of miscellaneous textiles, head thrown back against the wall as if struggling for breath, mouth open. His skin was waxen and he was quite obviously dead. All the same, Pelagius crossed the room in two swift steps, and took his wrist, looking for a pulse. The flesh was already cool: there was nothing whatever to be done. As he took a step back, Pelagius observed the little phial of tincture of opium, standing open by the bedside. He picked it up and found that it was empty. Comrij must have taken another dose, and it flashed across his mind that there was a question about the spirit in which he had taken it. Why had he quoted the 'Nunc dimittis'? Had not all his speech been about ending? But on the other hand his words could easily have sprung from the depression induced by catching cold. He had been ill, feverish, far from sober, impatient: all good reasons for taking an unwise second dose. And Pelagius had no desire to probe further: he felt a filial unwillingness to uncover the nakedness of Comrij's despair. He drew the sheet up over the old man's grey face and retired into the other room to think.

Calvinists do not pray for the dead; Comrij was either among God's elect, or he was not. In the course of his theological studies, Pelagius had fully comprehended the logic of this; but he recognized in himself an inescapable desire to do something – to offer to God, as if the Almighty were not able to see it for Himself, his own perception of the essential goodness and even greatness of the flawed, sour and disappointed man who had been his own second father.

With an odd, sinking sense of giving way to a shameful desire, he whispered, 'My God. *De profundis clamavi.* I do not question your will or your purposes, but will you graciously vouchsafe me a sign?' He still had Mariken's nuts in his pocket, where he had unthinkingly put them: he gathered them into his hand and performed the oracle. Two hundred and twenty-one, *Odù Òsa-Retè.* The words came dropping through his mind – If a man who sleeps alone sleeps badly, only God can wake him . . . a stranger came to sojourn, and asked for help to carry his burden. He was asked to sacrifice, and heeded the request. He prepared his burden and looked backwards and forwards, but no one was there to help him: he said, 'This load is now God's. Those who have no friends must put their trust in God.'

He put his elbows on the table, let his head fall into his hands and wept. Órunmila was all too clear. He had been no son to Comrij; for all that he had done in practical terms, he had withheld his charity, and the old man had struggled and lived and died alone. He sat at the table, unmoving, for hour after hour, neither thinking nor praying, in a state of blank, nightmarish distress. Only when the early afternoon sun lanced through the high window of the attic and gilded the table he sat at, did he stir himself. There was much to do: first of all, he must lay out his master's body.

In the days that followed he moved, like a man in a dream, about the practical business of getting Comrij decently interred. He had seen many a funeral since coming to Holland, slow and stately processions of black-clad burghers. But there was no one but himself to walk behind the coffin; there need be no sober funeral feast, for there was nobody to eat it. He sold Comrij's clothes, most of the furniture and his beloved books, and paid Mevrouw Mariken what she was owed. The books brought in guilders enough for a coffin, two decent men, the use of a handcart, and a place in the town burial ground. Walking back afterwards to 't Groote Vis, it occurred to him that he owned almost nothing except enough ready money to live on for a week, if he was very careful. No replies had ever come from the grandees to whom he had written all those weeks ago: in any case, he could demonstrate no rights over Comrij's intellectual legacy since the old man had not thought to make a will. At least, he reflected bleakly, he was not, in himself, an item of unaccounted-for property.

He trudged back up to the familiar attic. It looked very clean and very empty. He had packed the notebooks and the herbaria with their dried specimens neatly into piles: if they had a value, he had not the faintest idea how to realize it. The door to Comrij's room stood open, as the undertakers' men had left it, with his bleak little bed stripped and bare. His spirit seemed to have completely gone out of the place.

In Pelagius's pocket were five and a half guilders. Beyond that, there was no future that he could envisage. What could a middle-aged man of scholarly habits and inclinations with no patrons and no friends do to support himself once Mariken's patience wore out? For any sort of profession a recommendation would be needed and there was no one and nothing to recommend him. He must move into cheaper quarters, that was certain; but what on earth could he do?

As he sat and bleakly revolved his lack of prospects, he heard a tentative tapping at the door.

'Come in.'

The door opened a crack and through it sidled Mevrouw Mariken, carrying a covered bowl. 'Doctor. I thought you might like a bite.'

'Mevrouw. How very kind of you.' He was amazed and touched. Mutely, she held out the bowl. He took it from her and put it on the table. 'I am very grateful.' He looked at her gravely. She showed no sign of intending to leave and there was something in her face which made it look as if she had something more to say. 'Can I help you?'

Mariken clasped her hands, raising them to her lean bosom in an involuntarily prayer-like gesture. 'Doctor. What you said about my daughter . . . she's into the sixth month, and she's still got Hans-in-the-cellar.'

'I am very glad of it,' said Pelagius, a little nonplussed.

'Well . . . I was wondering if you could help Geertruyd.'

He stared at her, the saliva drying on the roof of his mouth.

She misunderstood him immediately. 'No, no, Doctor. I don't mean you should do it for nothing. She'll pay you. Well, we've all got to live, I know that.'

He was left absolutely without a coherent response. He had a flash of panic: what was he getting himself into? But money was money. He decided all at once. 'Very well, I will see her.'

'Oh, thank God, Doctor. She's downstairs. I'll bring her up.'

Mariken whisked out of the room. Pelagius cast a wistful glance at the bowl cooling on the table, emitting a savoury odour of stockfish. But if these women were determined to see him as a magus, they must not catch him with a spoon in his hand: that was elementary. Who was Geertruyd? One of the house's overplus of drab women, it was safe to assume, but which?

Some moments later, Mariken and her friend knocked on the door. He rose and bowed formally. Straightening up, he looked at her with something more than ordinary interest. He vaguely recalled seeing her before: she must live in the house, though they had never exchanged a word. She was fat, where Mariken was scrawny; the stairs had given her some trouble. It was not the firm, healthy, pink-toned fat of many Dutch women, but seemed to lie semi-liquid and lumpy under thin skin. Mariken's face was strained by chronic poverty and worry; this woman's eyes held a beseeching anxiety which spoke of something above and beyond the ordinary difficulties of living.

'Mevrouw,' he said formally, bowing a little.

'Doctor,' she replied, her voice hoarse with nervousness.

'You wish me to consult Ifá for you?'

'Yes.' Her round, fearful eyes met his own momentarily and skittered away.

Pelagius sighed and reached for the nuts. Some little time later, he reported. 'The *odù* is called *Ìretè-Túrá*. How can I say it? ... At the beginning, it says death does not recognize a healer. Olamba was killed, Eji-Agogo was killed. But Ifá was divined for Órunmila ... the death which would have killed Awo, the disease which would have killed Awo, has gone away. It is going, it has given way. Mevrouw, I think you are sick, but the oracle says there is hope. People have died of such things, but those who respect God and walk uprightly have been saved.'

'Oh, thank you, sir!' she whispered.

Pelagius, seeing the tears standing in her eyes, was surprised and embarrassed. 'Mevrouw, it is not me that you need thank. The words of God are spoken through Órunmila and

I give you the words which he spoke in the *odù*. I am only a vessel.'

'But I can feel the truth in what you say, sir. Look . . . I'm sorry it's not more.' Gracelessly, she rootled in her pocket and thrust out her hand with a handful of stuivers on the palm.

He took the money from her. 'I am glad of it, nonetheless. Walk in the paths of righteousness. Pray to the Lord that you may be healed.'

The door closed behind them. Listening to the two women's feet receding down the stairs, it occurred to him with some astonishment that he seemed to have acquired a possible livelihood without even going out of the house. He looked at what she had given him: twelve stuivers. A day's subsistence. He was hungry and there was food on the table. He found a spoon and began to eat Mariken's cooling *hutspot*, with a chill feeling beginning to form, as he chewed, that each mouthful further committed him to accepting her view of him.

The food, though Mariken was a good enough cook in the Dutch style, began to sit uneasily on his stomach. The words, 'Thou hast sold thy birthright for a mess of pottage', came into his mind and he put the bowl down, uneasily swallowing the food, which had turned in his mouth into an inedible bolus. The whole question urgently required examination and inward searching. He slipped down on to his knees in front of the chair he had been sitting in and rested his elbows on the seat, with his forehead leaned against his clasped hands, in order to think his position through.

To begin with, birthright, in the natural sense, he had none. The words of the psalmist were words he could take as his own: I am become a stranger unto my brethren: even an alien unto my mother's children. His birthright was as a son of God, a son of the covenant. The woman tempted me and I did eat . . . No! The words of Adam were a false leading. For was there not also the widow of Zarepthah, who sustained Elijah with the last food that she had? Mevrouw Mariken was nearly as poor. And Elijah brought the widow's son back from the dead in the name of the Lord. Moreover, in the next chapter, Elijah prophesied and performed great works of magic. Did he do ill in using the oracle, if he helped these poor women? After all, he was not encouraging the worship of false gods, but insistent that Órunmila spoke in the oracle only as a voice. He had studied Greek and Roman authors; and had learned from the professors at Leiden that pagan wisdom was not necessarily to be despised, even by a good Christian. He had been taught that a number of wise and virtuous men had had presentiments of the One God long before the birth of Christ. Surely he could not be wrong in believing that his own people were under the hand of God though they understood it not; did they not believe that Olódùmarè alone created the world and all that was in it, while the many lesser gods were merely His ministers and servants? Was there any reason to doubt that God had revealed Himself to Odùdúwa, the ancestor of the people, just as He had revealed Himself to Plato, Moses and Virgil? The Ifá oracle spoke nothing which was against the law of Christ: true, it recommended sacrifice in atonement for misdeeds and mistakes, but so did the Old Testament. The oracle of the Jews was overturned by the revelation of the New Testament, but did not thereby lose its validity. Finally, his thoughts circled back to the idea which had struck him from the beginning: did not the fact that God had guided the selection of *odù* so surely indicate that he was justified in continuing their use?

Considerably cheered, he rose from the cold floor and resumed his meal. If he retained a humble spirit and used the opportunity given to him as an occasion of instruction, all would be well. He had wanted to be a servant and a minister of God, and had been prevented from becoming one. Perhaps he should see in this unwished and unlooked-for development an indication that he was marked out as a minister of a different kind?

In the days which followed Mariken, it was to be assumed, spoke to her friends and the people she met in the market, for a number of feet stumbled up the steep stairs of 't Groote Vis, a number of hands knocked hesitantly on his door, never less than one in a day, sometimes two and, as the days went by, three or even more. Men and women trying to decide whom to marry, women trying to keep peace between a husband and a son at loggerheads, people in unsatisfactory work, people out of work, the ill, the mildly deranged. In fundamental respects, therefore, people very like the Oyo. He helped them to the best of his ability; and in the main, they seemed to go away comforted.

In his wanderings around The Hague, he was occasionally tempted into bookshops. He had sold all of Comrij's books at the time of his death and missed them acutely. It was a great pleasure to him to turn over old volumes, even knowing that he could not buy them: reading a few pages or even a paragraph, standing at the stall, would give him matter for meditation, something to turn over in his mind. Because his own people had used almost no writing – he had a very little knowledge of Arabic script, learned for horse-trading with the Muslim Songhai, little more than his numbers and a few words for describing horses – his memory had been well trained in his youth. Even a knotty paragraph of theological prose would sink deeply into his mind and remain there, if he gave it his full concentration.

On one such expedition he found about three-quarters of a little old book without its covers, which turned out to be most of Lactantius's *Divine Institutions.* He opened it cautiously and the broken-backed little volume fell into two halves in his hands, linked only by the undersewing of its spine. He had heard of Lactantius, in his studies at Leiden, as one of the earliest Christian apologists, but had never seen a copy of his work. He began reading where it had fallen open and found that the old philosopher was reviewing what pre-Christian writers had said of God and Christ. 'And the

Erythrean Sibyl, at the very beginning of her compositions, which were gifts of God on High, prophesied the Son of God as the leader and emperor of all, in these verses ...' he read on, fascinated, puzzling over the enigmatic poems in Greek which Lactantius went on to quote. Reading as fast as he could, skimming, trying to absorb the information, he came to realize that there had been a considerable number of pagan poets known as Sibyls and a whole collection of verse prophesies associated with their names. Another clause caught his eye: 'and the Libyan Sibyl; whom Euripides recalls in the prologue to his *Lamia*'. But Libya was what the Romans called North Africa. Were there African Sibyls? His hands tightened unconsciously on the battered little book.

'You can have that for a guilder fifteen,' said the bookseller, watching him. 'Seeing as it's so damaged.' He thought, put it down, picked it up, thought again and bought it. Taking it home, he read it with concentration and revolved it in his mind for several days. His first impression had been correct: there were many Sibyls and their utterances were consistently treated with reverence by this respected early Christian writer. For Lactantius at least, pagan prophets had a small but honourable part to play in the history of revelation. He got up and prospected in the cupboard. There was an old notebook, with some entries on pandanus and rattan, otherwise unused. He turned it round, so as to start from the clean end, and wrote a title in large, clear, elegant letters on the virgin page: *Liber oraculorum Orunmilae, aut, Sibylla Africana.* Then he began to translate the *odù* of the Ifá Oracle into Latin. The Sibylline verses gave him a model, and he felt the essential dignity of Ifá was best served by a classical tongue – moreover, he had been taught to write Latin, but not Dutch. Though his spoken Dutch was completely fluent, his spelling was so wildly approximate that on the few occasions when he had had occasion to write a few words they had often proved incomprehensible. It was soothing to him to write again; the mental discipline of calling up the *odù* and trying to render them into an alien tongue was pleasurable in itself to a man who had spent most of his life as a scholar. He worked away, slowly and hesitantly, filling the pages with his fine, upright Italic script, the *odù* rising like fish from the dark depths of memory. Each one was held in his mind, mulled over, the words scrutinized minutely, the translation completed before he set pen to paper. Some second thoughts there were, but what went down in the book was for the most part, complete.

There was, he came to realize as he worked, an intense satisfaction in thus bridging the vast gulf between his first and his second lives. His African knowledge, now distant by half the world and a quarter of a century, had never been of the slightest interest to anyone. Most of the people he had met in his life since then had wanted to exploit him, and a few had wished to teach him. Not one had ever wanted to learn from him. But the value, the human truths, of the Ifá Oracles were proved every day, in this alien land, as he sent the poor and the simple away comforted and sustained by the words of Órunmila.

As the weeks passed he became more and more confident of his new abilities. He found in himself, unexpectedly, a secret, reckless pleasure in showmanship that was alien to the cautious, scholarly ways he had learned so well. The element of dazzling improvisation, the speed at which it was necessary to think and react, exercised an aspect of his mind which had lain unused since his days as a prince and leader of men. He began to enjoy his own skill, especially since he now had the oracles in written form and was no longer absolutely dependent on his memory. Autumn was well under way and he had enough money from day to day to keep a fire in the grate and a coat on his back, so he had much to be thankful for.

One bright and frosty morning, when thin, clear sunlight lanced through his attic window and made a cheerful pool of light on the bare boards, it struck him suddenly that the *Theatrum* should have been printed. Perhaps he should go to Meester Claes and find out:

the book had been thrust to one side by the events of death, but now he came to think of it, it was unfinished business. It had cost enough of his life, after all.

The Hague was looking much better in winter light than it had in the dreary days of late autumn. He loathed the cold, but there was something actively pleasant in the clean tang of the air on this day when the shadowed areas of the streets gleamed white with rimy frost, but the sun was strong enough still to melt the areas it touched directly. He had not set foot in the Turfmarkt since Comrij's death and looked about him with interest.

He knocked on the workshop door and entered at the answering shout. The workshop was warm and stuffy from the heat of the braziers, and the sharp odours of ink and lye stung at his nose and eyes.

'Hey, it's old Comrij's man. How are you doing?' Meester Claes, in his shirtsleeves and busy as usual, seemed moderately pleased to see him, though with some reserve.

'I am very well, meester, and I have work.' He had guessed right; there was a perceptible relaxation in Claes's attitude now he was assured that he had not come begging to be taken on.

'Take a seat, Pelagius. A drop of genever, to keep out the cold?'

'No thank you, meester.' He sat down, still in his cloak and with his hat in his hand, though he was beginning to feel sweat gathering along his hairline. 'Meester Claes, what has happened to my master Comrij's book?'

'The book? Oh, yes. It's printed, I believe. The copperplate sheets went to van der Aa weeks ago.' Something seemed odd in his manner and Pelagius looked at him rather sharply. Claes was never fulsome, but there was a sort of blankness which he could not interpret: it was a little disappointing not to get a few words of compliment. But perhaps the man was simply hoping to get rid of him.

'Thank you. I will go to mynheer van der Aa, Meester Claes.'

'Fine, lad. I'll bid you good day, then. Glad to see you're getting on all right.'

Pelagius rose and bowed, and Claes let him out into the Turfmarkt. He walked over to the Prinsengracht with a vague, pleasant sense of expectancy. After the labours and setbacks of all Comrij's difficult and disappointed years, something had at last come to birth. And the plates were superb. Perhaps the book would be a success after all – to the profit of van der Aa, regrettably, but all the same, to be hoped for as a lasting memorial to his master.

He went, therefore, to van der Aa's shop. Most of what it contained was, apparently, paper. Like nearly all other sellers of new books, van der Aa stored his stock as heaps of folded folio sheets, thus allowing him to keep it on shelves of uniform size, and bound books individually for customers when they were wanted. But one corner of the shop contained bound books of all sizes for customers to look at. The well-remembered size of the folio plates ensured that Pelagius's eye rested only on the biggest of the volumes. There was nothing he could see that seemed to be the right shape; there were a couple of books large enough, but they were slender, and the manuscript which had gone to van der Aa had filled a whole satchel: he reckoned it should have taken up about a hundred pages. Though, on the other hand, the printed pages would be very large . . . He plucked a book off the shelf and opened it on one of the tables provided for the purpose. It fell open at the plate of the coconut palm and its fruit, which he had not seen for six months or more. He was delighted to see his own careful drawings, professionally realized. Though he had of course seen Gerrit's proof pulls months before, there was something different about the way it looked bound into a real book. Attractive, clear, comprehensible; it was work to be proud of. He shut the book and reopened it at the title page.

It was some little while before he could believe the evidence of his eyes. He stood staring in sick horror, bile rising in his throat. He could hear Comrij's voice in his head, shrieking hoarsely. The title-page before him was not *Theatrum Florae Indicae* and Comrij's name did not appear. The volume was simply called *Oost-Indische Kruyd-boeck*: plants of the Indies. With trembling hands, he turned the page and confirmed his worst fears. There were about twenty pages of text, in Dutch. He could hardly bear to look at them, but the glance he took told him that the work was simple-minded to a degree, and as often as not factually incorrect. To add further insult to injury, Comrij had spent an extra fifteen guilders on fine French paper for the illustrations and the letterpress was set on ordinary Bastard which was half the price. Grimly, he shut the book and knocked on the door which led up to the publisher's private quarters.

'I must see Mynheer van der Aa', he told the manservant baldly. The servant went away to take the message, and some time later returned and showed him into van der Aa's room, as before, where he stood waiting.

Eventually, the publisher made his smooth and smiling appearance. 'Ah. The good doctor's servant, I believe. How can I help you?'

'Mynheer van der Aa, I have just seen what you have done. Why have you not printed my master's book?'

Van der Aa sighed and sat down at his desk. 'Won't you sit? No? My dear fellow, I am a man of business and I must be practical. I showed your master's text to one or two learned men of my acquaintance and they saw, to be frank, little value in it. Too much theory, too much controversy. Debate and dissent among the learned is one thing, my friend, but your late master descended to a level of personal insult, and against most distinguished persons, which I could hardly put my hand to. And Paracelsus . . . I was assured on all hands that Paracelsus is no longer regarded as of great significance. Van Helmont's the man, they tell me.'

'You have betrayed my master's memory,' said Pelagius, controlling his voice with some difficulty.

Van der Aa flushed a little. 'He betrayed himself. The work was unprintable. I gave it to one of my young men and he boiled the gist of it down for me.'

'He did no such thing, mynheer. The work is atrocious and inaccurate in every respect.' Another thought struck him. 'And what about the money? My master paid more than two thousand guilders for the illustrations and you have put them to a worthless text.'

'I cannot see that it is any concern of yours,' said Van der Aa coldly. 'Dr Comrij has left no heirs and assigns that I know of. And in any case, do not forget that I have been put to extra expense commissioning the précis. I see little profit in discussing this further. Good day to you.'

Pelagius looked at him: he did not move, but van der Aa shrank back in his chair as if he was expecting violence, and half-raised a trembling hand.

'Remember this, mynheer.' His voice was deep, cold, and measured. 'The joy of the hypocrite is but for a moment. He will perish for ever, like his own dung, though wickedness is sweet under his tongue. The meat in his bowels will turn to gall, and God will cast the fury of his wrath upon him.'

Van der Aa staggered to his feet, pale and alarmed. 'Don't you threaten me!' he gasped. The servant, alarmed, appeared suddenly in the doorway.

'It is not I who speaks,' said Pelagius, putting on his hat. As he strode from the room, he saw, from the corner of his eye, van der Aa falling back into his chair, with his hand on his heart, and his man running to the corner cupboard.

He barged out of the house, blind with fury, and stalked down the Prinsengracht with long, hasty strides in the dwindling evening light. Grimly he calculated the sums involved. If van der Aa had done as he had contracted to do, then his share of the costs would have been nearly seven hundred guilders. He could hardly have spent two on the wretched *Kruyd-boeck*, which would certainly sell on the plates alone. Pelagius had no doubt that the text of the *Theatrum* has been destroyed: van der Aa's slovenly, indifferent attitude made that certain. The stumbling illiterate who had produced that travestied text would hardly have troubled himself to keep it. Waste; nothing but waste and loss. A lifetime's work, reduced to a set of pictures. Acquainted as he was with the vanity of human effort, the destruction of Comrij's work touched him to the quick. The only mitigating thought was that the old man had not lived to see it, though on the other hand, if he had been alive, van der Aa might not have dared to act as he had done.

When he returned to 't Groote Vis, he was hoping for nothing but a little time to himself to grieve in peace. But as he entered the house, Mevrouw Mariken waylaid him.

'Oh, Doctor!' He looked at her without enthusiasm. She was aware of his displeasure, but not abashed by it. She had always been polite to him, but made it clear that he was to her mind in a different class from Comrij. Now he was her sole tenant, she might have revised her attitudes, except that she had made herself responsible for finding him clients and her stance towards him had, in consequence, become proprietorial. 'You remember Mevrouw Geertruyd? My friend? She wants to see you.'

Pelagius sighed. He did not, on the other hand, want to see her and what was more, could not remember who she was, but he could not afford to turn Mariken against him. 'I will see her,' he said wearily.

He went up to his own quarters, lit a couple of tapers and tried to coax a little life out of the fire with the bellows and a couple of fresh turves, beginning to wonder what had happened to his client, as the minutes passed. He now kept the room arranged to suit its new purpose, with a chair on either side of the table, which held his *liber oraculorum*, his bowl of nuts and the candles, arranged so as to cast light on the face of his client. He was aware that little could be seen of his own dark face in such a light and had come to realize that the effect of his deep voice out of the shadows was enhanced the more obscure he remained. On the other hand, his clients' faces often told him a great deal.

He had been aware of a noise outside the door for some time; a dragging progress. The knock came at last, and he took a taper and rose to open it. It was Mariken's fat friend, his first client apart from Mariken herself, looking piteously up at him. Mariken was hovering behind her in the darkness of the stairwell. She had got a great deal worse since he first saw her. 'Mevrouw. Please take my arm. You must rest.' He guided her across the room to the chair, realizing that nearly her whole weight was resting on his supporting arm: she fell into it, breathing noisily. He put the taper back on the table, fussing with it, so as to look unobtrusively at her face as she sagged in the chair, mouth open, and eyes shut. There was death in her features; he saw the tracks plainly enough.

'Mevrouw, what can I do for you?' he said, when she showed signs of recovery. She opened her eyes and looked at him with the eyes of a trapped animal. She knew what he knew; yet she had dragged herself up those painful, endless stairs.

'Doctor, you must do something,' said Mariken. He jumped and turned towards the voice. He had completely forgotten she was there in his concentration on the sick woman. She was standing by the jamb of the door, hands clasped loosely in front of her.

'But I have done all I can do,' he said helplessly. 'I have asked Órunmila, and he did not say if she should be healed.' The force of her silent rejection hit him like a blow. There was something in the concentrated force of this woman which left him weaponless. He could silence her in debate or knock her down the stairs; either way, she would come back at him, furious, ignorant and determined. She was like a hungry ghost, absolute in her demand to be served.

Undaunted, she came forward. 'There's another thing I've heard of people doing,' she said. 'You put a bit of black ink in a saucer, and look in it. I want you to do it for us.' She did not even ask, but ordered him, as if she had the right to do so.

'Who is this woman to you?' he demanded in his turn, angered by her attitude.

She primmed her mouth, eyes hard as she stared him down. 'My no-good brother's widow.' Taking a step forward, she rested the back of her thick-knuckled, work-worn hand momentarily on the other woman's cheek. Mevrouw Geertruyd moved her head almost imperceptibly, leaning her cheek against the caress. Her eyes were still shut, it was if she had entrusted everything she needed to say to Mariken.

Defeated, he got up and found a bottle of ink, and poured some into a saucer. 'What do I do?' he asked.

'Look in it. You're a cunning man, you'll see something all right. Then you'll tell us what.'

The situation was so extraordinary for him, so dreamlike, he found it easier to accept it than to deny it. Resting his chin in his hands, he stared at the ink, then raised his head. Mevrouw Geertruyd was still sitting in the chair as shapeless as a large, pale pudding, but she was looking at him. He caught her gaze with his own; her frightened eyes flickered, then locked with his: they rounded and lost some of their strain as she fell into a posture of trust. Though he did not understand what was happening, he began to see what he must do to resolve the situation. 'You must look too, mevrouw,' he ordered.

She leaned forward, folding her arms under her substantial bosom as her flesh fell forward on to the table. Together they stared into the ink. The black pool of liquid stood between them, so positioned that it reflected neither their faces, nor the candle; absolute and velvet darkness. Outside the light had completely faded from the sky. The only light in the room was from the tapers, shielded from the ink by the interposing bulk of Mevrouw Geertruyd. It is hard to look into darkness and see nothing.

Suddenly she thrust out a hand towards him, still staring into the ink. He took it: the texture of her grasp was clammy, cold and unpleasant, and he could feel the tremor of tension which vibrated through her. Though she seemed bulky enough, her hand was swallowed up in his, it felt like a dead fish. The texture of her grasp changed; what was it? her pulse? Something was different, his palm perceived it.

'What do you see?' he said, on a guess.

'Jan,' she said hoarsely. 'He's there.' Her voice was full of fear; the hand in his was sweating like a sponge.

Mariken stepped forward, hands on her hips, glaring at the ink. 'Janneken,' she ordered with a big sister's authority, 'leave her alone. You can't have her.'

Pelagius held Geertruyd's slippery hand, fascinated. He could see nothing at all; but it was absolutely clear to him that a drama was being played out between the two women and their idea of the dead man which was using him as conduit. It was enough that they believed in his powers: evidently, it was only necessary to keep his grasp firm and let them do as they must. 'Tell him what you feel,' he said; his deep, even voice sounding with cool authority in the dark room.

'Jan, I don't want to. I'm sorry. I didn't mean any of it. I couldn't help it.' Her voice was gluey with tears and helpless with apology.

Mariken pounced again, shaking with vehemence. 'Jan, you've no right. She was a good wife to you. You've nothing to reproach her with.'

'Don't make me come to you.'

'You can't make her,' interjected Mariken fiercely.

Pelagius, without thinking, caught up in the situation as a whole, intervened. 'Jan,' he said firmly, 'Rest in peace. You belong to God, your wife is her own woman. Trouble her no more.'

'He's gone,' said Mariken. 'Oh, thank the Lord. He's gone.'

Geertruyd said nothing, but began to weep fat, soggy tears of pure thankfulness. 'He's gone. I can feel him not there.'

'Your fate is your own, mevrouw,' said Pelagius sternly. 'Do not blame on the dead what is yours to know and suffer.'

'Oh, sir', she said, turning to him with the tears still streaking her face, 'I'm not sorry for it. But he's been weighing on my heart.'

Mevrouw Mariken put her hand under Geertruyd's elbow, and hefted her to her feet. The deathly look had already faded from her face. Pelagius rose, taking a taper, to light them down the stairs, and observed, as she went, that her step was already firmer, her back straighter. Something had gone from her; he was certain it was through no craft of his own.

PURIFICATIO

IV

Earthly things do fade, decay,
Constant to us not one day;
Suddenly they pass away,
And we can not make them stay.
Elizabeth Stuart, later Queen of Bohemia, 1609

The fact that he had without doubt helped Mevrouw Geertruyd gave Pelagius a number of difficult nights. He was intellectually opposed to the notion of calling up spirits: the dead, his Calvinist training told him, should be sleeping in the Lord, though the African side of his mind was not so certain of this. He also remembered that the Witch of Endor had summoned the spirit of the prophet Samuel for King Saul; thus, on the authority of the Old Testament, spirits of some sort existed to be summoned. Some writers, as he recalled from his Leiden days, thought that all such spirits were demonic, but since St John in his gospel also said, 'test the spirits to see whether they are from God', he had it on the word of an apostle that some spirits could be benign. His conscience was troubled over the fact that he had apparently been seduced into conjuring, since any dealing with spirits was dangerous; yet he was not conscious, in himself, of any kind of magical process. Geertruyd, not he, had seen something, and what she had seen, he strongly suspected, was the embodied form of her own guilt. But it also became increasingly clear to him, as time went on and his practice as a dispenser of the Ifá Oracle grew, that he was able to help people in ways that none of his intellectual training enabled him to explain. It seemed obvious that his black skin had something to do with it: it marked him so clearly as alien, therefore mysterious and possibly magical, that it allowed his clients to resolve their own difficulties, unaware that they were doing so. Beyond that, he developed no very clear idea of what was happening. The whole business certainly allowed him to scrape along from day to day rather better than he could have hoped; but he had no sense of where it might all be going, except that he became increasingly certain that, in some fashion, he was serving the purposes of God.

Sitting one morning, musing on what the day might bring him, he was interrupted by Mariken. He could hear her beginning to speak as she came up the last flight of stairs: by the time she arrived in the room, she was out of breath, and he had understood nothing of her gasping communication.

He rose and bowed. 'Mevrouw.' He could see that she was holding something white in her hand.

'Doctor! A letter. The messenger said it was for Dr Comrij, so I thought you should have it.'

'Thank you, mevrouw.' He took it from her, and sat down again, breaking the seal thoughtfully, full of curiosity.

'He was a fine, handsome lad,' volunteered Mariken, agog. 'He had a lovely horse.'

'Thank you, mevrouw. If you could just leave me a little, to read it . . . ?'

Mariken departed, looking injured, while he broke the seal. The paper was stiff and expensive, and the script was of exemplary, professional clarity. As his eyes travelled over the lines, a number of emotions passed through his mind, perhaps the most clear cut of which was an immense weariness. The letter was from the Stadhouder, Prins Fredrik Hendrik.

Most learned and well-honoured Dr Comrij,

Your letter has only recently come to my hand. My duties in

the field have left me no time for any concerns but the most pressing affairs of state. Having now a moment of leisure, I would be glad to discuss with you the progress of the *Theatrum Florae*. As you rightly say, it is in the interests of our great nation that such a work should exist. While it may be that the purely commercial interests of the East India Company militate against supporting such ventures, it falls to the part of the Stadhouder to consider matters which are, while no less important, only indirectly profitable. I should be pleased, honoured sir, if you would wait on me at the palace, whenever you find it convenient.

Yours, &c., Frederik Hendrik.

How Comrij would have crowed and exulted. But now, what could he say? What was there to be said? He folded the letter and put it carefully on the table. In any case, he would have to wait on the Stadhouder and explain as best he might.

It was only a few minutes' walk from 't Groote Vis to the Kneuterdijk in terms of distance, but it was far enough in human terms. Leaving behind the crowded tenements of the myriad poorer folk of this town which was not a town, he walked into the precincts of the court. Like the *afin* of the kings of Oyo, the palace quarters of the Stadhouders sprawled over a considerable distance. Unlike his father's *afin*, and in Pelagius's view most indecorously, the palace area was open to public access and anyone who chose could walk in the Buitenhof or down the Vijverberg, the long walk down the side of the ornamental water which fronted the palace buildings.

When he presented himself at the palace, letter in hand, the Prince's signature got him through the doors without difficulty: he was told that his highness would be available for audience at two o'clock. At two o'clock he was duly ushered in to the presence.

He regarded his first European ruler with interest. Fredrik

Hendrik turned out to be a smallish man in vigorous late middle age, with a cavalryman's straight back, a plump, down-to-earth face, and a pointed beard and moustache, wearing a very beautiful brocaded coat. His expression was intelligent and enquiring, and it fixed on Pelagius, as he entered, with some degree of puzzlement.

'Who are you?' he asked, once Pelagius had made his bow.

'Monseigneur, I am the servant of Mynheer Comrij, who is now dead. My name is Pelagius. I worked with him on his book for more than twenty years. He left no heir in law, but in conscience I may speak for him.'

'I see. Tell me of this book.'

Pelagius sighed. 'I am sorry to say, Monseigneur, that I believe it has been lost. The plates, which Mynheer Comrij paid for, exist, but the printer, who is a Mynheer van der Aa, has disposed of the book and used the plates to illustrate a most inadequate text he commissioned himself.'

'I wondered if something like that might have happened', said Fredrik Hendrik. 'I have seen the *Oost-Indische Kruyd-boeck*. The learning which lies in the plates is prodigious, but the text is almost without interest. It made me curious. Who prepared the plates?'

'I did, my lord,' said Pelagius.

'They are excellent. You yourself must have a considerable knowledge of these matters?'

'The knowledge of an assistant only,' said Pelagius deprecatingly.

'And the *materia*, the objects for study, you still have something?'

'Yes, my lord. I have Dr Comrij's *hortus siccus* still and many of his notes, though his final thoughts on the questions he considers are lost.'

Prins Fredrik Hendrik leaned his chin on his hand, observing him carefully. 'I have a suggestion, mynheer. Deposit the herbaria at the University of Leiden, with the collection of the learned Dr Clusius. If you do not know it, Leiden is a small town, some twenty leagues from here.'

'I am familiar with the university,' volunteered Pelagius. 'I spent some time there studying theology, with a view towards ordination, before Dr Comrij returned and called me back to his service.'

'Oh, did you?' said the Stadhouder, regarding him with increased interest. 'Well, then, you will know the Hortus Botanicus. I will write to Professor Vorstius, who is the Prefect, and to Mynheer Hermann the hortulanus, and if you take your master's collection of dried plants up to Leiden, you will be offered a just price. I accept absolutely the words of your late master, mynheer. If we are to conquer the East, we must first understand it.'

Pelagius walked home, more depressed than elated, hardly remembering how the interview had ended. It seemed so easy. A mere half hour, and his life was completely changed. As the psalmist said, once the voice of a king was raised, the ways were made straight; but why could it not have been raised before? With respect to the Stadhouder himself, the answer was obvious: Fredrik Hendrik spent his summers fighting the troops of the King of Spain. He had certainly done so that year, as even a preoccupied scholar could not but know, since that particular summer his forces had suffered a major defeat and thousands of men had been captured by the Catholics: the pamphleteers and ballad singers had been busy, and whenever Pelagius was tempted into the bookstalls their crude sheets had met his eye at every turn. No wonder, then, that the Stadhouder had not had a moment to concern himself with Comrij's plans for the reform of medicine in Batavia. But he was only one of a dozen great men they had approached and the others had not been so hard pressed: could none of them have lifted a finger? Why had Comrij had to die in despair when salvation awaited them? In order to have faith, as a Christian must, he could only hope that some greater good lay hidden in a situation which, at that moment, seemed one of tragic irony.

When he opened the door, Mevrouw Mariken ran out to meet him. 'Doctor! have you heard the news?'

'What news?' he asked, confusedly wondering if somehow she could have heard of his own adventures.

'Mynheer van der Aa. They're saying he's had some kind of fit. And they're saying when you went to see him, you cursed him and the curse came like fire from heaven. He's like a little child, messing himself in his bed and he can't keep nothing down. Doctor, can you help him?'

Pelagius considered this news for some time. 'My hands are clean,' he said finally. 'I spoke only of the fate which the Lord has assigned to the wicked. If God has chosen to strike him, it is none of my doing. Who has told you of this?'

'His cook, Doctor. When they were all wringing their hands round the bed, she spoke to the manservant, and from what he told her she knew to come to me.'

He turned the facts, as they appeared to him, over in his mind. Van der Aa, fat, plethoric, an ideal subject for a stroke of some kind, had finally fallen over the edge he had walked along for many years. As a doctor, in all but name, it seemed to him most unlikely that he could effect any kind of cure. Moreover, there was the matter of Comrij. 'I have nothing to say,' he replied finally. 'I spoke only the words of the Lord, and if God has chosen to act on them, I cannot ask Him to stay His hand.'

Mariken said nothing, but curtsied: for the first time in their acquaintance, there was something like fear in her eyes.

Patience and circumspection had been ground into the bedrock of his nature. Though his first impulse was to leave immediately for Leiden, he remained in The Hague for a week to give Prince

Fredrik Hendrik time to honour his promise. During that week he busied himself packing up, sorting and organizing the dried plant collection, and the notes which went with it. Much of it had furnished his life for so long that he had effectively ceased to see it: when it was all bundled and corded for transport, there turned out to be a gratifyingly large pile. With the bundles of papers removed from their long resting places and heaped in the middle of the floor, the room was dusty and almost bare: to many it would have seemed depressing, but he was unconscious of its bleakness. Surveying the bundles with satisfaction, he reflected that after all something, and no small thing at that, had been saved from the wreck of Comrij and his book. It was even possible to hope, following his own devoted, ungrudged labours, that some doctor or herbalist of the future would read Comrij's all but illegible, indecisive notes and put some of his insights to a use that Comrij himself had never managed to achieve. In taking the *hortus siccus* to Leiden, he was sowing a seed in ground prepared for its reception. However dusty, dry and wrinkled it appeared, in God's good time some unimagined flower might come forth.

Standing thus musing, he distantly heard a thunderous knocking at the street door below and, moments later, Mariken's voice shrilling that the carrier had come. He shouted back down the stairs in answer and heaved one of the bundles efficiently to his shoulder. No point in wasting the effort of a trip downstairs.

His good mood lasted all through the labour of loading and the hiring of a horse. He departed The Hague with a light heart, pacing leisurely behind the slow-moving cart on an ambling old nag. The weather had broken: after a period of rain and fog the air was clear and crisp once more, cold enough for the warmth of the horse to be welcome against his legs, but thin, clear light was sparkling on the water of the polders. Winter was on its way; there would be black frost before long. As he rode through the town gate, he seemed to pass, as it were, through a cloud of the bitter despair and anger he had felt on his arrival. He had felt so strongly, he remembered, that his chagrin had seemed to lie like a solid lump of burning matter behind his breastbone: the memory was clear but far away. How little he had understood of the divine purpose. His heart stirred strongly within him; he removed his hat and bowed his head, leaving the horse to guide itself.

'O Lord,' he prayed, 'I am in your hand. Lead me as you will, so that I may serve your purposes.' The faces of those he had helped or healed came confusedly to his mind. Perhaps one of these, poor wretches that they seemed, had been a person of importance in the working out of God's scheme. Had his own misery and desperation been a necessary mechanism to put him in a certain place, so that some particular person could be healed? In his present exalted mood, he was full of hope and humble trust: a strange, light-headed sensation for a man so serious and deliberate in his ways. 'I am a feather on the breath of God,' he thought. 'Let Him move me where He wills.' First under his breath, then more confidently, he began to sing a psalm:

> 'His angels will direct my legs,
> and guard them in the stony street,
> on lion's whelps and adder's eggs,
> my steps will march, and if I meet
> with dragons, they will kiss my feet.'

When they got to the outskirts of Leiden, the light was already fading from the sky. They put up at an inn, where the surly carter promptly vanished into a raucous, gin-swilling crowd of his kind, while Pelagius sat by the window with a beaker of beer and his thoughts, politely fending off the vulgar curiosity of the landlord and the persistent overtures of a raddled, drink-sodden trollop curious to find out if he was made differently from a Dutchman. At last, it was time to go to bed.

The sleeping chamber contained three beds and a number of rustbanks: simple trestles with mattresses. The beds were to be shared, so he thought it prudent to settle on one of the narrow rustbanks. As he rapidly discovered, lying down in his shirt and breeches, there were bugs as well as fleas in the thin mattress. Since he had not ridden for a long time, the journey had left him stiff in the back and legs and that, combined with the vicious attentions of the insects, was sufficient to keep him staring open-eyed into the dark for hours. The blankets, at least, though odorous and far from clean, were sufficiently warm, which was something to be thankful for. Most of the clodhoppers who stumbled up to sleep alongside him dealt with their quarters' deficiencies by the simple expedient of reeling in almost insensible with drink. Their resonant snores gradually filled the room with a miasma of second-hand gin, tobacco and fetid breath. Indifferent, withdrawn into himself, Pelagius waited for morning and eventually fell asleep.

Early the next day he went to the botanic garden. He had been forced to root the carter from his bed, jaded and sullen from the previous night's carouse, and they had quarrelled. The prospect of parting company with him was not the least pleasant aspect of the morning. 'Wait here,' he commanded, pushing open a discreet small door in a wall. He had visited Dr Clusius's garden during his time at Leiden and was gratified to find it had changed little. He was looking down the length of one of the two main walks, trimly raked with crushed white shell. The other bisected it at right angles, creating four sub-gardens representing the four quarters of the world. There were small, narrow beds in each, planted with study specimens of various genera, though many of them were empty, or apparently so, in this winter season.

When he knocked on the door of the hortulanus, he was relieved to find that Hermann knew all about him and greeted him with courtesy. Summoning a couple of sturdy gardeners, he walked out with Pelagius to help unpack the cart. Once they had carried the last of the bundles through to the study room, it was finally possible to pay off the carter and see the back of him.

The fact that Hermann immediately instituted a thorough inspection of the *materia* seemed right and proper to Pelagius. Such matters should be treated meticulously. Some bundles were unpacked then and there and the state of the plants carefully examined, while all the dockets were gone into in some detail. To Pelagius's surprise, a copy of the lamentable *Kruyd-boeck* was produced and he was asked technical questions about the plates which brought a glow of pride to his heart. The inquisition took the entire day, but finally Hermann accepted that there was no more to be wrung from Pelagius's memory. Straightening up, he regarded Pelagius with an eye of kindly authority.

'Well, mynheer. This is an excellent collection, which will be a great addition to our resources. As you probably know, our own Dr Clusius translated the Jesuit Acosta's book on the medical plants of India. I know he wished to explore this field further, but he had no opportunity to do so. In these latter days, our own people have ventured so much in the East, the need has become still more pressing. I am empowered to offer you a hundred and fifty guilders. Is this satisfactory?'

Pelagius looked at him with astonishment. The financial aspect of the whole transaction had barely occurred to him. It was strange that it should not have, when for so long he had led a life of desperate calculations on small sums, looking twice at every stuiver, and the sum represented something like a year of survival. But the *hortus siccus* was a life: Comrij's, and an appreciable part of his own. He had not thought of it in that way.

'I'm not cheating you,' said the hortulanus sharply. He started, realizing abruptly that he had been staring at the man in silence for an indefinite period of time.

'No, indeed, Mynheer Hermann. I am very happy to accept your offer.' They shook hands and drank a ceremonial tot of genever together, then the hortulanus disappeared to some inner fastness, from which he returned with a small leather bag. He sat down at a desk and began counting out money.

'Did the Stadhouder pay for this?' Pelagius asked suddenly, struck by a sudden thought as he watched the blunt, careful fingers piling the coins into tens.

'He did. Prins Fredrik Hendrik's always been a friend to the sciences. Well, mynheer. Here is your money. You have brought us treasure indeed.'

Pelagius stowed the heavy bag carefully in the inner pocket of his coat and walked out into the Leiden dusk. From the Kloksteeg, he could hear the chime of the curfew. He must find lodgings, more acceptable, he hoped, than the previous night's had been. He was a wealthy man; or at least, he had more than enough, an entirely new sensation as far as he was concerned.

The next morning, after attending the morning service in the Pieterskerk, he took the painfully well-remembered walk down to his old professor's house in the Herengracht, and knocked on the door.

'Mynheer Pelagius!' said Sambucus, when he was shown in, dropping his pen in his astonishment.

'Professor,' said Pelagius, bowing low, hat in hand.

'What brings you here? Come, man. Sit down in that chair there, where I can see you, and the girl will bring us a morning draught.'

Pelagius sat where he was bidden and gradually, in the course of the following hour, told Sambucus most of what had befallen him since last they met, though he did not speak of his adventures with divination. Sambucus heard him out, nodding gravely with steepled fingers, asked occasional questions and forbore from comment.

'Your purpose is still to become a predikant in Batavia?' he asked, when Pelagius had come to the end of his tale. 'There is a crying need for them.'

'I suppose so, Professor,' said Pelagius, a little taken aback. 'It has not been possible for me to think in terms of what I might want. I have only tried to follow where I was guided.'

'Very right and proper. But if I understand you rightly, Pelagius, you are now a man of some means.'

'That is true,' he said slowly. 'I had not thought of it.'

Sambucus looked at him shrewdly, with a slight quirking of the lips.

'Mynheer Pelagius, you built a good and true foundation when you worked here with me. You were an excellent student. Has it struck you that if you were to write a thesis, print twenty copies and present it for examination, you could earn a doctorate? We have a university printer now, a man called Govaert Basson, his rates are reasonable as these things go. You could afford to do this, could you not?'

'Oh, yes.' If there was one thing of which he was absolutely certain, it was the economics of printing. Swiftly, the figures ran through his mind, as he recalled theses he had seen; octavo, perhaps two hundred and forty pages. Figures for the paper, the printer's costs, the binding, were not hard to work out: without the colossal expense of copper-engraved illustrations, printing twenty copies of a modest book would amount to perhaps forty or fifty guilders. He could afford it with ease and afford, also, to devote a significant part of his time to writing. He must speak, he realized – Sambucus was still looking at him, waiting patiently for him to reply.

'Honoured Professor, I am profoundly grateful to you. I think that you have pointed my way forward.'

'I would like to see you in doctor's bands, Pelagius,' said Sambucus simply. 'I think there is still much good for you to do in this world; back in Batavia, where our people are going to the devil for want of preachers. Our own ordinands do not want to work in a climate so hot, but since you are a native of the Tropics, your case is different. Remember the fate of the servant who hid his talent in a napkin and did not put it to its right use.' He shifted in his chair and sipped from his glass of genever, changing the subject. 'Several of your contemporaries have published their theses in the last year or so. Did you know Vollrad Schneewind, who came here from Württemburg?'

'I did. We were not close friends, but I remember him well.' A memory of the German came to his mind's eye: a tall, stoop-shouldered question mark of a man with a mop of white-blond hair, weak-chested and often ill. He had been interested in numerology and cabalistics, Pelagius recalled: on several occasions, they had talked late into the night about numbers and their significance.

'He published his thesis not long ago, and sent me a copy.' Sambucus leaned forward and indicated a plain quarto which lay on top of the pile of books on the table at his right hand. 'I was reading it only this morning. It seems that Dr Schneewind has joined the Brotherhood of the Rosy Cross, if indeed he was not always one such – the Rosicrucians are secretive fellows. There is much in his pages of the great instauration of learning, the return of justice to the earth and the final consummation of time. He was a good student, as you will remember, and the argument is learned and ingenious, though much of it was familiar. It struck me, as I was reading, that ours is an age of dream and visions. There seem to be portents and rumours of the end of all things on all sides. Tell me, Pelagius, are you persuaded by these Brethren, or any others of their kind?'

'Professor, I have read the *Fama Fraternitatis* of Christian Rosencreuz – as who has not? It may be that the world is hastening on its end, but how are we to know? Did not our Lord say, "Take heed, watch and pray, for ye know not when the time is"? It seems to me, therefore, that a wise man should always live as if he was in the last age of the world, but he should not seek to know if it is so.'

'Wisely said, Pelagius. I confess, I incline to your party. There is a Dr Samson Jonson in The Hague, a friend of mine, who is much given to speculation on these matters. I mention him to you now merely because now you have patronage in court circles you may meet him – he is chaplain to the exiled Queen of Bohemia, who lives in the town. He and I have spoken together of such matters for many a year, and though I commend his learning and his zeal, I have not come entirely to share his views. Now, mynheer, to your own purposes. If you were to write a thesis, have you any subject in mind?'

When Sambucus began the sentence, he had not had an idea in his head, but by the time the last word had left the professor's mouth he knew what he wanted to do. It struck him as curious, as if the idea had been lying hidden in his mind, waiting for its moment.

'Yes, Professor. I wish to consider the wisdom of virtuous pagans. Those men and women who were plainly guided by God and who we are enjoined to consider as precursors, though like Moses they saw only His hinder parts. How are we, as Christian men, to understand and use their knowledge? I am thinking of such figures as the Sibyls, for example.'

'Dangerous ground, Pelagius, dangerous ground, but interesting. A meaty enough topic, to be sure, and one that is little studied. Read that Englishman's book on natural theology – Audoenus, he is called, I think – it will give you a grounding. I will look forward to seeing your work.' Sambucus half rose and Pelagius, taking the hint, got to his feet and bowed himself out.

He returned to The Hague thoughtful, but in excellent spirits. It struck him, as he began tentatively to plan his future, that he was in the region of fifty years old – the precise date of his birth was not known to him. In all that half-century of life he had never really possessed the luxury of choice except in the most trivial matters, and he had almost lost the capacity to permit himself preferences. But once more, the life of solitary, dignified independence which was all that he had ever hoped for seemed to be within his grasp. Cautiously, and with the circumspection which was second nature to him, he began to allow his mind to play with the question of what he might actually want.

Some new clothes, he thought at once. Good-quality second-hand would suffice, but he must have respectable student's black again and at least one reasonable shirt. The clothes he was wearing had begun well enough, but they had lasted him since his arrival in Holland and had seen hard service: they were deplorably shabby. That was a simple enough matter, but as he rode towards The Hague, a bigger and less tractable question presented itself to his mind.

Should he move away from Mariken's attic and all it represented? A difficult decision and one which took him most of the way home. If it was a matter simply of what he would like, a side of himself which had hardly ever been allowed a voice, then he would move back to Leiden, where it would be easier to write, and make a clean break with the sorrow and anguish of his life with Comrij. But there was the question of money. He could print his thesis and maintain himself while writing it, but the examination itself would be expensive since he must entertain the Faculty, and the amount he would need would not be well within his control. He would need money, also, to get himself back to Batavia and he had no patron, though perhaps, if he worked hard and the thesis was a success, he might acquire one. To move to Leiden was a considerable gamble, requiring a very optimistic attitude towards the future. On the other hand, if he continued to practise as an oracle, then he would have money coming in, enough to live on, and could hoard his bag of gold against major expenses and future need. There was also the perception of his outward journey to bear in mind: was he, in some unknown and unknowable fashion, doing God's work, and if so was he entitled to abandon it? By the time he reached The Hague his mind was made up. If he remained in The Hague, he could afford to buy books, so he would stay where he was and try to the best of his ability to guess what God might want of him.

The return was less depressing than he had feared. Mariken was delighted to see him and had scoured every mote of dust out of his quarters to welcome him back: the room was reduced to bare, sand-besprinkled boards and whitewashed plaster walls, with a table, two chairs and a cupboard, but it was as clean as a dairy and the sun shone cheerfully through the small, sparkling window. In the weeks that followed, he began to put together a library, lingering long at the booksellers and carefully weighing up the merits of each purchase before committing himself, and began to read towards his thesis.

Sitting one evening, snug by his own fireside, reading Meursius's recent edition of Chalcidius on the *Timaeus* while the first proper ice storm of the winter rattled viciously at the window, he was surprised to receive a second summons from the Stadhouder. He went the next day, curious to know what the meeting might be about, wondering if perhaps, Prins Fredrik Hendrik had received a report from the hortulanus and wished to discuss it. But, as he straightened up from his bow, he saw that the Stadhouder's face was grim.

'So, mynheer,' he began abruptly, 'I was not expecting to see you again. I have summoned you here to explain yourself.'

'On what count, Monseigneur?' inquired Pelagius, as politely as possible, but in some perplexity.

The Stadhouder sighed and leaned back in his chair, regarding him fixedly. 'I saw fit to make enquiries into the doings of a certain Mynheer van der Aa, and I was told that he had met his end here in The Hague. I would have thought no more of it, if your name had not been mentioned. Then, since I had seen you some little while before, and had formed my own impressions, I made further enquiry. You seemed to me an honest man, mynheer, and you gave me to understand that you were also a Christian one. Be aware: I will have no warlocks in Holland, black or white. I want to hear your own account of the matter.'

Pelagius bit his lip, and raised troubled eyes to the stern face of the prince. 'Monseigneur, van der Aa's household believed that I ill-wished him, I know. I did no more than tell him that God would not suffer such as him to prosper in his wickedness and, as God Himself knows, I had cause. I believed what I said to be true and, indeed, it has proved so. His mischief returned upon his own head, and that is no curse for such as me to impose, or to lift, but the judgment of heaven.'

'That may be so, mynheer,' replied Fredrik Hendrik coldly. 'But they believed this of you because you were known to them as a warlock, is this not so?'

'Monseigneur, I am no warlock,' protested Pelagius. 'I believe most sincerely in God our heavenly father. Prayerfully, and with good intention, I sometimes consult an oracle on behalf of the sick which I learned in my own country. No magic is involved, but only a questioning of God's will, and through no virtue or power of my own I have helped many by this means. I have examined my conscience, Monseigneur, and I most truly believe that the oracle is from God.'

'I see.' The Stadhouder sighed again and paused to think. 'This is a difficult matter. I am accustomed to judging men, mynheer, and you seem to me to be speaking the truth as you see it. I will also say this, apart from van der Aa, I have heard of no harm that you have done. But have a care, Mynheer Pelagius. You walk a dangerous path. Good day to you.'

Fredrik Hendrik nodded abruptly and an equerry came forward to murmur confidentially into his ear. The audience was over.

Uneasy in his mind, Pelagius walked slowly home. Having arrived at his own conviction of the value of what he did, he was not to be downcast by the opinion of an earthly monarch, though he was disconcerted, and a little gratified, to find his small, scholarly life made visible to such a man. Perhaps perversely, he was inclined to take his encounter with the Stadhouder as a sort of confirmation. His conscience was entirely clear, so the warning he had been given, so oddly echoing that of Sambucus, did not disturb him. Innocent men have been accused before now, as he well knew, but he had come to be certain that in the matter of Ifá God walked with him and would not permit him to stumble.

The days went by and winter settled over The Hague, bitter cold, and a black, hard frost. After the New Year a fair amount of snow began to fall. At first it merely lay, or was brushed from the streets on to the frozen canals. Almost immediately, children began to take advantage of the piles of snow lying on the frozen water to make snowmen: crude constructions for the most part, merely one ball atop another, perhaps with coals for eyes. But as January gave way to February, Pelagius observed a curious new development on his occasional forays outdoors: snow figures, far more sophisticated in concept, which appeared overnight. He noticed one from time to time, but gave them no heed: it was too cold for an African to linger on the street. He continued to see patients, the news of his practice travelling by word of mouth from one poor soul to another, enough to keep himself in food and firing and usually to pay his rent: when it did not, he had a purse to draw on. Most of the time, he worked on his thesis, which began to engross his mind completely.

The problem of the virtuous pagans had been on his mind since he first consulted Ifá for Mariken's daughter. The evocation of the oracle had brought into focus for him a whole area of residual disquiet about the relationship between his identity as a son of the covenant and the worth and dignity of his own people. In Africa, though he had known it not, he had been a creature made in God's image, the beneficiary of the unimaginable mercy of Christ even while he played in the dust with the other children of his father, or sacrificed in ignorant worship before the figures of the *orisa.* He had not known God, but of a certainty God had known him. The priests had spoken of the *orisa,* but also, beyond and above them, of Olódùmarè, the Creator, who commands, acts, rules and judges. Was this not the eternal God, casting the shadow of His wings over West Africa?

It was with sober, scholarly delight that he began to weave his thoughts into an academic thesis, buttressed by argument and authority, which included learned essays on Plato's *Timaeus,* the First Eclogue of Virgil and the Sibylline prophecies. Once these sections were roughed out, he began on the most original part of his work, the section which, he hoped, would gain him the respect of the world of learning. He began to put together everything which he could find about the spiritual history of Africa: the ancient knowledge of the Egyptians, reverently discussed by Herodotus and Plato, the wisdom of the Queen of Sheba, the prophecies of the Libyan and African Sibyls and, above all, the story of the Ethiopian eunuch, who sought God unprompted by anything but the movement of his own heart. On the basis of these instances of the manifest working of God in the minds of individual Africans, cautiously but with increasing confidence he began to formulate the case for regarding Órunmila, the founder of Ifá, in the same light as the Sibyls, building his argument by slow, sure steps of logic.

Thus engrossed, he was distinctly irritated to receive the third letter of his life. This one, when he broke open the seal, did not come from the Stadhouder. It was written in a bold, rather careless italic hand, no secretary's script. Unusually, some great personage must be writing in his own hand. The letter was in Dutch, which he read only poorly, and the spelling was no better than his own when he wrote in that tongue. It took him a moment to puzzle it out, though it was brief and, once he had understood it, to the point.

> Learned Doctor Pelagius.
>
> Our cousin the prince has spoken of you. He says that you are a true seer. Please attend me when it is convenient for you, at the Wassenaer Hof.
>
> Yours &c.,
>
> Elizabeth, by the grace of God, Queen of Bohemia

He could give no further thought to his work, but it was with some reluctance that he corked his ink bottle and went downstairs to call on Mariken.

He found her in the kitchen, playing with a bonny lump of blonde baby swaddled in a cocoon of white bandages, while the child's mother dozed in a chair, overcome by the warmth, holding a half-finished shirt in her lap, which she had been making by the light of the fire. Her daughter and her grandchild, it must be: she had been born at the turn of the year, a little early, but quite healthy, and Mariken had been exultant. Born in the New Year . . . reckoning up, he decided she must be getting on for two months old.

'Doctor! Here's my *dochterken,* my little angel. Smile for the gentleman, my honey-lumpkin. If it wasn't for him, you wouldn't be here.'

Pelagius smiled politely as the baby's randomly wandering gaze fixed on his face in apparent puzzlement. 'Do not thank me, mevrouw, thank God the child seems so strong. I came to ask you a question. What do you know of the Queen of Bohemia?'

Mariken peered up at him from her seat on a low stool, completely at a loss, her gnarled hands automatically patting and soothing the baby's plump little bolster of a body. 'The Queen of Bohemia?' she said vaguely. 'Oh, yes. She's been in The Hague long enough. She was married to one of them princes. He went for to be King of Bohemia, I don't know why they didn't have a proper king of their own. The thing was, him and this Queen were good Protestants, and the King who died, I forget who he was, but he was a papist. So this Prince, he got his bottom on to the throne all right, but then the papists came back and fought him for it. They beat the stuffing out of him and he and his wife have been skulking in The Hague ever since, living off the Stadhouder, without a pot of their own to piss in. He died a while back, I think, so she's a widow, poor thing.'

Mariken's tone bespoke a genial contempt for kings and princes and all their ways, but Pelagius felt a twinge of sympathy for this unknown couple. He discerned, in her ignorant narrative, the shape of a grand design, aspiration, failure. Familiar: though in his own experience, such tales ended in slavery or death rather than in a palace in The Hague. But to eat the bread of exile is bitter, even in a palace. He began to feel that he had a very definite interest in meeting this woman.

'They call her the Winter Queen,' said Mariken suddenly, breaking into his thoughts. 'I think it's because it's just a winter they spent in Bohemia before they were chased out.' The baby began to wail and distracted her attention. Pelagius left her to deal with it and went up to his own quarters, deep in thought. Such a woman was a very different proposition from the Marikens and Geertruyds whom he knew: the occasion called for all his skills of showmanship. He smiled to himself, with a purely professional lifting of the spirits. Such a client was a challenge, but he was not without resources. Perhaps he would surprise this Winter Queen.

He went to see her the following afternoon. As he came through the Buitenhof, he observed that the great snowbank which had lain on the frost-burned grass for some time, the residue of daily path clearing, had received the attention of the mysterious nocturnal snow-sculptors. Their composition was long and low and not at first sight easy to interpret: two masses, interrelated, perhaps ten feet long in all. He stopped to give it a more careful inspection. Dark was already beginning to come down and candles glittered like little golden stars through many of the great glass windows of the noblemen's houses looming through the dusk, but the white snow held the last of the light. One mass came up and over the other, which seemed to protrude from a v-shaped gap. Suddenly he understood what it was intended to represent: a giant hand holding a scrubbing brush.

He thought at first of Mariken; an antic vision of overworked women meeting in the grey dawn to celebrate the instrument of their daily toil. Then the representation came into focus. It was nothing so innocent, but was meant for the hand of God, poised to scrub the world clean as He had done at the Great Flood. It came into his mind also that the image was an emblem; he suddenly remembered the motto that went with it, which Comrij had occasionally quoted: 'Afkomst seyt niet': origins count for nothing. The hand was scrubbing away aristocracy, the right of any one person to stand head and shoulders above his fellow man. A reminder that the stadhouderate was far from being universally popular and an image with ominous implications, found thus within a stone's throw of a royal palace. He was a little surprised that it had been left undisturbed; but it struck him that perhaps the Stadhouder felt it was best left to time and the weather. The effort of removing it might perhaps only encourage the mysterious individuals who had created it in the first place to further, and perhaps less indirect, forms of political comment. It struck him as a very Dutch gesture. Indirect, yet uncompromising, and requiring a great deal of tenacious and well-co-ordinated effort to bring about.

The Hof te Wassenaer was, like the house he lived in himself, old. Unlike 't Groote Vis, it had always been the home of aristocrats. It stood back from the road, guarded by a wall with a stone gateway. Entering the gates, Pelagius found himself facing a courtyard and at the far side, an enormous red brick house with steps up to the front door. A halberdier guarded the entrance, though his halberd leaned casually against the jamb and he appeared to be entirely preoccupied with his pipe. People were passing in and out, paying him no heed. As a visitor, Pelagius felt he should remain in the courtyard until invited to enter by a palace servant, but the behaviour of others suggested that the manners of the Queen were less formal than those of Oyo.

With some hesitation, he mounted the steps, the guard's gaze passing indifferently over him as he did so, and found himself in an oak-panelled hall adorned with dim, green Flemish verdure tapestries with paintings hung over them, which struck him as profligate. It had an elaborately carved, large stone fireplace, where a fire burned brightly, warming the air around it but fighting a losing battle with the draught from the door.

Pelagius stood, looking around him, ignored. The sound of argument drifted up from some lower region of the house, servants passed through on unknown errands, paying him no heed. He stood for some time in hesitation and when a fair and buxom woman in a silk dress entered the hall, looking past him at a pair of quarrelling, lace-collared small boys with lively disapproval, he approached her tentatively, removing his hat.

'My lady', he began, bowing respectfully. 'The Queen has asked to see me.'

The lady looked him up and down, her expression chilly and a little frown of perplexity appearing between her blonde eyebrows. 'Who are you? What is your name?' she asked, without courtesy.

'Dr Pelagius, madame.'

'I will tell the Queen that you are here. James! Francis! stop it at once, or I will have you whipped. Why did you not ask this fellow his business?' The woman shook a warning finger at the children, who parted sheepishly, and whisked back up the stair from which she had descended. As she turned her broad back, one of them put out his tongue at her. A few minutes passed, in which he looked at the pictures, before she returned: the little boys, after pausing briefly to stare at him round-eyed, had prudently vanished.

'Her majesty will see you now.' He followed her out of the hall, full of curiosity, and walked behind her into a room hung with black. The Queen was sitting at the far end, on a throne under a canopy: all he could see of her was her face and neck, palely glimmering, and hands clouded with point-lace. Walking up, he was conscious of the sound of his footfalls, and as he came nearer he was disconcerted by her style of dress. Dutch women, rich and poor alike, covered themselves modestly up to the neck and he was quite unused to seeing any female flesh other than hands and faces. By contrast, the Queen's dress was cut low enough to expose a good deal of her bosom in a fashion which seemed to him embarrassingly unsuitable. Three steps from her, he bowed low and stood with downcast eyes.

'Parlez-vous français, Maître Pélage?' came a clear, pleasant voice out of the gloom.

'No, your majesty. Only Dutch and Latin,' he replied in Dutch. He understood a little English and wondered whether to say so: Comrij, whose father had fled Scotland for the sake of religion in the days of the Catholic queen, had used Scots occasionally. Since he was far from certain he could string three words together in that tongue, he decided against volunteering the information. It would only create further confusion.

'*Dommage.* Well, mynheer, French is the language of courts and you are no courtier: Latin is the language of scholars and I am no scholar. We must compromise on Dutch, then, which is at least the language of the country. I speak it barbarously.'

'Your majesty, you are perfectly clear.' He spoke the truth. Her voice was distinct and her accent fell pleasantly on his ear, reminding him a little of Comrij. She mixed High German with Low German forms indifferently, but she was fluent.

'Tell me a story,' she said, after a pause.

V

All earthly pomp or beauty to express,
Is but to carve in snow, on waves to write.
Celestial things though men conceive them less,
Yet fullest are they in themselves of light:
Such beams they yield as know no means to die:
Such heat they cast as lifts the spirit high.

Thomas Campion, *First Book of Ayres*, 1613

Elizabeth surveyed him steadily from her throne, one hand absently caressing the warm head of a dog, almost invisible in the dusk, which leaned immobile against her chair. Though she could not see his face, his figure was impressive, tall and well built, and from his stance he was plainly not in the slightest degree overawed by her, though she was aware that he was a poor man and not used to courts. Fredrik Hendrik had told her a little of his history and had piqued her curiosity. An interesting fellow. Was it the authority of the preacher, or the seer, which gave him such confidence, she wondered, or was there something else about him?

'Dr Pelagius,' she said, 'they tell me that you can see beyond earthly sight. Is this not witchcraft? My father would have thought so.'

His deep, beautiful voice was calm and authoritative: he answered her question soberly and directly, without a note of apology, as if he were her equal. 'I am not a witch, your majesty. I do no *maleficium*. I do not call up spirits, or make use of the dead. But I believe that the Lord God has it in His power to send messengers who may not be seen by mortal eyes. Did not Abraham eat with angels and Jacob wrestle with one? Was not Joseph, the earthly father of Jesus, warned in dreams and visions? I ask that I might see, your majesty, prayerfully, and with humility, and sometimes I am vouchsafed a vision.'

'See for me,' she challenged him. He raised a hand in demurral, visible only from the movement of its white linen cuff.

'Your majesty, I am no mountebank. I cannot summon the vision, I must go where it leads and I can see nothing in this room. If you come with me I will go where the sending takes me, and perhaps see for you what you wish to have seen.'

Her chin rose and she sat still straighter in her chair, glaring at him. He was not even looking at her. With downcast eyes, he was looking at his own hands as they held his beaver hat by its rim, submissive, poised, perfectly respectful, but obdurate, and she was forced to concede. She looked away from him to the Countess of Löwenstein, one of her four maids of honour, who was standing by very correctly, her large, fair face unreadable in the dusk. 'Very well. Bess, my furs. Wrap up well and fetch Catharina. I want you both to come with me.' The woman, almost invisible in the failing light, curtsied and went to obey the Queen's orders. Pelagius bowed and retreated. As she left by the side door at the top of the presence chamber, he walked back down the length of the room and out into the hall, where he stood waiting.

Some minutes later, the Queen of Bohemia, cloaked in sable, flanked by two carefully blank-faced gentlewomen, joined him as he stood patiently in the oak-panelled front hall. He bowed as she approached and when her serving man threw open the great door, he offered her his arm.

It was neither light nor dark when they emerged on to the Kneuterdijk. The sun, well down the sky, was behind the tall buildings, but the sky was leaden grey with black rags of cloud. It was terribly cold and the cobbles were mailed with tiny pellets of ice: hail melted and frozen again, or aggregated knots of snow. The going was treacherous in the extreme: she took the arm he offered because she was uncertain of her footing. Through his broadcloth, her velvet, the stiffened, padded layers of cloth which protected them both from the savagery of a Dutch winter, she could feel, dimly, like a four-month child, the stirring of his breathing and was conscious, for a moment, of his strong masculinity.

Without hesitation, he piloted her across the Plaats and down the Vijverberg, followed by the women, now arm in arm with each other, whose presence he never acknowledged. They crossed the open space, walking as rapidly as the circumstances would permit down the narrow double allée of trees towards the corner of the embankment opposite the new Mauritshuis, where there was a ramp down to the water for the convenience of water cargo. The water was a solid sheet of ice, overlaid with a dusting of granular snow, and the ramp was as slippery as a child's slide. As he walked towards it without slackening pace, Elizabeth's arm muscles, with no conscious intention of her own, tensed to slow and, if possible, stop him. Looking up at his tall head, so elegantly poised on its long neck, she had consciously to relax her grip. She was used to strong-minded men, and his expression, withdrawn, concentrated, was far from inscrutable. He was a hunter, hunting: what spoor he was seeing, or what senses he was using, she could not guess, but she knew the mood, the attitude, well.

They descended the ramp with caution. Her shoes, narrow-heeled, skidded alarmingly, but her potential slide was arrested by an arm like an iron bar; she clung to it with both hands. She walked on the ice with mincing steps, like a cat, conscious of the freezing air striking up under her petticoats, afraid that she would slip and lose her dignity and afraid on a deeper, unacknowledged level that the ice would crack and swallow them. It was very cold. The state of the snow overlying the ice, sullied, marred with footprints and scored with the curving lines left by skates, showed clearly that many had walked upon it, but she found it impossible to rid herself of a conviction of its treachery. The ice was darkest blue, with glass-green highlights wherever the scuff of dirty brown snow was disturbed; she was as frightened as she had ever been in her life but too proud to show it.

Pelagius came to a halt in the middle of the ice. 'Your majesty. Here I am. If I can see what you wish to see, it is here that I can do it.'

Elizabeth took a step back, conscious of the presence of her maids of honour, comforting because they were hers and female, and also strengthening because she knew they were as frightened as she was and she would not shame herself before them.

'Master Pelagius.' Her voice came out thin, flattened by the ice, but confident. 'Show me my sons. I am afraid for them.'

His face, already serious, stiffened with concentration. He brought out a flask and as he opened it, turned to her, holding it out for her to smell if she wished. 'Only good Dutch genever, Your Majesty, nothing magical about it. We need a mirror, if we are to see.' The reek of honest grain spirit came to her nostrils as he tilted his wrist and spilt the liquor over the ice at their feet. As the alcohol spread out in a pool, it melted the superficial snow, the footprints and the dirt, to show the hard, glassy darkness of the ice with its sinews of currents and the little bubbles and fragments of frozen weed which were held in it. He reached out: only his glove touched hers, yet the contact of flesh was implicit. She was very conscious at the same time of the hand which held hers and of the fact that her feet were freezing. 'Look.'

She looked down. She saw the black fall of her dress and the sables in which she was huddled, she felt the hard grip of the ice clutching through the soles of her shoes. Before her stretched an inky pool of clear ice. She was worried about Charles Louis, wherever he might be, struggling to raise support among the deadly indifference of Europe's kings, and about her poor Rupert, prisoner in Linz: she tried to concentrate her mind, aware of the light hand engulfing her own. Charles Louis. Rupert. My darling boys.

There was something under the ice. In the complete darkness of the water a glimmer of light. Not a glimmer, a something. Pale, oval. Heedless of her dress, her stiff knees, Elizabeth slid down, as it became clearer and clearer to her. Under the ice, under armoured glassy inches, he came up: Fredrik Hendrik, her first born, her beloved, his skin leaden and pinched with the cold, hair waving like black weed, his lovely grey eyes filled with innocent astonishment. Help me, mother. Mother, why am I dead?

Elizabeth fell forward over the ice, grasping ineffectually for her son. It took all three of them, both ladies and Pelagius, to raise her. She turned, snow-caked and drenched all down her front, to weep hysterically on the countess's shoulder. Between them, the two women took her away, tacking and slipping erratically over the ice, while he stood, unrewarded and forgotten under the windows of the Mauritshuis, startled out of his wits.

As he plodded homewards, Pelagius tried to make sense of the encounter. He was heartily and sincerely ashamed of himself. He had succeeded beyond his wildest dreams, only too well, but in another sense, he had failed completely. He had caused pain where he hoped to bring knowledge or reconciliation, and it occurred to him uncomfortably to wonder what the Stadhouder might say if he got to hear of the incident. For the first time in his career as an oracle he was truly uneasy in his conscience: deliberately, he had courted the sending of spirits, arrogantly confident in his own inability to see anything, which had allowed him to convince himself of his own moral integrity while he exploited the weakness of others. It was the first time that he had made such a show of his gifts and he vowed to himself that he would never do it again.

A week later, after seven days of unease and the searching of his conscience in which he was unable to make effective progress with his thesis, the Queen summoned him for a second time, greatly to his relief. He hoped very much to make his peace with her, and if possible, with himself. The maid of honour Catharina, whom he had met on the ice, took him up the stairs to the private apartments and brought him to the Queen's closet, a small chamber which was at the same time magnificent and pleasant. A fire was crackling cheerfully in the grate and the room was warm, well lit and hung with pictures big and small. The melancholy eyes of a dark-haired man in military dress, hung in pride of place over the hearth, seemed to rest on him as warily he entered the precious little space. Two dogs, slim little gaze-hounds, curled round one another with their long noses on one another's backs in front of the fire, watched him curiously with their bright black eyes, immobile.

Elizabeth was seated by the window, very upright, in a chair of blue velvet. Bright, clear winter light caught on her brown hair, illumined her soft, middle-aged complexion and winked from the lustrous pearls around her neck and wrists. She put out a hand towards him in a gracefully impulsive gesture of welcome.

'Dr Pelagius. Please be seated.' The silent Catharina brought up a wooden chair, one of a pair which flanked the Queen's cabinet of treasures, and he bowed and sat as he was bidden. 'I am sorry . . .' her voice trailed off uncertainly. He observed her attentively. Sorry to have lost her dignity? Sorry for what she saw? Sorry for some other reason entirely? Her meaning and her intentions were equally far from clear to him. Elizabeth leaned forward and took up a plump little purse of Genoa velvet from where it lay on her work table, and held it out to him: he took it obediently. 'The labourer is worthy of his hire. I am in your debt.'

'Your majesty,' he began shamefacedly, 'I cannot regret enough that I caused you pain. It was wicked of me to use my poor talent in that way. I have scried often enough, but I will scry no more. I do not trust these visions; we cannot know where they come from. Please try to be easy in your mind and forgive my foolish arrogance.'

Elizabeth leaned forward in her chair. 'Dr Pelagius, do you know what I saw?' she asked urgently.

'Your majesty, your secrets are your own. I am the medium only,' he said soothingly, inwardly filled with shame.

She took a deep breath, clasping her hands together under her bosom. 'It was my first son that I saw, Dr Pelagius.' She indicated one of the many pictures on the walls, the smooth, pale faces which stared down at them from heavy ebony and gold frames. 'My Fredrik Hendrik. Twelve years ago, Doctor, he sailed to Amsterdam with my honoured husband, the Elector Palatine. There was fog and heavy frost. Their little boat was run down by a cargo vessel and they were thrown into the water. God preserved the life of my husband in those straits, but my son was not found until the morning. He was tangled in the rigging and his cheek was frozen to the mast. He was fifteen years old.'

He felt for her: the image she conveyed was a very clear one and he was stabbed with compunction. How stupid of him, and how arrogant, to take her to the ice. 'A heavy loss for you to bear, your majesty,' he said gently, 'but God disposes all things as He wills.'

'And I have sought to be resigned to His will, Dr Pelagius,' retorted Elizabeth. 'But when I saw him . . . it was as if no time had passed at all. I felt as I felt on the day that the Elector returned and told me what had happened. And on that day they feared for my life, or my reason.'

There was nothing to say in response to this, so Pelagius remained silent. Her dress was of black damask, rich and intricate, cut low enough to reveal the full, time-slackened swell of her bosom. Unwilling to raise his eyes to her face, he watched the play of light on the fabric as her bodice gently rose and fell with her breathing. A complex jewel was pinned to her breast, with a huge, pear-shaped pearl pendant from it. One of the diamonds in the mount caught the sunlight and winked at him like a tiny heliograph. The purse in his hand was comfortingly heavy: gold, it must be. Months of his frugal, contracted life lay within it, free of anxiety, books he could buy. He was duly grateful.

'Dr Pelagius,' she said suddenly, breaking the silence, 'I have thought for a long time about what happened. Please forgive yourself: I think that you are a vehicle for God's grace. I think, also, that you can show the secrets of the heart. I did not know that I was thinking of Fredrik Hendrik, but there on the ice, the memory, perhaps, lay sleeping in my mind where you could call it forth. I want you to help me, but I do not think I can bear to repeat what we did then. Have you any other . . . any ways of asking God his dispositions, without these hideous visions?'

'If your majesty pleases, I have another poor skill for her to try; the divinations of my own country.' He was deeply relieved, though his voice did not reveal it to her: he sent up a brief, but fervent prayer of thanks that he was permitted to redress his error.

'What do you do?' she asked, with ready, almost childlike curiosity.

'I should use palm nuts, but there are no palm nuts here in Holland. Yet my master taught me to think that what is true in one place is true in another. And for a certainty the truth of God is true over all the world and the men that are in it. So, sixteen nuts, your majesty. Hazelnuts will do very well; I do not think I betray the oracle. I hold the sixteen nuts in my right hand, then I hit my left palm with the hand full of nuts. Some nuts will fall loose, into the left hand. I do this eight times, noting at each time, the number of nuts which go from one hand to the other. The combination of the eight results determines which *odù* is the one appropriate to the situation.'

'And where are the *odù*, Dr Pelagius? What are *odù*?'

'They are something like the Sibylline verses, your majesty. They are very old. I am the son of a king and not a priest, but I learned the *odù* when I was young,'

'So you are a king in your own country!' she said with sudden interest.

'King no longer,' he replied, briefly but firmly, hoping to deflect further enquiry.

'I am Queen no longer, but majesty is a matter of quality, not politics.' She sat a little straighter and looked at him as if, for the first time, she truly saw him. 'Very well. My older sons are scattered abroad, Dr Pelagius. My second son Charles Louis is Prince Palatine since the death of my first-born, and he is working to regain his father's kingdom. He was always my little *politique.* He has his father's cool head and, I fear, a cooler heart. I have worried about him since the day he was born. He was a sad little scrap then, but I begin to think that now he has grown to manhood he can look after himself very well. He is probably still in Paris and I fear two things for him – that he will get no help there, or that he will get help, but he will pay for it with his honour. France is in the hands of Cardinal Richelieu, who does nothing without policy, and he will hardly countenance help for a Protestant prince unless he sees some gain by it. My third son, Rupert, is a prisoner in the castle of Linz, on the banks of the Danube. I have had no direct news of him for months, though my poor Thom Roe is wearing out his life working for his release.'

'War breaks kingdoms, your majesty, and it breaks the hearts of mothers.'

'Do you speak from experience?' she asked with interest. 'I hear bitterness in your voice, do I not?'

'My father was King in Oyo,' he explained reluctantly. 'The

Oyo Mesi, his council, I think you would say, favoured the son of his father's sister. It is the task of the *basorun*, who leads this council, to judge if the King's sacrifice is acceptable to God at the Orun festival. He gave a false judgment, your majesty, because he loved the man Egonoju. The next day my father was given parrots' eggs, a token that he should die. There were some of the people who supported me, as the heir of the King, and others who supported Egonoju. Many died. I was captured and sold down the river to the Portugals, and Egonoju became King. I doubt that my mother forgot me. She will have ended her days in poverty and bitterness when she should have been Iya Oba, the first woman in the kingdom. I am certain also that many another woman had cause to mourn the day of her birthing because of that lie.' He spoke with a bitterness which could not be concealed, and she regarded him with interest and a dawning compassion.

'I am sorry for it. But . . . war between kings and their cousins, Dr Pelagius, is the way of the world. My brother is King of England and Scotland. Do you know anything of my country?'

'No, your majesty.'

'My brother the King is at war with his people of Scotland, but there is no cousin risen up against him,' she explained. 'His Parliament there, his "Oyo Mesi", if I understand you, deny his right to rule as a king. You have seen many lands and many peoples, Dr Pelagius: have you ever heard of such a thing?'

'I have not. Among my people, the King is sacred. It is death to a common man even to see him blink. When he goes outside the royal palace he wears a crown with a fringe of cowrie shells, which hides his whole face, because no one who is not his wife or his child or his slave can look upon him. When I was taken to the other end of the world, I found that in the Dutchmen's Batavia, Jan Pieterszoon ruled with kingly authority, and, beyond the walls, the King of Bantam ruled much like the King of Oyo.'

Elizabeth raised her pale and beautiful hands: the fingers fanned out as she spread them in an eloquent gesture. 'What is this madness, then, which has come upon the Scots?'

'I do not know.'

'It is a *furor*. It is as if God has blinded them. And yet these blasphemous men of blood fight with the name of God on their lips. I cannot understand them. Did not God ordain monarchy for Israel? – There is no example for them to follow. They speak as if they are guided, but when I look deeply into the scriptures I can see nothing to support them. Our Lord was poor in this world, but it was He who said, "Render unto Caesar the things that are Caesar's".'

'It is the deception of Satan,' said Pelagius firmly. 'We understood Satan in Oyo, your majesty. We called him Èsù. He walks up and down the world and, where there is wickedness in the hearts of men, he stirs it: where there is mischief to be made, he makes it. Èsù is walking in Scotland. Pray God that your brother is strong and resolute.'

'As my sons must be. Dr Pelagius, cast your oracle, having in mind the Prince Palatine Charles Louis and Prince Rupert. Rupert's picture is just to the right of his father's. The Prince Palatine is on the wall behind me, wearing a russet satin scarf, the only one of my grown children who is not as black as pitch. Look at them well.'

Pelagius looked around the room in puzzlement until he saw her meaning: the room was ringed with youthful dark-eyed, dark-haired faces, pale-skinned, to his eye, though without the pink-toned fairness of the woman before him.

Then he brought his little bag of nuts from his pocket, selected sixteen and began to count with them. Elizabeth, sitting, and Catharina, standing against the wall, watched his dark, powerful hands as they banged together, the nuts slipping from palm to palm. He paid them no heed, rehearsing the numbers of each cast under his breath as it was made. He sat back, on the eighth cast, and looked up at the Queen.

'It is the second of the *odù* that is your guide, your majesty. This is what it says, in my own tongue:

'Márùnlelogójo igi oko
Òpè ati Ayìnré li o ru:
Oromodiè ninu won
Nitorinaa bi iji ba nja
Ogo mariwo a ni:
Oun sebo Òyokese.'

'These are solemn verses, and very sacred, so I have made them into verses in Latin, following the example of the oracles of the Sibyls. Do you understand Latin, your majesty?'

'If you speak slowly,' said Elizabeth apologetically. 'I did not learn Latin as a child – my father the King used to say that to make women learned and foxes tame but made them more cunning. When I became a Queen, I had to learn it, and I am an ill scholar.'

Pelagius nodded, and spoke slowly and clearly, the round, full vowels lingering on the air:

'"Arbor palmae, arbor ajinreae
sacrificium faciant, cum ceteris arboribus:
'si tempestas evoluit',
declarat filum palmae,
'sacrificium feci, ut periculum evadet'."

'I do not think there is a word in Latin or Dutch for the *ayìnré*, your majesty, it is a tree of my country. The oracle declares all dangers are averted for the palm tree and the *ayìnré* because they fear God and observe the law. Your sons are safe.'

Elizabeth's cheeks were a little flushed; she leaned forward staring at him excitedly. 'We say the same of the palm, Dr

Pelagius. The palm is a holy tree, it is chaste and it is also royal. It is an emblem for surviving adversity, because when it is weighted it grows up despite the weight: the motto which goes with it is "cresco sub pondere pressa". How strange that you should speak of my sons in such words.'

'You should not be surprised, your majesty, for customs differ, but God is the same everywhere and so is man. If the learned men of Europe are right to understand the palm tree as an emblem of constancy and trust in God, then that will be true also in the kingdom of Oyo.'

'You are right of course. It is foolish of me to think otherwise, but it is still strange. The first foolishness of home-keepers is to think that nothing will be the same five miles from home; the second is to think that everything will be different. You are a man of a bigger world than I, Doctor. You were born in Africa, you spent much of your life in Asia and now you live in Europe. You have walked in the three quarters of the world where I have travelled only in fancy. My world has been Europe alone, though God knows, it has seemed large enough.'

The stout woman, the one who had greeted him on his first appearance, came to the closet door, knocked, and opened.

'My lady. It is gone twelve o'clock.'

'So late? I am sorry, Bess. I did not observe how time was passing. Dr Pelagius, will you dine with me?'

'Most happily, madam.' He rose and bowed to her, and offered her his arm, as he had seen great men do in Batavia: she set three light fingers upon his sleeve and walked with him out of the room and down the stairs. As they paced down the stairs in unison, there was a sudden rush of wild, jerky movement from above, a monkey bounding from some coign of vantage to the newel post and from thence to Elizabeth's welcoming embrace: it clung to the lace of her collar with tiny, near-human hands, chattering and making fierce faces at the stranger.

'Jack, Jack. Mind your manners,' she chided. 'Dr Pelagius, this is my monkey, Jack. He is a fine fellow, but humoursome. He can bite hard, so do not touch him until you are firm friends. Did you have monkeys, in the country you come from?'

'Yes, we did.'

'Did you have one?'

'I do not think I understand, your majesty. We have no monkeys quite like your Jack and we do not keep them with us. There are black and red monkeys in the forest and it was our tradition that women who suffered twin babies gave reverence to them because my people believe that twins are born again as these monkeys. Then there are also monkeys of other kinds.'

'So do you make pets of the others?'

'No, your majesty, we eat them.'

'But how horrible!' she ejaculated, the fingers of her free hand flying to cover her mouth.

'Monkey is very good,' he insisted perversely. 'This Jack of yours would be tender and sweet. In Oyo we would stew him with a little palm oil and guinea-pepper, and eat him with pounded yam.'

She turned away from him, addressing the animal in her arms, half-distressed, half-teasing, miming disgust. 'Jack, do not listen to these horrors,' she admonished. Indifferent, the little beast sprang from her arms again and ran away across the floor of the hall, as light as a spider. They had reached the bottom of the stairs. The maid Anna stood by the door to the dining hall, and they entered together.

He had never consciously wondered what it might be like to dine at a European royal table, but to his surprise he discovered that he had somehow acquired a number of preconceived ideas which, one after another, were shattered. When his father had shared food with his people, the occasions had been ones of deliberate decorum. The atmosphere in Elizabeth's dining room, despite the gilt leather hangings, was more like that of a common inn. He took his place at Elizabeth's right hand, at the top table, set along the shorter wall at the top of the room: though the people at the top table rose to greet her, the room did not fall silent, nobody else stood up, few even seemed to notice or acknowledge that she was there. Other tables stretched the length of the room at right angles to the Queen's own table. There was a guard, halberd in hand, at the door, who looked as if he was meant to keep people out, but some pushed past him, some, whom he challenged, stopped to argue while others streamed by unchecked. The room gradually filled with people talking loudly to one another, oblivious of their hostess.

'Dr Pelagius. Let me present you to my chaplain, Dr Jonson. The gentlemen beyond him are my secretary, Mr Dingley, and my chamberlain, Sir George Sayer. The ladies are my mistress of the robes, Mrs Broughton, and my maids of honour, the Countess of Löwenstein and Juffrouw Catharina van Eck, whom you have met already, Lady Dohna and Lady Sayer.'

Pelagius looked at the chaplain with some interest, recalling that his professor had spoken of him. He was a short, stout, red-faced man in preacher's black, who looked at him with flickering, puzzled eyes, but acknowledged his bow with a courteous return. Beyond him sat the secretary, a younger, plainly dressed man with a guarded expression, and a more solid figure with a flourishing moustache, who gave him only an abrupt nod. The women were grouped to the Queen's left, well-dressed ladies, ranging in age from Catharina, perhaps in her mid-twenties, to fifty or more: he bowed to them also and they curtseyed formally in return.

'Let us be seated,' commanded Elizabeth. 'Come, sit by me, Doctor, so that we can converse in comfort.' She took her place with dignity and sat with a slight smile, ignoring the revellers in the lower hall as easily as if they were so many chickens. He seated himself, as he was bidden, at her right hand. A manservant with a linen towel over one arm carried in a silver bowl of water and took it round the Queen and the other diners. Each in turn gravely dabbled their fingers. Dr Jonson said grace, two waiting women took their places behind the Queen's chair, on her either side, and a cup-bearer came forward and began to pour fine, yellow Rhenish wine into beautiful thin glasses.

A quarrel broke out further down the room: voices were raised in anger and the chaplain half-rose, then sank back into his seat. The Queen turned to Pelagius gracefully. 'My servants fight like gladiators, Doctor. It is very shocking.'

He was unable to gauge the relationship between her tone, as light as if she were deploring the weather, and her words. It was an extremely difficult remark to answer: should he agree that he found them impertinent and offensive? With a sudden flash of insight, it occurred to him that a widowed, dispossessed Queen might feel unable to control her household as she would wish. He smiled back at her, and pledged her, lifting the glass elegantly. The wine was good.

'You said you enjoyed hearing tales, your majesty. Shall I tell you of the palace, as we would say the *afin*, of my father?'

'Oh, yes. Did your father endure these cormorant hordes? Say that he did, Doctor, and I will pity him from the bottom of my heart.'

'He did, your majesty. We have a saying in my country, "Rúwàrúwa nile oba." It means, all different kinds of people abound in the palace.'

Elizabeth snorted with amusement, raising her glass to him. 'We should have that saying in Holland, Dr Pelagius. What kinds of people abounded in the palace of your father?'

'Many different kinds, your majesty. The lame, hunchbacks, the blind, the albinos and the deaf and dumb had a right to come to my father and seek refuge and residence in the *afin*. Once they were there, of course, they had little enough to do, so they quarrelled and fought among themselves. Then there were the men of art, drummers, trumpeters, craftsmen, flautists, artists of all kinds. They served the King, but they did not live in the *afin*, because it was the belief of our people that nobody but the King should . . .' he trailed off, uncertain how to express precisely what he meant. He began again. 'The King is a father to his country. He has many wives, like a patriarch of the Old Testament. The *afin* is a place of joy and a place for the King. No one must die in the *afin*. Royal wives, nearing their time, must go outside its walls to give birth. Nobody must weep and nobody but the King may have relations with a woman, so his artists and his grown sons and counsellors keep their households elsewhere in the city. The King is sacred and his palace is holy ground.'

'Yet at the same time you have this legion of quarrelling idlers!' Elizabeth marvelled.

'It is necessary. The King is the source of justice and of mercy. Those whom the King has pardoned also become servants in the *afin*.'

'It is necessary here also,' observed Elizabeth. 'I feed half the ruffians in The Hague, when I would sooner see them sent to the galleys, but it is not for a Queen to count stuivers like a housewife.'

One of the ushers was carving as they spoke. The meat before him was burned black on the outside and as he sawed away at it, the slice, as it dropped away from the bulk of the joint, revealed on its inner side the jellied, bluish-crimson aspect of near rawness. Elizabeth looked at it with disfavour, but accepted the offering with the same obdurate, graceful indifference with which she ignored her quarrelling pages and the drunks in the lower part of the hall who were calling loudly for more beer.

'Dr Pelagius, perhaps you might care for a little of the oatmeal pudding,' she said, gracious as if none of this was happening. 'And I believe that is a dish of parsnips stewed with milk, and by your right hand, there are marrow pasties.'

'James!' hissed the Countess from the Queen's other side. One of the small boys whom Pelagius had seen in the hall slouched up from where he had been leaning indifferently against the side wall: the stout Countess pounced from her place, and seized him by the ear in a way which was almost certainly painful. He twisted away from her, reddening, but came forward to serve, pink-faced and sullen-eyed. 'James, where is the bread?' the Countess demanded, when he had bowed to his mistress and put the cover back on the dish.

'Francis was getting it.'

'My lady.'

'Francis was getting it, my lady,' he said sulkily.

'Get it yourself, boy,' she snapped, with a dangerous edge to her voice.

Elizabeth watched him go. 'Bess disciplines these little younkers,' she commented. 'I have not the patience, but I am grateful and so should they be. They are the children of good families, but without her to whip them and teach them to mind their manners, I am sure they would all end up hanged.'

'Children should reverence their elders. How else can they learn to walk in the path of righteousness?' He spoke a little at random: there was an animal of some kind moving about under the table; he could feel its smooth, hot body pressing against one of his legs. Only he was disturbed by this: looking along the table, he could see that the others took it for granted. The chaplain was looking at him again: he caught his eye and the other man looked hastily away.

Elizabeth sighed. 'You are quite right, Doctor. I should take more trouble with them, but in truth, I prefer my dogs.' She took a piece of the half-raw meat from her plate and held it below the edge of the table: the narrow tip of a canine snout appeared momentarily beside his left thigh and daintily accepted the offering.

'Your own sons are all abroad, your majesty?' he enquired,

relieved at least to know what the beast was that was moving about at their feet.

'My oldest three,' she explained. 'I have many children, Doctor. They are bred at Leiden for the most part. The Stadhouder let me use the Prinsenhof for them and my little ones, Gustavus, Henriette and Sophia, are still there.' He looked at her, surprised. He knew the Prinsenhof well; a big, old building on the other side of the canal from the Aula Magna of the university. He had walked past many a time, but it had never occurred to him to wonder who lived in it. 'The three middle boys, Maurice, Ned and Philip, are in Paris, learning good French and better manners,' she continued blithely. 'My two eldest daughters are with me now, in the house of Lady Vere: there is no room for them here. Perhaps to you this house seems big enough, but you must remember that I lodge in only three-quarters of it.'

'Why is that, your majesty?' he enquired, politely puzzled.

'It belongs to Mynheer Cornelius van der Myle. He was sentenced to exile by the States-General some years ago and banished to the isle of Goree, which is off the west coast of Africa, somewhere near your own country, I believe. When the Elector and I came to The Hague, and the Prince of Orange looked around for a roof to put over our heads, he thought the Wassenaer Hof would be suitable, but it was not unencumbered even then: Mevrouw van der Myle was not forced to leave Holland and was permitted to keep rooms in her own house. I was angry at first, but it has turned out for the best: in brief, Doctor, we became fast friends, and I felt for her sorrow. I spoke to the States-General on several occasions, and when Prince Fredrik Hendrik succeeded as Stadhouder, Mynheer Cornelius was permitted to return. Now we all live together and rub along very well. They have the top floor and I have the rooms of state and my private apartments and rooms for my servants.'

'You are very generous, your majesty.'

The Queen looked a little surprised and slightly offended. 'All my life, it has delighted me to oblige my friends. In this case, it is no more than a matter of common justice. So, as I was saying, my daughters are quartered elsewhere, and I am thankful to say that I do not have to see them more than once in the day.'

'But are not your daughters your comfort?' asked Pelagius. He found it hard to understand what she was telling him: her attitude seemed different from that of any mother he had ever known.

Elizabeth laid down her fork and took a sip of her wine. 'My daughters are my cross,' she replied curtly. 'The boys are bad enough, but at least they can stir about for themselves. I look at the girls and sometimes I think that my heart will burst. The eldest, the Princess Palatine, is a scholar. She was bred up by her grandmother in Heidelberg and educated with her brothers, so she is far cleverer than I am. My second daughter, Louise Hollandine, has a pretty skill with a pencil and sits as a pupil to Meester Honthorst. Henriette is growing a beauty, and my pert baby Sophia bids fair to become a wit. They are all charming, they are all lovely, they all carry the royal blood of England, Scotland and the House of Orange, and yet I cannot find them husbands. I am poor, Dr Pelagius, and no prince will marry my dowerless daughters. Perhaps if the Prince Elector regains the Palatinate, there may be hope at least for the youngest, but I am mortally afraid that they will all wither on the vine. I am angry and sad for them, and every time that I see them I end by finding fault, so they fear me more than they love me. But when they have made their curtsies and gone, I know in my heart that the fault was not theirs.

'I want so much for them to have what I had in my day, and my girlhood was an enchantment, Doctor. I danced in masques at my father's court and my dresses were of silk and tissue, wonderfully made and embroidered with pearls. When I was sixteen I fell in love with the man I was to marry and the trousseau I took to

Heidelberg cost eight thousand pounds in good English gold. Now I am an old woman and it is my daughters' turn to glitter and shine. They should have been the best matches in Europe and I cannot give them one dress, or even one *day* of the life which is appropriate to their rank. Is it any wonder I cannot bear the sight of them? My sons are nearly as bad. They are beggars in the courts of Europe, when they should be captains of armies and patrons of the arts.'

He looked at her in silence. He could see very well what she meant, and understand the frustration of a generous heart with nothing to give. It seemed impertinent to offer any comment, so he changed the subject as best he could.

'What is a masque, your majesty?' he enquired.

'It is a kind of play. Do you know what a play is? Do you have them in Oyo?'

'I know what a play is, your majesty, but I have not seen one,' he replied patiently. 'We do not have such things. We do tell stories, of course, and we dance, and there are poets, and *arokin*, who recite the praise of the King.'

'Like the bards of Ireland,' she commented.

'Perhaps, your majesty. I do not know about Ireland.'

'I have not been to Ireland either,' explained Elizabeth, 'but I have read Stanihurst's account of it and he says there are poets there whose business it is to praise the King. But that is by the by. It was masques I wanted to tell you about. A masque is a kind of play, not for common actors, but for the court, with splendid scenes and devices and poetry. My mother loved such things. She used to devise them with her writers and scene-painters, and then we would play in them with the ladies of the court on festival nights. I have always loved the theatre. I remember from when I was a girl, the King's Men gave fourteen plays at Whitehall at the time of my wedding, just before I left England for ever. Two of them have stayed in my mind, Dr Pelagius: I sent afterwards to buy a book with the words. In one, which was played on my betrothal night, there is mention of a daughter of a King, who married the Prince of Tunis. Some person says of her that she sailed "ten leagues beyond men's life" – I was going no further than Heidelberg, but I was only sixteen. My poor mother was there and I saw tears in her eyes when the player said those words. It was the truth, for we never saw each other again.'

'And the other play?'

'The other play was called *Othello*. The heroine was close to my heart, also, because she was curious of the world. She fell in love, listening to stories, and I have always dearly loved to hear a tale.'

'What happened to her?'

The Queen's lips parted and then she seemed to catch back what she intended to say. She made no answer, but turned to her ladies. 'Bess, it is time we removed.' The Countess got to her feet, and pulled out the Queen's chair so that she could rise easily. With Pelagius on her left hand, followed by her ladies, she led the way upstairs to her private room.

Pelagius trudged after her, uncertain what he should do. His instinct, based on his own sense of decorum, hinted that he should modestly retire, since he had been with the Queen for some hours. He saw her settled in her withdrawing room, with her women about her, and once she was comfortably seated, he made his bow.

'Oh, must you go, Doctor?' she asked, with open disappointment. 'I would like to hear more stories about your kingdom.'

'I am your humble servant, your majesty. If you summon me on another occasion, I will be very happy to entertain you.'

Her head came up and it seemed for a moment as if she would insist on detaining him, but she capitulated gracefully. 'Farewell, Doctor. Thank you for your oracle, and for your company.'

* * *

When Pelagius had gone, Elizabeth sat for some time musing. Gradually her ladies began to disperse. Mrs Broughton excused herself and went about her work. Lady Dohna also excused herself, saying she had letters to write, leaving Lady Sayer sitting reading by one window and the Countess of Löwenstein by the other, setting in the sleeve of a smock. It was a peaceful scene of quiet industry, but not entertaining. The Queen suddenly stirred and turned to the patient Catharina, who had taken her seat by the Queen's seldom-disturbed tambour frame, and was filling in the outline of a leaf with Hungarian stitch, and decided to send her for Madam van der Myle.

There was a certain coolness, as she knew, between Judoca and all of her own ladies, except for Catharina. She had never enquired into it; it was, perhaps, a tension born of their overcrowded life. But in consequence, it was her habit only to use Catharina as an intermediary and here she was, conveniently to hand. 'Catharina, would you ask Mevrouw Judoca to come to me?' Catharina curtsied and some minutes later returned with Judoca van der Myle.

She entered the room smiling, a broad-beamed woman with a mass of frizzed, fairish hair, wearing a blue silk gown. As always, she was wearing the wrong jewellery: she had a taste for dainty little ornaments which were out of keeping with her bulk and her plain, somewhat sheeplike features and, as usual, when Elizabeth first set eyes on her, she longed to remove most of her little pins and necklaces and throw them away. But once that moment of fastidiousness was over, her heart warmed to see the affection on the other woman's face.

'Please sit down, Judoca. Did you see my black magician?' she asked.

'Is he the man who frightened you so much?' asked Judoca in her turn, her tone disapproving, as she brought a chair over to where Elizabeth was sitting, and settled on it confidentially. Catharina, meanwhile, moved her own chair away a little, politely out of earshot, and returned to the embroidery, while Elizabeth was vaguely aware of Lady Sayer and the Countess gathering their things and quietly leaving the room.

'Yes. But I am not angry with him. He is a most interesting man.'

'Oh, my lady. You are always curious for the new,' said Judoca, her voice as near to critical as she ever permitted herself.

'True enough, Judoca. But what would my life be without new things? Waiting and watching. Writing letter after letter, playing with my animals. And what do the answers to these weary letters tell me? That I am a useless creature and I can do nothing to help even those I love best.'

'You are downhearted today,' observed Judoca, looking a little concerned.

'Yes, I am. My African doctor has told me that all is well with Charles Louis and Rupert, and I think I believe him. But he has made me think about the children. I had another letter this morning, about Gustavus Adolphus. He has been having convulsion fits again, and I am in two minds whether he ought to be here, or whether he is safer in the country. He is happy at the Prinsenhof, I know, but I think of him often. And I worry about the older ones. It is hard to keep a cheerful countenance, watching them wear away their youth. Sometimes, it is very hard not to think that God has forgotten us.'

'Never say that, my lady,' said Judoca firmly. 'We cannot know His purposes. I grew up thinking that ill fortune could never touch me, but when my honoured father was executed, I thought I would die of grief. My Cornelius consoled me for that loss, then the States exiled him to Goree and I was in despair. It may be well enough for such as your black doctor, but I truly thought he would die out there of heat and the bad air. You brought him back to me and spoke for us when we had not a friend in the world, out of nothing but your own good heart. God will test you, my lady, but he will not let such virtue go unrewarded. Remember the words of the psalmist: "I have not seen the righteous forsaken, nor his seed begging bread."'

Elizabeth shrugged. 'That is well said, Judoca, but we have done nothing else but beg our bread since the Battle of the White Mountain. Oh, I know that I am melancholy because it is winter and I am mewed in the house, but Dr Pelagius has stirred up old, sad thoughts. I try to console myself with the hope that God has only done all this to try us, and that for the love of His church He will yet give us the victory; but how long, O Lord, how long? Why did God permit my beloved husband to break his noble heart, when he was the sword arm of His righteous purpose? I have been asking this of God and my own heart for eighteen years and I am no nearer to an answer.'

'There will be an answer, my dearest lady. We cannot see far enough to comprehend His ways, but we may be sure that the whole of our lives are part of some greater purpose. The Lord will never cast you away. You are one of His elect.'

'You are always my comfort, Judoca. I think I will see my African again: I have a presentiment that he may be able to see how we are guided.'

'Well, it can do no harm,' observed Judoca indulgently. From time to time, Elizabeth was aware that though they were much of an age, the other woman spoke to her as if she were a child. She had an insinuating, nurse-like way with her, which was perhaps why Mrs Broughton and Lady Dohna considered her sly. Elizabeth disliked flattery of the ordinary kind, but in a life often barren of comfort it was pleasant once in a while to be petted. 'Oh, my lady,' said Judoca suddenly, breaking into her reflections, 'I have just remembered something I meant to tell you. I was speaking to François Aerssens van Sommelsdijk, and he mentioned to me that Dideric de Baer had a painting he was thinking of selling. A very fine old Flemish piece – he got it when we liberated Den Bosch from the Spaniards in '29. I thought it might interest you.'

Elizabeth's melancholy was instantly dispelled: with lifting spirits, she turned eagerly to her friend. 'I must see it, Judoca. Can Aerssens arrange a viewing?'

'I don't know where the picture is at present. But I will certainly find out, since you are interested. Do you want to write, my lady, or shall I?'

'Oh, I will write.' Elizabeth went to her escritoire and opened it. Catharina raised her head immediately, but once it was clear that her mistress did not want anything she turned back to her needle. 'I will tell him I want to see it as soon as possible,' she said, taking pen in hand. 'If it is good, I must have it. I will find the money somehow, even if I have to sell something. It is not an extravagance. It would make a present for my brother, if Charles Louis needs to sweeten him one day. My brother has become a great collector – he favours the Italians, but he is always interested in anything truly good of its kind.' She was writing as she spoke and soon finished her letter, signed it with a flourish and waved it gently in the air. When the ink was dry, she folded it, sealed it and handed it to Judoca.

'I wonder how soon he can send it,' she said wistfully. 'I am so tired of having to wait. And the Stadhouder might want it: I doubt if I could outbid him.'

'My lady, I will do my best. I have not told the Princess of Orange and I asked van Sommelsdijk not to mention it to her.'

'Never fear that Amalia will come to hear of it,' said Elizabeth dryly. 'But perhaps we can put some water in her wine.'

'Oh, my lady. I am sure that if you want it, you will get it. After all these years, you are still the Queen of Hearts. There's not many can resist you.'

Elizabeth could not help but be pleased, though she did not deceive herself. 'A poor, fat old woman?' she asked.

'Oh, my lady. It is not the years that matter. It is a question of worth.' Whether Judoca was right or not, she was unquestionably sincere. As always, it was very comforting.

VI

Where are all thy beauties now all hearts enchaining?
Whither are thy flatt'rers gone with all their feigning?
All fled, and thou alone still here remaining.

Thy rich state of twisted gold to bays is turnèd;
Cold as thou art thy loves that so much burnèd:
Who die in flatt'rers arms are seldom mournèd.

Yet in spite of envy, this be still proclaimèd,
That none worthier than thy self thy worth hath blamèd
When their poor names are lost thou shalt live famèd.

When thy story long time hence shall be perusèd,
Let the blemish of thy rule be thus excusèd,
None ever liv'd more just, none more abusèd.

Thomas Campion, *First Book of Ayres*, 1613

Pelagius walked back to 't Groote Vis. Snow had fallen again during the hours he had spent closeted with the Queen: he kicked up little puffs of it with the toes of his boots as he walked. Everywhere busy women bundled in shawls and wraps were out with their red hands, their cold-mottled faces and their brooms, shoving the new-fallen snow off the street and into the canals, where perhaps the silent commentators would make use of it.

The scrubbing-brush image came into his mind as he watched them work. Who was Elizabeth to speak so slightingly of stuiver-watching housewives? Yet her extraordinary spirit seemed almost to give her such a right. He had read a little medieval theology as part of his course at Leiden, and he recalled that Aquinas had defined magnanimity as, theologically speaking, a virtue. It had not been a case he found wholly persuasive, but it had been interesting as a piece of argument. His understanding of it had been vitiated by the fact that he had never known what it meant to say that someone was great-hearted, but as he contemplated Elizabeth's grace, her generosity to the point of recklessness and her apparent inability to bear a grudge, he arrived for the first time at an inkling of what the notion might actually signify.

Entering 't Groote Vis, he bumped into Mariken, coming in with her broom.

'Oh, it's you, Doctor. Been hobnobbing with your Queen again?'

'Yes, I have seen Queen Elizabeth,' he confirmed.

Mariken sniffed and leaned her broom against the stair, where it dripped a cold puddle, pellets of ice still frozen to its bristles. Her hands were so distorted with chilblains that her fingers looked like twisted red roots. As she spoke, she automatically chafed them, her hard, workworn thumbs passing over and over the sore, broken swellings on her knuckles. Elizabeth's hands, he remembered, were lovely: white-skinned, with long, slender fingers and narrow, well-kept nails. 'I don't know how she has the face to live like that,' she said, her voice edged with rancour.

'How should she live?' Pelagius was somewhat offended on Elizabeth's behalf, but interested to know what lay behind the sharpness of his landlady's voice. It was quite evident that if Elizabeth despised housewives, Mariken, speaking perhaps for *vrouwen* in general, despised Elizabeth. 'She is the daughter of one King and the widow of another.'

'She's as poor as a rat,' Mariken snapped. 'Living on charity when she's got a good pair of hands! How she has the cheek . . . she should be selling herrings in the market and there she is, sitting on her backside in another woman's house, not doing a hand's turn.'

'But the daughter of a King cannot do such things,' he pointed out gently.

'I'd like to know why not. Why don't her family fetch her home to make herself useful?'

Pelagius thought of Elizabeth's life, what he knew of it and what he could guess. The scheming, plotting and contriving on behalf of the heir of the Elector: he was no stranger to such manoeuvures, among the mothers of royal children. It was work. Oh, indeed yes, it was work, but not of a kind which Mariken could be made to understand.

'Mevrouw Mariken,' he said gently, but with authority, "Judge not that ye be not judged."'

She jumped and bit her lip. The fearfulness he had occasionally observed in her since the death of van der Aa flashed across her face and she dropped her gaze and reached for her broom. It was as if she imagined he might do her some harm – pathetic, but supremely irritating. 'Mevrouw,' he added, attempting to soften his tone still further, 'I have reason to know that the Queen has as hard a path to walk as any woman in this country, though it seems to lead through pleasant places. Let us each look to the beam in our own eye.'

She did not reply, so he said merely. 'Dag, mevrouw,' and started up the stairs.

He entered the attic with a certain sober pleasure. It was still very nearly empty, except for the neat shelves of his few domestic possessions and the precisely ranged row of his books. He had sold Comrij's lectern. It was not his own preference to read or write standing up and, in any case, he could not have brought himself to use an item of furniture so sodden with failure and false hopes. The table was kept set for his Ifá consultations: when he read he sat in a chair by the fire, when he wrote he moved to the chair his clients used and put his notes away carefully when he had finished. Most of a lifetime in which he had had little or no space to call his own had left him obsessively tidy with anything he truly valued. No strong memories of Comrij, or the squirrelling disorder of his intellectual life, remained in the room. It had been hard the first time he spent a night in his late master's bed, but he had long since ceased to concern himself or think of it as such. He did not fear Comrij's ghost. All that could be done had been done, and while he did not forgive himself for his moral failings towards his late master, he could not think rationally that Comrij's spirit would have any further truck with him.

With a sense of relief he dismissed the Queen of Bohemia from his mind, and settled down to work. He was brooding about the Ethiopian eunuch, a keystone of his argument in the African section of his work, the section dearest to his heart. According to the Acts of the Apostles, a eunuch of Queen Candace of Ethiopia had come to Jerusalem on a purely spiritual quest. There he had met with the Apostle Philip, accepted baptism and returned, a Christian, to the service of his Queen. A most curious story. Just as the Magi had seen a star in the east and come to worship the Christ child, so this nameless man had come out of Africa to seek the service of the crucified Saviour, one of the first people ever to do so of his own volition, without any stimulation from a preacher or a miracle. An important moment in the history of Christianity, yet one which seemed hardly to have been studied. He made a mental note to ask Sambucus if there were any commentaries on the Acts of the Apostles other than those he had read, but he was moderately certain that, in developing a theological account of the event, he was virtually on his own. Two aspects seemed to him important. The narrative fitted into a history of parallels in the Bible – Isaiah's 'they all will come from Sheba carrying gold, incense, and myrrh, announcing greetings to the Lord', the account of the Queen of Sheba coming to Solomon, the visit of the Magi itself – all of which, in various ways, implied a receptiveness to God in the peoples of the south. Black people. Did not the commentaries identify the Queen of Sheba with the bride in the Song of Songs who says, 'I am black, but comely'? Did not the psalmist also say, 'Ethiopia shall soon stretch out her hands unto God,' and Zephaniah declare, 'they may all call on the name of the Lord, even far beyond the rivers of Ethiopia'?

The second strand of his argument was historical. Following a recommendation from Sambucus, he had acquired the Chronicle of Amandus of Zierikzee, which included as an appendix an account of the Ethiopian church, and a letter from the Ethiopian King Atani Tingil, baptismally David, to Pope Clement VII, which informed him that the Ethiopian people had become Christian after the return of the eunuch to his homeland, and a subsequent missionary visit by the Apostle Matthew.

Pelagius stopped to think. If all this was true, if the Jews had known of Ethiopia and the Ethiopians had known of God, how did this affect the history of his own people? The vastness of Africa unrolled before his mind's eye. He had several times been as far north as Bornu to trade for horses, which the Mai of Bornu had bought from the Songhai merchants of Gao and Timbuktu, far to the south, and once even he had been to Gao itself. He knew from the Songhai that beyond their great walled city of Timbuktu stretched the Sahara, and that some of the horses themselves, the Arabs and the Barbs, had come from Ethiopia and Arabia on the far side of the great desert. The merchants told him that they had taken months on the journey. It would necessarily have been a slow one from one watering place to another, since they would have been trying to keep the beasts in some kind of condition, but all the same he had a good sense of how far a horse might travel in a day and, even allowing for a deliberately slow pace, the distance was almost inconceivably great. He had never met an Ethiopian; though he at least knew from the psalmist that the men of Ethiopia were black like himself, rather than of Arab stock like the Songhai. He was hardly the man to make the mistake of imagining that one kind of person extended uniformly over the whole continent, so this information was valuable. But all the same, the eunuch of Queen Candace was central to this part of his thinking. Ethiopia was in the east of the continent, at the top of the Nile. It was within the bounds of human possibility for this man, whom he imagined as something like an *ilari* – in Oyo these senior royal servants were eunuchs, confirming that he was probably right to imagine some similarity between the court of Ethiopia and that of Oyo – to make his way downriver and, from there, to the valley of the Jordan. Had an *ilari* of Oyo, in the far west of the continent, conceived the idea of such a journey, the vastness of the distances and the greatness of the perils which would have lain before him made it impossible to imagine how he could have reached his destination. But the story illustrated beyond doubt that the Holy Spirit had been at work in Africa, that, as psalm 68 predicted, Africans had indeed reached out to Him. To say that Órunmila, the source of the Ifá oracle, a child of the African west, was another such reacher out and intuitively a son of God, was an argument by analogy, but a strong one.

It was pure joy to him to sit for hour after hour, building his argument in careful steps of clear, straightforward Latin prose. He made, himself, almost no noise but the scratching of a pen. He had almost entirely ceased to hear the pigeons on the roof, out of long familiarity with their noises, and the distant screeching of Mariken; and the bawling of the grandchild, who seemed to be there as often as not, did not disturb him in the slightest. When Mariken brought him clients, he gave them his full attention and concentration. The moment the sound of their feet began to recede down the stairs, he forgot them completely and went back to work. In his newfound state of prosperity, with Elizabeth's money added to his savings, he had Mariken bring him food, empty his slops, do his laundry and sweep his floor. He seldom needed to go out: a walk for the sake of exercise, taken in a state of complete preoccupation, or a visit to the bookseller's, represented the limit of his excursions. He was barely aware of the passage of time.

When Mariken brought him another note from Elizabeth, refraining pointedly from comment, he realized that something in the order of five weeks had passed since he had seen her. Walking down to the Wassenaer Hof, he remembered the snow in the Buitenhof and the snow-sculpture which had been made there. Now it was simply wet; gusty, equinoctial weather with sudden rainstorms and unpredictable cold spells. The inhabitants of The Hague scurried along with their heads down like so many beetles.

He was taken up to the closet, where Elizabeth greeted him with pleasure. She was dressed as before, in black, but covered up, with a scarf of black and silver tissue wrapped high round her throat, and she looked tired and somehow a little crumpled. Her voice was hoarser than he remembered it and she was clearly aware that he noticed it.

'I have had a quinsy,' she explained, after he had paid his respects. 'I am subject to rheums in the winter months.'

'I am very sorry to hear it. I hope you are fully recovered.'

She smiled charmingly up at him. 'I am much better, and all the better for your good wishes, Dr Pelagius. Please sit down.' She turned to the maid standing by the door, awaiting her next request. 'Catharina. I will entertain the doctor myself. Come back to me just before the supper hour.' The girl's blank, solid face assumed as much surprise, perhaps, as it was capable of showing, but she curtsied in silence and departed, closing the door softly behind her. Pelagius watched her go with a qualm of anxiety. Even in Batavia, a lady of rank would never dream of shutting herself alone in a room with a male visitor and he could not imagine why the Queen had done so.

'What do you wish of me, your majesty?' he asked cautiously, once he had seated himself.

'I would like you to try your oracle once more, Doctor.'

'On whose account, your majesty?' he asked.

Elizabeth bit her lip and considered the question for some little time, looking down and absently scratching the neck of one of her dogs. 'I have given this much thought, Dr Pelagius. It seems to me that your oracle has said what it can of my sons' fortunes. It also seems to me that my eldest son's fortune rides on that of his uncle, my brother. We must look to my brother for support before we look anywhere else. Can you tell me anything of my brother Charles, King of England? I sent Catharina away because I want to keep your reply for my own ears alone. Catharina is a good girl, but she is a daughter of Holland. It is not fit for her to hear you on such a subject.'

'Very well, your majesty,' he replied, somewhat relieved by her explanation. 'I will do my best.'

Perhaps a little superstitiously, he had continued to use the same nuts throughout his career as an oracle, despite their unromantic origin in Mariken's kitchen cupboard. He oiled them a little once in a while and they had darkened and become polished with handling, so that they had begun to look something more exotic than ordinary Dutch hazels. He set them out on the table and began to make his count.

A little while later, he looked up and straight into the eyes of Elizabeth. She did not drop her gaze, but continued to look steadily at him, with an unself-consciousness which was almost inhuman. It occurred to him that the troubling clarity of her eyes was due to a single fact: they were for looking out of, not at. She seemed as innocent of any danger of self-betrayal as the kings of his youth who had kept their faces hidden behind veils of cowrie shells. But her face was its own veil, the veil of an eager and vital spirit. 'Your majesty,' he said slowly, his face troubled, 'Ifá has spoken. The *odù* is called *Ìrete'wòrì*.

'"Mundus spoliatur bello:
Insidiae destruunt populos.
Ita oraculum pro Olófin Iwàtuka divinatur;
Monitus est Olófin, ut proelium minatur.
Si Olófin victoriam vellet;
Sacrificiam magnum feceret.
Olófin oraculum audit;
Sed sacrificium non fecit."

'Your majesty, you understand Latin, do you not?'

'Interpret for me. I want to make certain that I understand you.' Her voice was hoarser than before: catarrh, or emotion?

'The oracle warns of war and plotting, your majesty. It says that war destroys the world and people are ensnared in plots. It speaks of a man called Olófin Iwàtuka: since I am reading this for your royal brother, Olófin Iwàtuka must represent him. Olófin is warned that war is threatening, and he is told: if you make sacrifice, you will gain the victory.'

'And does he?'

'He does not, your majesty.'

'And he is defeated?'

'The oracle does not say, your majesty, but it implies that it is so. I am very sorry to offer you no comfort.'

Elizabeth bit her lip. 'I am sorry to say, Doctor, it sounds very like Charles. He is the most obstinate of men, and all the warnings in the world will not budge him from his path. You do not encourage me.' She looked so downcast, he put out a hand toward her – the movement was quite involuntary. Drawing it back at once, he was relieved to see that she had withdrawn into herself and had not observed his gesture.

'May I read for you again? Perhaps the question should be less indirect – should I simply ask whether your son will regain the Palatinate?'

She looked at him again, almost visibly shaking herself free from the net of her thoughts. 'I do not know. If the answer is "no", Doctor, then I hardly know how I will be able to go on. No, that is cowardly. Consult your oracle, ask if Charles Louis will come into the kingdom of his father.'

Soberly, he performed the ritual, and spoke. 'The *odù* is *Òwónrín 'Kònràn:*

> "Dies est, dies hilaritatis:
> dies est, dies lachrymorum.
> Quis est dies hic?
> Oraculum divinatur pro Egasese:
> Inquit, 'quis dies est?'
> Dicatus est, est dies hilaris, dies ludique.
> Monitus est sacrificium fecere.
> audit, et sacrificavit."

'I interpret in this way, your majesty. There will be joyful days, days of laughter, and there will be troubled times and days of weeping. The future holds much that is good and much that is bad – of course, almost any event may seem good to one person and bad to another. But we have asked if the Elector will come into his kingdom and we are told that to Egasese, who is the subject of this *odù*, the day is one of joy. We are also told that he was advised to sacrifice and did as he was told, which being interpreted means that he followed the behests of God. Surely this means that your son will be crowned, though the road to his coronation may be a bitter one.'

'Oh, God be praised', said Elizabeth explosively, 'There will be an end to my grief.'

'Your majesty, do not forget there will also be a day of weeping.'

'With what you say of my brother the King, Doctor, I am sure the days of weeping will be many. But it is my son who is above all my hope and care. The fortunes of my other children rest on his shoulders.'

Pelagius bowed as he sat. 'I am honoured to have brought you better tidings.'

Elizabeth was transformed. She sat more uprightly and the glowing vivacity so characteristic of her had returned. 'Well, Doctor. I think you have done me more good than a summer's day. You have given me a thread of hope, a clue to lead me through my labyrinths of policy and plotting. Well, let us talk of other matters. Tell me about yourself.'

Pelagius looked down at his hands. What could he say? The Queen, surely, would be bored by the question of virtuous pagans, which preoccupied him almost entirely. And his life otherwise was almost non-existent. Her curiosity was of a different order from that of Comrij and far less offensive because rooted in an obvious and very personal good will, but he could not think what she might want to know.

'You are very silent, Dr Pelagius,' she said gently, after some time had passed.

He looked up at her a little helplessly. 'Your majesty, it is very difficult for me to oblige you in this way. All my life I have been a man without a voice. Even when I was *aremo*, which is to say heir to my father ... you must understand, in my country, the King is very sacred. So in certain ways, because he is so sacred, the King is king in the palace and the *aremo* must be king for the people. And thus an *aremo* walks with death at his heels. He must be his father's dog, busy and vigilant, but an *aremo* who is too much a king in his father's lifetime shortens his own days. So when I was *aremo* I was a good steward and careful, and my lips were kept shut on my thoughts. Later, in Batavia, my hands and my will belonged to Master Comrij. I was a good servant to him also, and obedient, because it was honourable to be so.

And thus, through the days of my life, I have learned the ways of silence.'

'But I want you to talk, Dr Pelagius,' she insisted. 'I want to know you.'

He shrugged a little and laughed. 'I find that I am thinking of my father, my life as *aremo*. There was a thing I wanted to say, which would help you to know what I have been – something my mother used to say, warning me to walk warily: "Alájobi ni 'pa 'yèkan." Do you understand me?'

She bit her lip, for once looking a little angry. 'Of course not. What does that mean?'

He sighed. 'Your majesty, I am not mocking you. I can put the idea into Dutch words easily enough – it is that when a man is related to the King on his mother's side, this relatedness may bring about his death. But what it means is part of the whole meaning of Omoloju, the man I was. These Dutch words which I have just uttered signify very little, but it is no better if I use the words of Oyo, because if I say *aremo*, you hear "prins", I say *afin*, you hear "paleis". Yet all these things are the same and not the same. I know my great ignorance, as a stranger and a sojourner in this country. I am reminded every hour of all that I do not understand. I think, with respect, it is not so easy for you to observe how little you can know of who and what I am.'

Elizabeth remained in brooding silence for a time, then suddenly began to speak. 'I am not learned as you are, Dr Pelagius, since my noble father would not have me a scholar, and I have travelled only in Europe, but I would not like you to think me entirely ignorant.'

'Your majesty, I would not presume to think any such thing,' he protested.

'When I was a child in the care of Lord Harington at Combe Abbey,' she pursued, ignoring his reply, 'I wanted to know all about the world. He let me have a little kingdom of my own, on an island in the lake. I had all the different animals and plants there that I could get and in the cottage I called my palace I had the skins of hummingbirds and other bright creatures from very far away. Perhaps I had some from your country. I read books of travels. I tried to make my island into a world in miniature, a microcosm. Lord Harington bought one of the Dutchman's new microscopes for me and I explored the world of tiny things. He had a telescope and I looked at the stars. I had many books and many curiosities from everywhere in the world. I liked to think of strange places. In my imagination, I possessed the whole world.'

But you did not, he thought to himself, not without pity. You possessed an idea and imposed it on the rich strangeness of all that there really is. She reminded him momentarily of Comrij: perhaps this way of thinking was a basic vice of the European mind? It was a point he felt he could hardly make, though he was coming to feel considerable affection for her and believed it to be reciprocated. 'I find that I am thinking of St Paul,' he said mildly. '"For now we see though a glass, darkly; but then face to face: now I know in part; but then shall I know even as I also am known." There will be a time when all minds and hearts will be open. God's elect will be transparent to Him, and also to one another. Perhaps one day you will know me as you wish.'

'Oh, Doctor. How gently you rebuke me!'

'Your majesty, I do not rebuke you at all. It would be impertinent in me.'

She shot him a faintly ironic glance and looked down at the dog that was leaning against her chair, caressing its head while it shut its eyes in a trance of animal satisfaction. 'Do you not care for animals, Pelagius?' she asked, changing the subject. 'You do not look at my pretty Apollon as you enter or give him your hand. I have loved dogs all my life. They are innocent beasts, and once their love is given it is set. Walking as I do among politic men, I value them more and more.'

'Your majesty, to me, a dog is a dog. I do not think of them as you do. But I have always cared about horses.'

'Horses! My great weakness. Do you ride?'

'I cannot afford to keep a horse, your majesty. But my own people were horse lords. There is something in the air of western Africa which is enemy to the horse – they can only live in high and open regions, and the northern uplands of Oyo, where the chief strength of the kingdom lies, is country of this kind. Even so, we could not breed horses very readily, but every year we imported Arabs and Barbs from the north. The Songhai bought horses and sold them to the Bornu, and the Bornu sold them to us. There were a thousand horses in my father's *afin*, each one with his own slave to bring him *burgu* grass and water.'

'So you were a *ridder*, my Pelagius,' she said, wonderingly. 'A "knight", we would say in English.'

'"Knight"? I am not sure that I understand you, but I was most certainly a rider – my people fought on horseback, my lady. There is a saying, "Tani i ba elesin jagun papa?" – Who can beat a warrior who is a horseman on a plain? Our horsemen were as numberless as the sands of the sea and our enemies feared us. Our accoutrements were a lance, a throwing spear and a sword, while our foot soldiers fought with the bow.'

'Your battles sound very like those of my forebears. Crécy, Agincourt, were won by knights, armed with lance and sword, and bowmen. It is only this last hundred years that we have come to use guns. How very strange, Pelagius. The more I discover about you, the more I find likeness.'

'But it is not quite so simple, your majesty. I have looked at the pictures and tapestries in this mansion of yours, and it is obvious from what they show that if you could have seen me as I was in my youth, dressed for war, you would not have thought of your ancestors.'

Elizabeth waved a hand dismissively. 'I am sure you looked very fierce and strange, Pelagius. But the differences are of the surface. The similarities are essential. And the most essential thing to me is that you love horses! We must go hunting together. You have hunted?'

'Of course, though not in Europe. Poor scholars do not do such things.'

'With the boys away, I have a stable full of hunters eating their heads off, growing fat for want of exercise. Let us rumble away our griefs together, one day soon. The weakness of my lungs does not permit me to go freely abroad while it is so cold, but as soon as it is spring, let us hunt together.'

There was a knock at the door: Catharina, come to say that it was the Queen's supper hour. Pelagius excused himself from attending her and walked home in the dusk, thoughtful. He was far from sure that she would remember her promise, but the idea of a good horse was a pleasant one to play with. For the time being he had much else to think about. Packing away his memories and hopes, he turned his mind once more to his researches.

March turned to April; the blowy showers, having chased away the snow, gave way to mares' tail clouds streaking a pale-blue sky and the fresh, cool air of early spring. The pigeons were mating on the roof of the attic, a noisy process involving heavy clatterings of wings; ducks quacked and quarrelled in the canals; and everywhere in The Hague, small birds as light as leaves chittered, fought and made love. One morning early in the month Pelagius was surprised at his lodgings by a messenger with a bulky packet. Opening it, he found a brown leather jerkin and russet riding breeches, not new, but in good condition, a pair of boots and thick gloves. There was also, rolled into the middle of the bundle, a short, huntsman's sword in a nest of worn leather straps. A little piece of paper, folded into a cocked hat, fell to the floor as he picked up the jerkin to measure it against his chest. He retrieved it and read it. It said only, 'Dear Doctor, I will not have you peril your preacher's blacks to give me pleasure. We will hunt on Wednesday.' The thought was a truly practical one and she must have observed him carefully: the clothes looked as if they would fit, though he was a head taller than the average Dutchman. He was deeply pleased and touched.

When he entered the gate of the Wassenaer Hof shortly after dawn on the following Wednesday a lively scene met his eyes. The courtyard was full of people, horses and dogs, huntsmen consuming a morning draught as they stood, grooms walking their shiny, well-kept beasts up and down, horses, horses everywhere, Elizabeth's dogs milling underfoot, excitement in every line of their bodies, and other more business-like hounds, leashed in pairs, which sat and yawned, awaiting their moment of glory. Some men were already mounted, walking the well-fed, under-exercised animals to calm them.

He waited by the steps, until Elizabeth emerged in a plain black habit and high-crowned hat. A groom leading two fine beasts came forward, doffed his cap to her and helped her up, looking away politely as she sprang up to the saddle. She rode astride, he observed. Sitting high on her tall chestnut mare, she looked about her, until her eye lighted on Pelagius.

'Oh, there you are, Doctor! Those are my tall Rupert's hunting clothes – I hoped they would fit and I am glad to see that they do. This bay is for you to ride. His name is Sparrenbord and he is a good horse for a true rider – he is strong and steady, and goes well, but he can be froward. Do not let him think he is master.' Pelagius nodded and vaulted on to the bay's back. Taking the reins in his hands and feeling the animal's mouth, he wondered how to follow her advice. Having observed the saddling up of the occasional livery hacks he had ridden in Holland, he had observed that a Dutch bit was very different from those he had known at home and gave him very much less control. His own people used a style of bit in which pulling on the reins exerted pressure both on the horse's palate and behind its chin: no animal, however temperamental, was capable of resisting such pressure, which was used only at critical moments – ordinary guidance was achieved with thighs and knees. He looked down at the horse a little dubiously. Sparrenbord was very different from the sorry, broken-winded old beasts he had ridden to Leiden and back. He was big and powerful, in the prime of life, a kind of horse he had only ridden in Africa, with a curb. Would Sparrenbord understand the language of the knee if he was used to being guided by mouth?

He held the reins slightly tensed, sensing the horse's movements as he nibbled at the bit, testing his control over his own head and neck. He began to hope that some communication was being established between them; that his hands and knees had not lost their cunning. Completely engrossed, it was some time before he looked up and saw Elizabeth smiling at him, laughing, almost.

'I live for this moment,' she shouted over the general Babel. 'The first hunt of the year, after a winter mewed indoors. If you are in doubts, Doctor, give Sparrenbord his head. He is very well affected to my Dido and he will follow her.' She clicked her tongue and set her handsome mare in motion, settling her to a smart trot. One by one, the horsemen wheeled and fell in behind her in a jingling cavalcade. Sparrenbord was eager to be gone and there was no difficulty in putting him in line; the only difficulty was preventing the animal from breaking into a canter. The short sword jounced uneasily at his side, distracting him: he was not used to carrying a weapon of any kind.

As they crossed the Voorhout, Pelagius was assailed by a sudden memory of the day, so long before, when he had stumbled on such a cavalcade returning, and almost been ridden down. Had that been a year past? More? – Certainly when Comrij was still alive. How could he have believed that he would be a member of such a company? Yet here he was. The thought was only a momentary one: there was far too much going on in the present moment to allow him the luxury of recollection. After some minutes of moving smartly along at trot, he began to think that he had the horse's measure. Sparrenbord went easily and was responsive to commands. He began to enjoy himself.

When they reached the deer park, no great distance from the town, the hunt servants uncoupled their hounds, who fanned out in businesslike style, noses down, tails high: men and dogs began to beat the coverts. Their distant shouts came to the ears of the hunt, who stood waiting and peering into the misty, early-morning distance, the horses shifting from foot to foot or strolling, jingling their harness.

'Look!' cried Elizabeth. Pelagius's gaze followed the direction of her upflung arm, just as the thin, distant note of a hunting horn came to his ears. Three deer had broken cover, distant brown bodies bobbing over the grass, propelled in great bounds and pursued by the dogs, the white rump patches flashing as they ran. The hunt rumbled into action, streaming out over the park.

He urged his willing horse into a full gallop, heart pounding as if he were a boy in his twenties, lost in the pleasure of movement, the pure exhilaration of action engrossing his mind, preventing conscious thought. He did not even remember Elizabeth: his senses were filled by the horse beneath him, the ground to be negotiated and the occasionally glimpsed white, bobbing rumps of the distant deer. There was a ditch ahead: he checked the horse a little, more confident now with how to use the reins, and had the satisfaction of feeling Sparrenbord collect himself, gather his hind legs beneath him and fly over the obstacle. A grunt of triumphant laughter was jolted out of him as they landed. Exhilarated with speed, he felt as if the years had fallen away from him; they had been years of spare but regular diet and work – why should he not have kept his strength?

The deer disappeared into a stand of trees: he was well up with the other horsemen by now and thundered into the wood on their heels. Branches whipped at his face and he began to worry if his horse might catch his foot and stumble, dangerous at such a pace: he slowed to a canter, half-observing that others were doing likewise. The horse's neck was wet with sweat and he sawed irritably at his bit, excited and resenting the check, sending flecks of foam flying back to dew Pelagius's clothes and face. In only a few minutes' traverse, they were through the coppice and back out into an open ride. Another horse came up to run shoulder to shoulder with Sparrenbord: he spared it a glance and saw that the rider was Elizabeth.

'Bravo, Doctor!' she shouted. 'You handle your mount like a true knight.' She was transfigured. The exercise and the wind had blown roses back into cheeks which he had only ever seen pale, and her eyes were sparkling like topaz. Like himself, she seemed to have shed ten years or more in the chase. He tried to smile at her politely and found that he was grinning uncontrollably with sheer pleasure: he could feel the muscles tensing under his ears and he could not even discipline his face to make an appropriate response. Elizabeth went off into gales of laughter and took off her hat to him, doffing it elaborately, with an ironic, gentlemanly flourish. Then she clapped it back on anyhow, regardless of her chignon, dug her heels into her horse's sides and galloped away. Not to be outdone, he stirred up Sparrenbord and followed at his best pace.

As they galloped, they gradually left the woodlands behind and passed into featureless, open country; the stands of trees thinned and declined to scrubby bushes and sparsely clad, sandy soil alive with rabbits – their holes were everywhere, an appreciable hazard, and more distantly rabbits themselves could be seen, standing bolt upright like exclamation marks before diving with a flash of white scut into a friendly burrow. Sparrenbord and Dido were well in the van of the horses, though the hunt was spread out, each beast taking his own course, rather than bunched together as if it were a race. Faintly, he heard a thin shout and looked over his shoulder: Elizabeth was staring urgently at him. Once she was sure she had caught his eye, she beckoned, a sweeping, whole-arm movement, and turned Dido's head, urging her mare off at a tangent to the main direction of the hunt. Without any kind of guess at what might be in her mind, he followed her. The two horses scoured off together, raising a cloud of the thin, sandy earth from their spurning hooves. The ground was beginning to rise, the gentle hills increasingly pronounced.

Elizabeth and Dido breasted a rise and vanished. Following on Sparrenbord, he was astonished to find himself charging over the crest of a sand dune; before him was nothing but grey-white sand, marram grass and the grey and open sea. Sparrenbord dropped back on his haunches and slid down the dune stiff-legged, in a cloud of sand; in front of him, at the bottom of the slope, he could see Dido and Elizabeth recovering themselves and setting out diagonally across the beach. The tracks of the mare's hooves made a strong line across the wet sand. He could do nothing but follow, trusting and uncomprehending; overhead, the gulls screamed and rocked in the sea wind.

Only when Dido was galloping along the very edge of the sea, with the waves wetting her hooves as they swept in to the shore, did Elizabeth begin to move parallel to the dunes. He took up his position behind her, his nostrils full of the scent of salt and sweat, his ears with the splashing racket of their progress. It was not until they had maintained their lonely course for some time that the reason for her manoeuvre became apparent. Out of the corner of his eye he saw one of the dunes seem to erupt; over it came a stag, hotly pursued by dogs, making for the sea. Elizabeth was riding crouched low over her mount, hell for leather; he dug his heels into Sparrenbord's side, urging his best speed from him. The three flying animals moved to a point of convergence. He heard a long, shrill scream; it was Elizabeth, sounding almost like a falcon, a chilling noise, and he yelled himself, as loudly as he could, hauling his sword one-handedly from the scabbard and waving it threateningly. The stag was very near: he could see its flanks heaving like a bellows, and a ring of white all round the dark, unseeing eyes. The mouth was dry, without foam, and the tongue protruded, looking like a piece of old leather. At almost the last moment the animal seemed finally to register their presence, and without checking wheeled in a great arc, away from them, away from the sea and back towards the dunes.

He risked a look back at Elizabeth, aware that she was no longer beside him. She was bent double over her saddle, coughing her lungs out, gripping the reins in fisted hands, as Dido lost speed. He checked Sparrenbord without mercy and circled back to her, his heart in his mouth. Both horses came to a complete stop.

'Your majesty! Are you well?'

The Queen continued to cough, but after a little while, raised her head and gave him a watery smile. Her cheeks were red under a mask of sandy dust and streaked with tears, though her eyes were bright. 'I should not have screamed like that,' she croaked, 'but they will take to water if they can, when they are hard-pressed – dogs are ill swimmers, and if a hart goes to the sea, they are often drowned.' She fumbled for a flask which hung by her side together with her sword and uncapped it with shaking hands, needing both hands to get it to her mouth. The action reminded Pelagius of his own thirst: he had not thought to bring anything. He ran his tongue over his own dry, gritty, salt-crusted lips, and patted the damp neck of his horse who must, he reflected, be even thirstier. Elizabeth seemed to have regained her vitality. She put away her flask and sat up straight, urging Dido into motion. 'Come, Doctor. We must be in at the death.'

They cantered together along the shore. It was not hard to know where to go; they had only to follow the tracks of the stag and its pursuivants clearly marked on the sand. A confused ululation of baying dogs and yelling men drifted out of the dunes. When they came up, they found the stag was at bay in an angle of sandy soil, with dunes at his back. Horns lowered, feet scraping threateningly, he menaced the dogs, who danced about, prudently just out of reach, uttering horrible growls and snarls and making occasional dabs at his muzzle. One dog lay dead and crumpled, its blood staining the sand.

'Oh! It is Jupiter,' cried Elizabeth, her voice grieved. One of her own? – He could not be sure, though it was a type she favoured. He watched, curious as to how the situation would resolve. The end, when it came, was unexpected. A man appeared suddenly at the top of the dune and slid down in a cloud of sand; the stag, preoccupied with the enemies in front, had no time to turn. He hit the beast squarely at the shoulder, bringing him to his knees, and stabbed him in the neck. Bright red blood spurted in a long curve, ebbing and pulsing as the great heart began to fail. It was over. The hunt raised a cheer and hunt servants waded in, whipping off the dogs and leashing them, while slowly the stag fell on his side. Off to one side, someone raised a horn to his lips and blew the mort.

The rest was businesslike butchery. The stag's body was turned over, an undignified jumble of stick-like limbs and lolling genitalia, and a slit cut in the skin of the belly to ascertain the depth of fat. 'He is well in grease, for the time of year,' commented Elizabeth approvingly, watching the process with a professional, housewifely eye: with some amusement, Pelagius reflected that if she had had any inclination to it or seen it as consonant with her dignity, she would have been perfectly capable of running her establishment with tolerable efficiency. Then the beast was disembowelled on the spot and the carcass loaded on to a horse, while the hounds, who had been whining softly, straining on their leashes, were allowed in to the mess, gorging themselves, with wagging tails.

'We must water the horses,' said Elizabeth. 'I know where there is a stream. Do not let Sparrenbord drink too deep, or he will get a colic.' Gradually, the hunt drifted off in search of fresh water; a pause in the business of the day. He felt a pleasing sensation of repletion, as they ambled off, an almost erotic sense of prolonged physical excitement reaching a successful climax: the sense of blank, spent lassitude was familiar. Jogging along, he was very conscious of his body, as he had not been for years. In all the time he had been in the Netherlands, he had had no sexual contact, had hardly thought of it. The hunt was bringing him alive, an effect he would not have predicted, and a startlingly inconvenient one. He certainly could not take a wife until he was back in Batavia, salaried and with a position, and a man of God such as himself could not consort with whores . . .

'When we have breathed the horses,' said Elizabeth, cutting disconcertingly into his thoughts, 'we will draw for another stag.'

Ignis Amoris

VII

My sweetest Lesbia, let us live and love,
And, though the sager sort our deedes reprove,
Let us not weigh them: heav'ns great lampes do dive
Into their west, and strait againe revive,
But, soone as once set is our little light
Then must we sleepe one ever-during night.

Thomas Campion, *Second Book of Ayres*, 1613

Pelagius plodded home through the evening, aware of his stiffening muscles. The following morning he found himself so sore he was barely able to get out of bed. Forcing himself to his feet, he hobbled into the study, where his borrowed jerkin and riding breeches hung on the back of the door reeking of sweat and horses: since they could not readily be cleaned, the stable smell was, it struck him, now a permanent part of the atmosphere of his room. On the whole, a pleasant addition. He shuffled round and round, moving, at first, like an old man walking on ice, supporting himself against the wall, the knots in his knees, thighs and back gradually, painfully, loosening. As soon as he felt able to tackle the stairs, he drove himself out to try and walk off the stiffness, resolved to take more exercise and keep his body supple. Elizabeth had invited him to come again the following Wednesday; he must keep himself in readiness.

As spring wore on, he hunted with the court every week, an eagerly awaited pleasure punctuating long days of intensive work on his thesis. On his second outing he observed that Prins Fredrik

Hendrik was one of the party, portly and formidable even in plain hunter's russet. Feeling the Stadhouder's stern eye upon him, he bowed formally in his saddle, and received the satisfaction of an acknowledgment. From week to week, he came to feel increasingly accepted within Elizabeth's circle, which was, he came to realize, not so much a circle as a series of individual connections to the pole star at the centre. He also ceased to be 'Doctor' to the Queen, who began to address him as 'Pelagius'. It gave him a secret pleasure to hear her using his name.

As they jog-trotted homeward after perhaps the third or fourth of these excursions, a cavalcade of tired mounts, their necks sagging a little from weariness but their ears pricked as they hastened eagerly towards their stables, Sparrenbord picked up his pace, seeing Dido ahead of him and came companionably alongside her. At once, Elizabeth turned in her saddle to acknowledge him. Though she was, of course, bedraggled, with brambles tangled in her skirts, she was looking far better than she had in the winter. Looking at her, her bright face dirty as a child's, her mouth just perceptibly quirked in the quizzical half-smile which seemed to be its most natural expression, he spoke the thought in his mind, without any of his usual circumspection.

'Your majesty must know that they call you the Winter Queen. But seeing you today, I cannot think that winter is your season. You have been transformed by the spring; your youth is renewed like the eagle's.'

Her fine eyebrows rose, and the smile broadened, as she accepted his remark without coquetry. 'My dear Doctor, we will make a courtier of you yet. A fine speech, but I know that I am old. My sun will not renew.'

He bowed in reply, without protesting. He liked that clarity in her; but he held to his first thought. He did not blind himself to the visible signs of age in her, but to his eye her soul shone clear of the accidents of the body.

'Will you dine with me tomorrow?' she asked. 'My old friend Lord Craven is come from England. He was sorely wounded in that action of my sons' which left Rupert a prisoner, and he did not wish to hunt with us today. I would like you to meet him.'

'Yes, your majesty. I would be happy to come.'

The following morning Elizabeth finished her letters by ten and sent Mr Dingley away, heavy-hearted. There was no good news on any hand. Rupert was no nearer freedom, she hated and feared all that she heard from France of Charles Louis and his doings, her little Gustavus still gave cause for anxiety, and her brother's quarrel with the Scots seemed to be going from bad to worse. But for that morning she had done all she could. There was a boat standing off Helvoetsluis which would be going to England on the next morning's tide: she had taken the opportunity to write to her brother and to Archbishop Laud, whom she profoundly distrusted but wished to conciliate, and had sent Dingley to take the letters down to the captain. Nothing remained to do that morning but to pass the time before dinner, so she remained in her closet, reading Du Bartas's long poem on the creation of the world, a work she had been picking at for months. Frederick and her mother-in-law had been both fond of it, so she kept hoping that she would come to like it more than she actually did. When Lady Dohna knocked on the door and came in, she sat up a little, not displeased by the interruption.

'Madam, Dr Jonson would like to speak with you.'

'Thank you, Cordula. Tell him to come up.' She marked her place, shut the *Semaines* without regret and laid the book in her lap.

'Dr Jonson,' she said, once the preliminaries were over, 'what do you want from me? I hope all is well? Have you news?'

He bowed a little as he sat. 'No news, my lady. Rather, I have come to you with questions.'

'How is that?' she asked curiously.

'Your majesty, what can you tell me of your black acquaintance?'

'Do not fear for me,' she said immediately, rising to the defence. 'He is a most learned, godly and sober man, not a charlatan or a trickster.'

Dr Jonson raised a hand protestingly. 'Please do not misunderstand me, your majesty. I am glad, of course, to hear this from your mouth, but I was aware that he was doctorandus of the University of Leiden. I publish in Leiden, as I think you know, and I have friends there. I have long been acquainted with his tutor, the learned Sambucus, who speaks well of him.'

'I am glad to hear it. How, then, can I help you?'

'Your majesty, what manner of man is he? I have a reason for asking this.'

She exhaled gustily, with a note of laughter. 'I wish I knew. He says so little! But I will tell you what I know of his life. He is an African and he was born to rule. His empire was called Oyo: I have looked in the atlases of Ortelius and Mercator, and I cannot find it, but I am sure he is no liar – he says it is away from the coast and none of our people go there, so how could it be mapped? But it is clear from his face and his manner that he is of royal blood. He was the heir of the king, but a cousin of his father betrayed him and sold him to the Portugals. He was sold into the Dutch spice islands, where he was bought by a deep scholar, who baptized him and set him on the road of learning. He spent many years in the Indies, studying medicine and the plants of those regions. Then he conceived a desire for ordination and came here to study. Some time after that his master took him out of Leiden, to work with him upon a flora of the Indies. He was reduced to great want and in his poverty turned to an oracle of his own people to put bread in his mouth. He has consulted for me. It is a form of *sortes* and I see nothing in the oracle, or his interpretation, contrary to the truths of revealed religion.'

She spoke a little firmly and again Jonson made a gesture of deprecation. 'Your tale interests me very much,' he said. 'It marches with what I know of him from Sambucus. You feel that he is a remarkable man, do you not?' Elizabeth nodded, her eyes fixed on him. 'And you feel also that he is a godly one?' he persisted. 'Yours is a wise and discerning heart, my lady.'

She turned the palms of her hands upwards, helplessly. 'What can I say? He seems to me a man of the greatest integrity, a true believer. Have you heard otherwise?' She began to have a curious sense that two conversations were happening at the one time: the words she and Jonson were uttering and other words which seemed to flow beneath the surface.

'No,' he said heavily, 'but what I am thinking needs to be weighed and tested with the greatest care. Even now, I fear to say too much. Do you recall the *Chymische Hochzeit* of Christian Rosencreuz, and the *Atalanta Fugiens* of Dr Michael Maier? Have you read Mede's *Clavis Apocalyptica*?'

'The Elector discussed it with me a good many years ago, and I have some knowledge of the other works you mention. Mr Twisse, who was my chaplain in Heidelberg, was acquainted with Mede and they corresponded.'

'Mede looks to a great instauration of learning, which will march with the reformation of the church and the world, the creation of the new Jerusalem and the reign of the Just King. His work is subtle and he speaks much in parables, but the intention of his writing is clearly to be seen.'

Elizabeth regarded him steadily. 'I know these things. When I was a young bride my dreams and my waking hours were full of such visions. We truly thought, the Elector and I, that we would trample down the ungodly and bring the nations to Christ. But what of it? The Elector is dead and the dream lies in ruins. So the glory of this world passes away.'

'But not the glory of God,' said Jonson firmly. 'Your majesty, consider Pelagius and consider also the words, "The hour is come, and not the man."'

Elizabeth found she had put her hand involuntarily to her throat. 'Dr Jonson, what are you hinting?'

'I am not hinting, but advising you to look at this man and think about him. As you know, I also have studied the alchemical arts. Behold, we have a king, the son of a royal house, a dreamer. Like Joseph of old, he was reduced to the nothingness of slavery, which is a death in life. It may thus be said that he has undergone the *nigredo* of the philosophers, the corruption from which cometh life. He was reborn into Christian life as a prophet, a man who walks with God. And further, your majesty, he carries within him the knowledge of three different spheres, Africa, Asia, Europe. The world is a great globe and in all its quarters Christian voices are raised in prayer. As the psalmist declares, the glory of the Lord is declared among the heathen and the ends of the world have seen the salvation of our God. For years I have thought and prayed and studied on these matters, and I have come to a great question: in the days of your youth and mine were we presumptuous in seeking to fulfil God's purposes for this great, rolling ball on the basis of dispositions in Europe alone? Was our vision too narrow?'

'These are wild words, Doctor.'

Jonson bit his lip, and looked down at his folded hands. 'They are not uttered without long thought, your majesty. This Dr Pelagius is but a poor man, living at his own hands. We must ask, then, could such as he be emperor of the Last Days? We should recall that our Lord himself was a poor man, living among humble people. The Jews in their blindness saw him not, but looked past him, straining their eyes for a Messiah in purple and gold, with chariots and horses and a sword in his hand. We mock at their folly, but should we not have a care, lest once again the King that is to come is one whose kingdom is not of this world? Are we, in our generation, snared in the same error? I have another question, which goes with my first.

Are we right to interpret what we read in Revelations as earthly power and glory?'

Elizabeth rubbed her brow with her fingertips, massaging the temples. 'My dear Dr Jonson, I do not know if you have said too much, or not enough. My mind is in a maze.'

He rose and bowed respectfully. 'I will leave you now, your majesty. Keep my words in your heart and, when opportunity offers, observe this Dr Pelagius with all the care you may.' Softly, he left the room: the Queen sat on, paralysed with astonishment, holding her book without opening it. It was a long time before she bestirred herself and then only when there was another knock at the door of her closet.

Judoca opened the door at once, before Elizabeth had replied, and slipped into the room, her face animated. She curtsied perfunctorily. 'Madam, I have news for you.'

Elizabeth shook herself free of the formless half-thoughts and emotions which had been crowding round her and gave her friend her attention, intrigued by her manner. 'Judoca. What is it?'

'The Duke of Gelderland's painting. It is in The Hague, at a house on the Voorhout. Do you want to see it?'

'Of course.' Elizabeth stood up, and shook out her skirts briskly. 'Call one of the maids and let us go as soon as possible. I have cobwebs in my head, moping here like an owl. I should like to go out. Tell Lord Craven I will see him at dinner.'

Pelagius came to the house for twelve, crossing the courtyard, entering the hall without looking about him. As he came in, he saw Elizabeth descending the stairs with a train of followers behind her, on the arm of a pale little man with a sensitive, suffering face ornamented by a neat, small beard, dressed with sober magnificence in drab brocade and a fortune's worth of lace. They moved slowly, concentrating on the descent, Elizabeth's arm, it seemed, more supportive of than supported by her cavalier. She looked up as they negotiated the last step.

'Ah, Dr Pelagius!' She spoke in English and he strained to follow her. 'Dear my Lord, may I present Pelagius van Overmeer, doctorandus in theology of the University of Leiden. He is a friend and I am infinitely obliged to him.' Switching to Dutch: 'Dr Pelagius, Lord Craven, ever a staunch friend to me and mine, who has spent much of his life and fortune in my service.'

Pelagius bowed low: Lord Craven acknowledged the courtesy with a stiff nod, his troubled dark eyes cold and suspicious, and moved on limpingly with the Queen on his arm. Pelagius fell into step behind the van der Myles, beside the chaplain, dimly aware, from the corner of his eye, of girlish figures descending the stair. At last, it seemed, he was to see the Queen's daughters.

The dinner was more decorous than the previous such occasion which he had attended. The noisy crowd at the lower tables were relatively subdued, perhaps by curiosity. The whole length of the upper table was set to accommodate the large group of diners and glittered with silver plate, while pages, ushers and footmen stood in readiness. Pelagius wondered what prodigies of discipline Sir George and the Countess of Löwenstein had expended, in order to achieve this spectacle. Lord Craven was settled, with a good deal of fuss, at the Queen's right hand, while her daughters took their places on her other side: he himself was seated at the bottom of the table beside the chaplain, Dr Jonson.

He regarded the girls with covert interest. Both were tall and well grown, with dark hair and sad, dark eyes. The Princess Palatine was a rather heavy-featured, long-nosed young woman of perhaps twenty, with sallow skin. She had nothing of her mother's vitality: in purely physical terms she could have been attractive, had she not looked depressed and a little sulky. Princess Louise was more like her mother in appearance: her face was sensitive and open, with a wide mouth, but her expression was vulnerable and anxious, without any of Elizabeth's confident appeal. They were good-looking enough, as far as faces and figures were concerned, but drooping beside their mother they made a cheerless pair. He began to have an inkling of why she might find them irritating.

Dr Jonson rose by his side and said a long grace in Latin. When he resumed his seat and the meal had begun, he turned to Pelagius, continuing to speak in the Latin language.

'*Salve, magister.* Professor Sambucus has told me a little of your work. How does your thesis proceed?'

Pelagius bowed where he sat, privately astonished. '*Gratias ago.* Thank you for your interest, Doctor,' he replied warily. 'I think it is not far from completion.' In the noise and clatter of the room, they were slightly isolated at the end of the table, able to talk almost as if they had been alone together.

'You are studying natural theology, are you not?' pursued Jonson.

'That is so,' Pelagius confirmed. Looking around him, it was clear that the etiquette of the meal was to take portions from the dishes that were immediately to hand or to ask a servant to bring some particularly favoured item to within reach. He helped himself at random to the nearest dish, a tart with a filling of some dark green vegetable. He was surprised, putting a forkful in his mouth, to find that it was rich and unctuous with almost no detectable vegetable flavour, and to encounter lumps of some intensely sweet substance, unfamiliar to him.

The chaplain was observing him and the expression on his face as he chewed must have given him away. 'Spinach with marrow and candied eringo, Doctorandus,' Jonson explained. 'A *quodlibet* for a feast; a "kickshaw", we would say in English.'

'Eryngium? Sea holly?' There was nothing in the soft, overly sweet stuff he had swallowed to suggest the tall, spiky plant he associated with the name.

'Ah. I had forgot you were a botanist. The roots, I believe, prepared with sugar. They are nourishing and restorative, especially to the aged and those that lack natural moisture, but less healthful, perhaps, to a man in his prime, particularly a man of the cloth, since they are heating. There is a veal fricacee before me, sir, may I help you to a little?'

'Thank you, Doctor. I am not accustomed to these courtly dishes.' He sampled cautiously the hashed veal which the chaplain had put on his plate: it was highly flavoured, bound with a rich, buttery sauce. Too rich: a man could eat little of this food and stay in health, he thought, though up and down the table he saw the company doing full justice to the dishes before them. He ate a few mouthfuls and found he had had all he wanted. Dr Jonson, at his side, was bolting his food with a carelessness which reminded him of Comrij, indifferently greedy, and beads of sweat were already beginning to show at his temples. One of the pages, James, or was it Francis?, came by, proffering a basket of fine, white manchet bread; he took a roll gratefully and began breaking it into small pieces: it would serve to disguise his lack of appetite.

Dr Jonson laid down his fork and took a long swallow of wine. 'I was asking you about your work, Doctorandus. Tell me, what is your argument and what is your conclusion?'

'My subject is the natural turning of all peoples towards God, Dr Jonson.'

The man's thin lips thinned further and his eyes were suspicious. 'Do you then contemn the works of those that preach and teach the Faith?'

Pelagius, in his turn, raised his glass and took a sip of wine. It was not clear to him whether the chaplain was seeking a quarrel or merely a discussion; when he spoke, his tones were equable, but not apologetic. 'I do not. It is my dearest hope that, once I am ordained, God will grant me the grace to become such a teacher, bringing His true word to the peoples of Batavia.'

'But mankind is blinded by sin, Doctorandus Pelagius,' objected Jonson. 'The creation of fables is natural to our race: we are lovers of stories from our childhood. There is a spark of the divine in every child, for it is made in the image of God, but there is also a wilful leaven from the Father of Lies. In the childhood of mankind poets imagined gods and demons in every river and mountain, and thus the nations were perverted with lying stories of Jupiter and Minerva, Bacchus, Venus and all their false crew. The Jews alone held fast against this storm of error, but when the Light came to the world, their darkened eyes comprehended it not and centuries of steadfastness were blotted out in one great fault. What say you to this?'

Pelagius took a deep breath. 'I respect your argument, which is also that of Dr Owen, but there is light in the darkness, Dr Jonson; the natural light of human reason and the enlightenment given by God. I do not deny the error, but everywhere men can be found whose eyes have been washed clean. You speak of the lies of the poets and the fables of Minerva and Venus: but did not Plato and Aristotle, who were brought up on these fables, speak out against them and for the One God centuries before He walked on this earth? In the East the Hindus worship demons in the forms of monkeys, elephants and men with many limbs, but philosophers that I have spoken with see a shadow of the Trinity behind these profligate delusions. The Buddhists, similarly, have inklings of a single God and declare that it is the destiny of the virtuous to participate with Him in the beatific vision. The Muslims, like the Jews, are fatally in error, but they believe in the One God and they are left-handed sons of the covenant God made with Abraham. Remember that there were even those among the Jews who turned to Christ: the apostles were born into that faith. I do not know about the gods of the north, but in Africa, though my own people bow down before idols, our priests speak of one God, the Creator of heaven and earth and all that is in them.

'Wherever I have walked, in this one world of ours, I have seen ignorance and folly. There are many men and women here in this Christian nation, Dr Jonson, no less mired in superstition and vice than the Bantamese or the people of my own country; does not half Europe accept the idolatrous perversions of Rome? Sin is strong and men are weak. But the Lord chooses His own. He chose Elijah and the other prophets, and also Plato and the Sibyls. When Jeremiah was in prison, an Ethiopian eunuch who was in the palace went to King Zedekiah and begged the release of the servant of the Lord. Why did he so? When our Lord was in the hands of Pontius Pilate, his wife sent word to the court, begging his release. What prompted her in this but the stirring of God in her inwards? I do not deny the need for teaching. But if we consider the wife of Pilate, we see that she was not simply a fertile field for the sowing of grace. Grace was already planted and growing in her heart, and the words of a preacher would but have nourished it and brought it to flower.'

Jonson was listening intently to his reply, but made no overt sign of his reaction. When Pelagius had finished speaking, he stirred, and reached for a decanter. 'You argue well, Doctorandus. A little more wine? Come, drink with me.'

'Thank you.' He accepted the wine – a peace offering? – and pledged the chaplain, raising his glass.

'And you?' enquired Jonson baldly.

'I do not think I understand you,' he replied warily.

'You were born into heathenism,' persisted the chaplain. 'Tell me. What did you know of God?'

Pelagius looked at him in astonishment. 'It is not an easy question to answer,' he said carefully. 'It was long ago. I was heedless and caught up with the things of this world, but then I was a young man and rich, a warrior, and a prince, and I rejoiced in horses and fine garments and in the strength of my arm. Did not our Lord say, it is easier for a camel to go through the eye of a needle, than for a rich man to enter the kingdom of God? I was deaf to the Lord, but it may be, not because I was a son of Oyo, but because I was the son of the king. I remember that I wished to know many things: I spoke often with the Ifá priests, who interpreted oracles for the people, and I talked with the Songhai, who were Muslims, about their God, but the Lord did not touch my heart. I dreamed that when I was King, I would bring many men to the palace to tell me what they knew: it may be that this desire was a spiritual thirst, though as I remember I thought of it only as a desire for knowledge. It was once I was humbled and brought low that I turned to the Lord.'

Jonson remained silent for some time, and when he spoke it was, surprisingly, to quote psalm 105. 'He sent a man before them, even Joseph who was sold for a servant, whose feet they hurt with fetters, he was laid in iron: Until the time that his word came: the word of the Lord tried him. The king sent and loosed him, even the ruler of the people, and let him go free. He made him lord of his house, and ruler of all his substance, to bind his princes at their pleasure, and teach his senators wisdom.'

Pelagius's eyebrows rose. 'We are all lords and rulers, Dr Jonson, for God has made us His children, heirs of God and joint heirs with Christ. Who could want more? For myself, I ask only that I be given the grace to bring others to the knowledge of this heritage.'

'And is that not the power to bind and loose, promised by God to His servants?' said Jonson. A movement further up the table caught Pelagius's eye: an usher was drawing back the Queen's chair. All along the table, diners scrambled to their feet, with a great scraping and scuffing of chair legs; the usher darted forward to help Lord Craven, who was in difficulties, his small figure awkwardly poised as he struggled to get his weight on to his stronger leg. Once all were securely afoot, Dr Jonson pronounced a closing grace and the Queen left the room.

Pelagius followed her out, deep in thought. The chaplain seemed disinclined for further conversation and, with an abrupt farewell bow, whisked off about his own affairs. Elizabeth and her party went into her throne room, while the Van der Myles were climbing the stairs, presumably returning to their own quarters. He hesitated in the hall, reluctant to attend Elizabeth's public audience. His relationship with her was a personal one, nourished by their common passion for hunting and by precious, private conversations in her closet. He knew that her life had a public face, but he had no further curiosity about it. He had seen kings speaking with their people from his earliest youth. More a matter of concern for him was the conversation with the chaplain, which he did not understand. Perhaps the man had wished to assure himself of his orthodoxy? But the trend of his questions was odd and his aims not immediately apparent.

Pelagius made his mind up. He would go home, and return to work. Perhaps he would reread *De Theologia Naturalis*: had he missed something in Owen's work which Jonson had expected to hear?

He heard no more from the Wassenaer Hof until the following Tuesday. In the intervening period he reread Owen and satisfied himself that, although he was not fully in agreement with the man's arguments or his conclusions, he had missed nothing essential. His own work was complete: the thesis had gone to the printer's, but he was preparing himself for the public examination, in which he would have to defend the points he had made. Revisiting Owen on natural theology was timely and he was duly grateful to have been reminded of the work.

When he next heard from Elizabeth, it was not with an invitation to hunt, but with a summons to her closet after dinner. He went with some curiosity, and took with him his bag of oracle nuts. Did she, perhaps, wish him to consult Ifá for Lord Craven, if he was still with her, or in response to some news he had brought?

But when he entered the closet in response to the Queen's message, it seemed to be neither of these things that had led her to summon him. She was alone, sitting in her usual chair by the window, but he sensed excitement in her. Catharina van Eck, having brought him in, retreated to her usual position by the door, where she stood with her hands loosely clasped awaiting instruction.

The Queen's eyes, fixed on his face, were bright and her lips pressed firmly shut: she looked like a little girl possessed by a secret. There was something new in the room, an easel, with a picture on it covered by a black cloth.

'What is this?' he asked, indicating it.

'Look and see.'

He lifted back the cloth and looked at the picture. It was not very large, less than three feet high, and was in three parts: the largest in the middle. He touched one of the outer panels and it moved gently, hinged, he saw, to shut over the main image. A ruinous hut, in it, a thin, pale girl enveloped in an enormous blue cloak, a thin, naked, unnaturally alert infant sitting upright on her lap. Behind her, peering through the windows of the crazy dwelling, a gang of mocking figures, jeering spitefully: she seemed unaware that they were even there. Before her, though her sad eyes looked through and past them, were three great men in elaborate clothes, two grovelling at her feet, one standing. His attention was caught by the standing figure. He was black-skinned, dressed in a white robe, apparently made of a material resembling suede or deerskin, with fantastically elaborate sleeves of seaweed and thistles, so long that the ends trailed on the ground.

'Do you see why I wanted you to see it?'

'Does it represent the visit of the Magi?'

'Of course. But do you not see the third King is just like you?'

'Perhaps,' he said doubtfully. There was a tall, thin mirror on the narrow strip of wall between the closet's two windows and he moved to where he could see himself, posing soberly so that he could see his three-quarters profile.

'It is easy to see that you do not often admire yourself,' said Elizabeth, amused. 'Now that you see yourself, can you also see the resemblance? It is you yourself, dressed as the King of a far country.'

'Yes,' he said slowly. 'It is very strange. How did this come about? Who is the painter?'

'It is painted by Jerome van Aken of den Bosch: it is already more than a hundred years old, I believe. I heard that the Count of Gelderland was thinking of selling it and had it brought here. Once I saw it, of course, I was mad to get it. Amalia wanted it as well, but I outbid her.'

'How much did you pay for it?'

'Five hundred guilders.' Pelagius swallowed, his mouth dry. Enough money to repair ruined lives, such as his had been until Providence ordained his rescue, for this piece of painted wood. The idea was obscene.

'Is it not beautiful?'

'Yes.'

'You do not like it.'

'My lady, I do not think that I understand it,' he protested. 'I do not know how to value such things. I know that the kings of the world came to do homage to our Lord and this knowledge is precious, but I do not know why anyone should picture it in this way.'

'You have a very austere mind, Pelagius.' The Queen rose and came to stand beside him with a whisper of stiff silks. He could smell her perfume and, under it, the human smell of her hair; her heavy skirts brushed against his leg. Standing so close to him, he was conscious of her height, the robust strength of her body. 'It helps us to remember what we might otherwise forget. It illustrates the great paradox of the faith. Mary is dressed like a queen to show that she is the Mother of God, honoured above all other women, yet she is dwelling in this hovel. See, Joseph is on this side panel, dipping up water to wash the Christ child's dirty linen in the stream, as if these scions of the house and lineage of David were no better than the poorest of the poor. The soldiers and the peasants who will one day crucify this child are already showing their cruelty, but those with eyes to see, the Wise Kings, are bowing before Him.'

'Why is his face so vicious?'

'Not Balthasar's?'

'No. The white king's – the one in red.'

'It is a mystery. It is, I agree, and the king in green looks as stupid as a stock. The painter Jerome was a man of very subtle mind. I do not know who the half-naked man in the doorway can be, either. He has the face of a wicked idiot. Perhaps he is meant for the king of the beggars. Perhaps Jerome is telling us of the nature of man before the coming of this royal baby, who sits so still. It will take me a long time to riddle out the mysteries of this picture. And while I am thinking about it, you see, I am also thinking about God and His purposes in the world.'

But five hundred guilders! he wanted to say, but did not. Money, he knew, was all but meaningless to her. She was not paying attention, in any case. 'I am trying to think where to put it,' she said. 'I want it in here. Perhaps if I move that picture of me to my bedroom, it could go in its place. It is very difficult. It is a good picture and I liked that embroidered jacket – it is pleasant sometimes to remember the days of my youth, before I wore black. But if I move the Stadhouder or Amalia they might be offended, and I want my family about me.' She was peering closely at the picture, her face smooth and absorbed. Suddenly she glanced up at him: he took half a step back, startled. 'It will also make me think of you. He looks so like you,' she said, a little shyly. 'It is not just a matter of features. He is a man of sorrows, his face is bewildered with grief.'

'Do I look so sorrowful?' he said gently.

'Oh, Pelagius. Only once have I seen you smile.' She was looking directly into his face as she spoke, her changeable eyes clear and filled with honest good will; the first human soul for more years than he could remember who had any concern for his feelings whatsoever. It was no effort for him to smile at her with real affection. The effect was unexpected: her eyes flew wide, startled, and colour rose into her cheeks. She put a hand up, as if to ward him off, as he instinctively extended his; their fingers knocked together with a shock.

'I am sorry, your majesty,' he said quickly, wondering what he was apologizing for.

'Catharina! A glass of Canary, if you please. I am a little faint.' The waiting woman whisked out of the room and Elizabeth retreated to her chair. 'I am so sorry, Pelagius. Your smile is a sweet one. But your teeth are so white! I was surprised, for a moment.' She was still a little fluttered and her cheeks were pink.

Pelagius became aware that his body was reacting to her femininity, to his great embarrassment, though the weight and thickness of his clothing at least prevented any fear that he might betray this to her. With a sudden moment of insight, he divined that something similar must account for her reaction. She had stood so very close to him, thinking about nothing but her picture; then suddenly she had realized that he was a man. He was filled with sudden happiness.

'I should warn you, your majesty, I think I may smile again.'

The maid Catharina, coming in again with a tray, stood astonished in the doorway, as the Queen began to laugh; clear, joyous, ringing laughter, like a boy's. Pelagius stood in the middle of the room, grinning cheerfully down at her. She roused herself and blotted her eyes.

'Oh, that has done me good. I have not laughed so since . . . oh, not for many years. Let us take a glass of wine together, Pelagius. Catharina, bring him a chair.'

Catharina poured another glass of wine and brought up a chair. He sat, lifted his glass and raised it to her. 'Your health, your majesty.'

She acknowledged the toast, with a courteous nod of the head, and sipped at the pale wine, holding the glass elegantly by the edge of its foot. She set it down and rose: he stood up automatically.

'No, be seated, Pelagius. I have just thought of something.' She went to the cabinet in the middle of the far wall, a stupendous affair painted to resemble tortoiseshell and standing on spiral-turned, gilded legs, and unlocked it, throwing open the doors. He had never seen it opened, and looked on with interest. The inner sides of the doors were painted with a pastoral landscape, and within was a series of little drawers decorated with marquetry in ebony and ivory, and an arch-headed niche, backed with mirror glass, which held a nautilus shell mounted as a cup with an elaborate silver-gilt foot. She pulled the drawers open one after another, searching for something. 'Ah! I have it.'

She returned to her seat and held something out to him. He set his glass down and took it from her. He examined it curiously, turning it about in his fingers. There was a transparent disk, a little over two inches across, engraved with figures. One man, standing beneath a tree on the banks of a river, a branch in his hand, a group of figures on the other bank. Their bodies were thin and angular, their gestures were vivid: command on one side, pleading, perhaps, on the other. He frowned in puzzlement.

'Moses?'

'I think so. "– when they came to Marah, they could not drink of the waters, for they were bitter. And the people murmured against Moses, and said, what shall we drink? And he cried unto the Lord, and the Lord shewed him a tree, which, when he cast it into the waters, the waters were made sweet."'

'Even so.'

The crystal was set into an elaborate frame of gold, surmounted by an eagle. She watched his face as he looked at it. Finally he laid it down and looked at her. 'You must explain, your majesty.'

'The crystal is very ancient. It is said that it was made for the Holy Roman Emperor Louis the Pious, the grandson of Charles the Great, so it is eight hundred years old. You make me think of the Emperor Louis because it was said of him that he never showed his white teeth in a smile. It belonged to the Emperor Rudolf, who treasured it because it was a link with that first Holy Roman Empire. He had the mount made by his master goldsmith, Anton Schweinberger. When I went with the Elector to Prague as Rudolf's heirs, I found it in the imperial treasury. I was a giddy young girl then, so I used to tease my monkey with it, by catching the sun in the crystal and making spots of light dance on the floor for him. As chance would have it, I kept it by me for that reason. When we fled from Prague, we took almost nothing, but I found much later that I had it in my workbox. Today, when I saw that Jerome had made his black king hold a crystal toy mounted with a golden phoenix, I thought of the Emperor's bauble. I wanted to see it in your hand, Pelagius.'

'It is beautiful', he said. 'Beautiful, and very curious.' He picked it up again, and held it out to her. Gently she pushed his hand back towards him.

'It is for you.'

'But your majesty, I cannot take such a thing!'

'I wish it. I command it.' She was smiling, but perfectly serious. 'I delight in making gifts, Pelagius. Oblige me, if you please.'

'Thank you, your majesty,' he said, a little helplessly. 'But it is too valuable for me. It is a royal treasure.' He was still holding it in the tips of his fingers; it made him uncomfortable, but he did not feel that he could put it down. 'It is too costly.'

'But I am not asking you to buy it, Pelagius! Only to accept it as a gift.'

'It is not a right thing for me to have.'

'You think too much about money, Pelagius,' she chided him. 'A scholar and a philosopher should hardly notice it, surely? I know you have lived as a poor man and I can see that you have done it with dignity, but it has left a mark on your mind. Why is it the value of this crystal that you notice, and not its beauty, or its long history?'

'Your majesty, I think that money means something very different to you and to me,' said Pelagius slowly. 'A man who has the experience of being sold learns a lesson about money. He learns, in that moment, as he stands naked before strangers, that all he has is a price. Value is his only defence against abuse, or even death.'

Elizabeth was silent. 'I see,' she said finally. 'Pelagius – what did you cost?'

'When? When I was sold to the Portugals, my value was twenty thousand cowries and a string of fine coral beads. My people love good coral. In Batavia I was worth fifty guilders. The sum has a meaning for me.'

'I can see that it would. But it is not very much, for a man.'

'Many are sold for less.'

'Perhaps I should say, it is not very much for a prince.' She sighed, looking down into the wine in her glass. 'Pelagius, you make me think of such troubling things.' She raised a hand pre-emptively, seeing him about to speak. 'No – do not apologize. It is right that I should think of them. We hoped to serve the Lord, the Elector and I, but our hopes collapsed in ruins at the White Mountain. I have lived on, to beg for my children, and to eat the bread of strangers, and I have thought myself scourged by the Lord. But I have not suffered as you have suffered. I cannot imagine it. You were born a prince, as I was. How was it that your heart did not break, when you stood on sale?'

'I do not know, your majesty. I was young and the young are hard to kill. As I have told you, my life as *aremo* schooled me in patience. There was, I suppose, always some spring of hope in my heart. At first, perhaps, I had some thought of rescue or ransom, if the followers of Egonoju had been bested by men loyal to my father's house. Then later I found that I had acquired the habit of endurance, which grows upon one little by little. And once I was baptized and instructed in the faith, I had the hope which I share with you, and with all Christians. I saw many of those who were enslaved with me die of despair, your majesty, on the ship, or once we had got to the Indies. They sat still and the light went out of their eyes, and some while after they died. Perhaps it was because I was a king's son that I did not. I had the habit of thinking myself a person of importance and in the pride of my youth, I could not believe that I was utterly cast away. Then, of course, I found that I was not.'

She was gazing into his face all the while he was speaking, her face soft with compunction, the lovely hazel eyes glimmering brighter, then, as he finished speaking, spilling over with tears. She set her glass down; wordlessly she held her hands out to him and he clasped them. Her hands felt very small, soft-skinned and warm; they filled him with tenderness. Without thinking, he released her right hand, and reached very delicately to touch the soft, wet skin beneath her eyes, catching the drops on his fingertips. She tried to smile. 'Forgive this foolishness, Pelagius. I am weeping for your youthful hopes, I think.'

'Foolishness, perhaps, but it is good and merciful in you to feel for the pain of another. Even a pain that is long past.'

She released her left hand gently and felt for a handkerchief.

Covertly, as she turned away from him to wipe her face and blow her nose, he touched his fingers to his lips, tasting the salt of her tears.

VIII

You meaner Beauties of the Night,
That poorly satisfie our Eyes
More by your number, than your light, –
You common people of the skies;
  What are you when the Sun shall rise?
You curious Chanters of the Wood,
That warble forth Dame Natures layes,
Thinking your Voyces understood
By your weak accents; what's your praise
  When Philomel her voyce shall raise?
You Violets, that first appear,
By your pure purple mantles known,
Like the proud Virgins of the year,
As if the Spring were all your own;
  What are you when the Rose is blown?
So, when my Mistris shall be seen
In Form and Beauty of her mind,
By Vertue first, then Choyce a Queen,
Tell me, if she were not design'd
  Th'Eclypse and Glory of her kind?
Sir Henry Wotton, *On his Mistris, the Queen of Bohemia*, 1651

She hardly knew when he went. She was confusedly aware of his tall body rising and blotting out the light, his bow, his deep voice, his firm, quiet tread, and aware, also, that her own voice was mechanically replying, saying what was expected. When at last he had gone, she clasped her hands together, bit her lip and tried to collect herself. The unexpected touch of his fingers on her face had sent a wave of scalding heat through her body; she was shocked at herself and at the violence of her feelings. It was inconceivable to her: that whole aspect of her selfhood was dead and buried with Frederick; angry and unconsenting, she recognized the slippery warmth between her legs and rejected it with all the force of her will. 'This is absurd,' she thought to herself vehemently and scrambled to her feet.

'Leave me, Catharina,' she commanded. The girl slipped out at once: she paid her no heed. She felt she must be throwing off scent like a bitch in season. Ranging randomly about the room, she looked up for help at the portrait of Frederick which hung over the mantelpiece. It was a good portrait; the sad, dark eyes spoke to her as they had spoken in life. He had been a man of melancholy habit; she had so often been aware that it was her will, her energy and her lust for life that had had to do for them both. But the trust between them had been absolute since the moment when they had awkwardly collided, two children of sixteen, he seeking to kneel and kiss the hem of her skirt, she to curtsy and offer her cheek: they had met in the middle, both off-balance and with the massive ordeal of a royal wedding before them, they had put out their hands to steady one another and instantly, in the meeting of their eyes, sworn mutual loyalty, a loyalty which had never for a moment been broken. How could her body, now, betray her mind, her vows, after nearly thirty years?

Out of the corner of her eye, she saw the new painting on its easel and turned to cover it. But she paused as she put out her hand and looked again at the black king. Another pair of dark and sorrowful eyes, another sensitive mouth compressed with virile resignation upon secret and bitter thoughts. So alien: the bronze-dark skin, the soft-looking, close-curled hair whose texture she could not but imagine under her hands, the subtly different tang of his sweat. And so familiar, in his honour, his pride, his sad submission to the will of God. A melancholy scholar, who was also a prince and a warrior. She swept the cloth brusquely over the picture and left the room, then stopped the first servant she met.

'Tell Mrs Broughton I am going riding. She must come to my bedroom and prepare my habit. Then tell a groom to bring Dido to the front door and a mount for himself.' The maid curtsied, and fled; evidently aware of the haste and irritation which she was unable to conceal. She climbed the stairs to her bedroom, unpinning the lace from her neck as she went. By the time her mistress of the robes arrived, looking a little startled, with a riding habit over one arm, her collar and cuffs were reposing on her dressing table, with a precious heap of pearls glimmering beside them. 'Unlace me, please.'

Mrs Broughton was a woman of rank and had been in her service for twenty years: she was more a friend than a servant. Normally, dressing and undressing was an occasion for gossip and banter, enjoyed by them both. But she knew her mistress well enough to read her expression. Elizabeth climbed in grim silence out of the stiff pool of black brocade which fell at her feet, standing in her smock as Mrs Broughton, blank-faced, fitted the plain black twill habit round her, settling it at the waist with experienced, knowing tugs at the laces. Once the Queen was dressed, she curtsied without speaking, schooled, professional, discreet. Elizabeth sat on a stool, allowing the other woman to catch back her side curls, and rearrange her hair in a simple chignon.

Gazing bleakly at her own reflection, as Mrs Broughton held the hair away from her face, she observed the heaviness which had come upon it, the time-defeated sag of the flesh along her jawbone and under her eyes. Her nose had taken on something of the beakiness of her mother's. 'I was beautiful once,' she thought; a sad thought in a way, but also, perversely, a relief. Twenty years before she had looked in mirrors more often, and the face of her youth was still present to her mind's eye. Her hair had been paler then, and much longer, an amber river when it was let down and combed to hang free. Her face had been delicately modelled, with an aquiline little nose and a lovely, creamy complexion. Oh, yes. She had been called the pearl of Britain and rightly so. She had been fit to be loved and she had been loved. But it was over.

She rose from the stool and Mrs Broughton handed her her cloak and her high-crowned beaver hat. Leaving the mistress of the robes to tidy her things away, she walked down to the hall and out into the courtyard. Her favourites Celadon and Babbler and several of the other dogs, who had been lounging before the fire in the hall dozing and scratching, scrambled hopefully to their feet and followed her out. She ignored them, but made no attempt to prevent them from joining her. Piet was there with Dido and one of the carriage horses. He bowed awkwardly, with the reins in his hand, and boosted her up to Dido's saddle. 'Just a ride,' she said, once he was mounted. 'I need air.'

He saluted. 'Right you are, m'lady.' She dismissed him from her mind: he would follow where she went and that was all that was needed. Setting Dido to the trot, she breathed deeply, letting the sensation of the moment flow over her mind. It was a fine day and the ground of the deer park was hard, drumming beneath the horses' hooves. The dogs ranged widely about them, pursuing the rabbits who bobbed and scuttled beneath the trees, circling back, tongues lolling, after each futile expedition. They made her laugh; she enjoyed their pleasure, the mindless, animal contentment she shared with them and with the smoothly cantering mare. It was only with reluctance that she turned for home, sensing the first symptoms of weariness in her mount. But the cobwebs were blown from her mind and her body. She was her own woman once more.

When they returned to the Wassenaer Hof, she slipped from the horse's back, patting the sweat-slicked neck and rubbing the long nose. 'Goodbye, Dido. Brave girl, good lass.' It was only when she was walking up the steps, acknowledging the bow of her halberdier with a lift of her gloved hand, that the name of the horse jumped in her mind and fell into focus. Dido, widowed Queen of Carthage, faithful to the memory of her dead husband, had yet fallen in love with a stranger prince, a teller of tales. She looked back at the mare with regret as Piet walked her back to the stable. I shall have to sell her, she thought. Perhaps I should bring one of the children's horses up from Rhenen. There is Jewel, she is tall enough for me, and poor Rupert is not here to ride her. The light was fading from the sky. The hour for evening prayer was approaching and she must change. Followed by her pack of tired hounds, she picked up her muddy skirts and hurried up the stairs.

Washed, changed and restored to herself, she began her evening prayers with her usual reverence, perhaps even with an unusual degree of concentration. I must not think of my own desires, she admonished herself, but of the purposes of God and how I may serve them. Lighten my darkness, I beseech thee, O Lord ... the grave and familiar cadences of Chrysostom's prayer composed her mind, and she gave her full attention to Dr Jonson.

The text for the evening was psalm 72, painfully familiar. 'The righteous king shall come down like rain on the mown grass, as showers that water the earth. In his days shall the righteous flourish, and abundance of peace, so long as the moon endureth.' It was an unfortunate choice, which rubbed painfully against the sore places in her mind. She and Frederick, as they debated the offer of the crown of Bohemia, had been possessed with that psalm, which seemed to speak directly to them with the voice of God. How devoutly they had hoped to bring peace and plenty, justice and godly rule to the Empire. She remembered Frederick's dark eyes flashing with the light of a prophet as he told her, 'It is a divine vocation, which I have no right to reject,' and the letter which they had received from the Archbishop of Canterbury to advise them that accepting the crown was a religious duty. Inevitably, Frederick had followed where he seemed to have been guided and disaster had followed. All those years ago: she had been so young that it had never really occurred to her that they could fail. She cast a moment's unindulgent thought towards her youthful self. She had survived the births of three children and the death of her mother when she and Frederick had sat together and spoken of the crown of Bohemia. How wise she had seemed to herself, how competent to advise her husband. How little she had known.

After the service, as the servants filed out, she continued to sit in her black velvet chair of state in the chapel. It was pleasant just to sit, she was tired from the afternoon's riding. Jonson busied himself with the furniture of the Lord's table, setting the books straight, snuffing the candles. When only one remained alight, he looked across at her as she sat quietly in the dark, clearly wondering if she wanted him to go and leave her sitting, or to speak to her. 'Leave it,' she called softly, her voice clear in the small room. 'Bring a chair and sit by me.'

He bowed. 'Your majesty.' He drew up another chair and they sat together in the quiet semi-darkness. The room was a black cave, with dim trails and patches of light; reflections from the highlight-points of polished, dark, carved wood and gleaming silver. With the thick door shut, the racket of the hall was stilled; they might have been sitting together in a forest.

'Dr Jonson, why did you choose that particular psalm?' she asked.

'Because it is a thought I wished to share with you, your majesty. It is the duty of all men and women to walk uprightly in their ordained paths and fear the Lord, but to the princes of the earth much has been given and more is expected beyond the service of the common man. You are the guardian of a precious destiny.'

'Dr Jonson, I am not,' she protested. 'I have been weighed in the balance and found wanting. I am the stone the builders rejected.

All that there is for me now is to dwindle out my days in peace. My every second thought should be my grave.'

'Your majesty, it seems to me your melancholy misleads your tongue. It is the stone the builders rejected which was made the cornerstone of the temple.'

It was strange to talk in the near dark. The chaplain's quiet voice came to her out of the night: she spoke in return, dropping her thoughts like pebbles into the quiet black pool of the darkness, too weary to censor her tongue. 'We each have our day, Dr Jonson. Women come early to their flowering, then their petals fall. Before I was twenty, I felt the world turn under my hand. I am past forty now. It is for my daughters to eclipse me.' Even in the dimness, she sensed, or saw, the impatient jerk of his head.

'No, your majesty.' It was not like him to contradict her so flatly and she looked at the pale oval blur of his face in astonishment. He continued doggedly. 'Your majesty, it is well known to you that the philosophers have long seen your path as one marked by destiny. You will recall the ancient prophecy, from the time of Edward the Confessor, "The Rose of England beareth the Cross of Christ to foreign lands?"'

Elizabeth sat a little straighter, her hands still in her lap, a small crease beginning to appear between her brows. 'I remember it.'

'As I reminded you some while ago, Mede looks to a great instauration of learning, which he linked with the reformation of the church spoken of in the prophecy of King Edward's time. There are others I could mention, but in short many learned men, your majesty, have seen in your marriage the fulfilment of the great prophecy of the Last Days, and hailed the Elector and yourself as the Just King and Queen. The work of my learned friend Dr Fludd points also in the same direction; but that is not the whole of the tale. It must be remembered, also, that there are prophecies which relate peculiarly to your own royal house, your majesty, and to yourself in your own person. Are you not the Rose of England?

All the people and nations wait with longing hearts for the return of Astraea and the reign of divine justice upon on earth, but we, above all, must concern ourselves with these matters. The learned Dr Maxwell has declared, "from the rose of England shall proceed the reformation or purgation of the Church of Rome", and there are other prophecies, relating to England more generally. It is said on many hands that England is the land chosen by Jehovah to be the scene of the restoration of all things. I have also seen it said that it is a scion of the Stuarts who will reign in Jerusalem when the Jews are converted at the end of time, and even that this Stuart prince will be Emperor of the world. I have worked and thought, your majesty. You know I am a practitioner of the spagyric arts. I have consulted the stars. We are moving towards a great conjunction.'

'Speak,' she said coldly.

She sensed, rather than saw, the movement of his hands as he threw them up. 'Your majesty, I would not dare to speak, if I did not perceive some prompting from your own heart. The man Pelagius –'

'What of him?' she demanded, her voice, in her own ears, a little shrill.

Jonson's voice came low and urgent from the dark. 'You know well. I have had speech with him, when you were dining with Lord Craven. I have tested him; he is humble and walks with God. And yet he is a king and soon he will be a priest in the order of Melchizidek. All the writings of the philosophers speak of the wedding of a king and queen. The renewal of the world must depend on their conjunction ... my dearest lady, I believed, as you did, that the Elector was the man. But he was not. You know in your heart he was not. We cannot know why the Lord refused his sacrifice, and I can only think that it was because he was no more than an earthly monarch. But my precious lady, you are still the vessel of all our hopes. Remember, your father betrayed us all, whoring after Spain. Noble Prince Henry is dead. Your brother who lives is married to a Catholic and his wife rules him in all things. Your son is in France bargaining for his inheritance, and who knows if they will pervert him? You alone stand as you have always stood. In your lovely youth, my lady, you were often enough hailed as Astraea, but as the years pass and you remain staunch amid the storms and errors of the world, it seems to me more than ever that there is something in you that is touched with divinity. I have read and scried and prayed, and it is manifest to me that your destiny is concerned with the salvation of the world. Watch, I say to you, watch, You do not know when the bridegroom may come.'

Elizabeth stood up. 'Dr Jonson, this is blasphemous nonsense. I cannot listen to it.'

But as she was sweeping out of the room, she heard his voice pursuing her, low and calm. 'I speak not as a man, your majesty, but as your spiritual adviser.' And what, she thought angrily, as she climbed the stairs, has the spirit got to do with it?

It was only as she was going to bed that it occurred to her that the next day was a Wednesday. Pelagius had a standing invitation to the hunt, she would see him. If she did not stay at home. She lay awake for hours, staring into the dark. Perhaps she would be ill. But even as she slipped to and fro on the borders of sleep, she knew herself too well. The vigour of her body would deliver her to the next morning, well and strong, and never in her life had she refused a challenge. She did not see that it would be possible to avoid the encounter.

They hunted the next day: to her surprise, she enjoyed it. Dido was brought out for her and it seemed ridiculous to reject the poor beast, though she was resolved to replace her within the week. She saw Pelagius as he came into the courtyard and greeted him civilly. The warmth between them lay latent, like a fuse; she commended, in her heart, his discretion as he turned away from her courteously and gathered Sparrenbord's reins into his hands. In the hours that followed, she saw him at intervals, his dark face rapt with concentration, riding with skill. He did not seek to course at her side; he was merely a figure in the mêlée or in the crowd assembled at the death.

Yet, when they were jogging home and Sparrenbord sought his accustomed place by Dido's side, she did not turn away from him. Two thoughts strove confusedly in her mind. On the one hand there was Jonson's vision of the apocalypse, a vision which in one form or another, had haunted and informed her life for twenty years. On the other was Pelagius himself. In sober daylight, free from the womanly nonsense of her private imaginings, he was a plainly dressed, decent, dignified friend, whom she had come to admire and respect. The easiness of their companionship seduced her, so remote was it from the dreams of Jonson and, behind him, the voices from her youth – Maier, Fludd, and Rosencreuz. Pelagius was too much himself, too sane, for such things. Almost, she convinced herself that there was nothing in her thoughts of the previous day but a freak of the blood. He was so cheerful, so much at his ease, she could hardly trust her own memory.

When they got back to the Wassenaer Hof, he jumped down neatly from his horse and bowed to her once the groom had helped her down and she had straightened her skirts.

'I must say farewell, your majesty. I regret that I will not be able to attend you next week. I am going to Leiden to defend my thesis.'

'Oh! it is finished then. Oh, Pelagius, I am so pleased for you. I am sure it will be a triumph.' She hardly noticed as Piet collected the bridles of their weary horses, wheeled them round, and took them off to the stables. 'Come to my closet. We must drink to your success.'

He followed her in to the hall. Jane Sayer and Catharina van Eck came down to meet their queen, beaming and proprietorial. 'Jane.

Take Dr Pelagius to my closet and attend him there. Catharina, come and shift my clothes as fast as you can. I do not want to keep the doctor waiting.' She whisked up the stairs, followed by the taciturn Catharina, while Pelagius followed at a slower pace with Lady Sayer. As she hastened away, she heard him speaking.

'My lady', he said, a little apologetically, 'Is there anywhere I could wash my hands and – ?' the voice tailed off politely.

'There is a little closet here on the stairs, Doctor, with a close stool. I will leave you for a moment, and then knock on the door and bring you water and a towel.'

'You are very kind,' she heard him say, as she turned the corner of the stairs. Poor Pelagius, she thought. I gave no heed to his comfort, thinking of my own. At least he has the wit to manage for himself. She and Catharina had reached the door to her own room. She skimmed her hat on to the bed and began to jerk at the fingers of her gloves.

Only fifteen minutes later she joined Pelagius in her closet. She made a regal entrance, though, catching sight of herself in the mirror which hung between the windows, she noticed that the curls which should have been tumbling down to her shoulders still clung damply to her hastily washed neck. He stood in the centre of the room with his hat and gloves on the side table, awaiting her with perfect self-possession. He bowed as she came in. Lady Sayer had already left. Catharina entered behind her with a decanter and two glasses. She set them on the table, curtsied and, unbidden, departed, closing the door softly behind her.

'Shall I serve you?' asked Pelagius quietly.

'Thank you.' She seated herself, avoiding looking at him as he approached near to her chair in order to pour the wine, fluffing her skirts so that they fell in correct folds. She took the glass he handed to her and raised it, pledging him as he picked up a chair, looking at her for permission as he did so, and seated himself catercorner from her.

'My best wishes for your success, Pelagius. Tell me what you are doing next week; I do not think I quite understand.'

'Your majesty, I have published my thesis.'

'Oh! I would have liked to see it.' She was genuinely disappointed. She would have liked to feel that he wanted to share it with her, useless gesture though it would have been. Not that he was a man for useless gestures, she reflected wryly.

'I am sorry, your majesty. I could not think that you would be interested. I will bring you a copy. It is all in Latin, of course,' he added.

'Perhaps I could not read it as you would, Pelagius, but I would have made shift to understand a little,' she said, piqued. 'Or I could have asked Dr Jonson to explain it to me.'

'I am very sorry. It was remiss.'

She gestured regally, waving off his apology. 'It is your humility, Pelagius, or your *mauvaise honte.* I absolve you of bad intentions. But now your thesis is published, why must you go to Leiden?'

'I must defend it, your majesty. With my professor as sponsor, I must present myself before the Rector and other learned men and answer questions on the subject I have chosen.'

'It is a combat of words,' she said, interested.

'In a way.'

She sipped at her wine and smiled at him.

'What is your subject? I do not think I have ever asked you.'

'Natural theology.'

'Why?'

He looked up in shock, his eyes widening so that she saw the whites flash. 'Do you know, I do not think anyone has ever asked me that? It is to me the question of questions. Because I need to know what it means to be both a son of the Covenant and the son of the King of Oyo. Because I am an African. My work has been directed towards understanding the existence of my people, so far from Christ but not from God, and explaining, as far as I can, the oracle which I perform. I do not think I have wholly succeeded, but what I have come to understand is that there is some divine purpose in what I do. I do not know what it may be, but I know in my heart that I am moving to the purposes of the Almighty.'

'How strange. That is what I feel too. You know – do you not? – perhaps you do not, it was long ago – in brief, Dr Pelagius, we were the hope of Protestantism, the Elector and I. Prayerfully, with the certainty that we were the sword of the Lord and of Gideon, we went to take the Empire, and bring it back to the ways of God. The sequel you must know. We fled from Prague, the Elector broke his heart, and I lived on, working to restore his children as best I could. I remember that, all through that dreadful journey, it was not the cold or the fear or the child I was carrying that dragged at my heart. It was that I could not understand how God had permitted the Catholics to conquer. For more than twenty years I have thought about this. God rejected the sacrifice of my beloved husband, as he rejected King Saul. I have long wondered what David is to arise in his place, for that God has turned His face from His people I cannot and will not, believe.' Jonson's words rose in her mind, as if he were putting them in her mouth. 'There are many prophecies of the House of Stuart, Doctor. There are even those who say that the last Emperor of the world would be of our house, the King who the prophets say is to reign in Jerusalem and bring the Jews to God. I do not know how to interpret these visions, or how to think of them.'

'Your majesty', Pelagius said very gravely, 'do not think of them. Do as you must, following the promptings of your heart, after prayer and searching of conscience. It is not earthly wisdom which will help you. It is of no avail. For my own part, I have thought from time to time, in my ignorance, that I could discern the purposes of God. I became a slave and it is a terrible thing for a prince to fall into slavery. When I became a Christian, I looked for the hand of God and it seemed to me that I was called to become a preacher. I imagined, foolishly perhaps, that there was meaning in my suffering. If there is a meaning in my life, it is not for me to know it.'

She leaned forward, urgent with communication. 'But, Pelagius, I am in no better case. I have thought such things for nearly half my life – it is eighteen years since the Battle of the White Mountain, and I am past forty. All I can think, my dear Doctor, is that this defeat, this suffering, though it seems so great to us, is a tiny detail in the great purposes of God. Something else is meant for us. Have faith.'

'Faith?' he said suddenly, with immense bitterness. 'I am not guided in this matter. But I have faith in you.' She looked at him, startled, the hazel eyes flying wide, an unbecoming flush rising on her neck; their eyes caught and locked; she held out her hands and tried to smile.

'Pelagius, I am a poor creature to be any man's guide.' Slowly, for the second time, he took her hands, which shook in his grasp.

'You are a rock, madam. You do not know your own strength.' His grip tightened very fractionally, she did not think he was aware of it. Reckless, holding his gaze with her own, she rose and took a step forward; there was nothing he could do but rise and step forward in turn.

The blood sang in her ears, she could feel the lace on her bosom, coarse against the backs of her wrists and behind her hands, crushed between their two bodies, the movement of his chest and the slow hammering of his heart. She looked up at him, deliberately holding his gaze. 'Pelagius, my dear, I am yours if you want me,' she said gently. She saw him swallow, then he bent his long neck and kissed her.

When she pulled away at last, he released her at once: she stepped back from him reluctantly, so as to look up, though she kept her grasp on his hands. 'Pelagius, we must speak with Dr Jonson. I am not a private person and I must act under advisement.'

'Elizabeth?' For the first time, a little tentatively, he used her name. 'I must be guided by you. I do not know what you can do. But you are my earthly happiness, my *schaatje*.'

The low-Dutch word, my treasurekin, sounded comically in her ears: almost, she felt inclined to reprove him for it, but the tone of his voice set the incongruity to one side. Time enough to teach him the language of love she had bathed in all her days, pleased and unmoved, even, her thought ran on, if she cared to. He was alien to what she had known and his alienness included a Dutch which was of the city, not the court. It did not matter. He was something other, and something more, than all the poets who had sung her beauties in days gone by.

She drew a deep breath. 'Leave me, my darling. I must talk to Dr Jonson. He has been saying in veiled terms for some little while that we should marry. I would have paid him no heed, if my heart had not gone out to you, but when head and heart speak together, what can I think but that there is more to it than the lust of the flesh and our own wills? You are powerfully strange to me, Pelagius, and I to you. If we are drawn together, over all that separates us, there is something beyond inclination. Your love fills me with a happiness I thought never to know again, but I must be politic. I am not at all ashamed of you,' she finished unhappily, 'but I am the mother of a prince.'

'I understand,' he said at once. 'You are a woman of most honourable and upright mind, my Elizabeth, and there are promises for you to keep. I must not tarnish what men think of you, for fear it harm your children.'

She came towards him again and leaned her forehead against his chest: he put his arms round her. 'I am ashamed that I must think so,' she said, her voice muffled against the black cloth of his waistcoat. 'You are not my private indulgence.' She looked up suddenly, relaxing into the circle of his grasp, slipping her own arms round his waist. 'I would say, you are the next task set for me by God, but I have come to love you so much that you seem more like a gift.'

'I will go', he said, making no move to release her. 'You must not be found like this, it is beneath your dignity. And mine.'

A faint sense of the absurd stirred in her heart. He was virile, she could feel it in his responsiveness; she knew herself as quick and slippery with life as a young girl. Yet they stood facing one another, two middle-aged souls, so bundled in heavy breeches and petticoats that even crushed against him as she was, she had to guess his response to her. How foolish they would look, if anyone were to walk in. Reluctantly his arms slipped away from her and she moved over towards the fireplace, looking back at him wistfully. 'Pelagius, my mind is split in two. I injure nobody if I do not love, but if I love I risk harm to the children of the Elector, whom I loved most dearly. Because I am engaged to the children above all as a sacred trust, truly, if I were a private citizen, I think that I would harden my heart against you. Yet I am the daughter of England and there are considerations and duties for me which go beyond the ordinary tasks of a widow and mother. I fear, from what Dr Jonson has said, that when He comes, the Lord might demand from me a talent I have hid in a napkin. The destiny of my house lies on me, for I am ashamed to say I am the only one of us who still stands without staggering from the principles of the Reformation.'

'Dr Jonson has spoken to me also,' said Pelagius slowly. 'He may be right. God knows, my dearest one, my personal inclination is towards you, as it has never been towards any woman in my life and there is nothing in my heart or my conscience to set against him. If this is what God wills for us, so be it. I have not your responsibilities, Elizabeth, I could not bear to say nay. If there is anything to stop us from joining as God joins men and women, it must come from you.'

'I do not think it does. But I must go to Dr Jonson and I must ask him to pray with me. And you, Pelagius my dear, must go, lest we become a scandal. Come back to me tomorrow morning after prayers and we will see what may be contrived.'

After Pelagius was gone, she sat for some time in a state of blank astonishment at herself. Uppermost in her mind was a passionate certainty of the rightness of what she was doing, however unlikely it might be; but as the immediate excitement of her lover's presence began to fade, the practical implications began to rise before her in all their complexity. She must talk to Jonson; but above all, she must talk to Judoca. She rose and went in search of Catharina, and sent her to fetch Judoca. There was half an hour still before dinner.

Judoca entered and curtsied, her plain face a little worried but full of good will.

'Sit down, Judoca,' directed Elizabeth, and paused, uncertain how to begin her tale.

Judoca seated herself in the chair Pelagius had so recently vacated, and looked at her shrewdly. 'My lady,' she began, 'I think I can guess something of what you want to tell me.'

Elizabeth sat bolt upright, the blood draining from her cheeks. 'What . . . ?'

'No, no, have no fear,' said Judoca hastily. 'No one is speaking of you. Catharina is a good girl and she does not gossip. But she watches over you and she talks to me from time to time because we are related. She is the daughter of my husband's sister, you know.'

'I had forgotten,' said Elizabeth faintly.

'My dearest lady, if you have forgotten what the house of Van der Myle owes to you, I assure you we have not. Nobody has breathed a word of suspicion anywhere in the house. But Catharina has been with you when you have entertained Dr Pelagius, she has seen your face and heard your voice. When you brought him in this last time, she opened her thoughts to me. Have no fear; we will never betray you. We owe you so much, I feared we could never repay it.'

Elizabeth drew herself up proudly. 'I acted from common justice, Judoca. Do not speak as if I have bought your silence, or I will be sorry for it.'

'You have not bought us, my lady,' said Judoca with unusual dignity, 'but we will serve you for love. Forgive me if I speak out of turn, but you are in love, are you not, with this African doctor?'

'Dr Jonson tells me I must marry him,' explained Elizabeth stiffly. She detested the note of conspiracy in Judoca's voice, the hole-in-corner dealings into which she was forced, and could not bring herself to look at the other woman. 'It is not a question of lust, or a freak of the flesh, though I most truly love and admire him. But Jonson tells me something great will come of it. You know, he is a student of the mysteries.'

'I don't try to understand such things, my lady,' said Judoca frankly. 'But I have known you for nearly two decades, and in all that time, I have never known you act dishonourably. If you think you should have him and Dr Jonson thinks you should have him, then we must all do what we can.'

'I cannot take him openly,' explained Elizabeth, 'lest I hurt the cause of the Prince Elector, or even my brother.'

'Yes, yes, yes,' soothed Judoca. Her solid, sheeplike face was compassionate, but avid: the aspects of the situation which most repelled Elizabeth evidently gave her considerable satisfaction. 'I have an idea. You know, I have a little closet near to my room, at the top of the stairs. My eldest daughter used to sleep there until she married; now I read there sometimes, but I do not use it much. There is a desk there and a box bed set into the wall, and it has a key, which I will give to Dr Pelagius so that he has a room to use under this roof. If I tell my husband you wish it, he will not say me no. People come and go in this house all the time. If the room is kept locked and we are careful, who is to know that he sleeps here? And if they do know, who can say any ill of it? He will be in my part of the house. My husband is a sound sleeper and I am a poor one: he never rouses if I get up in the night.'

'It is a good plan,' said Elizabeth a little doggedly. 'Thank you.' She rose and tried to smile. 'Now I must go and speak to Dr Jonson.'

Pelagius walked through the streets of The Hague like a man in a dream. Images crowded his mind: Elizabeth in all her attitudes, but most particularly as she looked up at him, her face full of sweetness. A tag from a poem came into his mind, one of the Kisses of Joannes Secundus which had struck him when he read it as well turned, but no more: 'Alas, what discontents arise, betwixt my emulous lips and eyes!' He knew now how Secundus had felt.

The practical aspects troubled him very little. They were for Elizabeth to deal with and he trusted her completely. He was sorry only that he could not help her; but the idea of bringing her to his attic in 't Groote Vis was obviously absurd. Common sense told him he would have to return to her. She would need her things about her, the dresses, the jewellery and the waiting women who tended them and her. Moreover, there was nowhere in this town full of eyes where they could be less under observation than in her ramshackle and disorderly household. Whatever life they had together they would have to have under the roof of the Wassenaer Hof.

He felt himself completely in God's hand. The situation was unlikely beyond computation: the daughter of the King of England had fallen in love with him; they would marry. He was the instrument of a great purpose; no other explanation was possible. Retrospectively, it explained everything. The poverty, which had forced him to take up the Ifá Oracle, his practice as a seer and all that went with it, which had brought him into Elizabeth's life and then into her very arms. If God had marked out the path, all he had to do was tread it, alert to the whisperings of divine guidance.

He slept very little and spent most of the night in prayer for himself and Elizabeth, trusting himself without reservation to the Almighty. He rose at first light and washed himself with care in front of the fire, standing nude and goose-pimpled in his washing tub with a pail at his side, scrubbing his flesh with a cold, wet linen towel. He shaved meticulously, beat and brushed his clothes until they were as clean and fresh as he could make them, and oiled his shoes. A poor outfit for a bridegroom, but she did not take him for anything but what he was. He could not even buy her the traditional pair of wedding gloves, but he would buy a little paper of cloves or cassia to sweeten his breath, then he would have to consider himself ready.

He arrived at the Wassenaer Hof after prayers, as she had directed, and Catharina took him up to the closet, where he found Elizabeth sitting with Mevrouw Van der Myle. She had also slept little, he observed: her eyes were puffy and she had lost much of her usual animation, she looked rather plain and distressed. His heart went out to her; he longed to kiss the tired eyes. With the Dutchwoman's interested gaze upon him, he felt unable to do any such thing, so he bowed formally, and remained standing.

'Pelagius, my dearest. You know Judoca.' He bowed again and she acknowledged him. Elizabeth's voice was clear and rather impersonal; it had lost the vibrant overtones of their intimacy. He divined suddenly that she resented the intrusion of this woman into her privacy, no less than he did himself. 'She has a solution to our chief difficulty,' Elizabeth continued. 'She has found a little room for you at the top of the house. It is small but adequate, I think and it has a key. You may use it when you wish. Tonight, after supper, go up to this closet. There are candles there; you can work, perhaps. When the house is quiet, Judoca will bring you to the chapel. She and Catharina will be witnesses and thus, I hope, we can keep the matter to ourselves.'

He bowed again by way of reply, embarrassed. 'My lady,' he enquired, 'what am I to do with the rest of the day?'

'I think we had better spend not it together,' said Elizabeth. 'I will bid you to supper.'

'It is well,' he said abruptly.

Mevrouw Van der Myle stood up and smiled at him. To his ruffled sensibilities, it was the smile of a bawd. 'I will show you your room,' she said. 'Come with me.'

Pelagius, once introduced to his room and given the key, made his escape as soon as he might. There was nothing for it but to return to 't Groote Vis. He took the opportunity, meeting Mariken in the hall, to tell her that he thought he might be going on a journey: if he was not in his room at curfew, she was to shut the house and assume that he would not return that night. She nodded, shut her mouth abruptly and went back to her quarters without speaking, to his surprise: he was unaware of the urgency of his voice and manner.

The discipline of long habit enabled him to spend the day reading. It seemed to him best simply to read the Bible: the books of Genesis and Exodus, then the long narrative of Samuel and Kings. He was sensitive and alert to God's choices: the refusal of Cain's sacrifice and, later, the preference given to Jacob over the first-born Esau, and the choice of Joseph, the youngest, over all his brethren. Above all, the raising of David as king in the place of Saul, the Lord's Anointed, and his house and lineage. David was set in the place of Saul and his son, Solomon, was the greatest king in the history of the world. The stories had been familiar to him for half a lifetime; now he looked at them with different eyes, trying to imagine what any of these situations would have looked like to a contemporary. Could any of the people of Bethlehem, who knew David as the son of a poor man keeping his father's sheep, have guessed that he would rise to be king over Israel? Still less could they have imagined that his kingship was a moment in the great unfolding of God's plan for the salvation of mankind. It was not right to expect God's dispositions to be transparent.

As the light began to fade, he shut his bible and went out into the street. He watched the people hurrying homewards, respectable women with their baskets, men with their pipes, drunkards, prostitutes, shopkeepers, day-labourers. What great convulsion of divine purpose would it take to raise them all to the vision of God? Watch, I say to you, he admonished them silently. Watch and pray; you know not the day nor the hour. He walked at his leisure to the Wassenaer Hof, filled with a strange, febrile excitement.

Supper was a considerable test of endurance. Elizabeth sat with Mevrouw Van der Myle, talking in low tones; he sat at a distance with the chaplain, unable to look at her or to eat more than a token mouthful. He made a pretence of disturbing the food on his plate and drank a little wine. Dr Jonson was not moved to conversation: he sat hunched over his plate in preoccupied silence, forking in food with mechanical regularity. Once Elizabeth had left the hall, Pelagius escaped to Judoca's closet, his stomach churning, and locked himself in. Someone had left him a flask of wine: he spared whoever it might have been a grateful thought. He sat on in the one chair, too nervous to think in any connected way, listening to the feet that trampled past the door of his room and the distant noises of the household as it wound gradually through the end of its day towards silence and repose.

After an interminable length of time, he heard a soft tapping on the door. Opening it, he found Judoca Van der Myle, with a taper in her hand and a black wrapper about her bulky body. Her eyes seemed bigger and darker than usual in her large pale face, and her expression was very serious. She was wearing list slippers: he followed her without a word as she padded noiselessly down the stairs, moving as quietly as he could. The fire was burning brightly in the hall: the halberdier who should have been on watch outside was comfortably asleep in a chair with his booted feet stretched to the blaze, his pipe still in his hand. A slumbering tangle of dogs lay on the warm hearth. There was a pewter pot on the floor beside him and there was no change in the rhythm of his breathing as they crept quietly past him. Not even the dogs bestirred themselves.

In the chapel two lights burned on the Lord's Table. He heard Judoca van der Myle locking the door behind them: Elizabeth was already there, a black shadow in the darkness, kneeling on a cushion with Catharina standing behind her. He could see Dr Jonson standing with his book, wearing a preacher's long black gown, with white linen bands at his neck. When Pelagius approached softly and knelt down at Elizabeth's side, he opened his book and began to read.

The wedding service was conducted in Latin: Elizabeth spoke her vows, quietly but firmly, in English; Pelagius answered her in Latin. The homily, though, was in English: obviously Jonson hoped that he would be able to follow in that language more easily than Elizabeth would understand Latin. He found it difficult to grasp and resolved to ask for a written version when opportunity permitted. Jonson spoke softly, but with passion, his voice carrying clearly in the silent night.

'My lady Elizabeth, and Master Pelagius, you have come together before me, even as Solomon came together with the Queen of Sheba, in a mystic union. Take heed and understand that the actions that you perform in the flesh as very man and woman are at the same time, signs and tokens of the Holy Spirit's work towards the unification of all nations before the Throne of the Most High, for the affairs of man are mirrored by the movements of nature, and the restoration of the inward and spiritual man will ever be mirrored by a physical renewal of the outward body. In the same way, the renewal of mankind, the head and centre of God's creation, will bring about for us, as Lord Verulam promised, a great instauration of the world. The processes of alchemy are a sign for us, of the regeneration of the world and how it may be achieved. We begin with matter in the alembic: sealed, and placed in a furnace, it undergoes *nigredo*, the breaking down of previous order into primal chaos. On a spiritual level, the dark night of the soul; on a physical level, death, or slavery. This is the First Work; from it is born the Black King. Master Pelagius, you will recognize yourself. Then within the dark matrix, the matter remakes itself, and *albedo*, or the White Rose, appears. There are no coincidences in this; only deep correspondences ordained by God as signs. It is no accident that the rose is the badge of the Tudors and that you, my lady Elizabeth, are the white rose of England. So the White Rose is the Second Work. The Third Work begins with a royal wedding. The Black King, whom some authorities refer to as Saturn or the Old Man, is united in the Fire of Love with his blessed queen, the White Rose. From their union, the ultimate perfection will be effected and the Philosopher's Stone will be born. The fulfilment of this promise lies in the will of God and the womb of time, but if you remain steadfast and pure in heart, this consummation may be granted to you. Let us pray together that we may see in our lifetime the footsteps of the Righteous King upon Mount Olivet.' He switched to Latin and repeated his last sentence softly, obviously fearing that Pelagius might have failed to understand him. 'Magister, oremus ut videntur in diebus nostris vestigias Justi Regis in Montem Oliveti.'

He knelt: Elizabeth and Pelagius slipped from their chairs to kneel side by side. Afterwards, when they had signed the loose page Jonson had prepared, and Judoca and Catharina had witnessed it, she curtsied to him, and slipped away, followed by her waiting woman. He felt Judoca's clammy hand on his wrist.

'Wait with me,' she whispered. 'When it is time, I will take you up.' Jonson bowed to him and left the chapel in the wake of his mistress. Pelagius sat on, counting his heartbeats, watching the last candle as it burned low. Only when it was guttering towards extinction did Judoca light her taper and lead him from the chapel.

He followed her up to a room he had never before entered, the Queen's bedroom. When they reached the door, she made him a deep curtsy. 'I will call for you again, in the dawn,' she whispered, and withdrew. He lifted the latch and entered without knocking. The monkey, at least, seemed to be elsewhere, though as so often, a heap of little dogs lay curled together on the hearth in front of the fire, which had collapsed into a glowing heap of charcoal. He could sense Elizabeth watching him from the great, crimson-hung bed, and dimly make out the white of her face and her night smock.

As expeditiously as possible, he took off his clothes with fingers made clumsy by tension. The sensuous cadences of the Song of Solomon were looping through his mind: 'until the day break, and the shadows flee away, I will get me to the mountain of myrrh and the hill of frankincense . . . I have put off my coat, how shall I put it on? I have washed my feet; how shall I defile them?' When he was stripped to his shirt, he moved hesitantly towards her. Silently she threw back the cover to admit him. His eyes had adjusted to the dim glow from the fire and he saw her at last. The flickering light was kind to her; her face was candid and sweet as a little girl's. Very gently he touched her frizzled hair, tacky beneath his fingers with pomade and powder, and then her neck. Her skin was soft and a little crumpled, like fallen rose-petals, so soft that only its warmth and the pulse beneath his fingertips allowed him to be certain that he was touching her at all. She put her mouth up for a kiss and in a little while, between them, they got her night smock off over her head, followed by his shirt. Beneath the sheets he began to explore her well-used body, the heavy breasts, liquid beneath his hands, the soft, silken-textured, ponderous flesh of belly and flanks. He could hear her breathing coming shorter and rejoiced. Though he was so stiff it was almost painful, he leaned on one elbow over her, deferring perversely, out of a lifetime of having being taught to wait, fluttering little butterfly kisses on her cheeks and eyelids until she embraced him frankly with her knees and pulled him on top of her. Sliding into her body was a moment of such relief and sweetness it brought a rush of blinding tears to his eyes. Elizabeth moaned softly, clutching at him, and the dogs stirred and whined on the hearth. They lay rocking together until he could hold back no longer and spent himself with such force the climax seemed momentarily to empty the blood from his body.

IX

Here lies a she sun, and a he moon here,
  She gives the best light to his sphere,
  Or each is both, and all, and so
They unto one another nothing owe,
  And yet they do, but are
So just and rich in that coin, which they pay,
That neither would, nor needs forbear nor stay.
John Donne, *Epithalamion on the Lady Elizabeth*, 1613

In the first week of his ambiguous new life Pelagius went to Leiden to defend his thesis. Since the marriage he had lived and moved in a trance of human happiness. The thesis was no longer at the centre of his concern, though he was far from indifferent to it as the public judgment of a lifetime's experience and thought. Perhaps because he was no longer anxious about it, his defence was a notable success. Sambucus was delighted.

'When do you think you might return to Batavia, Doctor?' he asked at the formal dinner after the defence.

Pelagius gaped at him, struck dumb. He had been so caught up in the flux of events that he had not quite realized what he now saw clearly, that he would have to give up the idea of becoming a preacher. 'I do not know,' he said finally.

'But it was always your intention, surely?' persisted Sambucus.

Pelagius sighed. 'It was. But I have acquired duties here, a practice. There is much in my life here which I had not expected to find.'

Sambucus peered at him, the small, kindly eyes shrewd. 'I never thought, Pelagius, that I would see you distracted by the things of this world. You of all men should be able to value an earthly court at its true estimation. "Aulae magnificum nomen, seu gloria vanae, est levis, est mendax, nil pietatis habet."'

'Honoured Professor, it is not as simple a matter as you imply,' he said, profoundly uncomfortable. 'I am the guardian of secrets which are not my own. I may not tell you what constrains me, but for the time being I must stay where I am.'

Sambucus unexpectedly put a hand on his sleeve. 'I think well of you, Pelagius. Your mind is an honest one and I flatter myself you have been well taught. For all I have said, I trust you to think without prejudice. But my dear son, watch and pray. Think always whether you are doing what God wants of you or following inclination.'

'I ask this every day, in my waking prayers.'

'Then I am satisfied. If your conscience does not sleep, then you are doing your best according to your lights. No man may do more.' Sambucus paused to pour more wine, and when he spoke again it was on a different tack. 'It has long seemed to me that your naming was no casual matter,' he observed. 'I was thinking it again, this afternoon.'

'I was named simply as "a man from the ocean", I think. I do not believe that Master Comrij had anything further in mind,' said Pelagius cautiously.

Sambucus waved a hand dismissively. 'To be sure. "pelagaus" in Greek is the great ocean and so Pelagius is a name for a man from beyond it. But there are secret currents in the ocean and in the minds of men; and both are set there by God. I need hardly tell you that Pelagius was the great opponent of St Augustine. I was thinking, as you were speaking this afternoon, that there are some curious sympathies of approach between the arch-heretic Pelagius and yourself. The heresiarch, I recollect, declared that man can take the first steps towards salvation by his own efforts. Is this not very much what you are arguing for your virtuous pagans? I fear that your work may be misused by enemies of the Gospel. It was, I think, Pelagius who was the first man in Christian history to ask whether men who are apart from the Gospel are necessarily bound by the power of sin, and with that thought in mind it seemed to me that there were tendencies in your work which might be dangerous indeed.'

'I have read Vossius's history of the Pelagian controversy,' admitted Pelagius, 'but I do not admit that Pelagius is a model for my writing. As Protestants, we repudiate utterly the doctrine of salvation by works and Pelagius's understanding of divine grace is gravely defective. In a work such as *Ad Demetriadem*, if he is read as a moralist, rather than a theologian, I think his work is to be respected. He has a good plain style. In no other respect do I see sympathy between my work and his. In a way, I suggest that our ideas are opposite. He is concerned with the ability of an individual to save himself by his own actions. I, on the other hand, am concerned with the outpouring of grace on those who have not had the benefit of instruction.'

'Excellently answered. But it also struck me, while you were speaking, that there is a certain irony which your own work brings out,' commented Sambucus drily. 'It is the African Augustine who has commanded the history of Christian philosophy, Protestant and Catholic alike, while Pelagius, a man of Britain, is all but forgotten.'

Pelagius raised his eyebrows. 'Augustine was a Roman born in Africa, not an African.'

'And you, my son? After all these years of study, are you an African or something else?'

'It is not easy for me to answer such a question. I think perhaps I am more Dutch now than I might like to imagine. But above all I am a citizen of the Heavenly City and in that city, there is neither Jew nor Gentile, nor black, nor white.'

Sambucus's question stayed with him as he trotted back to The Hague on Sparrenbord's strong back, eager to see Elizabeth. The thesis justified her taking a public interest in him; they would dine together and, unless something intervened, he would spend the night at the Wassenaer Hof. The idea of homecoming filled him with simple joy. There was a house and, in it, a woman who was his wife. He had hardly hoped to have anything so like a home in this world: it was a peculiar one and his relationship to it necessarily shadowy and eccentric, but with Elizabeth to return to it was home indeed.

His emotions were not those of Africa, it struck him. The relationship was an impossible one in African terms; the intellectual companionship between them was something he would hardly have thought to seek from a woman of his own people. Although he had had a household of women in his days as *aremo*, their lives had been very separate from his and his only close relationship had been with his mother. Now it occurred to him that, although he still thought of himself as African, and his dark skin inevitably caused others to see him as African even before they saw him as human, as a man who was deep in love he was newly conscious of the Europeanization of his heart. It was a man whose notions of love were formed by the Song of Solomon, by Catullus and Joannes Secundus, who was making his best speed towards Elizabeth's arms.

'I have had an idea,' said Elizabeth, when at last they were in bed together. They did most of their talking there, closely embraced and quietly murmuring in the silence of the night. 'My secretary Mr Dingley is still in England. Perhaps you could become my secretary for Dutch and Latin? There is a room by Dr Jonson's quarters you could have. It is well furnished because I kept it for my younger sons to use and there is no one in it at present. When Dingley is here he will write English and French for me, as before, but it will give you occasion to live here with me. You can come to my room every day after prayers and no one will think anything of it.' They were in bed, talking in whispers. Pelagius settled his wife's head more comfortably into the hollow of his neck and thought about it. It seemed sensible enough, though he felt a little pang of regret at the notion of giving up Mariken's attic. It was cold, it was uncomfortable, he had often been acutely unhappy there, but it was private and he had come to enjoy his privacy. He knew very well what it was like living in a palace.

'It is well. Is there room for my books? I have perhaps a hundred. Not a great number.'

'Of course there is room! The Prince Palatine and Rupert are both readers, there will certainly be a book press, and if there is not we can move one in. Do you not have anything else?'

'A change of clothes. Your crystal bauble. The hunting habit you lent me. Some linen. I have not needed much.'

'Oh, Pelagius. What a life you have led.'

'I want for nothing,' he insisted. 'You must not trick me out like a child. It will provoke talk and it is not necessary.'

'I suppose you are right, my dearest heart. But my greatest pleasure is in obliging my friends.'

He laughed a little, under his breath, and hugged her closer. 'What more can you give me, Elizabeth? You have given me your own dear self.' She turned in his grasp to kiss him and they talked no more that night.

They sorted out the details the next morning. It was a fine day; he did not even bother to wear his cloak as he set out to walk across The Hague. Nights with Elizabeth were not nights for sleep and he was a little light-headed with pleasant fatigue. He had reconciled himself to the prospect of dismantling his establishment: how nearly, he remembered suddenly, he had removed himself to Leiden when he had received the money for Comrij's plant collections. The direction of his life seemed to depend on tiny promptings, such as the second thought which had kept him in The Hague – a reminder how carefully each choice, so seemingly free, must be weighed and pondered. For now, it was clear he must commit himself to Elizabeth, let the future hold what it might.

He walked back to 't Groote Vis, where he had not slept for two nights – the first had been spent in Leiden, the second at the Wassenaer Hof. A familiar journey, which his feet seemed virtually to walk by themselves: it struck him that he was perhaps making it for the last time. He stopped in the marketplace and arranged for a carrier to call around midday. When he got to the house he knocked on the door to Mariken's quarters.

'May I come in, mevrouw?' he asked, when she opened it.

'Oh, it's the doctor! Come in and welcome.'

The kitchen was filled with bustling feminine industry. The married daughter was on her knees by the fire, changing the baby on a rush mat. The door through to the yard was open, for the light, and the woman Geertruyd sat in the entrance with a lacemaker's pillow on her knee, working on a coarse length of edging lace, her shadow falling across the clean, scrubbed flagstones. Beyond her he could see two women in the yard itself sitting with a basket of straw between them, making handbrooms with swift, efficient twists of their workworn, practised hands.

They all looked up as he entered and offered him a diffident chorus of greeting. He bowed to them all impartially. Mariken herself was dressed to go out, with a woollen cap on and a warm shawl pinned firmly across her thin chest. A businesslike basket waited for her on a chair by the door. 'I will not keep you, mevrouw,' he said politely. 'I have only come to tell you that I am leaving the house. I have gained my doctorate, mevrouw, and I have been made Latin secretary to the queen.'

She gaped at him. When she had regained the power of speech, she whispered hoarsely, 'You're going?' A susurrus of alarm and consternation arose on all sides; the broom-makers in the yard scrambled to their feet and crowded into the doorway behind Geertruyd. 'But, Doctor. What if people need you? We can't go to that place!'

'Mevrouw Mariken, you will all manage well enough, as you did before you met me,' he replied firmly, though he felt a touch of compunction at their naked distress.

'You saved Geertruyd's life!' wailed Mariken. 'What if something happens to the baby?'

Exasperation began to turn to anger. 'Nothing will happen to the baby. I have told you often enough I am no magician. Trust to God. Go and see your pastor, if you are in doubt. Walk uprightly. I wish you all well.'

'Please don't leave us,' said Geertruyd hoarsely. The baby began to wail, sensing the atmosphere in the room.

'I must,' he said coldly. 'Mevrouw, I have paid you for this month. I will take my books, but everything else that is up there, the sheets, the furniture, is yours to keep. Go with God.' He was furious: there had been a time when Mariken could order him about, but that time was past. As he fully expected, she retreated from her defiance of his will and burst into noisy sobs. All the women were in tears; the baby, neglected and indignant, was screaming with the regularity of an engine. He gathered what dignity he could and fled upstairs.

It did not take him long to pack. His notes were always orderly and the books were neatly on their shelves. It was a quick enough business to rope them into bundles. There was nothing personal in the room apart from papers, nothing for which he felt sentiment except the Queen's bauble and his bag of hazelnuts, both of which he stored carefully in his pockets, wrapped in handkerchiefs. In the days of his extreme poverty everything that belonged to Comrij, and hence to his earlier life, had been sold. He bundled up the best of his clothes and the hunting gear. Then there was nothing to do but lean on the windowsill, looking out over the rooftops of The Hague towards the Groote Kerk, and wait for the carrier.

His return to the Wassenaer Hof was less dramatic. He knew where his new quarters were; Catharina van Eck came out to help him, observing his arrival, and with her to superintend his movements, no one thought for a moment to challenge his right to be there.

'If you want drink, go to the cellar doors, mynheer,' she told him, as he turned to thank her after paying off the carter. 'If you want food outside dinner hours, go to the kitchens.'

'Thank you, Mevrouw Catharina.' He smiled at her; she did not smile back. He looked at her in some perplexity. Such a quiet, plain girl, withdrawn and secretive in her ways. She was one of the secret keepers and, as such, she held the power of life and death over him; he had not the slightest idea what she thought of the situation. Elizabeth had explained that she was bound by family to Judoca Van der Myle. He would have known how to interpret this had they been in Oyo, but how much pressure did such loyalty bear here in The Hague? He could not know for certain and the thought was disquieting. He would have liked to engage her in conversation, but already she had curtsied with downcast eyes and turned to go. The door shut behind her and he was left to take possession of his new home.

The room was a comfortable one. There were pictures on the walls – a large landscape, of some part of the world unknown to him, and portraits, from the looks of them, more of Elizabeth's innumerable family – and the walls were panelled. There was a highly carved oak four-poster bed, furnished with thick, dark-blue woollen curtains trimmed with rather tarnished gold braid. He had a writing table, with a small lectern upon it, covered with a precious Persian carpet. There were four carved wooden chairs, two armchairs upholstered in blue velvet, a heavy oak chest, a linen press and a bookcase. He put his books in the bookcase and his two shirts in the linen press, which was well supplied with sheets, towels and shirts of far better quality and condition than the ones he had just put in it. The curtains, also dark blue, were thick and heavy and in winter would keep out the draughts. On that early summer day, with blue skies showing beyond the casement, the darkness of the walls and the furnishings made the room a little gloomy, but it offered him luxury beyond anything he had ever known. He sat cautiously in one of the armchairs, allowing the padding to embrace him, rubbing his hand absentmindedly over the silky velvet of the armrest. Soon, he knew, he would be sufficiently at home to ignore these trappings and get on with his own work. He was tired, though. Now that he was seated in a comfortable chair, with no very pressing task before him, he felt fatigue draining through his body like a heavy liquid, immobilizing him. He had had very little rest for several nights, first on account of his examination, since then, on account of Elizabeth. Despite himself, his eyelids drooped, and he dropped into sleep where he sat.

As the weeks went by, their lives began to establish a rhythm. He began to try and make sense of Elizabeth's chaotic household. There were at least forty people living in and around the Wassenaer Hof, not including the Van der Myle household; fifteen officers, from the chamberlain down to the pages (who counted as officers, since they were the children of good families), and about twenty-five servants. He also began to learn English and French and, with the help of Dutch and Latin respectively, found that it was not difficult for him to achieve reasonable fluency as a reader, though speaking came more slowly. He discovered, to his surprise, that he had acquired a servant, a civil young man called Gilles, whose job was to look after him and Samson Jonson. Gilles, as he rapidly discovered, was a French speaker, Huguenot by origin, so, mindful of Elizabeth's remark that 'French is the language of courts', he bespoke an hour of Gilles's time each day after dinner to practise speaking and hearing French, and got on reasonably well. Almost by accident, in the course of these stumbling conversations, he told Gilles about his knowledge of plants and found that, thereafter, he was universally assumed to be a physician.

His feelings about this were mixed. It was with profound regret that he relinquished the work he had long thought he was put in the world to do. But such a position was out of the question, not merely because in that particular household Jonson already occupied it, but because the attitudes unconsciously betrayed by everyone he spoke with, even Sambucus, made it clear to him that an African predikant would not be acceptable in Holland. Exoticism gave him a certain advantage as an oracle, perhaps even as a doctor, but it disqualified him as a spiritual leader. His interest in medicine for its own sake was not great and recalling his long study of plants reminded him of a phase of his life he would rather have forgotten, but as he considered the idea further he was not entirely sorry to have acquired a reputation as a doctor. It gave an additional reason for his presence in the household and he was moderately certain that his actual knowledge was on a par with that of most physicians. People began to knock on his door, seeking assistance with the treatment of everyday ailments, and his suggestions were on the whole successful rather than not. Bowing to the inevitable, he bought new copies of Mattioli's *Materia Medica*, the *Regimen Sanitatis*, and Clusius's *Rarorum Plantorum Historia*, which had all been in Comrij's library, and dealt conscientiously with the problems which came his way.

He was able to call on the Queen each morning to work on her diplomatic correspondence and began to learn more of the politics which were her constant concern. Apart from these meetings they lived separately, with circumspection, seizing, when Elizabeth judged that they safely could, a precious night. Pelagius set the question of his ordination to one side for the time being and spent most of his time reading, first in Latin and Dutch, then, as his grasp of French and English strengthened, in those languages also. He read political histories, books on the law and anything he could find which would tell him more about the situation they faced. In mid-June Dingley returned from England, bearing news of her brother's treaty with the Scots. Elizabeth was at pains to establish that he was not supplanted, and after initial mutual suspicion he and Pelagius established a distant, but adequately cordial, relationship.

It would in any case have been hard to maintain a coldness in the face of Elizabeth's high spirits. The Scots had come to terms, the threat of an unnatural war was ended. The news was also immediately relevant to her own most pressing concerns, as she explained to Pelagius. The truce with the Scots meant a real and renewed hope that her brother might help Charles Louis. 'There is yet more,' she said excitedly. 'The Scots are as good Protestants as they are bad subjects, and many of them fought for Gustavus Adolphus in the late wars. They are a nation well trained to war and they are now in arms, with no enemy in view. My good Dingley tells me that Leslie, the Scots general in chief, has offered to go with his troops to the aid of the Prince Palatine. If my royal brother will but give his consent, then Charles Louis may be marching into his kingdom within the year, with an stout army of valiant Scots at his back. I have never thought it possible that he may fully be restored other than by arms.'

'Do you think that he will, my Elizabeth?' asked Pelagius.

'It is on the knees of God,' she replied, less cheerfully. 'As I have told you, he is my good brother and I love him well, but he is a man of most obstinate spirit, and too much inclined towards the counsels of his wife. She is a daughter of France and a strong Catholic, and she leads him always towards friendship with Spain and France. And so, like Solomon, he is led to bow before false gods and I fear very much that the sacrifice he may come to offer is my poor son and the Protestant cause. In the spring I was greatly grieved to hear that he was set on an alliance with Spain and was seeking to raise arms and even troops in the Spanish Netherlands. The Stadhouder took it very badly, and though he is my own brother, it is beyond my understanding how an English king could stoop to sending foreign papist troops against his own Protestant subjects. I am sure it was all the advice of the Queen which made him so far forget himself. But this Scottish peace is the sign of a better mind in him. He made it of himself, for all that the papists and the clergy could do to prevent it. Let us pray that it is the sign of happier times.'

The summer wore on and turned very hot. All the windows of the Wassenaer Hof stood open in the hopes of catching a draught of cooler air and Elizabeth teased that he had brought African weather with him. One warm, breathless midnight, once they had satisfied their most immediate desires Elizabeth turned in his arms. He could feel her breath on his face, and knew that if there had been any light in the room at all she would have been looking into his eyes. He was drowsy and at peace, but he could sense that she was still alert and slowly began to recover himself from the drift into sleep.

'Pelagius, if you had loved me in Oyo, what would have happened?'

Fuzzy with drowsiness, he struggled to bring the question into focus. On one level, it was absurd. Women of her age did not marry and to marry the ex-wife of a king would unquestionably have led to death or, at best, castration; none of which he wished to discuss with her in the dark of the night. He sighed. 'I or my father would have spoken to your father. We would have paid the bride price. You would have come to live in my house.'

'Do you not have a ceremony, even for kings?' she asked.

'No. But the bride is dressed in rich clothes and her friends walk with her to her new home, dancing and singing. Why do you ask?'

'I was thinking of how our marriage might have been, if things had been different. Were you married, Pelagius? I have never thought to ask you.'

'Yes. I had ten wives. It was the custom.'

'So many! Like a king of the Old Testament. But did you love them?'

'Not as I love you. I did not think to, though, of course I enjoyed their beauty. In my country women honour their husbands, and love their children. They spend most of their time together, while men live amongst men. I hardly knew them. You are the first woman since my mother whom I have truly loved.'

'What would have happened to them?'

He shrugged, aware of her head on his shoulder. 'They must have been given to Egonoju.'

'Poor girls.'

'I do not think they felt anything for me and they would have wanted nothing better. At least they would still be women of the *afin*.'

Elizabeth was silent for a while, then stirred and slipped her arm across his chest. 'I have been thinking how we would have married, if you had been a prince of Europe. I have told you about masques, have I not?'

'Yes. The first time I dined with you. I have forgotten nothing you said that day.'

'If we had been married as a prince and a princess should be,' she said wistfully, 'we would have had a masque. Lying awake by myself, in the nights when you were not here, I devised a masque for us. Do not laugh at me.'

'I would never laugh at you, my darling. Tell me about the masque.'

'This is what I would have liked. We would have nine and nine masquers from among the quality, with singers for Flora and Night and other gods, and musicians dressed as sylvans. There would be a full consort, hoboys and lutes with sackbuts and viols, and singers.

I think we would discover Flora in a delightful valley, with flowers all about her, dressed in shot green and golden taffeta, caught about with a veil of gold tissue embroidered with flowers. She would sing a song, then would come in Zephyrus her husband, dressed in silk robes of sky colour, and sing a duetto with her in praise of marriage. Flora would take her leave and then the scene would change, the green valley and all the flowers would vanish away, and Night would appear, crowned with the moon, with nine maiden Hours in her train, dressed in black silk and spangled all with golden stars, and behind her, in the centre of the stage, nine golden trees. She would complain for the loss of the virgin bride, snatched away from her service, and then she would explain that the nine trees were once bold knights who came to woo her maidens and were thus transformed. Then Zephyrus would speak for them and Hesperus, the evening star, friend to all lovers, would come down and add his voice. In the end they would melt Night's heart and she would call the trees to dance. The music would play and, as it played, she would sing and trees begin to move at her command. Three by three, the trees would come forward to be cleft and from them we would see the men masquers step out, clad in green taffeta, cut into leaves and laid on cloth of silver. As they come forth, they go down to the dance, with the black maidens of the Night. Once that dance is over each knight in turn comes by the House of Night and, each to each, his Hour gives him his helmet and plucks off his robe of leaves, disclosing him in carnation satin. So then they pass down to the grove of Flora, singing as they go, and from her grove Flora returns to company with Zephyrus her love, and Hesperus gives his hand to the fair nymph of Night. All the Gods pass down the middle of the dance and say farewell, leaving the masquers to their dance. It would be a brave device and most beautiful.'

He heard her out in some astonishment. 'I cannot think how it would be.'

'Oh, Pelagius. We must act a play for you. I have acted with the children on occasion and we are tolerable fair performers. You must try to see it in your mind's eye. Imagine. You are in a great hall, lit with many candles, in a chair of estate, with me at your left hand, and before you is a stage with screens on either side, raised, with a hill upon it, and a descent, curtained off from your gaze. The musicians are in their places when you enter and they begin to play when you first come into the room. When all is still, the curtain is withdrawn and Flora is seen, a maid in her first youth, with golden hair tumbling about her, crowned with flowers and glimmering in the light of the candles. When she moves, the shot taffeta catches the light and glitters, and the flowers embroidered on her veil look as if they are real flowers dancing in the air. Half the figures on the stage seem to glow with their own light; the gold and the silk and the spangles, and of course the pearls and diamonds which they wear, gather the candle flames into themselves. The other half are dressed in black, so as they pass and repass among the other dancers they seem like shadows, touched with little stars. And at the end, when they had danced upon the stage, the dancers would descend to your level. An Hour of Night, who would be a masked and lovely noblewoman, would curtsy before you and draw you in, while a masked Knight of the Sun took my hand and led me up the dance. Soon all would be dancing, with you and I at their head, while the musicians played their songs of love and night. When the revels were ended, you would not know if you were in the United Provinces or the Land of Faery.'

'And was this a common thing?'

'Only at the marriages of the great, naturally. Such things are devised for the marriages of princes. I wish I was a poet, Pelagius. I would make the songs for the masque and sing them to you, but I am none.'

He kissed her by way of answer and held her until her even breathing told him that she was sleeping. When he was sure that she would not be disturbed by his movement, he slipped cautiously out of the huge bed and dressed himself in the dark. He must always return to his own room, they had decided together; never could he simply allow himself to drift into easy sleep, to be wakened only by the sun. She had given him a black velvet dressing gown to wear on these nocturnal journeys: enveloped in its heavy folds and wearing list slippers, he knew himself to be silent and all but invisible. There was often movement in the house at night. Laundresses and chambermaids crept about with candles, sometimes at surprising hours. The chaplain was also given to night wandering: he maintained a small laboratory in the stable block, where he performed alchemical experiments and from time to time spent part of the night observing the stars. Thus, although in a more orderly household even his soft footfalls might have provoked investigation, he received no attention at all as he went quietly back to his own bed, moving with ease in the darkness.

For Elizabeth, the summer seemed a charmed one. Her personal happiness and the significant upturn in her son's fortunes left her profoundly thankful, her prayers centred only on the hope that this better luck would continue. Her love for Pelagius was a constantly unfolding presence in her mind. She had enjoyed his tact and his sensitivity since they had first met: now, as she watched him bend his powerful, well-trained intellect to the history of the times, it became clear to her that as he became more inward with her affairs and those of the Palatinate, he was becoming an adviser whose words she could trust absolutely. The more private side of their life together was also a source of renewed, secret joy. For all the gravity of his ordinary demeanour, there was an endearing playfulness in his lovemaking which opened her up like a flower. There were moments when, as she sat in the dining room or the throne room, she became suddenly aware of him as he ate, spoke, or listened with still attention. A wave of tender sensuality would pour over her as her gaze rested on his unusually small and elegant ears, his long, sinewy hands, or the play of muscles in his neck. It was fortunate, she reflected wryly, that the news out of England was such as to justify bouts of apparently causeless good humour.

There was also news from the devastated lands of the erstwhile Palatinate of a kind which filled her with secret hope. The great fortress of Breisach and the swords of the mercenary army which held it were for sale to the highest bidder. She had been not a little pleased and relieved when Breisach was taken: its capture blocked the 'Spanish Road' which allowed Philip IV to pour men and money into the Spanish Netherlands, and she knew only too well what this meant to her genial Dutch hosts. It had fallen to Bernard of Saxe-Weimar, who was in the pay of the French and she had resigned herself to seeing a French garrison installed there, since they were at least better than the Spaniards. But Count Bernard had died without handing over the fort and had simply left it to his second in command, who had let it be known that as a Switzer he had no reason to prefer one master above another.

Shortly after hearing this news from Fredrik Hendrik, who had informed her immediately, she had received an almost illegible cyphered letter from Charles Louis, the badness of the hand bespeaking a consuming impatience battling with the slowness imposed by the cypher; she, Dingley and Pelagius had puzzled it out between them. Her son, whom she sometimes thought over-cautious, was for once incandescent with enthusiasm. If only his uncle would support him, he wrote, he intended to offer himself as commander. Though the commander was Swiss, the army was largely composed of Rhinelanders, his own true subjects, who had seen their country devastated by Spanish armies. He hoped to appeal to their heart and honour, and regain the Palatinate with their help. If King Charles permitted General Leslie to give him further aid, so much the better. He was post-haste for the coast, intending to take the next boat to England.

The letter was always in her mind, as she went through the business of her life from day to day. She was profoundly concerned for her son, of course, but paradoxically easier in her mind about him than she had been for years. Had he troubled to take her advice, she would have advised him to do exactly as he had done. She had spent a lifetime in the heart of European politics, and one of the few things she remained completely sure of was that to win it was sometimes necessary to stake all on a single throw of the dice. She had begun to worry a little that unlike his reckless brothers, the Prince Palatine, who needed it above any of them, did not have the temperament of a man whom soldiers would follow. Caution and calculation might be necessary for a commander, but to win over Count Bernard's *landesknechts* he would have to touch their hearts. She was glad to see him so gallant and positive.

As always, when one worry receded others came into prominence. Her mind rushed optimistically over the many problems that lay in Charles Louis's way, beginning with his uncle, and began to play with the idea of her daughters' prospects. If all went well, and Charles Louis regained the Palatinate within a year or so, then his oldest sister would be perhaps twenty-two or three and Louise about twenty; a little elderly for royal brides, but not shamefully so. It was a great pity that Charles's oldest son was only nine; he was the same age as Sophia, but her brother would never consent to a younger daughter for the heir of England. There were few enough Protestant princes and Catholics were not to be thought of. The Prince of Orange was twelve, with a brood of sisters, and there were no sons of Sweden, only the child-Queen Christina. Momentarily, her thoughts switched back to her son. Christina would have been a good match for him, if he had not been promised his cousin, the Princess Royal. Her own girls would have to see who was to be had. In better times she would not have looked so low as mere counts and electors for them, but perhaps their best chance was to look among the members of the Protestant League and their sons. And

Charles Louis would need firm allies among the Protestant princes of Germany.

With a sudden access of cheerfulness, she decided to take Elizabeth and Louise down to Amsterdam. News would come there as fast as to The Hague and they could look in the great warehouses of the Dutch merchants. It was time they had new clothes; since, God willing, it was perhaps to be hoped that before too much longer there would be occasion to show off their good looks. Their court clothes were all erstwhile dresses of her own from the days of her marriage, cut down and remodelled. They were beautiful stuffs, but not in the latest mode, and the colours had not been chosen to suit them. It was as well to be prepared.

It took several days to arrange the trip. She sent a note to the Princess of Orange, and Amalia promptly offered the use of a house on the Herengracht belonging to her own family, the van Solms, as well as a great deal of well-informed advice. There were other arrangements to be made as well, but at last Lady Vere brought Elizabeth and Louise down to the Wassenaer Hof in the early hours of the morning, and they embarked together in her big travelling coach, drawn by six horses, accompanied by Catharina van Eck as gentlewoman, and two maids. The day had dawned clear and cloudless, promising blazing heat, and the vehicle was closed and dark: even with its windows open, it was stuffy already and would certainly get hotter. The maids were accommodated on the boot, which exposed them to the dust of the road, but at least gave them the benefit of whatever breeze was stirred up by their horses' stately trot. Elizabeth was inclined to envy them. All the ladies carried fans, and for a time the only sound in the carriage was the steady flutter as each of them attempted to stir up the languid air. The heavy vehicle rumbled down the open road and the merciless sun beat down on its dark roof. By her side the taciturn Catharina sat in silence, fanning herself and gazing out of the window. Opposite her her daughters, who had preserved a wary silence since their initial respectful greetings, began to droop. Louise, who was pale, got paler and the Princess Palatine began visibly to sweat, while her nose reddened and her skin went blotchy with the heat.

'You must sit more upright,' said Elizabeth severely, straight-backed, conscious of her linen damply adhering to her back and buttocks. 'Why have you got that nose?'

'You would like her less without one,' said Louise softly, through her teeth, as both daughters hastily straightened their shoulders.

Elizabeth affected to ignore her. Louise was in some ways her favourite daughter and was allowed a certain amount of licence. 'It is very unbecoming. God knows, I do not want my daughters tricked out like French harlots, but surely there is something to be done about your skin. Perhaps it is a question of diet. Do you eat onions?'

'No, mother,' said the Princess Palatine, almost inaudibly.

'You must be eating some heating food,' Elizabeth persisted. 'Eat only white meats for the next month and see if you get any relief. I do not like to see you sweat so. It must come of superfluity. Salts of alum are good to close the pores. I have some Montpellier powder from Florence, which Amalia thinks still better. She is of a heavy habit, and suffers in this weather, but you are if anything, over-thin – I do not see why you should need to sweat. All the same, I will send you some.'

'Thank you, mother.'

Elizabeth glared at them both with lively and impartial disapproval. The Princess Palatine's obstinate spiritlessness invariably irritated her and Louise, who was better company, had, as was her deplorable habit, dressed with such carelessness that as she wilted unhappily in her corner of the ovenlike carriage she seemed in danger of coming apart at the seams. Elizabeth was already beginning to regret the impulse which had led her to pawn a diamond bracelet on their behalf. Both of the girls were gazing diligently down into their laps, avoiding her eye. Perhaps it would be as well to change the subject. It was too hot to find fault and she was sick of it. 'Louise, how goes your painting?'

'Well enough, mother,' her younger daughter replied diffidently, though she looked up and her expression became more animated. 'I go to Meester Honthorst every day and he says he is pleased with how I do.'

'What are you working on?'

'I am making a portrait of Rupert, mother.'

'How?' said Elizabeth, astonished.

Louise flushed. 'I have been experimenting with portraits from memory. And Meester Honthorst has studies, as he has of us all, which help me. But I have taken the head from Meester Gerard's big picture of us all – the one where we are approaching the portals of Paradise and you are in a chariot drawn by lions looking at Father. I am working it up as a portrait study with Meester Honthorst's help. I have put him in military dress, with a red sash. I think it is quite like.'

'My dearest Louise,' said Elizabeth, rather gratified, 'you have always been clever with a likeness. I only hope that soon you will be able to compare it with the original. But it is feeling in you to do this work.'

Louise's blush deepend, an unbecoming tide of scarlet, rising up her neck. 'It helps me to think of him.'

'He is your favourite brother, is he not?' asked Elizabeth gently.

'Yes. He showed me how to draw when he saw I had a taste for it and gave me paper. I hope he will like his picture.'

Her mother sighed. 'He has a pretty skill himself. I hope it is helping him to fill his days, poor boy. He must be eating his heart out in idleness. Thom Roe is gone to the Emperor again to try and get him home. Perhaps this time he will succeed.'

'Mother,' said her oldest daughter suddenly, 'have you any news?'

'Not of the most recent, Elizabeth. I am waiting for word from England of how your brother's great enterprise is faring. We may get it from Amsterdam as soon as anywhere. News comes swiftly to the Bourse.'

It was not very far in leagues from The Hague to Amsterdam, but with the heat of the day, and the constraint of her daughters' conversation, it felt like far enough. When she disembarked at the van Solms' house on the Herengracht in mid-afternoon, it was with profound relief. Once they had rested a little and refreshed themselves with orange-flower water and a change of linen, it was possible to consider a glass of watered wine and a small but elegant late lunch of eggs and poached chicken. There was a dish of leeks also: Elizabeth, whose complexion was proof against all such dangers, would have liked some, but felt that to set an example to her daughters she should pass them over. She took a sip of wine instead and found it oddly metallic. Strange that the wine would not be good: she had never known a van Solms indifferent to the pleasures of the table. She observed that both the girls were drinking it without complaint, though that told her nothing since she had never encouraged complaints from her children.

'Elizabeth, how does the wine seem to you?' she asked.

The Princess Palatine looked a little startled, as she often did when directly addressed.

'It is very good, mother.'

'Louise?'

'I think it is delicious.'

'How strange. It seems to me a little spoiled. Of course, this is tainting weather. Nothing in my own cellars pleases me and perhaps last week's thunder has got into this wine also.'

'May I pour you some water, mother?' asked Elizabeth.

'Thank you, my daughter.'

When the meal was over, rested and refreshed, they donned gloves and thin dark veils to protect their complexions from the sun, and with their maids in attendance strolled at their leisure down to the Warmoesstraat, the centre of Amsterdam's trade in fabrics and furnishings. The warehouses, when they reached them, were glittering caves; large, square buildings, with big glass windows in their mansard roofs, pleasantly dim and cool after the glare of the streets. They were bound for the warehouse of Mynheer van den Heuvel, which, Amalia had advised her, had the best stock of dress fabrics outside Paris. Within minutes of their arrival, Mynheer van den Heuvel himself had appeared, with suspicious alacrity and profuse offers of hospitality, and bowed low in greeting before his honoured guests, who were looking about them with interest.

On the wide shelves reposed bolt after bolt of the most beautiful fabrics in the world. There were taffetas and tuff-taffetas, grosgrains, shot-silks, damasks, satins, velvets, still more precious Genoese cut and figured velvets, fine tissues embroidered with golden spangles and oes, cloth of silver, cloth of gold, and brocades from Prato, Lyons and even China; a rainbow of desirable stuffs, worth a king's ransom. Though Elizabeth was vowed to her black, she was not past feeling their sweet seduction. Tawnies, russets and carnations had always suited her. It was hard to finger the silky perfection of a bolt of orange-tawny damask, appraising its quality, and not to imagine how she would look in it. She shook her head, dismissing these pleasant fantasies. What need had she to care for such things when she knew herself most passionately loved? The thought of Pelagius sent her mind wandering in another direction. There was a dark-red grosgrain on another shelf; a deep, full colour, rich as good Burgundy. She could see Pelagius in a suit of such a colour. It would bring out the warm tint of his skin. Or perhaps he would look still better in creamy white, for drama, like the black King in the picture. No, she must not. She could see his expression too well, if she were to do any such thing. She dismissed the thought and looked after the girls, who were wandering dreamily up and down, gazing about them as if they had been transported to Paradise.

'My darlings,' she announced firmly, 'you are to have two dresses apiece. I am tired of seeing you in black and drab.'

'Two!' whispered Louise. Elizabeth's heart melted at the sight of her ecstatic face, though as seemed fatally inevitable with her daughters, her delight in their pleasure was immediately tempered with annoyance. The daughters of the Elector and nieces of the King of England should not be so pleased with so little. At their age she had bought two dresses a month. She fought down her reaction. It was not fair, and worse than unfair, to twit them with what she could not give them.

She looked around and van den Heuvel snapped his fingers. One of his attendants rushed to bring her a velvet armchair. Sinking into it, she dismissed her thoughts and prepared to enjoy herself. 'I think you should each have a formal and an informal court dress,' she declared. 'Elizabeth, you must have cool colours. Any shade of yellow is poison to you, it brings out the sallow lights in your complexion, and as long as your skin is subject to this blotching, you must avoid all manner of reds and pinks. Wear sea-green, and you will look like a lovely mermaid, or perhaps you might wear watchet or ash-colour. Louise, you are always pale, so with your dark hair and eyes, you can wear a true crimson or a carnation. If you choose such a colour, you will set off your sister well.'

Their choice took the rest of the afternoon. After prolonged and happy argument and innumerable changes of mind the Princess Elizabeth settled on an exquisite murrey-purple damask embroidered with arabesques of black and tiny silver stars, to have undersleeves of oyster-coloured satin. Her undress was steel-blue silk. Louise Hollandine chose a Genoa velvet in coral pink and grey, while her second dress was to be a carnation satin. Then there were pearlings, strings and laces to be thought of. By the time they were walking home in the cool of the evening, tired but triumphant, Elizabeth had spent not merely all the money her bracelet had brought her, but half as much again. She did not grudge it. When the dresses were made up, the girls would look as well as they possibly could. It would be foolish to repine at any expense which gave the poor creatures a little sense of their own consequence.

She listened tolerantly during supper while her daughters discussed with enthusiasm the fine points of fashion and cut, offering an occasional suggestion. She was still not feeling quite well; she wondered if the heat of the day had perhaps upset her. After supper she brought the evening to a close and went to bed early. As Catharina unlaced her, it occurred to her that she had never spent so long with her daughters without a quarrel. She appreciated the amendment in them. Soon, she thought hopefully, she would feel that she could take them anywhere, and watch them with pride.

In the morning she felt still worse. Her stomach was upset and at breakfast she could do no more than eat a little manchet bread and drink plain water. They were still sitting over their breakfast, when Catharina announced a visitor. She was surprised to see the handsome, shrewd and consequential figure of Baron van Heenvliet, the Dutch Ambassador to London.

'They told me at the port you were here, your majesty,' he explained. 'I have just landed from England and I thought you would want the news.'

'Bless you for the thought, Baron. How is the Prince Palatine, and what is happening? Please sit down and breakfast with me. Elizabeth, pour Baron van Heenvliet a glass of Rhenish.'

The Baron pulled out a chair and plumped wearily into it, accepting the glass which she gave him. 'I fear the news is none of the best, your majesty. Your royal brother is possessed once more with the notion that a Spanish alliance will do him service.'

'Oh, God help us now,' said Elizabeth softly. Simultaneously, her daughters laid down their knives as quietly as they could and sat rigid in terrified silence, their big dark eyes flicking from face to face.

'I am sorry to tell you this, for I think it is against both his dignity and his honour,' said the Baron heavily. 'As you well know, the Spaniards can bring no more men by the "Spanish Road". But we stopped three English vessels at sea a fortnight ago and found that there were fifteen hundred Spanish soldiers aboard them, bound for Flanders. We remonstrated, as you may imagine. In the last few days we have heard from the Channel scouts and my own sources in England that the arrangement continues. Spanish soldiers are entering the country at Bristol and Liverpool and marching across England by way of London to Dover, where English shipping is supplied to them, on royal authority, to take them to the Cardenal Infante in Flanders. I have protested as strongly as I may, and he is deaf to all that I can say.'

'Where is the Prince Palatine?' asked Elizabeth. Her lips were trembling, she struggled to control them.

Van Heenvliet sighed and shrugged, his clever, fat face compassionate. 'He is still in London. But if your royal brother has put his faith in the Cardenal Infante, what hope is there that he will assist the Prince Palatine to cross the interests of Spain?'

As Elizabeth sat, impassively as she hoped, absorbing the diplomat's words, a great darkness seemed to come over her eyes. Her blood was roaring in her ears; before anyone could move she fell heavily from her chair in a dead faint.

When she came to herself, some time later, she was in bed, feeling deathly sick. She sat up tentatively, feeling the room swimming about her. Catharina sat quietly in one of the armchairs with a piece of sewing in her hand, watching her.

'Has he gone?' she asked hoarsely.

'Yes. The Princesses have gone out to walk with Maria and a footman. I told them I would be with you and there was no need for them to stay in. There is a doctor coming in the afternoon. You should rest till then.'

Elizabeth settled wearily back on her pillows. 'He will tell me nothing I do not know, Catharina', she said grimly. 'When he comes, tell him to go away. I am childing. God knows, by now I should recognize the signs.'

Rex Rubeus

X

> But what a mighty state is this I see?
> A little world that all true worth inherites,
> Strong without art, entrench'd within the sea,
> Abounding in brave men full of great spirits:
> It seems this Ile would boast, and so she may,
> To be the sovereigne of the world some day.
>
> Sir William Alexander, 'Doomsday', 1614

Pelagius added himself discreetly to the group of maids of honour and servants who streamed out of the Wassenaer Hof on to the steps as his wife's coach rumbled into the courtyard. She had left bright-eyed, a little weary-looking, but merry, and he had fully expected to see her return in the same gay spirits, showering her friends with unnecessary and embarrassing gifts. His heart jolted as she climbed down from the carriage, for she seemed to have aged ten years in half a week. Her pale face was grim and somehow flabby, as if the spirit had gone out of her. Her daughters, getting cautiously down after her, seemed united in a determination to make themselves invisible. The cringing wariness of their movements was only too legible to an ex-slave and for a fleeting moment he pitied them. That his beloved wife possessed a temper was something he did not doubt, for all the noble sweetness and generosity of her behaviour from day to day. He longed to know what had happened and dared not ask. Catharina van Eck caught his eye as she disembarked after the three royal ladies and made an almost imperceptible gesture with her head. Taking the hint, he withdrew himself discreetly from the busy activity around the coach, and when she picked up her skirts and went up the stairs and into the hall he drifted in casually after her.

'Go to the chapel in an hour,' she said under her breath as he passed her. He made no acknowledgment, but went his ways, distracted with worry. Catharina was as good as her word. An hour later, as he sat in the chapel with a copy of the Psalter, trying to concentrate his mind on psalm 97, she slipped quietly into the seat next to his. Looking straight in front of her, her hands clasped loosely in her lap, she told him the news in an undertone; first, the disastrous setback to the Prince Palatine's plans, and second, the news which most closely touched himself.

For the first time since Elizabeth had become his wife, Pelagius found himself absolutely unable to share her mood. It was obvious that she was racked with grief, anxiety and anger about her eldest son; but, while he had every sympathy with her feelings about the Prince Palatine, for himself he was jubilant to know of her pregnancy. A child of his old age, and hers, another Isaac, the focus of the momentous hopes which had brought them together and perhaps the bearer of a mighty destiny. Beyond and almost above these all-but unthinkable aspirations for his son was the simple fact that in all the years since he left Africa he had hardly dared even to think that he would ever see a child of his own. He had left infant children in Oyo, but that was another life: if they had survived their babyhood, they would have grown up in another man's house knowing nothing of him, they were no longer his. He had long since ceased to concern himself with his childlessness, but it was clear to him in that moment that, from the joy he now felt, it had been oppressing his heart. He had no worries for Elizabeth. She was not young: though she was not yet a Sarah, there was an element of the miraculous in this late-conceived baby. It was not that he was unaware of the risks run by a woman of her age, but it seemed to him that this pregnancy was in a very specific sense in the hand of God, who had so mysteriously brought them together. He could not bring himself to believe that the Lord, having brought this second chance about, would let their enterprise fail. He longed to go to her; but Catharina had told him that she had gone to bed, and without her express invitation he could not follow her to her room.

In the event, he was summoned to her bedside that evening by Lady Dohna in his semi-official capacity as physician to the household. It had already occurred to him that this was a possibility, so he had armed himself with a flask of chicory water, soothing, cooling and very mildly sedative.

When he was admitted, he found Judoca van der Myle sitting with her, her large countenance flushed and alarmed, and Lady Dohna, quietly efficient, hovering armed with Hungary water and a vial of sal-volatile. Elizabeth was propped up among her pillows wearing a chic black satin jacket over her night smock, pale, sweaty and tearstained. Even in his extreme preoccupation he glanced around the room with momentary interest: although it was the background to the most secret and precious core of his life, he had never seen it so fully lit with candles. The bed, as he well knew, was crimson velvet trimmed with gold fringe: he now discovered that the walls were hung with crimson watered silk against which her pictures and mirrors, in black or gilded frames, made a handsome show. 'The Visit of the Magi', the picture which, he knew, she thought of as his portrait, was among them.

He came to her bedside and sat down on a hard chair which had been placed there for the purpose, and took her wrist gently, his thumb on her pulse. He could feel her trembling. The situation was a most awkward one: gentle Lady Dohna was fluttering at his elbow, concerned and ready to be helpful, and there was no way consistent with decorum or even courtesy of asking her to leave. Elizabeth's heart was a little fast, but perfectly steady, greatly to his relief. It was clear to him that, although she was very upset, she was in perfectly good health. Her eyes looked larger than usual as she gazed urgently at him; trying to divine whether he was aware of the situation and he racked his brains for a way of reassuring her. 'My lady, I have already spoken to Juffrouw Catharina, to ask if there were any events in your journey which might have disturbed your health,' he began cautiously and had the satisfaction of seeing the strained expression go from her eyes. 'I am most heartily sorry to hear the bad news from England.'

Elizabeth shut her eyes momentarily, then sat more upright in her bed. 'It is the work of that Delilah,' she said through her teeth. 'She is the wife of my brother and the mother of his sons, but I could watch the papist witch burning alive at Tyburn. She has perverted him and she will bring him to ruin.'

'My lady, do not distress yourself,' he said anxiously. 'I have brought you a soothing cordial.'

Elizabeth pushed her hair back from her face with both hands. 'This bitterness is bad for the soul,' she said wearily. 'I should not give way to it, but there is no charity in my heart towards that Frenchwoman. I cannot believe that Charles of himself would favour the King of Spain over my son. The whole Protestant world is leagued against the Spanish Empire, and my good friend Fredrik Hendrik is spending gold and men like water to keep them south of the Scheldt – and yet there is my brother, the Defender of the Faith, breaking rank with the godly kings to grovel before His Most Catholic Majesty. It is only women who delude men so.'

'What do you think the Prince Palatine will do?' he asked, pouring a little of the chicory water into the silver cup which stood on her night table.

'I do not know,' she said, accepting the drink he handed to her and sipping from it. 'If Charles my royal brother is in treaty with Philip, then in honour he cannot at the same time help the Prince to set a gate across the Spanish road. So it may be that the Prince Palatine will return here and seek the help of Fredrik Hendrik.

But the Stadhouder must guard the length of the Scheldt and at the same time do what he can to bar the Channel to the troops my brother is convoying. His army is committed on land and his navy is busy at sea. This is a small enough country, God knows, to stand against the Hapsburg Empire. I have spoken often to him of the Palatinate, as you can well imagine, and although he is fully sympathetic, he has never felt that he could afford to help us. My best hopes are that he will see the value of Breisach as a defence for himself and aid Charles Louis, or that General Leslie will put his fierce Scotsmen at his service for the sake of the Gospel, whether my brother wills it or no.'

Setting out these possibilities seemed to be calming her a little. 'Yours is a valiant heart, my lady,' he said, trying to control the tenderness of his voice.

Her eyes kindled. 'It has need to be. While we all live, there is hope for another throw of the dice. We must go on. Did you not tell me that Charles Louis would return to his kingdom? I have faith in that promise, but I thought for a moment that it would be soon, and for his sisters' sake and mine I hoped with all my heart that God would make straight the way.'

'Madam, I think you should rest. If you should want me at any time, I will be in my room and I will come to you on the instant.' Having given her as broad a hint as he dared, he rose, and bowed his farewell.

As he had hoped, he heard a soft tapping at his door some time after midnight. He was sitting in his shirt and breeches in the still heat of the night, trying to collate the various and contradictory advice of his medical books about the diet and regimen of pregnant women. He opened the door, only to see a dark form vanishing quietly round the corner; Judoca or Catharina, it must be. Putting his all-concealing and far-too-warm dressing gown on over his shirt, he padded out circumspectly into the sleeping house.

A minute or so later he let himself into Elizabeth's bedroom as quietly as possible and heard her stir. He saw the spark of a flint in the darkness, then a moment later a taper blossomed into light, illuminating the great red bed and Elizabeth. He locked the door behind him and went across to her. She held out a hand to him and he knelt beside the bed to kiss it.

'Pelagius, come to me,' she said, 'I am sick with fear.'

He shrugged out of his dressing gown, breeches and slippers, and joined her in the bed, wrapping his arms around her and rocking her like a child. 'What is it, my darling? What do you fear?'

'This is a bitter jest, my dearest. I think that in my heart, I did not believe that this would come to pass, or perhaps I did not think how it would be. And now I am childing, when everything falls to ruin all about me. Pelagius, what are we to do?'

'My darling, if God has opened your womb, we must believe that it is for a good end,' he said, as encouragingly as he could.

'I have not forgot Dr Jonson,' snapped Elizabeth. 'Those were pretty dreams he wove about us. But I am a mother already and I fear that God has turned His face from the Prince Palatine. He is at a crisis of fortune, dragging all his brothers and sisters behind him, and here am I, with child, risking a discovery which will disgrace us throughout Europe and, perhaps, my own life besides, when I should be putting him first and thinking of him only.'

There was nothing he could say to comfort her, so he stroked her hair and remained silent. Her view was understandable enough, though he did not share it.

'Oh, this was madness,' she continued bitterly. 'All my life I have acted before I thought and this time I am prettily rewarded. I cannot see how we may escape this snare.'

He was deeply hurt and she perceived the minute tensing of the arms that held her, though he tried his best to conceal his thoughts. Even in her distress, she responded at once. 'Pelagius, my dear heart, our love is the one thing I do not regret. But I was right to ask myself, when first we spoke of it, whether I would injure my children. I fear that I have and that my honour is compromised.'

'God will find a way, if He wills it,' Pelagius assured her, willing himself to believe it.

'He may indeed, but at what cost?' she said despairingly. 'It may be that this child is all that Dr Jonson hopes, and in time to come he will set his throne upon Mount Olivet. But you know as well as I do, even if God has marked out this baby for great things, that does not mean that He will spare me and mine. Meanwhile, I have Charles Louis to set upon the throne of his father.'

As usual, she saw clearly enough. The problem was unanswerable. All he could do was to hold her and offer what comfort he could. After some minutes of silence he realized she was weeping. He let her cry, blotting her eyes with his shirt and murmuring inarticulate words of comfort.

'You had better leave me,' she said once she had recovered herself. He kissed her tenderly, got up to dress and padded silently back to his room, exhausted with emotion.

In the next few days the natural resilience of Elizabeth's spirits reasserted itself. She went into a very private conference with Judoca, and reckoning up they decided that the baby was probably due in March.

'That is much to the good,' observed Judoca. 'My lady, you are often ill in winter. If you keep much to your room after the New Year and go out very little, or not at all, no one will think anything of it. It is the dark of the year, after all, and your room is not well lit, especially if you are seen only in bed with the curtains about you. If you so choose, none need see you in daylight. And the fashion of your dresses lends itself to such a deception. Since they fall from the shoulders at the back, and are caught beneath the bosom at the front, they show very little of your shape. If you draw in your busk as far as may be, you will do very well and I will help you all that I can. When we are nearer the time, I will find a nurse for the child and a place for them to live.'

For answer, Elizabeth reached out and clasped her hand.

'I have another thought besides that,' Elizabeth remarked more cheerfully. 'I could not have believed before this that I would ever be thankful that my poor mother died of a dropsy. But if anyone observes my new thickness, then I will say it is a dropsical humour. It is common enough in this country, and some are cured of it, so if I appear fat and then lean, I have but to say that I have found a remedy.'

'And, God be thanked,' added Judoca, 'childbed has never borne too hardly upon you.'

'That is true. The Elector once said, "C'est une grande grâce que Dieu vous fait." I had but four hours' travail with Louise, and two with Sophie, though I suffered very much with Nennie. Still, that is only one childbed out of thirteen which went at all amiss. Perhaps I still have the trick of it.'

As the summer went on, she ceased to worry unduly about the pregnancy. As it had done thirteen times before, her body adjusted quickly and easily to the presence of a child and she suffered very little from sickness. There was a plan in place for later in the year, and in the meantime she was well enough not to have to think about the baby and entirely preoccupied with the unfolding disaster which was English foreign policy. She was incensed, but not surprised, to hear that in August, an attractive, smooth-tongued young Italian nobleman came as a personal envoy from Pope Urban VIII to the English Queen, or that the King received him as if he had been veritably an Ambassador. Stony-faced, she absorbed the news that Queen Henrietta Maria had appealed with some success to English Catholics for money with which Charles could make war on his Protestant subjects of Scotland, and with less equanimity that Spanish troops continued to be convoyed to Flanders in English vessels, since the latter action left her prostrated with embarrassment before the Prince and Princess of Orange.

In September came news of the Battle of the Downs: the almost total destruction of a second Spanish armada, sent this time against the Dutch, within sight of Dover and under the eyes of the English fleet, by Admiral Maarten van Tromp. The Hague rang with celebration for nearly a week and Elizabeth, exasperated beyond endurance by her brother's conduct, felt more inclined to participate in the rejoicings than she thought it politic to admit.

It was, however, with grave misgivings that she heard that the Prince Palatine, despairing of any further good to be got in England, had taken ship for the Continent, hoping to make a direct appeal to the troops still garrisoning Breisach. As she explained to Pelagius, she was no little concerned about the forlornness of the enterprise, but she also had anxieties of a kind which surprised him. 'My royal brother, I thought, could have helped him more, but still it was for the Prince to stand by him against the Scots,' she said firmly. 'I did not think it was much to his honour to leave him at that time.' Pelagius looked at her, astonished, and she realized belatedly that her viewpoint was one which could not legitimately have been deduced from the hard words she had uttered in the past month. 'The Prince Palatine is the vessel of all our hopes,' she tried to explain. 'I love him best of all my children, but I do not understand him. His father was the soul of honour, and at Vlotho last year, he was truly his father's son – honest Thom Roe told me his attendants needs must drag him from the field after the day was surely lost. But when he is not in the press of battle, he is soured by too much policy and makes his reckonings like a little shopkeeper. There is too much calculation in his action.'

'But surely', asked Pelagius, 'a dispossessed prince must be wise and walk warily?'

'That is so, of course. But if he is too wary, he will lose all. If he is not noble, poor as he is, why would anyone risk his life for him? He must be magnificent if he is ever to be rich, and any action which savours of meanness makes me fear for him.'

It was one of the moments when she feared that their experience of life was too different for her to understand him. He looked at her for a long time, the black eyes searching her face, before he nodded.

The sequel was even harder for her to grasp or endure. Charles Louis, as he came to Boulogne, was greeted with a salvo of gunfire, and the honours due to a reigning monarch. He went at his leisure to Paris, and reported that his young brothers were shaping well. He hoped to meet with Richelieu before too much time had passed. The brief letters, ever more confident, which he sent were dissected at the Wassenaer Hof, syllable by syllable, where they caused much building of castles in the air. Then in November another letter came from France, which put an abrupt end to all her hopes. It was written from a royal prison at Vincennes; and said with bitter brevity that the Cardinal, having almost made final his own plans for Breisach, thought it best to detain him for some while. A letter followed, three days later, from his three young brothers, to say that they were also under house arrest, and did not know when they might be released.

The Princess of Orange came and wept over her, addressing her as 'Niobe', but she was very far from being turned to stone by her griefs. With the help of Mr Dingley and Pelagius, she sent a storm of letters all across Europe, expressing in well-turned sentences the rage of a mother who was also a statesman. Yet in time that situation, like every previous intolerable moment, transformed itself gradually into being the way life was. The other news of the late autumn, that King Charles had recalled the Earl of Strafford from Ireland to aid him, merely served to confirm that nothing was likely to improve in the foreseeable future. As both Ambassador Heenvliet and Sir William Boswell, the English Ambassador to The Hague, told her regretfully, Strafford was internationally known to be wholly devoted to the Spanish interest. The only remotely good news which came to the Wassenaer Hof was that Maurice had been released from house arrest, whereupon he promptly enlisted in the army of the King of Sweden; adding to their concerns the daily fear of news of his death from typhoid, exposure or wounds.

At the beginning of December Elizabeth, her daughters and Lady Sayer were sitting playing draughts before supper with sleety rain hammering on the windows, when the absolute ennui of the passing, newsless days fell on them all with the weight of an avalanche. Elizabeth, the Princess Palatine, watched her mother's grim face warily as she made a final move, winning the game, and Lady Sayer swept the pieces off the board. Unwell as she clearly was and had been for some time, the shifts in her mood weighed heavily on her women and her daughters. The Queen stirred restlessly as her maid of honour began to set out the pieces once more and stretched herself. 'Oh, I am weary of this life. We must do something to keep ourselves amused, or we will all die of melancholy.'

'What are you thinking of, mother?' asked Elizabeth cautiously.

'I think we should have a play for Christmas.'

'But is it right at such a time?' As usual, her mother refused to be contradicted. Her eyes kindled and she roused herself to opposition.

'Why not, when there is nothing whatever we can do? Just a play for ourselves to help us keep in spirits. God knows, I have cause enough to be sad, yet I am still of a humour to be as merry as I can, in spite of fortune.'

'Which play are you thinking of?'

'I do not want a tragedy or a history. We have enough of both. I know the very one. Which is the play where the child says, "a sad tale's best for winter"? I saw it before I left England, and again when the English players came five years ago. You and your brothers saw it with me at the Mauritshuis.'

'It is called *The Winter's Tale*, mother.'

'Well, that is very pat,' said Elizabeth, pleased.

'But can we perform it?' her daughter protested, 'I think we would need the boys.'

'Oh, I am sure we can contrive,' said Elizabeth airily. 'You have played breeches parts before. All the ladies must act. We will have no audience, but just ourselves.'

The Princess Palatine surveyed her mother dubiously. She was not looking particularly well and her figure was still unnaturally bulky. The confinement of winter never suited her: probably when the warmer weather came and she was able to get out again the basic strength of her constitution would reassert itself, and this dropsical weight would fall away from her. Meanwhile, the prospect of something to do seemed to have given her mother renewed energy. Somewhat against her better judgment, the Princess Palatine began to look forward to the idea of another play. The little ones would enjoy it so, she told herself.

When Pelagius next saw Elizabeth, he found her in her closet with a heavy volume in folio on the table by her side. She turned to him smilingly. 'Dearest Pelagius. I have decided we should have a play to help us through this sad Christmas. Please take this book and read the one I have marked, so you will understand what is on hand.'

Not without curiosity, he accepted the book and spent the rest of the day studying the play with attention. His only acquaintance with drama, beyond Elizabeth's occasional remarks, was Seneca's *Thyestes*, which he had once read for its style. By comparison, the work before him was a bewildering riot of characters and action, stretching across perhaps twenty years and half of Europe. It seemed at first, wilfully confusing, but on his second read-through, he realized that of all the literature he knew it was most like the *Aeneid*, with which perception he began finally to enjoy it.

He went down to the withdrawing room before dinner, filled with curiosity, taking the book to return to her. He found Elizabeth in state, in her favourite chair, with the Princess Palatine and Louise at her side, together with a sizeable proportion of her household officers, the Mistress of the Robes, the Countess of Löwenstein, Sir George and Lady Sayer, James and Francis the pages, and Mr Dingley. He was puzzled at first as to what they had in common, then suddenly realized that in that French-speaking household they constituted all those who were at home in English, with the exception of Dr Jonson. She looked up as he came in and smiled warmly at him, holding out her hands for the folio.

'My dear Pelagius. You are in good time: we are thinking of our parts.'

'If you are acting, your majesty, I think you must mean to be Hermione?' he guessed.

'Bravo. Louise will be Autolycus because she can sing and my tall Princess can be Florizel. My good Jane has agreed to play Pauline. Little Nennie will make the sweetest of Perditas and Gustavus can be Mamillius, if we are patient with him. I want you to be Leontes – I am sure you could be stern and jealous like the Grand Sophy, and put us all in fear.' Her tone was jocular, but her hidden meaning was clear to him: he was to play her husband and, for the first and perhaps only time, speak words of love to her before an audience, even if they understood it not.

He looked at her in dismay. 'But the play is in English,' he protested.

She dismissed this with an airy wave. 'You can read English and I have reason to trust your memory. I will teach you your part, have no fear.'

'But madam, I cannot do this,' he said, upset and deeply embarrassed. 'I know it is the custom of your country and your house, but for a man who has studied divinity and still hopes to become a preacher, it is wrong to move emotion with a fiction and to personate another. I had not thought that you would ask me.' Elizabeth sat very still and upright, her cheeks gradually colouring to crimson, looking at him with angry eyes which threatened tears. He was miserably conscious of having appeared to rebuke her before her household. 'I do not hold this as a reproach to you,' he said unhappily, 'but it is not right for me.' The discomfort in the room as a whole was almost palpable; though it was full of people, they seemed to be frozen like statues and there was no sound but the crackling of the fire in the hearth. Trapped in an endless limbo of embarrassment, a way out occurred to him, so he seized it. 'Perhaps I might personate Time?' he asked awkwardly. 'The difficulty is not there, for the figure of Time is an allegory and not a man.'

The Queen's expression relaxed a little and the room seemed to breathe again. 'I see there is no use trying to persuade you to further parts,' she said coldly, evidently furious. 'You are Time, then. Mr Dingley, will you play Leontes? We must have an older man in the part.'

The unfortunate Dingley flushed and stammered, but the Queen was inexorable. 'I hope you will not tell me it is against your principles,' she said with steely sweetness.

'No, but –'

'Then that is settled,' she snapped. 'We will cut the play as short as may be, and divide the lords and ladies and clowns up between ourselves. Our numbers will not suffice for the dances, so we must give them the go-by.'

The Queen's determination was not to be moved. It swept them all forward and from that day on the play absorbed almost the whole time of the English-speaking part of the household. The following week the youngest children came from the Prinsenhof with their three governesses, an elderly and upright lady called Mme du Plessen and her ugly, middle-aged daughters, Mademoiselle Plessen and Mme Ketler, and Pelagius met for the first time the gentle, ash-blonde Henriette, called Nennie, poised between child and woman and as pretty as a toy, pert, nine-year-old Sophie, and the seven-year-old Gustavus, a grave child with an old man's deliberate movements, who seemed, to Pelagius's compassionately diagnostic eye, unequivocally marked for early death.

Nennie, for all that she was only fourteen, had an executive ability beyond either of her older sisters or, indeed, her mother. She marshalled the mistress of the robes, the sewing woman, and four or five maids, and led a patient inquisition into the most distant recesses of Elizabeth's and her brothers' wardrobes. For much of December she was to be found composedly enthroned in a corner of the withdrawing room with Mrs Broughton and the sewing woman in attendance, taking up, taking in and remodelling old clothes so that they would all be suitably dressed for the occasion. For Pelagius, she found a white woollen dressing gown lined with silk shag, which had belonged to her father. He attempted feebly to insist that he would wear his own decent black, but in the face of Nennie's gentle tenacity he had to confess himself defeated. It was hard to refuse a little creature who looked so like a flower.

The gown which Nennie had found for him was a garment of great splendour: the back was pleated into a deep yoke, giving it a dignified fullness, and the wide sleeves were turned back with decorative loops and buttons to display the magnificent lining. The state of the hem suggested that when worn by the Elector Frederick, it had swept the floor: on him it came some way above the ankle. It was strange for him to handle something which had belonged to Elizabeth's first husband, in the most literal sense, to measure himself against him; and it caused him to ponder deeply on the history of the Bohemian venture. For all Elizabeth's unquestioning loyalty to her husband's memory, the judgment which was forming in his own mind, based on his reading, was not a wholly favourable one. He was coming to see the melancholy Elector as another Comrij; a man of ability and intelligence, with some fatal flaw in self-mastery or lack of authority which led him to fall short of his aim. A man from whom God had turned His face. Once he had feared that he himself might be such a man, but this fear was gone from him. The path of his life was so extraordinary that he had come to believe that he was among the elect.

As the month wore on, the wisdom of Elizabeth's decision to turn the house upside-down with a play became increasingly apparent. No news of any kind came: imaginative and loving as they all were, all they could do was envisage the Prince Palatine, Rupert, Ned and Philip all still trapped in their various prisons, while Maurice faced all the ordinary risks of a soldier. Condemned to waiting and inactivity, the sad little household would have had nothing to do but worry and bicker had they not been given something to think about.

The Princess Palatine undertook to cut the play for domestic performance and worked with great efficiency to minimize the number of characters and problems they would face. Once she had adjusted the play to their capacities, she co-opted Pelagius and Mr Dingley to help her write out parts, and he found to his surprise that he liked her. Naturally, he had always seen her through her mother's eyes, since they had barely exchanged a word; but now he saw her plainly dressed and unself-conscious, with a lock of her dark hair falling in her eyes as she bent over the page, she was far from charmless. Indeed, had she been male, he would have found her very easy to talk to. His reassessment of her dated from the first day of their work together, as the three of them were clustered together around the Queen's folio Shakespeare, which she had meticulously annotated in her small, clear script. As their eyes passed over Leontes's obscene imaginings, she indicated, with no more than a tell-tale, unbecoming mottling of her nose and cheeks to indicate her embarrassment, that the most offensive passages must be cut. He surprised himself with a sudden effusion of respect for her girlish dignity and an affection which he never afterwards saw any reason to withdraw.

Rehearsals proceeded, on the whole, smoothly. While Elizabeth had charge of the text and Nennie of the costumes, Louise did what she could for the scene-painting and talked the grooms and outside men into some pretty contrivances of lath and canvas for her to decorate.

The only real contretemps in the whole rehearsal period was caused by Pelagius himself. Having a well-trained memory, he had had no difficulty in committing Time's speech to his mind – indeed, having copied out a good deal of it, he had a virtually complete grasp of the entire play. He had accordingly been excused rehearsals until it came to time for the first complete run-through on Christmas Eve. He had spoken the speech over to himself several times in the privacy of his room and felt passably confident about its delivery.

They were in the presence chamber, where they intended to act. The rehearsal went well enough, up to the point where Pelagius was to speak. He entered on his cue, took a deep breath, and began: 'I, that please some, try all, both joy and terror, of good and bad that makes and unfolds error –'. His voice trailed off, for he could see his Elizabeth staring at him, white to the lips, looking as if she were about to faint. 'A chair!' he said urgently, and Louise, about to enter as Autolycus, ran to fetch one, which her mother dropped into as if the strings of her knees had been cut. He took two strides and knelt at her feet, taking her cold hands to chafe them. 'What is it, my lady?' he asked urgently.

Elizabeth smiled as best she could, her face still almost unrecognizable with shock. 'Pelagius, you spoke in my father's voice.'

He looked at her helplessly, unable to hide his bewilderment. For the first time since they had met, she looked at him with a kind of cringing, superstitious fear, as if she thought he might truly be a warlock.

'Dr Pelagius,' said Mr Dingley, his tone unreadable, 'you have a strongly Scottish accent, which has surprised her majesty.'

He looked at them all, as surprised as they were, before he managed to collect his thoughts. 'It is not witchcraft, your majesty,' he explained. 'My patron, Dr Comrij, was the son of a Scot. He spoke to me sometimes in that language. Since I do not speak English, I suppose I have pronounced the words in the way which is familiar to me. I am sorry.'

Lady Sayer, who had left the room silently as soon as Elizabeth was helped to a chair, returned with a glass of brandy and handed it to her mistress. After a sip or two, her cheeks began to return to a more normal colour, though her eyes remained dark and shocked looking. 'No, Pelagius,' she said, smiling more naturally, 'there is no need to apologize. You could not know what the sound of your speech would mean to me. I am the only person here who grew up with Scots in my ears.'

'Would you rather I withdrew myself?' he asked, a little hopefully.

'Oh, no. Not now I am expecting it. After all, I am the daughter of Scotland, born in Linlithgow. For me at least, it is fitting that Time should speak with a Scots voice.' She paused to drink a little, and when she spoke again, it was in a different tone. 'And', she added bleakly, 'it may be that Time speaks with a Scots voice to my brother, also.'

They ran through to the end of the play, but they had no heart for it.

The actual performance was, for Pelagius, one of the strangest experiences of his life. They were using the daïs in Elizabeth's presence chamber as their stage. A number of chairs had been taken from the dining room, and those who were not actually acting in any scene sat in them to watch, together with a number of other ladies of the household who were not taking part, Catharina van Eck, Mme Plessen, Lady Dohna, Judoca van der Myle, a couple of her daughters and her waiting-woman. They began in mid-afternoon, with the light fading fast. A row of candles was ranged along the edge of the daïs, and every floor-standing candelabrum in the Wassenaer Hof had been moved down to stand around the edges of the stage.

The first three acts meant very little to him. He had been moved by the play as a piece of writing; but it was hard to see that the personation was anything but a meaningless frivolity. Elizabeth was a dignified Hermione, but seemed simply herself, speaking the words of another; while ugly Mme Ketler was an implausible Polixenes, wearing her own skirts and a man's hat and waistcoat. The embarrassed Dingley uttered Leontes's speeches of obscene jealousy and rage in a strained, artificial voice which left them hanging in the air, disassociated from the speaker. The girls and the pages ran to and fro in a variety of hats, unconvincingly representing a nameless multitude of lords and ladies, with the assistance of Mme Plessen's daughters, the Countess of Löwenstein (who, as he had discovered in the course of rehearsals, was an Englishwoman, born Elizabeth Dudley), Sir George and Lady Sayer.

He was touched by Gustavus as Mamillius; a child who was soon to die, acted by a thin, fair little boy whose future was hardly less certain. His sister Elizabeth had cut his speeches down, fearing there might be too much for him to learn, but he delivered them stoutly and with dignity in a small, clear voice. At the end of the scene, the hoyden Sophie was merely absurd as the bear, extinguished beneath a sable shoulder cape of her mother's, jumping about the stage with shrill, excited squeals, while her sister Louise as Antigonus, clutching a wooden doll wrapped in a shawl, was hard put to it not to laugh.

At last, it was his own cue to rise, wrapped in the Elector's white gown and give Time's speech, explaining that for the last act the scene must be imagined sixteen years later. The candles standing around the makeshift stage made it hard to see out to the chairs where Elizabeth sat with her pretty children and her friends. Alone on the stage, as he spoke, the words began to have a meaning for him. He was no longer thinking of the unconvincing doll which had been the focus of the last scene, but of the child Elizabeth was carrying in her womb. Like Perdita, his son would grow up remote from a mother, in secret. What would his life be like? For this all too real child, who must be launched forlorn upon the world, would there ever be a point where loving parents would reclaim him? Momentarily, the confident faith in the dispositions of Providence which had sustained him up to that point, deserted him completely, and he was painfully affected by the impossibility of seeing any child's future, for good or ill. Shaken, he brought his speech to an end and strode off the stage.

He watched the last act in an emotional turmoil, generated, to begin with, by his own thoughts. But when Nennie entered as Perdita his heart turned over. Her silver-blonde hair was hanging loose, and her dress, cream satin embroidered with flowers, was of a fashion which even he could see was archaic, with a long narrow bodice and a drum-shaped skirt. The bodice was too big and stood away stiffly from her bird-boned, fragile chest: she did not so much seem to wear the garment, as inhabit it. He felt a gentle touch on his wrist: Elizabeth was leaning forward, her eyes bright with emotion. 'That is a dress from my trousseau,' she whispered, 'when I was young and little.' He nodded, absorbed.

With her long dark hair bundled up under one of her brothers' hats, the tall and bony Princess Palatine made a surprisingly convincing boy, at least to the eye, and she spoke well. As Florizel, wooing her little sister, she was charming; the actual affection between them lent a conviction to her sexless, boyish gallantry, while Nennie was infinitely touching. The oversized, but exquisite dress lent her a pathetic dignity. Hovering as she was on the verge of taking her place in the Queen's household as an adult, marriageable Princess, she was Perdita to the life, at once stately and childish, naïve and graceful. His heart ached for her and for them all and silently, but fervently, he prayed that the children's futures would be happy.

Elizabeth took her place on her own throne for the final scene and the pageboy James covered her carefully with a silver gauze veil until it was time for her to appear. Dry little Mr Dingley spoke Leontes's words of penitent loyalty and love with a spirit he had been unable to bring to the first scenes of deluded jealousy; and when Elizabeth, as Hermione, stood up and took her secretary by the hand with a familiar gesture of confiding affection, he found himself blinded with a sudden rush of hot tears.

The rest of Christmas passed without incident. News came from England in the New Year that the King and his court had also been acting at Christmas. The court had performed the most elaborate masque ever staged. It was called *Salmacidia Spolia,* and represented the furies of disorder and rebellion stilled by 'the great and wise Philogenes', which Pelagius interpreted for the Queen as 'the King who loves his people.' Elizabeth listened in silence to the written account of the spectacle, which included the descent of Henrietta Maria from the clouds, dressed as an Amazon in carnation silk and silver. When Dingley had finished his narrative, she said simply, 'And on the money spent on this trumpery, the Prince Palatine could have taken Breisach.' Leaning heavily on the arm of her chair, she got up and left her closet: to Pelagius's troubled eyes, for the first time, her walk was the walk of an old woman.

Three days later, she was laid low by an infection on the chest and took to her bed. Pelagius attended her daily. Her ladies nursed her efficiently through a serious but in no sense dangerous attack of the rheum, which caused her to spend night after night propped up on pillows, breathing in steam from bowls of boiling water, held for her by the devoted Lady Sayer, to loosen her cough. But in the course of that week, as he visited her room, it became increasingly clear to him that the true nature of her condition was no secret to any of the matrons who bustled in and out of her bedroom; but that none of them spoke of it, even to one another. A close atmosphere of feminine secrecy filled the room like an odour, tenacious, invisible as a cobweb. He found himself hesitating as he entered the room. The sensation was a familiar one, which he recalled from the Queens' quarters of his father's *afin*, and he felt, as he had sometimes felt as a child playing at his mother's feet, that his presence and his good will were taken account of, but that he was not in any true sense included within the circle.

Incorruptible loyalty was not a feature of European culture which had impressed itself upon him, yet he realized, watching Elizabeth with her women, that the loyalty to death of an Oyo *ilari* was not unknown in these colder regions. It was also evident that, if there were anyone who might provoke such a sentiment, it was Elizabeth. Watching her with her women, he began to understand her indirect criticism of the Prince Palatine.

The Queen's illness threw him into more contact with the maids of honour than previously and he began to learn a little of their past history. He discovered that pretty Lady Sayer had been a penniless Bohemian noblewoman, the daughter of a Baron Rupa whose eloquence had been widely held responsible for Frederick's election as Emperor, who had subsequently been reduced to destitution in the cause of Bohemian Protestantism. In the aftermath of the Battle of the White Mountain, Elizabeth had kept the girl with her to share her own meagre fortunes. When subsequently she married an equally penniless Englishman, Elizabeth had appointed them both officers of her household. Other stories were similar in their implications, however different in detail. The profoundness of the mutual obligations between Elizabeth and her ladies reminded him less of the feminine intrigues he had encountered in various parts of the world than of Plutarch's *Life of Alexander*. If the Prince Palatine were petty and ignoble, he reflected, it could not have been for lack of example.

Once her chest was completely recovered in the first week of February, Elizabeth refused to get out of bed. When none but members of her most intimate inner circle of women were by, she was often found waddling furiously up and down her room, desperate for lack of exercise, but she was not to be seen by anyone outside her household, or by any man other than Pelagius. Pelagius therefore, in the capacity of her physician in ordinary, parried a variety of alarmed queries from the Prince and Princess of Orange and other old friends in The Hague, such as Sir William and Lady Boswell, Lord and Lady Vere and Secretary Huygens, to say nothing of a motley variety of international friends and acquaintances. Their visits and notes were brought to him by Mr Dingley, in what rapidly became a daily conference, and he was as reassuring as he was able to be.

Her ladies took turns to entertain her, while she kept to her room, grew larger and fretted over the news. Judoca, meanwhile, held long, private conversations with Pelagius in her closet. She had a complete scheme worked out for the welfare of the child, which she explained to him in detail. There was an impecunious young couple called Berckman, living in Middelburg, the capital of Zeeland, whose family connection with the van der Myle household went back for three generations. The wife had recently given birth; the child was well, but she was strong and sturdy. There would certainly be milk for two. They had agreed to take the child who was to come, knowing nothing of its origin, and foster it. Pelagius was not wholly happy about the plan. Middelburg was far to the south and seemed to him dangerously near the Spanish Netherlands: he would have preferred to see his child fostered at the other end of the country. But the van der Myles' connections were with the south: if the baby went to Middelburg, it would be easier to get news of it. In the end, he was forced to concede, but he insisted that he himself must take the child to its new home. In his mind was the thought that if he was in any doubt about the situation, he would take the baby north again, and make his own arrangements.

At the end of February Elizabeth gave Judoca one of the best of her remaining jewels, a linked chain of diamond knots with nine big, pear-shaped pearls hanging in the loops, which had belonged to the first Queen Elizabeth. Judoca brought it to Pelagius to show him, before taking it down to the Jewish diamond merchants of Amsterdam. She returned with four thousand guilders – the baby's patrimony – well pleased with herself. As she explained to Pelagius on her victorious return, the Jews were connoisseurs of diamonds, but they loved fine pearls still better. Since the nine pendants were beautifully matched and of the finest quality, she explained at unnecessary length, she had been able to drive a very hard bargain. Looking at her bland, smug face, he thought, as he uttered the necessary words of thanks and praise, how much he had come to dislike her. He detested the way that she was so instrumental in his relationship with his wife and he did not for a moment believe in her disinterestedness. Under the cover of their conversation, he gave his full attention to her: not to her words, but to what he understood of her essential personality and, on the whole, he was reluctantly reassured. He perceived that the affection she felt for Elizabeth was in its way, genuine, but that other, stronger considerations of policy also served to keep her trustworthy. She was glad to serve the Queen, but glad, also, to hold a secret of such weight that it would bind Elizabeth to her need. She was a woman who grew fat on secrets, like a spider in a hole.

The arrangement Judoca and Elizabeth had made was to him an uncomfortable one, but he had to assent to it. It was absolutely clear, talking to Elizabeth, that she had never looked after any of her previous children except the oldest and it had not occurred to her for a moment that she would look after this one. One after another, even though there had been no need for discretion, they had left her care almost as soon as they had left her body and been brought up at a distance. It seemed to him incomprehensible that any woman would wish to do this; though it was also incontrovertibly the case that this apparently doubtful procedure had left her with ten live children out of thirteen births. Only two of the whole brood had died as babies, a record which any woman of Oyo would have been hard put to match. Whenever he was assailed by doubt, he told himself this over again, though it never helped to reconcile him to the plan.

In February the peaceful rhythm of the household was violently interrupted by a hammering at the door late one night. The sleepy halberdier opened up reluctantly to find that he was confronting an immensely tall, slender youth of almost twenty, black-haired, hawk-nosed and furious at being shut out: Maurice had come home, the first of the wandering sons, after eighteen months abroad. The whole of the Wassenaer Hof was set by the ears as maids and matrons ran up and down in their night smocks and wrappers, preparing a bed for him in Judoca van der Myle's closet.

While this was going on, he ran up to his mother's room and dropped hastily on one knee to kiss her hand. He was shocked to find her apparently so distorted, though she was bright-eyed and tears poured down her cheeks with joy and relief at the sight of him.

'What is this, mother?' he asked, once the first exchanges were over, sitting on the edge of her bed and peering at her anxiously by the light of her candle as she sat up, huddled in a satin jacket, with the quilts up below her chin.

'I am become broader than I am long', she confessed, with a touch of her old jauntiness. 'Your grandmother the Queen died of the dropsy – I fear this is a humour of the kind.'

'May it be averted from you, mother! Do you feel very ill?' he asked anxiously.

'Ill enough to keep my bed, my dear son,' Elizabeth said firmly, 'especially since I am not fit to be seen. Winter does not suit me now I am old and I dread to catch an ague or a rheum as well as this affliction. But I have hopes of a cure, and so does my physician. Perhaps when it gets warmer, I will be more myself. Leave me now. I must rest and so must you.'

Full of apprehensions, Maurice accepted his dismissal and went to bed. He spoke the next day with his mother's new physician, a tall, austere-looking African with the carriage of a soldier, who, it was rumoured in the household, possessed an esoteric knowledge of the herbs and remedies of the East.

'Your mother is in no immediate danger, Prince,' he said. His deep voice had a calm authority which was reassuring; the dark face was hard for Maurice to read, but there was no hint of wavering or duplicity in its firm lines. He disliked the man on sight and thought him a most inappropriate and eccentric addition to his mother's household: if his mother had had any toleration whatsoever for interference in her affairs, he would have told her so. However, for all his alarm and his basic inclination to distrust a black man of whom he knew nothing, he found he was soothed despite himself. 'This has been a difficult winter for her, with you and all your noble brothers in prison,' the black doctor explained. 'Day and night her thoughts and prayers have been for the Prince Palatine and you, her younger sons. Her spirit, perhaps, has acted on her body. Do not fear for her. I have hopes of a cure. Her constitution always responds well to the turn of the year and if the anxieties of the winter are lifted one by one from her mind, I think all will be well.'

Maurice, though he tried not to show it to this strange individual, found the explanation a sensible one, which squared with his own knowledge of his mother's constitution. His mind was greatly relieved: while he sometimes found his mother irritating, he was unable seriously to imagine a life without her care, her humour, her occasional storms. Bidding the man a scant farewell, he went his ways and began to think what he might do with himself without Rupert, whose faithful lieutenant he had been all his life.

The days stretched before him, blank and dull. He had a number of friends in The Hague, hard-drinking young noblemen; after some trouble before he went to Paris he had more or less promised his mother he would see them no more. He did not want to upset her while she was ill, but what was a man to do, moping alone with a pack of women? His mother, with whom he would normally have hunted, was in bed, one sister did nothing but read, the other did nothing but paint, and the babies were babies. Drinking, whoring, hunting and talking about politics would at least fill his days until he took another commission, something he did not intend to do until he saw which way the wind blew for his oldest brother: he was not a disloyal boy, and would rather fight in a family quarrel than another man's. He salved his not over-active conscience by telling himself that his friends would at least ensure that he got all the news that came to The Hague, and dropped by degrees back into his old life, coming and going at all hours with a noisy group of friends, frequently drunk, and adding yet further to the disorder of Elizabeth's chaotic household.

It was on 24 March, a windy night, with a storm chasing the last black rags of winter from the sky, that Judoca finally knocked on Pelagius's door.

'Her Majesty tells me she is unwell,' she said. Pelagius looked at her alarmed, until he divined her meaning from the archness of her expression and his heart leaped.

'Does she want to see me?' he asked.

'Yes. Not to stay with her, of course. This is woman's work. Do not worry, I have seen a good few babies into the world.'

He followed her upstairs. His books recommended a number of aids to successful childbirth, but he trusted none of them. Unless, God forbid, anything began to go wrong, she was best left to the wisdom of the body. When he went in to see her, he found her sitting up in bed, pale, bulky and sweating along her hairline, but cheerful.

'I think all is well,' she said. 'It feels like one of my good deliveries. When Nennie brought me such grief, I knew it by now.' She took a deep breath and shut her eyes. The mound beneath her smock shuddered like an independent creature, which, he reflected, it very nearly was. Once the throe was over, she opened her eyes again and gave him a weak smile. 'You must go,' she said firmly. 'This is my affair.'

He left the room and went back to his own quarters. He spent the night mostly in prayer, interspersed with bouts of organization. He packed a few days' necessities into a leather satchel and dressed himself for a journey. As dawn broke over The Hague and the chill, grey day began, he stole softly out to the stables in his shoes and saddled Sparrenbord with his own hands. He heard the grooms stirring in the loft above the stables, but such was the slackness of the household, especially since the return of Maurice, that since neither dog nor horse raised a clamour they did not bestir themselves. Leaving the beast tied in a corner of the courtyard, he returned to his room to wait, watching the sun's progress up the sky, unable to settle or even to sit down.

At a quarter to six there was another knock on his door. He opened it, his heart in his mouth. Mevrouw Judoca stood in the entrance, with a shapeless little bundle of blankets in her arms, and stepped hastily into the room as he shut the door behind her. 'Madame is well, she is sleeping easily,' she whispered.

'How is the child?'

'A fine boy. He has been washed and oiled and his navel string is tied. She has fed him, he should sleep for a little.' He barely heard her: he had assumed absolutely that he would have a son. Hastily, he sat down, kicked off his shoes and pulled on his long riding boots.

'Please come out with me,' he said, as softly as he could, 'then you can shut the gate.'

Together they crept down the corridor and out to the hall. The halberdier, as usual, was stretched at his ease, his snores deep and resonant. He had not wakened when Pelagius went out to saddle his horse, nor did he on this occasion. Pelagius untied Sparrenbord and vaulted on to his back, with his satchel over one shoulder. Judoca handed him up the blankets which contained his child and he settled the weight into the crook of his left arm. He watched warily as Judoca struggled with the bolts. As soon as the gate was open wide enough to admit him, he walked Sparrenbord through, hearing it close softly behind him.

Above him the sky was streaked with the violent orange-pinks of full dawn and it was still very cold. Lights were being kindled here and there in the servants' quarters of the houses along the Voorhout. He set Sparrenbord to a smart walk, consumed with impatience. As long as the child remained silent, it was safer to walk; even at dawn a horseman with no sign of urgency about him would attract no attention. Fortunately, the rhythm of the horse's movement seemed to be lulling the baby. He felt nothing from within the blankets at all and began to be a little alarmed.

He was deeply relieved when, once he was safely outside the town gates and trotting along a polder, the bundle of blankets gave voice; the appalling, squeaky, catlike cry of a newborn baby. There was nobody within earshot. He unfolded the blankets one-handed and for the first time looked at the face of his son. The absence of movement was explained at once: the child was wrapped in swaddling clothes, and immobile as a small log, with nothing but his face protruding from the carefully wrapped linen. The face was as red as the newborn sun, squalling and indignant, so distorted by grief that it was impossible to say what the child actually looked like. But every cry indicated his health and spirits. Cautiously, Pelagius looped the reins over his arm and gave his son his little finger to suck. The tiny mouth fastened on it avidly and a wave of tenderness swept over him. With the backs of his free fingers, he caressed the soft little cheek. 'I must name you, my son,' he said softly. 'You cannot have a true birthname, since your mother did not know to name you when you came out of her, but your praise-name is Alako, the child to be cherished if he lives, and you are Oranyan, and you are Balthasar, little one. Sleep now.'

In a moment or two the baby realized that no nourishment was forthcoming. Rejecting his father's loving finger, he heaved a deep breath and began to scream again. Pelagius set his teeth, reclaimed the reins and set the horse to a canter. After some little while, the jolting so affronted the child that he went back to sleep out of pure bewilderment. With his heart in his mouth, Pelagius cantered towards Rotterdam as fast as the faithful Sparrenbord could take him.

XI

Doing, a filthy pleasure is and short;
And done, we straight repent us of the sport:
Let us not then rush blindly on unto it,
Like lustful beasts, that only know to do it:
For lust will languish, and that heat decay,
But thus, thus, keeping endless holiday,
Let us together closely lie, and kiss,
There is no labour, nor no shame in this;
This hath pleased, doth please, and long will please; never
Can this decay, but is beginning ever.

Ben Jonson, translating Petronius, *Anthologia Latina*, 1, 2, dcc

Pelagius made the best speed he might, but ever after his flight to Middelburg remained in his mind as one of the most nightmarish of a life punctuated by terrible journeys. When he got to Rotterdam, he left a spent and limping Sparrenbord in the stables of an inn, to be cared for till his return. Balthasar was screaming again by that time; with the aid of the innkeeper's concerned and sympathetic wife, he tried to feed him with a little sweetened pap on a spoon, which the child was unable to take. They fared slightly better soaking the corner of a handkerchief and poking it into his mouth, since he was eager to suck, but by the time they gave up, he had consumed perhaps a teaspoonful of the liquid and the linen round his face was saturated.

'That's all we can do,' said the innkeeper's wife, standing back with her hands on her matronly hips, and surveying them dubiously. 'There's no one here I know of with a child on the breast. Best just to go on and get him to his nurse as soon as may be.'

'Do you think he is in danger?' asked Pelagius.

The inn woman bit her lip, her broad, honest face troubled. 'He's strong, he should do well enough. I remember with one of my daughters, my milk didn't come in for nearly three days. I thought she would starve, but she has two of her own now. God deals kindly with babies. Pray to Him and put the child in His hands. Have courage, mynheer.'

Through all the business of hiring a boat to take him to Middelburg and the long hours he spent sitting in the stern tenderly huddled around his distressed and screaming son, his mind recurred again and again to the good woman's words, which were all he had to sustain him. He knew almost nothing about babies. The children he had fathered in Africa had never left their mothers and he had never expected to know anything about them until they were of an age to conduct themselves with dignity. Comrij's household had been childless. He thought again of Perdita in the play, taken from Sicily to Bohemia, unfed, without a woman to care for her. Only in the feignings of a poet would she not have died. His heart was in his mouth as he tried unskilfully to soothe his child and protect him from the wind and spray. After his sleepless night and long ride, he was deadly weary and Balthasar's every cry seemed to pierce his aching head like an arrow.

The voyage through the delta of the Scheldt down to Zeeland was a strange one, which made him, in his sleepless and hypersensitive state, think of a journey through the land of the dead. The islands that they steered between seemed barely to hump themselves above the waterline, like sleeping whales; the sea, the river mouths and the land met ambiguously, flat, silver-grey sand lifting barely clear of the grey tide. Inland, beyond the wide sandbanks, were polders, furred with the grey-green leaves of willow and alder, fields as flat as millponds, and sometimes, in the distance, the lofting spire of a little church. It was a region where land might become water, water land; shifting and impermanent. Only the movement of the sun allowed him to maintain a sense of direction. Towards evening, the boat approached Middelburg, which was not, as he had thought, actually on the sea, but approached via a channel, with the bulk of the island of Walcheren between it and the Spanish Netherlands. He approved of this: within the maze of water and islands, the town was still further withdrawn, as secretively as a snail in its shell and therefore the more defensible. As they came up to the town itself, he looked on it with approval: what was spreading out before him as the *jacht* approached the Buitenhaven was a star town, in the most modern and approved style of military fortification, with the high, solid walls run out into flèches at the corners and surrounded by a canal, giving the defenders a complete field of fire against anyone who might be attacking. The dark snouts of cannons were visible to his left, aiming down at approaching vessels, and he could see a secondary canal system inside the wall. As the little *jacht* ran in towards its harbour, the steep, high, walls frowning down upon him began to make him feel easier in his mind about leaving his precious child there. Even for the amphibious Dutch, a town circled by the water was safer than one approachable overland and the good burghers had defended themselves well. And at the very worst it would be possible to flee to England, no great distance away on the other side of the Narrow Sea.

Once he had paid off the skipper of the *jacht*, he climbed the narrow steps up from the mooring on to the Oostpunt and made enquiries for the house of Cristoffel Berckman, called 'De Zeepketel', near the Spanjardstraat. Balthasar seemed to prefer the motion of a walker to that of a boat or a horse and became quiescent as soon as his father was afoot. All the same, it seemed an interminable length of time, though it was actually about forty minutes, before he was able to knock on the door of a tiny dwelling ornamented with a worn-out soap kettle. The Spanjardstraat itself, where he had wasted a lot of time, contained homes of some size, but the building before him was tiny, nothing but a two-room ground floor and an attic. It was also tucked into a corner of the Zuikerpoort, primarily a warehouse area; there was, he thought contemptuously, a pathetic pretension in the way that Berckman had sought to associate his mean little home with the settled prosperity of the Spanjardstraat. The baby, to his relief, was asleep in the crook of his arm as he knocked.

Berckman, Pelagius knew, was a notary by profession, a modest and ill-rewarded branch of the law, especially for a man just beginning his career. The size of the house alone revealed he was far from being prosperous. When Berckman opened the door, he was revealed as a lean, fair young man somewhat disfigured by a red birthmark stretching across much of his nose and left cheek, wearing the night-cap-like 'paternity bonnet' which the Dutch used to mark the dignity of new fatherhood, his face blank with astonishment at finding himself confronting a strange African looming out of the darkness. The small, bare, room behind him spoke of respectable near-poverty: it contained very little furniture, but there was a tall, carved walnut linen cabinet against one wall; a clear indication that the young couple cherished pretensions towards middle-class status.

'Dr van Overmeer?' Berckman enquired dubiously. The birthmark made his face hard to read, but his attitude spoke of caution and reserve.

Pelagius bowed in return, setting down his satchel, ignoring the obvious embarrassment of his host. 'Mynheer Berckman. I have brought you your foster-child and I am deeply obliged to you.'

There was a tapping of feet on the steep stairs and Susanna Berckman came down to make her curtsy. She was a large young woman, a little taller than her husband, neatly and simply dressed in a grey twill gown, with a low bodice laced up the front, worn over a plain linen smock which came up to her collarbones and ended in a simple band, with no ruff or collar. Looking at the splendid swell of her bosom, Pelagius found himself in no doubt that she would be able to feed two with ease. Surprise was written on her face also as she saw him, but her eyes travelled immediately to the burden he carried, and it was quickly set aside by simple interest in the child she had agreed to nourish. He bowed to her also and held forward the smelly bundle in his arms.

'Mevrouw, here is the child.'

She came forward shyly and took the baby from him, peering at him curiously and carrying him nearer to the single lighted candle they allowed themselves.

'He is very red,' she said a little doubtfully.

'That is not a sign of illness. His skin will darken. Remember, he is partly of my race.'

At that, both the Berckmans glanced at him simultaneously: sly looks from under the brows. The playwright's words came back to him again, the words of the shephered who took up the infant Perdita. 'This has been some stair-work, some trunk-work, some behind-door-work . . .', he could see some such thought in their eyes and deliberately stared back at them, his face cold and expressionless. It occurred to him to wonder whether Judoca had thought to mention that the child was partly African. From their reactions to him, probably she had not. They looked away, discountenanced.

'Well, let me get him comfortable,' said Mevrouw Berckman, after an awkward silence. 'Poor child, he has been long enough without care. What is your name, *schatje*?'

'His name is Balthasar Oranyan van Overmeer,' said Pelagius firmly.

'Balthasar, then. You want a change, don't you, little one?' She carried the baby off upstairs, and Berckman motioned stiffly for

Pelagius to sit down in one of the room's two chairs, pouring them both a frugal tot of genever.

Pelagius sat where he was bidden and fished in the inner pocket of his waistcoat. 'Here is a letter for you, from Mevrouw van der Myle.'

The little notary took it with a bow and moved the candlestick nearer, holding the letter under the light and reading it with great attention, his lips moving soundlessly. Once he was fully master of its contents, he looked up at Pelagius, his pale blue eyes unreadable.

'Tell Mevrouw Judoca we will ask no questions.'

All the same, questions hung in the room in a thick, buzzing cloud; Pelagius could feel them. He dreaded saying too much, but there were some points it was necessary to make clear. 'All I will say to you, Mynheer Berckman, is that in sending this child to you, Mevrouw van der Myle is fulfilling an obligation of her own. The boy was born in wedlock and he was not begotten in adultery or shame. The reasons why his mother cannot care for him are not dishonourable ones. You will oblige us infinitely if you make no further enquiry.'

Berckman bowed in assent. 'I did not think that Mevrouw van der Myle would dishonour my house, poor as it is,' he said, though it was all too clear that he had suspected no less, and perhaps still did.

Pelagius reached into his pocket again, and brought out a netted purse. 'Two hundred guilders for nurse's fee. If you accept this money, mynheer, you are bound in honour to nurture this child on the conditions Mevrouw van der Myle has made.'

Berckman's eyes were drawn irresistibly to the money in Pelagius's hand. Pelagius felt a momentary sympathy with him. Two years before his own life had been transformed with a bounty of a hundred and fifty guilders. He could see that the notary was in two minds about going back on his bargain, he also knew only too well what such a sum meant to a poor man. 'I accept,' said Berckman hoarsely.

Pelagius handed him the purse. Prudently, with none of the lordly trust which Pelagius had become accustomed to, he emptied it out on to the table, and counted the money. Only when all two hundred coins were neatly marshalled in piles of ten did he nod and seal the bargain with a sip of genever.

'What was our foster-child's name again?' asked Berckman. 'Balthasar –?'

'Balthasar Oranyan. His second name is one from my own people. Oranyan was the first king of Oyo and the child is a child of his lineage. The sword of Oranyan is held by each king of Oyo, one succeeding another down the centuries. Balthasar will do well enough for every day, but when he begins to understand I want him to know he is descended from kings.'

Berckman looked confused and might have said something, but before he could set his thoughts in order Susanna called down the stairs.

'Mynheer van Overmeer, would you like to come and see your son?'

In her simplicity, Susanna had assumed one thing which he had not said. He hesitated; half-thinking to disguise his relationship with the child, then abruptly changed his mind. He rose, and crossed the small room in two strides. 'Your permission, mynheer –?' Berckman nodded, and Pelagius mounted the stairs to the couple's bedroom.

Besides the bed, a simple one with plain serge curtains, the room contained a cupboard, a chest, a rush-bottomed chair and a wicker cradle conveniently adjacent to the bed itself. With the walls sloping sharply in on either side, there was room for little more. Susanna Berckman was sitting beside it with a rushlight in her hand and a pile of crumpled linen by her side, and the room was heavy with the smell of babies. As he advanced, he could hear Berckman coming up the stairs behind him.

'He nursed well,' Susanna reassured him. 'He is a fine, strong boy and well made. He has taken no harm.' Circumspectly, Pelagius came forward and peered into the cradle while she held the light for him. Two babies lay side by side, his own tiny son, with his red little face relaxed in natural sleep, and a slightly older child, pink-cheeked, with a tuft of blond hair. He looked anxiously for a likeness and failed to find one. The mouth, perhaps, was a little like Elizabeth's and the set of the eyes in the head, but in the wavering light it was hard to be certain.

'Well, no one will take them for brothers,' observed Berckman, who had come up beside him. Pelagius was absolutely unable to interpret the remark. Simply literal, jocular, or carrying a hidden resentment of the indignity his poverty had forced upon them? He would have had to know the man a great deal better to be able to tell.

He straightened up and looked at Susanna Berckman. 'I am sure you will care for him well, mevrouw. One final thing, before I go to find lodgings for the night.' Berckman looked a little alarmed as he reached into his pocket once more. 'Here is a trinket for you, a gift of thanks from Mevrouw Judoca.' She put out her hands, as simply as a child, and he dropped the gift into them. It was a necklace of flowers made of small turquoises and seedpearls, of no great value, but pretty enough in its way.

She looked down at the toy in her hands, her face lit softly, lips parted, as if she had glimpsed Paradise. 'Oh!' was all she said, holding it lovingly. She seemed to have been stricken dumb. He bowed to her, and to Berckman. 'I must go, mynheer, mevrouw. It is getting late, and you will need your rest.'

Berckman saw him down the stairs and bowed him out. It was dark and fairly cold outside. He spared a moment, walking briskly off in search of the friendly lights of an inn, to offer up a grateful prayer of thanks for the fact that the day had been dry and reasonably clement.

For all his physical weariness, he lay long awake, worrying about his son. The household was all that Judoca had promised, Susanna Berckman was a good, simple soul, sound as a nut, abundantly in milk, and kind-hearted. He could have hoped for no more. But there were aspects of Cristoffel Berckman's personality and, more specifically, his attitude towards his bargain, which stirred a vague disquiet. The child must stay where he was; the experience of getting him there had taught him that it would be foolish to think of moving him unless in direst emergency, while he needed what only a wetnurse could give him. All the same, he was not happy. He was haunted by the notion of the baby: if he had been in the same house, he would have got up and lit a candle to see his son and make sure he was still breathing. The women all seemed to think he was a fine child, but he was so tiny and fragile! Wretched and distracted, Pelagius turned to prayer and finally fell into an exhausted sleep.

The next day, he attended morning prayers in the Pieterskerk, and called on the Berckmans as soon as was decent. He found Susanna kneeling by the bed where Balthasar lay unwrapped on a towel, about to swaddle him, and he took the opportunity to look at his child in daylight for the first time. He was quite dark and the trace of hair on his little skull was black and curly, but the large eyes were like his mother's in shape. To Pelagius's anxious but inexpert eyes, he seemed to be as he should, without any obvious blemishes. He watched with interest as Susanna transformed him once more into a stiff little bundle: she swabbed the baby's buttocks with olive oil to protect him from his own ordure, and carefully tucked an inner napkin around his loins before binding his legs together and his arms to his sides. Then, when he was as straight as a doll, she wound another long linen strip around his whole body. The procedure was to him a mystifying one, though he knew it was customary, but he liked the way she handled the child, with decision and good will.

'There's my lovely boy', she murmured, tucking the linen firmly round him. 'How your mother could give you up –!' If there was a question implicit in her prattle, he thought it wisest to overlook it.

'How long will you bind him like this?' he asked.

'Three months. Then he will grow straight.'

Pelagius held his peace. There was no point in questioning the practice, when it was customary, and it was clear to see that it did no harm. He cleared his throat, and addressed her as soon as she looked up.

'Mevrouw Susanna, I will take my leave of you. I must return to The Hague, and report to Mevrouw van der Myle that all is well. I will return as soon as may be, to see how he does. If you have any cause for concern, please will you send word? Here is another ten guilders for the cost of a messenger: keep this money against need and if you ever have cause to use it, I will make sure you have more. The child is motherless, mevrouw, but he is not unloved.'

'Thank you, mynheer,' said Susanna Berckman, blushing a little as she took the money from him. 'He is a good boy and I will care for him like my own. If we have any cause, never fear that I will let you know.'

Elizabeth lay in bed, wishing that Pelagius would return. In the aftermath of her long ordeal, endured in stoic silence, she could feel the memory of pain gently leaching out of her abused body and remembered, with remote interest, that this had happened after each of her childbeds, as if the experience was somehow beyond the grasp of memory. She was heartily relieved that the baby was born and, as it seemed, the business managed so discreetly that no word had gone beyond the four walls of her bedroom. Though she was perfectly well aware in one corner of her mind that all her ladies knew of her state, she continued to cherish the illusion of complete secrecy. She had been assisted in her travail only by Judoca and the faithful Meg Broughton, who as the guardian of her most intimate toilette was hardly to be deceived about the change in her figure and other still more private matters, so had necessarily been taken into her confidence. Loyal to the core, Meg had maintained absolute discretion and had asked no questions, not even the identity of the clandestine husband to whom she had necessarily admitted.

The actual birth, fortunately, had been neither difficult, nor unduly prolonged. Worrying through the last months of her pregnancy, she had dreaded her first breech birth or some other such complication, which would have needed an experienced midwife, but in the event her body's natural facility for childbirth had been unimpaired by her advancing age and her last son had come into the world with no more than the inevitable pains.

She had been greatly relieved to see, also, that in the candlelight the baby was reddish, with a deeper hue only faintly discernible in the thin skin. Pelagius was as dark as mahogany and she had feared that the baby, as it came forth, would show its parentage to her dear Meg with embarrassing clarity. She was not ashamed of her marriage, but she was well aware of how it might look in the eyes of others. Fortunately, the baby had looked little different from the swarthy children of the Elector, and he had been taken to his father long before day could reveal his true colour. She stirred restlessly. He had been a pretty enough creature and in a purely animal way her body longed for him. She had never had any liking for babies, or patience with the details of their care, which she happily relinquished to others. Her children were objects of her loving concern from the moment of their birth, but she did not want to have them about her in the fetid intimacy of maternity. They became interesting to her once they walked and talked, and more so as they approached adulthood. But her body had another tale to tell, for the moment, in a way that was familiar: she felt shaky and inclined to weep and her breasts were aching and swollen, longing for a little mouth to relieve them. Judoca, who had breastfed her own children and believed firmly in doing so, was concerned lest the milk strike inwards and give her a fever, so she had made her a poultice for her breasts with lettuce and dittany, which was at least cooling. She wondered what the women had given out to the rest of the household to explain the comings and goings – a relapse, it might be, into her old chest trouble. Whatever they might be saying, there was nothing she could do about it; she would have to trust them. She composed herself to rest as best she could, holding the poultice against her sore breasts as she wriggled down the bed onto her back and tried to sleep.

On the twenty-seventh Pelagius returned. She questioned him minutely about the arrangements at Middelburg and was satisfied with what he had to tell her, though she had a sense that there was some reservation in his mind.

'Pelagius, what is troubling you?' she asked.

'I have never in my life wished so fervently I could be in two places at once,' he confessed.

'Do not worry,' she reassured him. 'I am the mother of strong children. From all you tell me, he is well placed and has all that he will need.' She could see from his face that he remained unconvinced and changed the subject.

'What news of the world? Have you seen Mr Dingley?'

'Yes. No news from France or Linz, but a little news from England. The Earl of Strafford is gone to Ireland, to raise an army for your brother against the Scots.'

Elizabeth sighed grimly. 'It is to be war, then, and I fear that Charles will find the Scots are pretty fighters.'

In the course of the week that followed Pelagius was astonished to find that Judoca had concocted a story of remarkable ingenuity. As he was excitedly told by a number of individuals, he himself had heard of a man from the Indies, newly arrived in Middelburg, who had with him some marvellous herb of the East sovereign against the dropsy. Without a moment's delay, he had flung himself upon a horse and galloped post-haste to possess himself of this treasure. He had returned with it in triumph and effected a wonderful cure. Her majesty's body had begun to void dropsical waters by the gallon and she bid fair to make a full recovery. Listening to this farrago, and cursing Judoca in his heart, he had never been more glad to know that Europeans found his face hard to read.

He found himself showered with embarrassing congratulations from all sides, including a personal note of thanks from the Princess of Orange and, more problematically as the story went its rounds, with wistful enquiries from sufferers asking if he could help them to a cure. His principles were entirely against lies of any kind, but in the circumstances he had no choice but reluctantly to commit himself to this patent nonsense, which offended both his moral sense and his intelligence, though it could not be denied that it solved the present problem. To well-wishers, he wrote brief and modest notes of thanks, firmly assigning the Queen's recovery to the will of God. To the dropsical unfortunates, he wrote with regretful courtesy to explain that the wonderful specific had been a compound called the Golden Pearl, known to the physicians of the King of Bantam, and he himself did not know how to make it. Only a single, precious dose had survived the voyage. He suggested that, in the absence of the Bantamese sovereign remedy, they might be relieved to some extent by foxglove tea, taken with caution, and given over if it produced any symptoms of dizziness or ringing in the ears. Thus, since he had read good accounts of foxglove as a specific, he hoped that he might be doing evil that good would follow and that God would forgive him.

His first thought and his last thought every day were of Balthasar. It was a source of endless regret to him that he had no one to speak to of his child. Judoca, whom in any case he did not like, patently regarded Balthasar as no more than a problem to be solved, and was no little pleased with herself to have solved it. Elizabeth, with her long experience of successful maternity, was not inclined to talk of the baby and shared his concerns only up to a point.

To his surprise, he found that the only person to whom his words seemed to mean anything was Dr Jonson, who questioned him eagerly about the child's appearance and health.

'He is healthy and red-skinned, you say? That is excellent. From the conjunction of the White Rose and the Black King, comes the Red King. In all the spagyric arts, vermilion is the colour of approaching perfection.'

'But Dr Jonson, the child is simply the colour that he should be,' protested Pelagius. 'I am black and his mother is white. His skin is between the two, according to nature.'

'To be sure. But as you of all men should know a thing can be at one and the same time a natural phenomenon and a sign. He was born on 25 March, which the chronographers tell us is the anniversary of the creation of the world and is also the date tradition gives to the conception of Our Lord. Those are facts, but would you not say that they also comprise an omen?'

Pelagius looked at him with barely concealed irritation. He had never been intellectually a wholehearted convert to Jonson's alchemic theories, but his intellectual misgivings were as nothing beside the doubts which assailed him now. To Jonson, Balthasar was fundamentally a symbol and perhaps, at some unimaginable future date, very much more. But whether the child had been born white, red, black or blue, to his father, he was now an individual, however helpless. He now found that it was with the child himself that he was concerned above all. Whether he was an instrument of the inscrutable purposes of God was still something for the future, but that he was himself a motherless and helpless baby was obvious and, for the time being, all that mattered.

What most dismayed him, in his new and overwhelming preoccupation with the child in Middelburg, was that Elizabeth did not share it. 'Can you not see, if Balthasar or his posterity becomes Emperor of the world, it will not be of our contriving?' she explained with infuriating reasonableness. 'It is not for us to make or unmake such things. We must do our best to keep him safe from harm and, above all, educated in religion. Beyond that we can do nothing but make sure he is well and fat. If God is to make something of him, He will do so. For now, I have business aplenty.'

Pelagius was seized by a moment of despair. He had never thought they could quarrel, but, staring at her in speechless distress, he knew they were perilously close to it. It was not indifference in her which distressed him so: he knew she cared for the child, as she had cared for all her children, it was merely her blithe relegation of his beloved son to a very small part of her overall concerns. The justice of her viewpoint was obvious: in the short term, there was little or nothing to be done but to wait, and in the meantime the fates of ten other living children clamoured for her attention. But while she was the mother of fourteen, living and dead, he was the father of one. Balthasar was infinitely precious to him.

In mid-April, when Balthasar was three weeks old, the Parliament opened in England. No sooner were the members in session than they began to shower the King with remonstrances against his policies. It was impossible even for Elizabeth, with all her experience, to see what the next turn of events might be. The news from England, faithfully supplied by Sir William Boswell, English Ambassador to The Hague, as it came in, was followed with breathless interest in the Wassenaer Hof. As the weeks crawled by, Elizabeth continued to vacillate between gloomy prophecies that her brother would declare war on his own subjects, and in more sanguine moments optimistic sketches of a future in which he came to a better understanding. As far as more immediate matters were concerned, it was evident by the end of April that she was completely restored to health. After four weeks of seclusion following the secret birth of her son, she resumed her active life, went to kiss all her old friends in The Hague and assure them of her complete recovery, and began to ride once more. But loving, frank, and friendly as she was, she gave no indication that Pelagius should return to her bed.

In the aftermath of her illness (as it was referred to in the household), Pelagius and Dingley had gone to see her together each day, to bring her the news and take her instructions. But at the beginning of May she sent Dingley to England. 'He is a relation of Sir Henry Wotton,' she explained to Pelagius on the day he left. 'Sir Henry, who is my very dear friend, is an old diplomatist, now provost of Eton. Between Windsor and London, I hope that my good Dingley will be able to come to a clear judgment of how matters are going between my royal brother and his people. I know many old and wise men who will speak to such a man as John Dingley what they would never write, even in cipher.'

She was looking well and the prospect of something to do had restored the clear-eyed vigour which she had temporarily lost in the long weeks mewed in her chamber. He looked at her, without replying: what she said was so self-evident it did not merit a reply. His focus was rather on the energy with which she had said it. He had not visited her bed since before Christmas; while he did not know what the customs were in Holland, it was clear to see that she had, in body and mind, emerged from childbed and was once again a woman. She looked a little older, but above all she looked her dear, indomitable self. He swallowed, looking at her mouth: his desire to kiss her so strong, that his tongue seemed to stick to his palate.

Emerging from his temporary trance of longing, he realized abruptly that she was reddening as she looked back at him, with tears forming in the corners of her beautiful eyes. Concerned, he got up to comfort her, but she raised a hand to prevent him.

'Pelagius, my dearest, I dare not.'

'But when?' burst from him. The old sympathy between them had reasserted itself; he understood her and knew she understood him.

'Oh, my dearest. I must not, in all conscience, not while I still have my courses. I know that now. You know I have always been sanguine, my beloved, and all my life I have acted before I think. My follies have given us Balthasar, and we may be truly thankful for him, since all went well. I know it was according to the will of God, and I can truly see His hand because we conceived him and I carried him and was brought to bed of him without anyone being the wiser. All the time I had a great belly, Pelagius, my heart was in my mouth, especially after Maurice came back to us. The girls are too innocent to know the signs, but I am sure that the boys are not. When we married, I did not think clearly enough about how it might be. I have never lived in such dread and, truly, I dare not risk another. It is not that I fear to hazard my body, but I fear for all the rest. We have more eyes about us, my darling. Maurice is back among his boon companions and he is jealous and hot-tempered. Ned and Philip are on their way and the Prince Palatine may soon be released. It hurts my heart to deny you, but the mother of a prince cannot toss away the world for love. We all live under necessity, my beloved, and my duty is clear.'

Bereft beyond description, he stared at her and she looked back at him, her topaz eyes candid and despairing. It was as if they were on either side of a glass. The truth and justice of what she said was beyond dispute, but he could not bring himself to assent. His had been a lifetime of patience, but all the bitter lessons he had learned were not enough to help him with that moment. When he could make himself move he went to her, careless of possible interruptions, and knelt before her in silence. He took her hand, warm and trembling in his, and kissed its fingers one by one. She sat as still as a stock, gazing at him, with tears rolling down her cheeks, but she remained silent, the air between them liquid and vibrating with love and regret. He felt tears standing on his own cheeks and looked straight at her.

'Get up,' she said, her voice low and quavering, 'you must not kneel to me. Oh, my darling. I wish I had died with Balthasar.'

He scrambled to his feet and stood before her, tall, frustrated and impotent. She looked up at him piteously and he saw her soft breasts rising and falling within the low circle of her black damask bodice. Unable even to say farewell, he stepped back so that he could bow to her and fled the room before he lost control of himself.

It was long enough before he was able to bring his mind to any semblance of calm. He prayed for hour after hour in his room, trying to use the familiar disciplines of worship to calm his mind, to no avail. God is a jealous god and, as he bitterly realized, he had set a degree of love on Elizabeth which should have gone to God alone. In his time of anguished grief and trouble, therefore, God turned His face from him, and there was no sustenance or help to be got in prayer. He did not go to dinner when the noon bell rang and when Gilles came to see if he wanted to practise his French, he sent him away.

The only thought which came to him in those long hours which was of any help at all was that it might be appropriate to consult Ifá. He got up and went to find his bag of oracle nuts, and his book. When he performed the divination, it led him towards oracle 118, which turned out to be one of a number of oracles which came in two parts.

> Ariba rubeus oraculum fecit
> pro Orí-Awo ex Omuko-epi.
> Dictum est: ut coronam parenti portet.
> Ergo, sacrificium feceret ut longaevus sit.
> Aurora oraculum fecit pro Adi.
> Adi Splendor Solis in matrimonium duceret.

Dicitur ut semper tremebundus est
In faciem uxoris ei.

Ifá had seldom been clearer. The first response related to a child; and filled him with happiness: Orí-Awo would wear the crown of his parent, so he should pray for long life. The oracle seemed, in its own way, to be confirming Jonson's thesis, arrived at on wholly other grounds. The second half, while not consolatory, was also helpful. It spoke of another person, Adi, who intended to marry the risen sun. The oracle merely advised him: if he did so, he would always tremble at the sight of his wife. The application to himself was obvious. He had chosen to marry the sun, so he must accept all that arose from such audacity. It held forth no answers, but at least it clarified his mind.

In the weeks that followed he decided that in his changed circumstances, since Elizabeth had less need of him, and they found it painful to see one another, he should at least follow her example and ensure that his other responsibilities were fulfilled. In the back of his mind, also, was a feeling that he would be wise to withdraw to some extent while Maurice remained in The Hague. It was plain that the boy, hasty-tempered and arrogant as he was, disliked him, in which he was perhaps prompted by some obscure instinct. He was anxious to minimize the occasions on which they met, lest despite Elizabeth's matriarchal authority, matters might come to a head.

With his wife's slightly puzzled assent, he decided to establish a household of his own at Middelburg, so that when Balthasar no longer needed the breast, he would have a home for him. She did not perceive any urgency in this while the child was still so young, but Pelagius himself was determined. He wanted the child to have a black servant to care for him. Balthasar's lineage on the mother's side must remain secret from him until he was old enough to have learned discretion, but at the same time he must be made to understand that he was a prince. Pelagius's own experience suggested to him that he would never convince any Dutch man or woman that it was possible to be both black and royal, and he wished Balthasar to be brought up by someone who recognized his rank. With that in mind, he began to look for a pair of servants of sound Calvinist principles, not obviously lung-sick, scrofular or syphilitic, of whom at least one was African by origin.

There was no shortage of black ex-sailors in the seaports of Holland, though black women were a considerable rarity. But the combination of black skin with sincere Christian commitment was considerably more difficult to find. After extensive enquiries, aided once more by Judoca van der Myle, he found a suitable couple. Narcissus had been born in Batavia, but was of Fula stock. His parents had been born in Senegal and had brought him up, so he knew a little about West Africa from their tales and he had heard of the kingdom of Oyo; he understood, therefore, who he was serving. His own history was an unlucky one. In his adolescence he had been a pretty and indulged page in a merchant's house in Amsterdam, where he had been passably well educated and instructed in religion, but his beauty had been destroyed in an accident when a set of bed curtains caught on fire. His face and hands were badly scarred and his injuries had left him with a slight limp, but he was not an invalid. Unwilling to be demoted to kitchen service, he had accepted a lump sum from his erstwhile employers and opened a modest chandlery on the Amsterdam waterfront. He had married a poor Dutch girl called Anna, a relationship which remained childless, and the pair had shown no great aptitude for business: Narcissus was clearly relieved by the prospect of abandoning his foundering enterprise and returning beneath another man's roof, and Anna, a prematurely aged girl with the eyes of a mistreated dog, was quite evidently abjectly grateful to know that a patron with powerful connections now stood between her and the prospect of starvation. Both so clearly preferred servitude to the risks and dangers of independence that temperamentally they were well suited to the role he had in mind for them.

Pelagius found himself a small, newly built house at the top of Spuistraat, not far from the Berckmans, and bought it for eight hundred and fifty guilders, using the money he still had from selling Comrij's plants and notes, the purse Elizabeth had once given him for scrying and money from Balthasar's store. Since it was new, he was at liberty to choose its name, and he called it 'De Derde Coninck': the Third King. As far as the citizens of Middelburg were concerned, the name would have an obvious reference to the Three Magi, but it also held a private significance in his own mind. The first two kings were Onfinran, his father, and James, Elizabeth's father. Balthasar was the third. The house had an attic, which he kept for himself, remembering wryly Mariken's attic at 't Groote Vis, and two floors, a first floor with two rooms, one for Balthasar in the fullness of time, and one for Narcissus and Anna, and a kitchen and keeping room downstairs. Though small, it was well built of good red brick and he was pleased with it. It cost him most of another thousand guilders to furnish it decently: he bought no silver, pictures or superfluities, but he bought a sufficiency of linen, delft, pewter, copper pots, kitchen stuff; decent, well-made things, good of their kind.

He was very preoccupied with the house through the rest of the spring and summer and went down to Middelburg as often as he could. He saw Balthasar frequently: the baby continued to flourish, and it was obvious that he was content with his foster-mother, who had become fond of him. Less happily, the man Berckman confirmed his suspicions by greeting the news that he was setting up an establishment for the child with ill-concealed relief. He was a narrow man, not likeable, and plainly resented the intrusion into his household, though Pelagius did not doubt that he would be honourable within the terms of his bond. He installed Narcissus and Anna in the new house in August and made sure that the two households became known to one another.

As far as the rest of Elizabeth's household in The Hague was concerned, Pelagius's increasingly lengthy absences from the Wassenaer Hof were explained by the news from England. In May Philip offered Charles four million ducats in return for a permanent guard of thirty-five English warships to convoy their transports through the Channel. With war in Scotland, there was no expectation on all sides that Charles would refuse, even though such an arrangement committed him to supporting His Most Catholic Majesty in a war against the Protestant League and threatened to plunge England into war with the Dutch. News from Amsterdam came readily enough, but there was much traffic between the English channel ports and Middelburg, and since it was so near Spanish territories much gossip to be had there; as things were going, it was understandable that Elizabeth should want a trustworthy, listening ear in that quarter.

Her personal affairs, to their joint relief, took a somewhat better turn. Ned and Philip returned to their mother in June, and in July he was delighted to be able to repeat a strong rumour that Cardinal Richelieu had set the Prince Palatine free at last. There was wild rejoicing at the Wassenaer Hof, though Elizabeth was a little dashed by the letter which came a week later from the Prince himself, which said that Charles I had refused to receive him in England, but Louis XIII suggested he would do well to stay awhile in Paris and he was 'not very unwilling'. Pelagius's heart ached for his wife, as she tried valiantly to seem neither upset nor insulted, and he began to conceive a definite dislike of this idolized child, whom he was yet to meet.

Apart from the return of the boys, the summer's news was almost universally bad. Over its course, the Baron van Heenvliet, working as that clever and able man had never worked before, succeeded in damaging the Spanish treaty beyond repair by ensuring that the ships to convoy Philip's soldiers would refuse to set sail: this he achieved by a clever combination of appealing to the sailors' Protestant sympathies, playing on their ingrained distrust of Spain, and offering the skippers substantial concessions from the Dutch East India Company. Elizabeth was profoundly relieved, from the point of view of a Palatinate partisan, though only too well aware that this left her royal brother committed to a war with Scotland which he could no longer afford.

The actual fighting began on 20 August, near Newcastle. Charles's forces suffered an immediate and overwhelming defeat; the Scottish General took Newcastle almost without opposition no more than ten days later. Charles Louis had returned from France earlier in the month, close-mouthed in defeat, and taken possession of the best bedroom besides Elizabeth's own, which was furnished in Palatinate blue. Elizabeth was angered and distressed by the spirit in which he received the news.

'I am not surprised,' said the Prince Palatine contemptuously. 'He cannot find a man to stand by him, except the papists, much good may they do him. He is not fit to rule England and his people are coming to know it, lords and commons alike. I have spoken with all sorts in my time in England. John Pym, the Speaker of the House of Commons, has sought me out, and I have been admitted to the counsels of godly, wise and sober men in the Parliament the King so despises. It is clear from all that they say that my uncle is a wittol. He is no more than a puppet in the hands of that painted dwarf, his Queen.'

Elizabeth looked at him with deep concern: they were sitting together in her closet. He was as good-looking as ever, well made, with a fresh, English complexion and something of her own turn of features. But his eyes had become narrow and wary at the end of this year of misfortunes, and the habitual expression of his mouth was a thin and bitter line. In some lights, his splendid youth deserted him and he looked like a sour old man; she remembered reluctantly that his brothers and sisters had nicknamed him 'Timon'.

'But my son,' she reminded him gently, 'he is still an anointed king. He is owed your respect. Do not speak of him so.'

Charles Louis raised his eyebrows, his expression sardonic. 'For how much longer? I will tell you a thing, mother, which Speaker Pym told me one day, when we were by ourselves. When Charles your brother was still in London, he came upon a window-pane with a writing on it, and shattered it with his own hand, but not before it was read. And what it said was, "God save the King, confound the Queen and her children, and send the Palsgrave to reign over us." There was a king once in Babylon, remember, who saw writing on the wall.'

Elizabeth stared at him, so aghast that her mouth was dry. 'Charles, my son, you must not seek to build on my brother's misfortunes! You have been eating his bread for twenty years.'

Charles Louis stared at her, his cheeks flushing with anger. 'Mother, we are not living in a romance of Arcadia! My uncle's difficulties are not misfortunes, they are mistakes. This is the wilful blindness of Pharaoh, rushing upon his own ruin. And would you not rather see me King of England than the papist brat of a French marionette?'

Elizabeth rose, took two strides across the room, and slapped his face, a blow delivered with the full vigour of her powerful arm. The impact resounded in the small room like a pistol shot and she heard his teeth clicking together as his head went back. Slowly, he rose to his feet, breathing heavily and glaring at her. His lip was bleeding, where his tooth had caught it, and she was very sorry to have lost her temper, though she stood her ground, straight-backed and undaunted.

After a long moment of silence, he stepped back and bowed with ironic formality. 'Good day to you, madam.' He turned and stalked from the room, slamming the door behind him. Elizabeth collapsed in her chair, her heart pounding.

They patched up their quarrel, but the underlying differences were not to be resolved. Elizabeth was forced to understand that there were elements in her beloved son's nature which were entirely foreign to her own, but he at least held himself aloof from the conflict: in her darkest moments she began to wonder if he might offer himself as commander in chief to the Scottish army and take arms against her brother in person. The news from England was of mutiny and desertion among Charles's conscript troops and ominously, given his reliance on Catholics, that in some places troops, if they suspected their officer of popery, had deserted or refused obedience. The degree of opposition to Charles's blind faith in Catholic help at home and abroad filled her with dread, since it gave ever more plausibility to the Prince Palatine's appalling idea that he might be welcome in England, a notion from which her judgment and her heart alike revolted. She made no attempt to discover what letters he sent; and was profoundly and unhappily aware that she was not in his confidence.

It was not that she ceased, in these long and dreadful months, to think about Pelagius or even about Balthasar. She knew the staunchness of Pelagius's love; throughout all the gnawing anxieties of her life, she felt herself gratefully sustained by his faith in her. But it hurt her to see him; she could not but remember that she owed him a debt, the debt of wife to husband, which she was unable to pay, a source of continuous heartache to them both, and also a niggling injury to her own honour. She had always detested being unable to give, and if there was ever to be a point where they fell into a state of sexless amity, it was clearly still far in the future. 'I see now why love is the business of the young,' said Elizabeth bitterly one evening, when the frustrations of their position were particularly acute and they were temporarily alone in the withdrawing room. 'They have time for it. It is misery to have a green heart and a grey head – I cannot give rein to my folly at my age. Even if it breaks my heart to be wise, I understand too much about consequences to let the heart have its way.'

Abstinence did not sour their love, but it marred it. The problem lay between them, resolved yet unresolved; an area of constant tension. At times even the meeting of their eyes seemed to provoke the whole mass of explanations, apologies and mutual reassurance to rise up and demand to be said over again, though in truth, there was nothing more to be said and considerable danger even in the saying. They hardly dared even to look at one another, lest their expressions betray them. She found herself looking at his hands because she could not look at his face, and knew that he did the same; in the agony of need she would pick a flower, smell it and touch it to her lips, then lay it down with apparent carelessness in the knowledge that he would pick it up; they each took care to cross one another's path, even, to catch the other's scent lying on the air.

It was easier, on the whole, when Pelagius was in Middelburg, though their letters had to be written with circumspection lest they fall into other hands. The Queen, like most of her court, was an avid reader of romances; and she had long been in the habit of referring to her family friends by nicknames, as an additional measure of security for her correspondence – the Prince Palatine was Timon or sometimes Tiribaze, dark Rupert was 'Robert le Diable', and the learned Elizabeth, 'la Greque'. In a similar spirit, the letters she exchanged with Pelagius made discreet reference to Joseph, a favoured prince who fell into slavery, and David because David was the father of Solomon: thus a mention, or a reference to either was understandable between themselves as a reference to Pelagius. Similarly, Elizabeth adopted the name of Candace, for the noble and valiant Queen of Ethiopia, and occasionally Pelagius would also speak of Adasobo, his own grandmother, who had ruled Oyo as regent when his father Onfinran had been a child. Thus they contrived to communicate in letters, which to other eyes would seem to say no more than was proper between a Queen and her physician.

But in some important sense Elizabeth began to feel that these letters were the last straw; that her whole life was spent on letters. She sat for hours each day in her closet, pen in hand, a veteran of thirty years of European diplomacy, still as active as ever she had been. As she had done since her marriage, and even more so since her widowhood, she collected stories and facts from all over Europe, she responded to the senders, passed on items of news to where they would do most good, advised, cajoled and informed, drawing on her formidable knowledge of personalities, locations, alliances, marriages and the myriad other factors which affected the decisions of the mighty. Her daily work was letters; all that she could do to help her children was to write yet more letters and, it bitterly occurred to her, now even her marriage was reduced to letters. How much easier, she thought, wearily composing yet another fruitless epistle to England, if she were in truth nothing but a writing hand and forty years' worth of experience and memories. Her body, her heart, were useless, and even positively dangerous, in this weary, endless struggle to explain and defend the Palatinate cause. She longed for Pelagius so much that she was more at ease when he was apart from her, the temptation visibly to lean on him was so acute.

XII

A Gyges Ring they beare about them still,
To be, and not seen when and where they will,
They tread on clouds, and though they sometimes fall,
They fall like dew, but make no noise at all.
So silently they one to th'other come,
As colours steale into the Peare or Plum,
And Air-like, leave no pression to be seen
Where e're they met, or parting place has been.

Robert Herrick, *Lovers How They Come and Part*, 1648

Two years later, in a dead haze of physical and emotional exhaustion, Elizabeth could still remember thinking like that. So much had gone wrong since then that, numb as she was, she felt a kind of wonder that the unacceptable could so easily become the ordinary then, as time went on, the life to which one looked back with a kind of nostalgia. Wearily, she set the cool heels of her hands in her eyesockets, covering her face and her hot, tired eyes, giving herself a moment of respite.

'Pelagius, my dear heart, I must write to Speaker Pym. My brother has nothing that he can spare for me and we must eat.'

'What would you have me say, my lady?' he asked, correctly secretarial as always. Only in the ultimate privacy of her bed did he abandon the formality of his address to her. They had not resumed their marital life in the ordinary sense; but in the previous year her fragile child Gustavus had died, and in her great distress following her bereavement, she had given way to Pelagius's insistence that he be allowed to comfort her. Not as a lover; sadly: they both understood only too well that as her world tumbled about her ears the risks were too great. But once the first vehemence of her grief had ebbed, they spent precious nights closely embraced, kissing one another with passionate affection, sometimes for hours at a stretch, but stopping short of the final act. Absurd, undignified, but a necessary indulgence without which she did not think that she could continue. As she nerved herself to the distasteful but necessary task of writing to the English Parliament, she hardly saw how she could have done without his silent presence.

'The address you have,' she said, giving herself time to think. 'Write it in English form, and when it is writ, begin, "Sir". Then a space. Then the meat of the letter – "I say nothing that you do not know, if I tell you that my affections are engaged on both sides of this conflict. But I must say to you and through you to the commons of England, that it is not just as a daughter of England I must come begging to the English people. It is well known on all hands that my life and all that is mine has been spent in the Protestant cause, and I need not recall to you that twenty years ago Parliament was to a man in favour of supporting the Elector's cause in Bohemia. You may also know that the learned and godly Dr Abbot, then the Archbishop of Canterbury, advised the Elector to accept the Bohemian crown as a religious duty. For all the weary years of his life the Elector never wavered from the divine commandment to serve God and His people which he assumed in those distant days, and since our defeat I have stood firm for the cause to the best of my poor ability. You need look no further than the late embassy of Prince Wladislaus for a sign of this – I have no husbands for my daughters, as you know, and I grieve for this as any mother might do, yet for the sake of religion, I refused his offer for the Princess Palatine."'

'Who was Prince Wladislaus, my lady?' asked Pelagius curiously.

'Oh, he was a prince of Poland. This is six years ago now, before you came to the court. He vowed that he would turn Protestant to get my Elizabeth, but his Council put water in his wine, and in the end he would not sign. Poor girl, she could have been a queen if things had fallen out otherwise. She has taken up philosophy, you know – she has some need of its consolations. I do not think she is entirely unhappy – oh, God help us all. But to our purpose. I must finish this letter. Go on: "Speaker Pym, for a quarter of a century, I have been, so men say, the emblem of the Protestant cause in Europe. In all these years I have not swerved or gone aside from the path which God has ordained. In asking that you should pay my pension, I ask for no more than justice. I am, etcetera." Have you all that?'

'Yes, my lady. I fear I must ask you to look at my spelling, lest I disgrace you,' he added apologetically.

'Oh, Pelagius, you do very well. If Dingley were not in England, I would not ask you to do this. But your hand of write is so beautiful, if I give but a moment to looking over your draft, you will write far better letters than I can do. Perhaps we should do them all together. Draft first, then I will look over your spelling, then perhaps after dinner you can make the fair copies. Put it on one side and begin another. I need to write to the Princess of Orange.'

'But surely you would rather do that in your own hand, my lady?'

'No', said Elizabeth firmly. 'I would have her remember my rank. We have been friends these many years, but when all is said and done she began as my waiting-woman. Things were well enough when she remembered it, but when she and the Stadhouder aspired to match their boy with the Princess Royal of England, then I saw she had come to a false understanding of her position. They should never have had Mary. I was glad enough to see my brother offer a daughter to the House of Orange, of course – if he had given them Elizabeth, it would have been an affront to Henriette, and a most welcome indication of a change of heart. But the match was too low for an oldest daughter, even if she had not been promised to my son. I cannot blame Amalia for doing what she could to bring this about, but she must know that I have not forgot and do not forgive. So I will write to her in the hand of a secretary and she will understand why. Begin with the address, and then "Ma chère Amalie". Princess she is not, and I would have her know it. "Ma chère Amalie, I hope that my niece continues well and in good spirits, but I desire to send you a warning in good time. The young Prince of Orange was most sweetly the little husband when I last saw the children together, so have a care to keep them apart. It is a sad thing if in marriages of state, the boy and the girl discover an aversion to one another, but if they fall in love, you may have difficulties of another sort. The Princess Royal reads romances, she knows that she is a wife, and for a mere younker your son woos most prettily. But she is still little and narrow. If you would see healthy children of her body, then exercise a wise severity, keep her by your side, and forbid your son her company until she is full grown. If she falls into the pouts for want of occupation, since she is lazy by nature and not greatly drawn to her needle or her book, let her play with your own little ones. It will accustom her mind and body to the use of babies, and allow her to pass pleasant enough hours without putting her in peril."'

'Is that the end of the letter?' asked Pelagius.

Elizabeth sighed. 'Perhaps not. Continue, with another paragraph. "My news from England is none of the most recent, or I would share it with you. I have had no word from Rupert and Maurice since they left England, and of the Prince Palatine, I know only that he is deep in the councils of Secretary Pym. The Queen of England, I believe, is still in The Hague: some of those that visit her come also to kiss my hand, but they disclose nothing of their business, and I do not ask what is not willingly told. She has had little luck with the diamond merchants, for they will not venture on pieces so valuable. My dear Amalia, I do not advise, but if I were in your place, I would not be instructing my jeweller. It is the crown jewels of England that she is cheapening; and I do not know that in law she has title to sell, even as the agent of the King. The Jews, I think, are of the same mind, and are giving her wares the go-by." – It is monstrous,' she burst out angrily, breaking off her dictation. Pelagius laid down his pen, and listened. 'Her mother was a Medici – it must be bankers' blood coming out in her, that she has shamelessly set up her stall like a market woman. It makes me sick to think of the treasures of the old Queen and Henry her father, and my father's own jewels, pawed over by the greasy hands of merchants.'

'But surely it is not folly, but necessity?' commented Pelagius. 'The Spaniards were to give your brother four million ducats for the use of his ships and he has not got the money because Ambassador Heenvliet spoiled the bargain. He must surely be wondering where the money for this war will come from.'

'Of course,' retorted Elizabeth, 'and if I look into my heart, that is precisely why I am so savage against Henriette. It is the fact that she is selling the royal jewels which tells me war is certain. He still cannot afford to make war, of that I am sure, but if he has this money in his grasp he may imagine that he can. That is why I seek to spoil Henriette's chaffering. If my brother's pockets are empty, he may be forced to think what he is about. Oh, it is a sorry tale. I cannot bear to think of it. Where was I?'

'"Give her wares the go-by", my lady.'

'Put a line through it, and through what comes before. I will tell Amalia to her face, but on second thoughts I do not want those words on paper. Stop after "I do not ask", then I will end it and sign it in my own hand.'

Pelagius made a note of what she wanted and added the draft page to the pile of letters for fair copying.

'Can you bear another letter?' she asked. 'We still have time before dinner.'

'Of course. Your majesty, I live to serve you.'

'Oh, Pelagius.' She looked at him properly and he raised his dark eyes from his work. They were alone because of the confidentiality of her correspondence; there was nothing to stop them from reaching out to one another and setting the world at defiance. Nothing but their own wills, duty and honour, the hard lessons of their savagely disciplined lives. Someone might come in at any moment; and they could not afford to forget it. All they could do for the moment was to look.

The moment prolonged itself until Elizabeth raised her hand a little, an all but involuntary protest. At once Pelagius dropped his gaze and she shivered a little, as if she was coming out of a dream. 'I had better write to Charles Louis. Begin, "My dear son".'

Pelagius waited, pen poised, for the dictation to begin, as the Queen sat, her face blank and slack with exhaustion, unable to continue. An appreciable space of time passed while she collected her weary thoughts. 'This will have to be cyphered,' she said suddenly. 'I cannot be sure that he will be the one to read it. Address it to Essex House, London, which is the last direction I had from him. Begin, "I send this in hopes that it will come to you. My son, I beg you on my knees to remember the commandment of Samuel: touch not the Lord's anointed. You dwell among men who are leagued against the king your uncle. They offer you fair words and seem to offer help, but trust them not. You know the Italian proverb, those who are kinder than usual either have betrayed, or will betray us. When you receive kindness from men who are your natural enemies, look for the serpent beneath the leaves, and remember: you are of kingly stock. To raise a hand against an anointed King in his own country is not merely to threaten him, but to threaten yourself, the memory of your father and the due order of the state. God knows I do not defend all my brother's actions, but in defending his right to act, I defend myself and you. It is your nature to be politic, my son; be true to it and look further than tomorrow and the next day. The men you are with will use you and destroy you, if they can, and they are not fools or simpletons – Secretary Pym is a man to be feared, and the best of those who follow him are men of stature and principle. If you can leave them with honour, do so, and in any case do not engage yourself further. My beloved son, I well understand your impatience. I was no patient creature, when I was twenty-five. It is time and adversity which have taught me to watch and wait – do not waste the lessons of my life. It is not as merely a mother that I advise you." I think I will end there. All that must be in cypher, then I will finish the letter with a postscript in my own hand. What is the time?'

'It is still half an hour to dinner, my lady.'

'Well, since I have written to the Prince Palatine, I had better write to Rupert. After the usual salutations, begin in this way. "My dearest Rupert, I was very angry with you when you left for England, and I am angry still, but I would not have you go into danger thinking that I do not care for you. It was like your knight-errantry to go to the side of your uncle and support him in his need, but it was also rank folly, when the Venetian Ambassador had said there was a place for you in the armies of the Doge. Once your word of honour was committed I would not have had you go back, but remember, there can be no true honour to be had in fighting your own countrymen, whatever their follies, whereas making war against the enemies of Christendom would win you renown, and at the last, perhaps, the name of hero. Of the promise extracted from you by Henriette I will not speak; but I will say to you, guard yourself in future against her designs. Make no more promises to she-Jesuits, but hold your tongue and do your duty. Look after Maurice. He has been your shadow all his life and he will be governed by you when he will listen to no one else. I pray for you both nightly."'

'Will you end the letter there, my lady?' asked Pelagius. 'Surely you might also add that he is making your own position extremely difficult?'

'I might, but I will not,' said Elizabeth firmly. 'His honour is committed, so there is nothing to be done.'

Pelagius nodded and completed the last sentence, putting the letter in the pile to be cyphered. The noon bell would strike before long; there was no point in beginning anything else. As he sat, with pen still in hand, his sensitive ears caught a sound. Or was it even a sound? It was, perhaps, an atmosphere of consternation which seemed to be rising towards them like the smell of smoke. It was a noisy and disorderly house, where servants quarrelled on the stairs and little if anything was done quietly and in due season, but the door of Elizabeth's closet was thick and well fitting, insulating her from the affairs of her household. There seemed to be nothing more than the usual faint intimation of domestic bustle coming through to them, but sensitive as he was, he found his gut suddenly clenching with apprehension.

'What is it?' said Elizabeth, alarmed, observing his tensely listening posture, picking up the contagion of fear. He did not answer her; straining with all his senses to perceive what might be coming towards them. It was a relief to them both to hear a light knocking at the door. Lady Dohna entered, her pretty face strained and anxious, and held the door open; a moment later, John Dingley appeared in the gap, weary and mud-stained, still wearing his riding boots and cloak, and bringing with him a heavy odour of horses, sweat and wet wool.

'What is it?' she asked again.

Dingley swept off his hat and bowed formally, his tired, sharp little face compassionate. 'Your majesty, three days ago, King Charles raised the Royal Standard at Nottingham. He has declared war in England.'

'Where are my sons?'

'Rupert and Maurice are with him. The Prince Palatine is in London.'

'It is ruin,' said Elizabeth blankly. 'No one can win this war. There will be destruction upon destruction and nothing to be gained.' The bell for dinner began to ring, startling them all. The Queen rose to her feet, straightening her back. 'We must go down,' she said firmly. 'Mr Dingley, you have travelled far and you must eat.' She went over to her exhausted secretary and, filthy though he was, smilingly put her hand on the arm which he had not dared to offer, so that he could escort her down the stairs. As Pelagius fell in behind them, with Lady Dohna pacing silently by his side, his heart jolted with admiration at her indomitable grace.

He was half-way down the stairs, when he thought of Balthasar. Suddenly he was beset with nightmare visions. What would be the wider effects of this conflict – would the Netherlands be drawn in, willy-nilly, the Stadhouder bound to support the father of his son's bride? Would the Cardenal Infante cross the Scheldt, with the Dutch thus distracted? But a second thought came to his assistance: the navy had been in the hands of Parliament since June; from Elizabeth's and her brother's perspective, a disaster which lengthened the odds against the King to an agonizing degree, but to him a blessing, since it was vastly less likely that the Parliament would involve either the Dutch or the Spaniards in their quarrel, with consequent risk of the war coming to Middelburg. All the same, the possibilities were terrifying. He was desperately anxious to question Dingley, but he would have to wait.

Moving in due order, the quartet entered the hall. Elizabeth's immediate entourage, assembled according to rank at the high table, were pale and grim-faced, in ironic contrast to the servants and parasites in the body of the hall, merrily oblivious to all that went on beyond the fringes of their own small lives. Elizabeth seated herself with grace, Dingley at her side, and quietly engaged him in conversation. Like nearly everyone at table, Pelagius drank a little more than usual and ate hardly anything. The ever-present dogs stirred beneath the table and whined softly, sensing the unease in the air. Pelagius sipped his wine and watched, his private thoughts in a turmoil which he was well able to conceal. For once, he need make no pretence of not watching Elizabeth: all along the table every face was avidly staring at the Queen, trying to guess all they could of the shape of the approaching calamity. Three glasses of Rhine wine had brought a more natural colour to Dingley's face. Elizabeth, it was clear, was scientifically extracting every scrap of information the man possessed; she had barely made a pretence of disturbing the food on her plate. From their looks as they conferred, heads together, none of the news was good.

The day wore on, wretched and indecisive. Elizabeth closeted herself with Dingley, while Pelagius made fair copies of the morning's letters and cyphered the letter to the Prince Palatine, wishing he were with her. The work at least allowed him to keep his sense of helplessness and humiliation at bay. It was at such times that he most bitterly resented the secrecy of their relationship – he longed to be with her, not only in order to stand by her side and offer what help he could, but also because his own interests and, above all, those of Balthasar, were also affected by the news from England. It was unfortunate, he reflected, that she had not been able to look over his spelling. He thought briefly of asking one of her English ladies to help him, but devoted though they were he rejected the idea: it would not be appropriate to show her private correspondence to anyone, so the most formal of the letters, that to Secretary Pym, he rewrote into Latin, a language in which he could trust himself.

Supper was an even more wretched affair than dinner had been. Elizabeth and Dingley did not appear at all, and those who did ate swiftly and distractedly. Even the boors in the body of the hall seemed a little subdued, as news seeped gradually through the network of gossip. When the household settled down for the night, Pelagius did not go to bed, but lit a candle and sat up in his black dressing gown, reading the most recent of the Diurnals to have come over from England, trying to gauge the mood of the country. As he fully expected, he heard a soft knocking at his door an hour or so after the household was still. He snuffed the candle and set forth, silent-footed, to Elizabeth's bedroom.

He let himself in and locked the door behind him, then joined her in bed. She was lying on her back, staring up at the canopy. When he put his arms round her and kissed her forehead, he found that she was not tearful, but tense-muscled and, as it seemed, almost excited. He could sense that she was thinking as hard as she could and had been for hours. Yet he knew how tired she must be: if she did not sleep, she would make herself ill. In this extremity, it was obvious that he must do all he could to help her. He settled companionably against her and prepared for a conference.

'How bad is the situation in England? Can your brother look to any foreign power for help?' he asked baldly.

'Where?' said Elizabeth immediately. He allowed himself a moment of self-congratulation that he had guessed her mood accurately, then concentrated on what she had to say: this was what he most wanted to know. 'He will get no help from Holland. Even if the Stadhouder wished it, the States-General would not aid so declared a friend of Spain. And Spain itself will not move to assist him because he is Protestant and has married his daughter into the House of Orange. I fear he has reaped the reward of all vacillators, which is rejection on every side. He might have looked to France, but there Henriette has wrought his ruin.'

'Why so? She is sister to the King. Surely he will want to help her?'

'She is also the blindly faithful daughter of that monstrous woman, Marie de Médicis. Her mother hated Richelieu, so she has always hated him in her turn and intrigued for his overthrow.

Now the Cardinal rules in France in all but name, since Louis lets him make and unmake policy. Heenvliet tells me that she has appealed to him and he will not listen to her pleas for help, which does not surprise me in the least. I have long thought that Henriette might bring Charles down at the last. She is a woman of no judgment.'

'What do you foresee, my darling?' he asked.

He felt her shoulder move against him as she shrugged. 'I cannot tell. Charles has no money to pay mercenaries and is not like to get any. I do not think that the war will go beyond the seas, since I cannot see that anyone will aid my brother. In any case, Parliament blockades the sea – Rupert was fired on when he went over, but his vessel outran the pursuit. As for Parliament itself, no European power will support a people against their anointed King. It will be a war of the English against the English, with the Irish and the Scots making what hay they can. My best hope is that it will be short. There are level heads and men of good will on both sides, and once the nation has let a little blood, perhaps their counsels will prevail. Surely, for all the calling of names, all but the rabble must understand that this is a ruinous course they are on?'

'Men at war do not always see so clearly, my dearest one,' observed Pelagius sadly.

'Ah, yes. That is true enough. But when it is his own house that is sacked, his own fields trampled and torn, even the boldest man of blood may stop to think a little. Most of the gentlemen's sons will be with my brother and that means that his cavalry will overmatch anything which Essex can put into the field. My hope is for a swift and crushing victory in battle, which will allow Charles to show himself magnanimous. Even he must know that his forces are not equal to annihilating the Parliament men, and even if they were, it would be foolish to destroy so much of the power and wealth of his own country. Surely he will seek an understanding with them, once he can do so from a position of dignity.'

'Do you think this will happen?'

'I do not know. But it is what I pray for. If God would only permit Henriette to drown on her way home, I would think it the more likely. Her counsel is always for war and my brother trusts her absolutely.'

As they talked, she had begun to relax; he could feel her softening against him. The tone of her voice was losing its nervous vibrancy and becoming merely sad. When her voice tailed off he did not reply, but stroked her cheek; she reached up for his hand and held it tightly.

'My darling, you must sleep,' he said, as softly as he could.

'I think I could sleep now,' she confessed, 'if you hold my heart.' He thrust his own sexual frustration resolutely out of his mind and kissed her in answer, wriggling into the posture which calmed her even in deep distress; lying behind her so that she was snuggled into the long curve of his body, his right arm round her, holding her firmly with his hand flat against her chest, wedged under the heavy breasts. He could feel the painful, spasmodic rhythm of her heartbeat, and knew that to her perception it was as if he was helping her heart in its labour. Its rhythm gradually calmed and slowed under his hand, and as it slowed her breathing became quiet and even. She was all but asleep, trusting as a child, and he thought again of Balthasar. Holding her thus, his cheek against her hair, profoundly alert to her whole breathing humanity, his love for her welled up until it made him almost dizzy. 'I married the sun,' he recalled, half-dozing, 'I must take the consequences.' He did not regret his bargain, painful as it was.

After he had achieved a good reading knowledge of the English tongue, Dingley had once shown him a poem written by his kinsman Sir Henry Wotton in honour of Elizabeth, a gesture of friendship, perhaps, or a gentle intimation of the nature of his own claim on her attention. In either case, the poem had remained with him, because it chimed with the words of Ifá, and because it expressed what he felt.

> You meaner beauties of the night,
> That poorly satisfy our eyes
> More by your number, than your light –
> You common people of the skies;
> What are you when the Sun shall rise?

For all the difficulty of his position, he had no regrets whatsoever. He had never had any great expectations of earthly happiness; that he loved, and was loved in return, seemed to him a fact extraordinarily beyond anything he could expect. He did not have the ordinary rights of a husband, but in the hand and heart of Elizabeth he had something far beyond them. The frustration and secrecy which marred his marriage were hard to bear, but not impossible for one so trained in renunciation and silence. And there was a world of difference between the willed self-discipline of a free agent, and the dreadful, blank repression of his erstwhile existence as a slave. He suffered and caused suffering in his beloved wife, but he did so as a continuous act of moral choice; something which his life had taught him to value in itself.

Like all other news which came to The Hague, the news of the war in England was, after the initial shock, gradually absorbed and accepted. To Elizabeth, what was most disturbing, in a way, was that in the town nothing seemed to have changed. At the Binnenhof the Stadhouder's court continued its stately round of levées, audiences and entertainments. As the year wore on to its close, the stout merchants and their stouter wives walked arm in arm beneath the lime trees to enjoy the air in the slanting, golden light of the late autumn afternoons, escorted by little pages;

fashions and foreign artists came and went, each a sensation in its turn, indifferent to the protracted agony of England.

Elizabeth began to feel doomed to continuance. The merchants of The Hague continued to give her credit despite her reduced income; the children continued to go their own ways and the news to get worse. Something in her nature longed for a final catastrophe, but all that there was was day-to-day endurance. And Pelagius. She saw him every day and he was the fixed point in her life. He had once spoken of her as his rock, she remembered. In this time of anguish, it seemed to her that their roles had been reversed. He was confident that she and her children would survive this calamity. 'But in what world?' she cried, in one of their precious midnight conferences. 'What will the world be like when this war is over?'

'My darling, that we cannot guess. But you will live, Charles Louis will live, Rupert will live. Ifá has said so. The only child too tender-hearted to survive these times is gone.' He was referring to Gustavus; the mention of him brought the tears welling up again. In those days she seemed to do nothing but weep, until she wondered if, like Niobe, she would turn to a statue of salt and a river of tears.

It was not until December that Pelagius was able to detach himself sufficiently from the urgencies of the Wassenaer Hof to go down to Middelburg. The king was established at Oxford, Rupert and Maurice at his side; the Prince Palatine had seen fit to denounce them. Another in the endless litany of toilsome episodes in which he must strengthen his wife to endure what her children did in the world. But the faithful Dingley was back in The Hague as secretary, and Elizabeth was in a state which made it possible for him to harden his heart and leave her. He had not been able to resist calling on Judoca's good offices to send a discreet messenger to Middelburg the day after Dingley's return from England; when the man came back to The Hague he was able to assure his anxious questioner that life in the Zeeland capital was undisturbed by the political convulsions across the channel; and moreover that Balthasar could now stand up by himself and say 'Da'. The money he had left with Susanna should ensure that, if the situation changed, he would receive news as quickly as possible, but all the same he longed passionately to see his son.

Now he would see Balthasar within the hour; he was impatient for the moment. It was turning very cold; as he sat huddled in the boat approaching the Dam, muffled to the eyes, he felt the cold air searching insidiously between his hat brim and the folds of his cloak, bringing a raw ache to his cheekbones and nose. But as the skipper ran the little *jacht* expertly into its mooring, he realized guiltily that he was happy. Surprised at himself, he turned his attention inwards, to examine his innermost heart. Mechanically paying off the skipper, disembarking and walking along the outer line of the city wall towards his own quarter, he bent his attention on his own state of mind, and this process of self-examination forced him to acknowledge the unexpected fact that, from a purely selfish point of view, he had been most strangely rewarded by God. The bizarre upheavals of his life over the previous three years, which had taken him from desperate poverty to the life of a royal servant and a secret marriage with the Queen of Bohemia, had most ironically left him, in one half of his life, as a respectably middle-class citizen of Middelburg with his own house, two servants, a son who looked likely enough to live and a modest medical practice which gave him an income to keep them on. The only private dream he had ever permitted himself, his theological work, and his hoped-for career as a preacher, he had abandoned without compunction for the sake of his wife and his son. The difficulties and anxieties which beset him sprang from the things it had never occurred to him to want at all – earthly love, which now occupied the centre of his being and earthly power: an adored wife he hardly even dared to look at, and a life in the eye of the storm of European politics, in perpetual fear of a discovery which would bring disaster and disgrace precisely where he most wanted to bring honour and assistance. In all of which he realized once more the profound ironies of the Lord. The moment of happiness floated away, disallowed.

He despaired of his own cold-heartedness. It seemed a kind of falseness in him that he could be happy at such a time. But while he shared all he could with his beloved Elizabeth, and sympathized profoundly with her anguish for her sons, the conflict did not touch him personally and if it did not spread overseas, which seemed unlikely, it would never do so. He had no feelings of his own for England, a country he had never visited, and no personal affection for the Prince Palatine, Rupert, or Maurice, all of whom had on occasion bored, annoyed or even insulted him. He was therefore anguished only vicariously, and for Elizabeth herself.

The early dusk of December was already falling, though it was not long since the town clock had chimed three. The cobbles beneath his feet were armoured in slippery ice and there was a freezing mist lying on the channel. As he looked down from the city wall, its foot was invisible, lapped in bluish-white, as if the city had been carried up above the clouds. The wind on his face was cold, with a prickle of icy moisture, and his earlobes began to ache. Huddled in his cloak, he walked along the wall towards the Veere gate, looking out over the water. The wind was blowing from the west, from England, and as he looked out, he saw it was bringing with it filmy veils of drifting snow, which slanted down to dissolve in the grey water. The brackish, rime-cold channel moved sluggishly under the veil of slush, not far off freezing. It was on such a winter's evening of bitter cold and light snow, he recalled suddenly, that he had first met Elizabeth three years before. How much had changed in that time, for him and for all Europe.

It was a bad winter. Somewhere across the Narrow Seas, Elizabeth's three oldest boys were all lying under arms, probably in the snow: if Middelburg had been further inland, it would certainly have been snowbound. He grieved for them impersonally; though none of the boys had endeared themselves to him, they were young and fierce and brave, and whatever happened defeat lay in store for one or more of them: he suspected it would be Rupert and Maurice. His own prayer was that, whatever else happened, Charles and Rupert would not actually meet in the field and break Elizabeth's heart.

As he walked, pacing deliberately under the snowladen wind in the gathering dark, the lullaby which Susanna liked to sing to Balthasar and her own Jan came into his head:

Zwarte zwaan, witte zwaan,
Zullen wij naar Engeland varen,
Engeland is gesloten,
De sleutel is gebroken.

'Black swan, white swan, both of them to England gone, England's lost and locked away, there is but a broken key.' It was an old song, with a wistful tune, and Susanna had, perhaps, been additionally attracted to it because she had both a black and a white child to tend. In the weary nights in which Balthasar had fretted for his foster-mother, Anna had often sung it to calm him. It was strangely apposite in the present crisis; the idea that the key to England was broken seemed as good a way of expressing the truth of this ineluctable war as any other.

Thinking of Elizabeth's sons and their own baby, he was struck once more by the terrible disjunction between any parents' hopes and intentions and the lives their children would come to lead in the chaos of their times. In his days as a student, he had recognized this intellectually and deduced from it the logical next step, which was to place his hopes entirely on God. But now, enmeshed as he was in the bonds of human love, he understood at last something of the true horror of the world. It seemed to him suddenly that for men and women to love one another and beget children was a sort of deliberate blindness or obtuseness, something as ignorant as the growth of a plant: it was as unlikely that any one couple's hopes for their child would be fulfilled as that any particular seed would find its way to fertile soil. The songs of his own people came back to him, statements of faith in loving and begetting: 'Oh, how sweet is the touch of a child's hand', 'A child is precious like coral.' He knew the truth of them when he held Bathasar in his arms. And, furthermore, beyond his boy's preciousness for his own sake, he still held in the secret depths of his mind Jonson's dream that the child was the new hope of the world.

But now, with disaster crowding on them all from every side, he was beset by an appalled perception of the uncertainty of things. When Charles Louis was an infant in Heidelberg, as Balthasar was now, what future could his young mother have guessed for him? Not in her darkest moment could she have imagined that at twenty-five he would be lying under arms in an England at war with itself, leagued against his own uncle. His adored Balthasar was the vessel of all his hopes for the future, but he found himself visited by a profound and melancholy perception that, however passionately he loved the child, they would never have much in common: for all that he could do to prepare him for his destiny, this grandson of two great kings was no more than a Dutch boy-baby, growing up with Dutch lullabies in his ears in a small house in Middelburg. It was impossible, at the moment, to see how he could have anything but a small, frugal, ordinary Dutch life, though Ifá suggested otherwise. Who would Balthasar be, at twenty-five? Where would he be? What experiences would have shaped him? He hoped fervently that the working out of the child's destiny, however it might be contrived, would be less painful than his own; but even as he hoped, he knew in his heart that this prayer would not be answered.

Pelagius came down from the walls and turned up the Breestraat towards home: the snow had eased off with a temporary surcease in the wind, but it was getting very cold and dark. Threading through the narrow streets with the skill of long familiarity, he caught, from the corners of his eyes, momentary pictures of the domestic life of Zeeland, glancing through well-polished windows into small, clean rooms where the candles had just been lit. A child, kneeling with his face in his mother's lap, while she sat beside the fire and patiently rummaged his scalp for lice. An elderly couple, she apparently all but asleep, but knitting swiftly with the automatic skill of a lifetime, while her old husband puffed on his pipe. A woman making *poffertjes* over the fire while her children clustered about her, waiting their turn for the treat. Besides the sadness which was his permanent companion, he felt an immense sense of charity towards the accidents of life; all these Dutch people, in their neat little houses, striving in ignorant hope to live as best they might. All that he saw were scenes of absolute domestic peace. But next day, next year, these chaste and contented *vrouwen* might be screaming beneath Spanish soldiers; their men dead face-down in the streets, with half the town in flames. Nothing was certain.

When he got home, he looked through his own window before knocking on the door. In good Dutch fashion, the shutters were still open. Narcissus was sitting on a stool by the fire and seemed to be telling a story, probably one of his many stories of Anansi the spider, which they all enjoyed: the scarred face was inexpressive, but his hands and body were moving eloquently. Anna was not immediately visible, but Balthasar was there, toddling about in a blue linen smock, his solid little body tacking erratically back and forth across the floor on some mysterious errand of his own. Pelagius smiled to himself to see him and knocked on the door. On his entrance Narcissus sprang to attention and a flustered Anna appeared in the doorway to make her curtsy, bringing with her a strong smell of onions and winter cabbage, while Balthasar, intent on the adventure of setting one foot before the other, ignored him completely. He picked his son up, regardless of his indignation, and kissed him. He was becoming a very pretty child; his skin richly amber and his dark eyes almond-shaped under well-marked brows, like Elizabeth's own to an extent which was almost comical. His cheeks and mouth were shapely, and he seemed to have escaped the long, aquiline nose which, Elizabeth had once told him, she had inherited from her mother and passed on to most of her children. Balthasar, resenting his father's scrutiny, squirmed away from his death-cold lips and pushed him off: Pelagius set him back down, amused by his independence. The storm was rising again; flurries of snow spattering the window, hurled there by the wind as if by an invisible hand. He went to close the shutters, barring out all that might blow from England that night.

'I am glad to see you all,' he told Narcissus and Anna. 'I can see that Balthasar is well and happy. I will ask for your news later, but first I must go upstairs to work. Do not make any special preparations, but leave me a little of what you are eating yourselves.'

The last duty of the day was to write a letter. He sat at his desk in the freezing attic, lit a candle and prepared a fair sheet of paper, addressing it in his most beautiful italic hand, with deliberate care, and long, well-drawn arabesques on the 'M' and 'B' of the superscription.

To Her Sacred Majesty, the Queen of Bohemia,
te Wassenaer Hof
het Voorhout
s'Gravenshaage
December 1642

My beloved wife,

I have heard a little news out of England from the captains and fishermen as I came down. It seems to drift from dark to darkness, and I hope most devoutly that better tidings have come to The Hague. Would that I could write as you would wish, and as you deserve, of the halcyon days of a world made new. I fear that this letter will fall on your ears like the croaking of an old black crow; but I am afraid, my Elizabeth, afraid and sad. Only death could deafen my ears to you, my Queen, my sister, my beloved Candace, but as the mist comes from the sea in this bitter weather, I know that I will die here and be buried in this cold country where I have lived a stranger.

I have thought much since I left you, my darling, about the sweetness which you have brought to my life. I was trained from a child in the paths of duty, not pleasure: I have been wary and prudent. And once I had come to God, I fixed my hope on the world that is to come. I did not understand how it was permitted to me to be so happy: our God is a jealous God, and I come near to setting you as an idol in my heart. Yet I know, also, that we do His purpose and His will.

The child grows and flourishes, I see in him some of your own beauty. He has the wilfulness of his tender youth, but I hope that he will be humble and walk uprightly before the Lord.

My darling, if we are to see one another no more in this world, we will meet before the Throne. Set me as a seal upon thy heart, for love is stronger than death.

Pelagius laid down his pen and read the letter through carefully, more than once, then held it in the flame of the candle, watching it until he was sure it had caught alight and was consuming itself utterly. Taking a fresh sheet of paper, he began again.

To Her Sacred Majesty, the Queen of Bohemia
te Wassenaer Hof,
het Voorhout,
s'Gravenshaage
December 1642

Most honoured and noble lady:

Magister Pelagius van Overmeer presents his respects and begs to be remembered to her Sacred Majesty. There is a little news of the Prince Elector here: I am told that, anxious for the Protestant cause, he has spoken against those who support H.M. of England in his ventures.

He begs leave to inform Her S.M. that she is ever in the memory of her humble and most devoted friend, and also to tell her that the son of David, who dwells in this city, flourishes and promises well in that he resembles his mother. He looks forward to the day when she will be pleased to call him once more to her service, and assures her that:

He remains Her Majesty's most faithful lover and servant, to his life's end;

Pelagius, called van Overmeer

Wearily, he laid down his pen. There was no more that could be said.